THE REDEMPTION OF VALERIE TOLLIVER

A Novel

By Dennis Crews

For Terry, Wynnie and Joshua, who always believed.

ISBN 978-0-615-81969-3

Second printing December 2013
This novel is also available as an ebook at Smashwords.com

PREFACE

This story is about a remarkable time I lived through, and it's especially about my friendship with Valerie Tolliver—the last person in the world I expected to have anything of value to teach me.

Valerie is a coal miner's daughter, a coal miner's granddaughter and a coal miner's great-granddaughter too. How she came to be where I was is a story inside a story, and we'll get to that eventually. But not long after meeting her there wasn't much reason for me to think we'd had anything more than a chance encounter.

Val was a tumbleweed, I thought, running away from a troubled past. Unsophisticated (though far from ignorant), abrupt and uncouth, she didn't seem to have much going for her and the little she had was running out fast. How could I have realized what astonishing things her friendship would open to me? If I had, no doubt I would have run as fast as possible in the other direction. After all, personal growth rarely comes without cost. But sometimes the greatest gifts come in the unlikeliest packages.

Now quite a few of us have much to thank Valerie for. Some think Rollin King was luckiest of all—but I'm not sure that's the right way to view it. What happened to me was even more profound and I'm told it had more to do with divine grace than luck.

Lately I've been thinking that may be the axis the whole world turns on, with each of us a wheel in the machinery. My time with Val gave me a little glimpse of the clockwork, and my place in it. But that won't make a bit of sense without hearing the whole story, just the way it all unfolded.

1

There is no excellent beauty that hath not some strangeness in the proportion.

Francis Bacon

CHAPTER 1

Valerie burst from the back door of King's Tavern and stormed across the parking lot like a thunderhead ready to blow. I watched her with apprehension from inside my truck, pressing my back into the seat, but she had seen me already. She strode over to my window and stood there with hunched shoulders, rising up and coming down hard on her heels. She radiated a whole spectrum of emotions and if she were in a cage I wouldn't have dared putting my hand close to the bars.

"Old man King just fired me." Val's flat mountain twang wobbled somewhere between disbelief and indignation. "He called me a liability to the business just because I won't play ping-pong." She dug a wad of brown paper towel from her pocket to dab at her eyes. To my astonishment they were full to the brim.

I had come into town at the old man's request to check out a problem with the dumbwaiter, which had been stuck in the wine cellar for two weeks. It turned out to be nothing more than a tripped circuit breaker on the motor. My guess was that one of the summer workers had tried to crawl inside and ride it up but of course nobody admitted to any such mischief. I was leaving on tiptoes, relieved that the problem had been so easy to fix and that nobody had come up to make small talk—a razor's edge from making a clean getaway.

"Why won't you play?" I asked, hoping to steer the conversation away from Val's liabilities for fear of hearing more than I wanted to. Valerie is one of those people about whom nothing is simple, no matter how simple they appear to be. She didn't hear me.

"I've got to help Rollie," she started and then stalled. "You don't want to hear this, Ray. Just forget it, I'll be fine." She pulled her mouth up into a tight smile but a tear squeezed its way out the corner of her eye, made a crooked path around her cheekbone and hung there, trembling as she drooped her head. I watched it grow fat and plop onto the tip of her scuffed Doc Martens and waited for the other shoe to drop.

"You know how we used to go down to the wine cellar and poke around in the stuff from the old restaurant?" She sniffed hard, honking.

"Yeah?"

"Last week Tina and me found a secret compartment down there. There was a bunch of old papers and a real old bottle of cognac. It had a handwritten label that was all faded brown from 1769."

"No kidding?" Even if this was a diversionary story it showed more imagination than I expected. "And what did you do with it?"

"We drank it." Seeing the shock on my face she giggled once and said, "What do you think we did, stupid? We gave it to Rollie."

"And?"

"And what?"

"Well, what happened then?"

She tossed long black hair out of her face and gave me a cold look. "Why should I tell you anything? You'll be like everyone— you'll just think I'm crazy and laugh at me. I'm sick of being patronized—sick to death of it!"

Now that was the Valerie most people knew, volatile and defensive to a fault. But there was more to her than met the eye and I knew it even if the others didn't.

"Val, you know I've never laughed at you," I said, "but you're not giving me much to work with. So you found some old cognac and gave it to Rollin. Fine, he's the old man's son; now you're fired for not playing ping-pong. What am I missing?"

"Mister Rollin Bigshot King is up to his ears in trouble and he don't even know it, but I can't tell anyone a thing because everyone thinks I'm crazy. I'm just the hick chick from Kentucky who plays ping-pong wicked good and breaks dishes and embarrasses everybody. Nobody thinks I have the brains to make one worthwhile thought."

I was impressed. She had hit the nail on the head concerning her image problem; that alone was a paradoxical accomplishment that

4

rendered invalid most everyone's opinions about her. By now she was practically regarded as the village idiot. "Hick chick" was one of her more affectionate nicknames; there were others that weren't so nice.

She did play ping-pong wicked good though. Old man King didn't care much for pool or darts and when he opened the new place decided against all advice to put two ping-pong tables in the back room. It seemed like a joke at first in such an elegant establishment, but the game somehow caught on and now two more bars in town had ping-pong, with boisterous competition between them. At the end of her fraying rope as a waitress Valerie had arrested her fall by playing exhibition matches with winning customers. As her fame spread beyond the local scene it brought an unanticipated gloss of novelty, not to mention income, to King's Tavern.

Of course it didn't hurt that the tavern already had been covered with glory by every news outlet in four counties. Still, Val was more than good; she was gifted. For a while there had been serious talk of sending her overseas to play tournaments with some goodwill group representing small-town America. I thought that kind of stuff ended in the sixties, but like hippie clothes and lava lamps it seemed nearly every fad from those days was being recycled. Yet there were more than a few people who shuddered at the prospect of Valerie as any kind of ambassador.

No doubt she would have impressed them all with her lanky looseness and lightning speed—standing way back from the table, hands out from her hips like some cowboy gunslinger, only flicking her paddle around with the economy and precision of a knife fighter. Diving for the net her body moved like a whip, or maybe more like a striking snake. She never missed. How anyone so gawky and graceless under other circumstances could perform so flawlessly, often surrounded by noise, distractions and vulgarity directed specifically at her, was something of a high mystery to everyone. Her returns were miraculous; her slams reduced the most experienced players to slack-jawed disbelief. She remained unbeaten.

5

But away from the tennis table Val was a walking disaster. By turns timid and outrageous she was the very essence of chaos. She was agonizingly self-conscious yet when something riled her up her rage could send large men diving for cover. I personally saw her knock down a 250-pound steelworker who made the mistake of grabbing her rear one night after she started working tables at King's. One quick punch straight to the jaw and boom, he was on the floor. It made her somewhat of a celebrity for a few weeks until people found out what a thin skin she had.

Valerie was 27, a strict vegetarian and an unflinching champion of the underdog. Unfortunately she often misjudged people's intentions. Folks around town would not soon forget the incident during the mayor's dedication speech at the new library. When he'd spoken in hushed tones of seeing Naples for the first time with his wife, Val had leaped to her feet and demanded how a man in his position could so cheapen a woman's body as to speak publicly of her private parts. To picture her engaging in small talk with local dignitaries in China or students in Singapore made me cringe.

At the moment this talk about Rollin and the cognac was too vague to grasp; all I knew was that Val had been fired for withholding her one unequivocally known asset from her employer for reasons that weren't yet clear. I knew quite well that Valerie had more than one asset and realized the first day she appeared at King's Tavern that she was anything but dumb. But by now few would believe anything but the worst about her. It seems that a small town needs a pariah to heap its scorn upon; someone to soak up the self-loathing of a thousand small minds and absolve them of their own myriad flaws. Pick somebody who marches to a different drummer, beat them down until they become wretched, then see how much more attractive everyone else looks by comparison.

Yes, Valerie Tolliver provided a valuable community service, albeit unwillingly and without credit or compensation. Any insights I may have had concerning her other assets wouldn't have enhanced her reputation—not that I would have disclosed them anyway. Valerie herself was so unsure of people and their intentions, so

6

accustomed to being left out and made the butt of jokes, that her defenses marched noisily ahead of her, erecting walls, knocking down potential friends as well as enemies and generally provoking outrage.

I felt a wave of sympathy mixed with despair as I groped for an exit but she beat me to it.

"So now you're just going to ride off?"

"I've got to get back to my job, Val—I have an electrical inspection scheduled in a half hour."

She hung her head and released a gloomy sigh.

"Why don't you ride with me out to the job?" I offered. "We'll go somewhere afterward for pizza."

She studied her feet and then squinted at the late afternoon sun. "I don't know," she said in a hollow voice. "I need to talk to Rollie."

I pressed her. "Come on, Val, let it go for now. If you've got something to say sleep on it first. Maybe I can talk to the old man if you think it would help."

"Fuck him." She turned her head and spat onto the windshield of the silver Lexus parked in the next row. "He's such an asshole; now he's trying to take his own son down with him." Her voice was bitter.

"Val, I need to go. This isn't a good time for you to be alone. Come with me and I promise to do whatever I can to help."

It's a good thing I had no idea of the responsibility I had just taken on. How often is ignorance of the peril ahead actually mercy granted to each of us, without which we would be frozen in our steps!

~

We rode in silence for a few miles and I started thinking about the guys back at the job. What would they say when I rolled in with Valerie? The last thing she needed was to hear someone on my crew using one of the names she hated so much. I picked up my phone and punched the call button. After three rings Mike, my lead

7

carpenter, answered. I asked how things were going.

"All done, Bwana; for the last hour we've been outside working on the deck."

"Good," I said. "You can cut everybody loose if you don't mind sticking around for Clarence. I'll be there in ten minutes."

"He just called and said he couldn't be here till four-thirty."

"Four-thirty? Tell you what, Ace, if he calls again tell him we charge time and a half for overtime."

"Time and a half? We don't charge him anything."

"That's just the problem. I'll see you shortly."

I slowed for the turn off the state highway onto Hawk Road. It was beautiful country here—a parcel of unspoiled America not forty miles from Allentown, Pennsylvania. Old farms, Pocono Mountains on the horizon, spring-fed streams running through the woods, deer and foxes everywhere and even a few bears, although they tended to keep out of sight. Lately there was a rumor among my crew that a mountain lion had been sighted in the watershed above Gladburg.

My mother's family was from Wilkes-Barre and when I was a boy we had vacationed in the Poconos most summers. My memories from those times were of green woods, deep lakes and streams alive with trout and bass, and people whose lives revolved around blue-collar jobs. In a world where the past is paved over without a second thought the land up here seemed remarkably unchanged. Coming here from Washington, D.C. was like taking a step back in time, to a place where I could forget my failed marriage and everything that reminded me of it. It took me light-years away from my old job, which had supported my ex-wife's lifestyle but made me feel like a sellout.

As chief architect I had designed trophy homes for one of the capital area's most prestigious residential builders—looming, soulless monstrosities of crenellated brick, columned entries and colonial grandeur run amok. Designed for corporate climbers with no time for introspection or contemplation of beauty, for conspicuous consumers who wanted only to have the biggest, most expensive pile of bricks on the street. But the job had earned me a pile of money

8

and a reputation for reliability.

In the end most of the money walked out the door with Jillian when she left and now I was back to square one—only with the benefit of hindsight and a mind full of new ideas. I had come up here strictly for the memories. At first I saw just the run-down towns, the sagging subdivisions riddled with foreclosures, the wooded enclaves housing hollow-eyed commuters who bused by thousands to distant jobs in New Jersey and Manhattan. I never planned to find work, much less to stay, but somehow I landed in the one place where things were different. Gladburg was the exception, the standout in a depressed region, a town where anything seemed possible.

At first commercial renovation seemed the only wild card here. I was sure it would be the same dreadful stuff one sees in all places past their prime, but I was mistaken. Best of all there was room to move around, to get lost on back roads and find vistas that took my breath away. There was ancient land up here that spoke to me and gave me visions that didn't dissolve in the poisonous reality of yet another faux-colonial suburban abomination. My mind often superimposed architectural fantasies over the landscape; some of my best ideas came to me driving these old township roads. I was beginning to feel at home for the first time in years.

"Hey Val, how 'bout them Eagles?" I yelled.

She crinkled her nose and poked her tongue at me. I grinned. She knew I cared no more for sports than she did; it was one reason we had become buddies back when I was putting the finishing touches on King's Tavern. Everyone was overheated with football fever; we were two lone dissenters outside that subculture who exchanged wisecracking clinical observations on the behavior of our "subjects."

Val objected to sports on moral grounds, believing the concept of winners and losers to be hurtful and therefore wrong. I just thought it was pointless, a waste of time and money. At the top was a small group of people who grew rich stoking the fantasies of millions of others who bought vicarious thrills in order to make their real lives seem less empty. The game itself did nothing to change the world in any way that mattered. There would always be winners and losers; in America at least if you were a loser at one game you could try a different one. That's what more than half the people I knew had been doing for years.

Valerie scorned the concept of winners and losers yet she played her one game ruthlessly, leaving a string of losers in her wake. She exploited every opening, never showed mercy, but never exulted at winning. She remained completely detached, as if winning were the only possible outcome so the game itself hardly mattered—only getting through it. Sometimes if you watched her face while she played you could see a kind of pain there, an impatience to have it over and done. It rattled her opponents.

One thing was certain to me: Valerie didn't play ping-pong for fun. Like a force of nature she had to do it. A gangling collection of contradictions, she was inexplicable, even inexcusable at times, yet somehow strangely beautiful to me.

Val was silent but as we rode through slanting rays of golden sun I could feel her stress melting. It was too lovely a day to stay all squeezed up by anger. By the time we turned off Hawk Road onto the gravel lane to the job site she was looking up at the trees and sky, and even smiled shyly when I caught her off guard looking at me.

"Wait till you see this place," I chuckled. "The owner's a major league attorney. He'll probably want to leave Philadelphia forever after spending his first night here. I don't know how he'll pay for it without staying in the rat race though."

"Ain't that how it works?" Val shrugged. "Everyone's a slave."

"I'll have to think about that," I said. Was I a slave?

"You're a slave to what other people think about you. Or money or power, or some kind of dope if you just want to forget it all. Most people end up slaves more ways than one. I don't reckon I've known but one free person ever."

"And did this person have a job?" Why did every little conversation with Valerie have to veer off into a dissertation now? Was it possible to make small talk with her at all?

"Yes, but not like you'd think." She was looking directly at me

10

and I had the uncanny feeling she was answering the question I had thought instead of the one I had asked. She turned away with a tiny smile.

We bounced on up the drive through old growth oak and maple and a stand of great shaggy hemlocks. There was honking ahead and I slowed, pulling to the right. Mackey's old red Dodge barreled past. His grin flashed briefly through the windshield as we rolled up our windows against his dust. As we toiled up the grade a roofline came into view, then suddenly the whole house as we rounded the last curve. It looked like a jewel in the afternoon sun, like poetry in cadence with the surrounding landscape—even with piles of construction debris scattered about. Valerie stared.

"Like it?" I pulled up next to Mike's van.

"Wow," she said slowly, several times.

~

One phenomenon that has fascinated me endlessly since my first summer on a construction job is the potential of a building to become a different entity, apart from its design and occasionally transcending it, as it finds its relationship with the land on which it's built. I've always been in awe of Frank Lloyd Wright and that may be the main reason I started building again. It wasn't so long ago that I never wanted to drive another nail or lay another block, but the euphoria of seeing a structure and its setting come together with such harmony is a powerful motivation to keep my hands in the process.

Even after years of designing custom homes until now no design of mine had achieved such a quality in my own eyes. This house was another matter. Over seven thousand square feet yet it wasn't imposing, it was right. Looking at it you could almost imagine it had grown out of the hillside, so perfectly did it fit. I had taken a long time designing it; I'd even camped out on the spot several times while drawing the plans to see what the rising sun could tell me, to listen to the rocks in my dreams.

Valerie kept touching her fingertips to her cheek and staring. The house was a pair of gabled structures situated one hundred thirty degrees to each other, joined by a soaring glass atrium that faced south. State of the art solar design with a view to die for. An underground stream came to the surface and tumbled through the atrium. Behind it stood a massive stone wall with French doors opening into the big kitchen that overlooked the deck at the rear of the house. The gable of each wing faced a spectacular view, and each echoed the lines of an old stone barn visible in the distance on a neighboring farm.

Frankly bowing to the barn's quiet authority I had integrated stone with post and beam framing in the house. Its most striking feature was a tower rising like a silo from the rear junction of the atrium and the western wing, which terminated in a rotating, copper-clad observatory dome for the lawyer's big telescope. Right now the dome gleamed like a shiny new penny but in a few years it would take on the patina of time and become even more beautiful. A computer room was directly beneath the observatory, with windows on four sides and a commanding view in every direction. Floating steps cantilevered from the inside wall of the tower and ascended in a spiral, connecting all three levels.

The foundation and chimneys were faced with stone that my crew and I had spent weeks gathering by hand from the property. A low retaining wall of the same stone meandered about a hundred feet below the house, defining the upper yard from the broad apron of lawn that would eventually spread down to the woods. The eastern wing was topped with a cupola that brightened a reading loft over the master suite. The overhanging roofs were clad in diamond-shaped slate shingles, which subtly enhanced the angular relationship of the house's parts while lending to the whole an earthy, timeless quality. Everything came together serenely, a harmonious blend of traditional and modern geometry.

Valerie seemed to have forgotten her troubles for the moment as she and I crossed the rough ground past the dumpster and up to the garage, a three-car bungalow attached to the western wing. Mike's

12

big generator was still running just outside the first door and several extension cords snaked across the floor into the utility room. We knocked the dirt off our shoes and followed the cords into the house.

Mike did a double take when he saw Valerie, then grinned. "Hey, Val. What do you think of the view from here—nice, huh?"

She nodded, suddenly shy again. Mike had had his own problems with people in town and tended like Val to march to his own drummer. No doubt he had heard every story about her, but he kept his own counsel and treated everybody the same. Besides being a superb carpenter he was one of the few people I trusted completely.

"Any more word from Clarence?" I asked.

"Nope. You might want to do a walk-through and see if there's anything we missed."

I glanced at my watch—three thirty. "I intended to," I said, and then turned to Val. "Okay, ma'am—hold onto your hat and come see how the other half lives, or will if we ever get this place finished. The tour will be two dollars. Pay that guy over there—I believe I owe him a beer."

Valerie laughed and I turned back to Mike. "Want to come along?"

"I really ought to wrap things up on the deck. Just give a shout if you need anything."

Mike knew something was up with Val. He headed back outside to his tools while she and I walked into the living room. A tower of scaffolding rose between the trusses to where the painters had been spraying the ceiling a few days earlier. A pile of scaffold planks lay stacked by the tower and it occurred to me how glad I was to not be doing the high work myself any more. I saw Valerie looking at me closely.

"Quite a place, isn't it?" I felt a tiny stab of self-consciousness as the words slipped out.

"It's okay to be proud of this, Ray," she said.

I felt an inexplicable sense of relief that didn't last long.

"Now let's see the rest of it, mister Bwana."

"That's just workplace humor, you know," I said.

"What, don't you think it fits? You got your hotshot lawyer, you got your faithful manservant, plus you got all your lesser servants climbing around on the monkey bars doing all the dangerous work, and look who gets the credit. Must be nice, Bwana." A faint look of derision lingered on her face.

"Are you kidding, Valerie? There's not a motion happening on this site that I haven't gone through myself a thousand times. Rain or shine, summer and winter, sick and healthy. Furthermore my guys get paid very well, and you're not being very nice."

"Sorry," she sighed, and we walked upstairs.

I checked the electrical receptacles as we passed through each room. I made sure every switch was screwed in. It was mostly appearances at this point, but all my inspections passed the first time and I intended to keep things that way. Clarence knew how careful I was and that was beginning to make his visits a little easier.

I was one of the few people who knew Clarence had blown a twenty-year engineering career at Otis Elevator for approving unsafe system designs. There had been an accident with loss of life, and he left the company a haunted, bitter man. He seemed to hate his present job but be scared to death of losing it. He performed every walk-through with dour formality. Each sign-off was like a tacit admission of failure—his past failure which had led him to this place, compounded by his failure to find any mistakes during the inspection. He never signed off without a solemn lecture, how you never can be too careful because electricity can kill and so on. I always listened respectfully, nodding and assuming a grave expression; it was the only way to get him out of there.

The house had a formal library in the east wing plus a gym, sauna, theater and second kitchen below ground level, but Valerie acted unimpressed by any of it now. She had been quiet since her outburst but still peered over my shoulder at every switch and light fixture.

In the master bath I found an ordinary receptacle by the vanity rather than the required ground-fault circuit interrupter, an outlet that would kick off instantly if someone got shocked from it. Just the

14

kind of mistake that would make Clarence's day. After finishing upstairs we went down to the garage where I found a box of electrical components. Rummaging through it I found one lone GFCI outlet. I ran to the truck and grabbed a pair of pliers and a screwdriver from my tool box, and we headed upstairs again.

Back in the bathroom I unscrewed the receptacle, clipped the black and white wires from the back with the pliers and then unscrewed the ground wire. After skinning insulation from the clipped wires I was about to screw them into the GFCI block when I saw why it hadn't been used. There was a long crack running across the back of it, and when I squeezed it I could feel something crunch inside. Damn. Someone should have told Mike about this before leaving.

Suddenly I remembered where there was another GFCI receptacle. I'd been rooting around it for months every time I tried to find something in my glove compartment. I didn't even remember where it came from. By now it was almost part of my truck, in the same way a forgotten sneaker under the seat or a stray pack of guitar strings in the tool box seems to belong there for some reason.

"Hey Val," I said, "Would you mind running down and getting something out of my truck?"

"Sure—I mean no. I mean, okay, sure."

I grinned. "Only if you're really, really sure."

"Don't push it, mister."

"See this? There's another one just like it in the glove compartment. Just promise you won't get grossed out by anything else you find."

She studied the GFCI receptacle in my hand and chirped, "Okay." Then more darkly, "What else is in there?"

"Oh, probably a few spiders, dirty socks, a couple packs of condoms, maybe an old chicken sandwich—you know, usual glove compartment stuff."

"You are just horrible, do you know that?"

"Tell me later—Clarence is on the warpath."

"Yes sir, Bwana." She saluted, did a snappy about-face and

15

bopped out.

I marveled. Who knew what went through her mind? What was all this talk about Rollin, and the trouble he was in? What had upset Valerie so much? I was sure it was something more than being fired. Why had she quit playing ping-pong? If only she'd lighten up I might catch a glimpse of the strange logic that propelled her along her erratic path.

I heard Mike's saw on the deck and knew he was enjoying himself. I remembered the day I really began to know him. We were just starting to work on King's bar, and there was no mistaking the love in his eyes as he looked at the lumber I was marking. It was extraordinary wood, ancient, fine-grained chestnut from the American forest primeval. Felled more than a hundred years ago, logs buried in cold mud at the bottom of Lake Superior and raised a century later, perfectly preserved. I knew the guy who salvaged and milled them. There is no living wood like it any more, but that's another story. The point is, Mike knew that wood was special before anybody told him. That's why I wanted him working with me.

In the end it was Mike who had opened up the soul of that wood—who had carefully selected each piece according to grain and color, and designed and inlaid an intricate woven pattern into the entire length of that bar top. It was flawless old-world craftsmanship, far more beautiful than anything I could have done alone.

It was warm upstairs. I wiped a film of sweat from my forehead and leaned on the vanity top, clutching the stripped wires together with the screwdriver in my dampened palm, pulling them clear of the box. I ducked and peered in at the light switch and the neat loop of wires behind it, wondering who had run this circuit. I heard Mike's saw die in the middle of a cut, then Mike calling, "Hello-oo…" The generator was still running smoothly. I heard Val's voice, faintly: "Sorry."

Suddenly a lightning bolt ripped up my arm. My hand was on fire, my arm was jerking and I couldn't stop it. I opened my mouth to yell but no sound came out. It felt like a jackhammer was pounding me; I could see fire inside my fist but couldn't let it go. Finally I lurched back and the wires yanked out of my hand. I heard the screwdriver clatter on the marble floor and smelled ozone and burning flesh. Nausea swept over me. Somewhere far away Mike's saw started up again.

I reeled out of the bathroom and found the stairs. My ears were ringing and my right hand felt like it was still on fire. Don't look at it, I thought, find the breaker panel first. My God it hurts. I sank to my knees at the bottom of the stairs just as Val got there.

I must have looked bad. Val screamed for Mike; fortunately his saw cut was finished, he heard her and came running.

"What happened to you?" he said in alarm.

"Burned," I muttered. "Who wired the breaker panel?"

"Ah, shit!" he said. "We ran power upstairs through the panel today; I forgot to disconnect the line. Val tripped over my cord in the garage and she must have plugged in the wrong one. Let me see, Ray, let me look at it."

Val began to cry for real now. "I am so sorry," she said over and over.

I opened my hand but didn't look at it. My insides felt jumbled up; everything was shaking. Mike said, "What can I do?"

"Go upstairs and put that breaker in the master bath before Clarence gets here. Val, do you have it?"

She nodded mutely and handed it to him.

I shook my head to clear it. The pain in my hand was obscene but I couldn't afford to think about it now. "Get that in and then disconnect the line from the box," I said. "Matter of fact, disconnect the line first. I need to find something to wrap this up in."

"Right away," Mike said.

He strode out to the garage and turned off the generator and in the sudden booming silence I heard tires crunch on gravel. Clarence already? It was only four.

Mike walked back into the house. I headed out toward the drive with Valerie in my wake. She collapsed onto an empty bucket by the garage door, crying her eyes out. The dam had finally burst, and I had no idea how much hurt and injustice had been piled up inside,

17

how many tears it would take to wash it away, or even if it was safe to approach her. Nevertheless I walked back to her, crouched down and touched her cheek with my left hand.

"Val, it wasn't your fault." I spoke slowly. It took great effort to form each word. "Those cords all look the same; you couldn't have known."

"I tripped and pulled it out, Ray. If only I wasn't such a clodhopper—oh lordy, I wish I could die!" She gave up again to great shoulder-heaving sobs, and I stood up clumsily just in time to greet Clarence.

CHAPTER 2

Having taken the express elevator from the corporate heights to his present station, Clarence knew something of life's ups and downs. Yet nothing in his experience prepared him for the circumstance that confronted him now. He stood gawking; his adam's apple moved as he swallowed several times.

"Ah, Mr. Brauner, if this is not a convenient time…" Fear glistened in his eyes; he winced at his own words.

"No, please," I said, "come in." Mike would need just a minute at the breaker panel so I groped for something light to say, some pleasantry to hold Clarence for a few seconds. Unfortunately nothing came to mind except floating black spots and I just stared.

Hanging down caused my hand to throb unbearably so I curled it to my chest. Clarence looked at me suspiciously. "Is everything all right?" he asked. Valerie's crying diminished to a quiet largo and I, stricken dumb, wondered how the day could have gone so wrong.

I felt spidery threads wrapping around my head. I grew dizzy and felt myself floating up. The pressure of dealing with Clarence evaporated, and I relaxed. Looking down I saw three figures moving slowly around an unfocused point on the ground. I couldn't see their faces. One sat shrouded in grief; the other two stood with one clutching something to his chest. They were locked in some conflict I couldn't understand. The grief of the seated figure spread to the other two and enveloped all three in a cloud. She carried a terrible burden that threatened to crush her. The figure with his hand to his chest held something of need to her but he struggled with its weight; now he was staggering. The third figure seemed to have no role except to balance the forces of the other two.

The three began rotating faster around the unfocused point and as their speed increased that point deepened into a vortex. They spun faster, and as things around them began to be sucked into the hole I felt myself falling. I beat my wings to fly up but it was no use. I pitched forward into oblivion.

The pain in my hand roared me back and I felt gravel under me. I scrabbled around trying to find which way was up and heard voices. Mike had returned carrying a first aid kit and his battered water jug, to find a scenario rapidly approaching meltdown.

"Ray!" He grabbed my shoulders. "You're in shock. Let me help you."

He leaned me against the garage door jamb. Turning to Clarence he said, "We just had an accident and we're busy here. Can you please get on with it?"

Clarence nearly whimpered with gratitude as he bobbed his head and backed away from us in the waning afternoon sun.

Valerie had stopped crying and my head was beginning to clear when Mike knelt in front of me. He unscrewed the top of his jug, put it under his arm and took my hand. The cold water pouring over it shocked my palm and for the first time I looked at it. A scarlet brand from the screwdriver shaft was seared across my palm and the upper and lower pads of all four fingers. In the center of my hand where the wires had arced a raw concavity was oozing blood.

Mike found some sterile ointment in the first aid kit and squeezed the whole tiny tube onto my burns. There was a roll of gauze in the kit and it was just enough to wrap my hand all the way to the fingertips. After he finished bandaging me I took a long drink that emptied his jug and sat still, letting the textures of the landscape fill my vision. In the distance a pair of hawks wheeled over the valley.

The three of us sat without speaking until Mike said, "You okay, man?"

"Yeah." The ringing in my ears was gone; I had a handle on things now. "Sorry for losing it. I've been shocked before but not like that. It was almost like a dream."

"Forget it. I screwed up."

"We all get our turn."

"You don't even know what hit you."

"What do you mean?"

"That was two hundred forty volts, Bwana."

"Get out."

20

"You know all those rip cuts we had to do for the railing?"

"Yeah."

"I put my table saw on the deck to make them. The motor's on a two-twenty line in my shop so I just left it wired that way to save time. Runs like a sumbitch."

"But the plug—"

"It's rigged. I think that's why the breaker didn't trip." He nodded toward the generator.

I looked over and saw a fat cord about three feet long locked into the 240-volt outlet. It ended in a hand-wired standard receptacle into which an extension cord was plugged. Another identical extension cord lay nearby unplugged. Now it began to make sense. I started laughing, and laughed till tears were running down my cheeks. Mike started too and we sat there like a pair of idiots, laughing till our sides ached. Valerie stared at us.

"I sure am glad you told me that, Ace. Now I don't feel so bad," I finally said.

"You took one hell of a jolt. I need to get that breaker in now."

"Go do it—and tell Clarence I'm fine."

He scrambled to his feet and I sat still, truly relieved. At least I hadn't lost it over ordinary house current. Two hundred forty volts is a force to be reckoned with. Now Clarence's dry lectures didn't seem quite so irrelevant. Funny how little attention we pay to life's warnings until we get knocked backward by the very thing we've ignored over and over.

I studied Valerie's profile. She was hugging her knees, facing the horizon with her blue eyes fixed on infinity. A tiny breeze gently lifted locks of wavy, raven hair away from her face. Her full lips were pulled in slightly, giving her face an unusually pensive look. She was beautiful; there was no denying it. But her beauty was so overwhelmed, so obscured by the chaos that surrounded her most of the time that nobody saw her that way. In a flash of insight I saw her as an exotic creature displaced from her natural habitat. Like a caged leopard, or some exquisite life form brought into an unforgiving, alien atmosphere she was slowly suffocating, and the realization touched my heart.

"What did you see in your dream?" Her calm voice surprised me.

"What dream?"

"You know, when you blacked out."

"I'm not sure," I said. "I've never had anything like that happen before but it seemed like I was floating up over everything, kind of looking down. Then I got dizzy and my lights went out."

"Mmmm. I know." She didn't move but kept her gaze to the horizon.

"What do you mean, you know?"

"It's happened to me."

"No kidding? What did you see?"

"Sometimes you learn things you don't want to know." She turned to look at me and smiled sadly. "I'm awful sorry about your hand. You really ought to see a doctor about it, don't you think?"

"I'll survive. I still owe you a pizza, remember?"

"Ray, you don't owe me nothing. Look at all the trouble I already caused." Her mountain twang grew husky. "Just get me out of here before something worse happens. I ain't nothing but trouble for you."

"Valerie," I said, "you and I need to talk."

~

When Clarence finished he wouldn't even look me in the eye. He glanced at my bandaged hand, paused and then forgot whatever he was going to say. He signed the permit and darted out to his sedan like a scared rabbit. Mike wrestled his table saw from the deck onto a piece of cardboard just inside the glass door. We dragged the generator into the garage and locked the house while Valerie leaned on my truck smoking a cigarette. I told Mike I'd see him in the morning and we all took off.

As we wound our way back to the highway Valerie said, "Let's not go to town. Let's go somewhere neither of us have been."

"Okay." I turned away from the lowering sun and drove with no

22

particular destination in mind.

"Are you sorry you brought me along?" Val was appraising me.

"I'm not sure how I feel," I said. "I don't really understand what's going on; I think I need more information."

"Gold star for Bwana—he's being honest."

We drove through mellowing light and about thirty minutes later found ourselves playing hide-and-seek with a stream that twisted in and out of the woods to the right of the roadway. We were nearing Stroudsburg when I spotted a sign that read "Millstone Brewery & Ale House." A clearing opened in the woods and there beside the stream sat a renovated millhouse. It was a brew pub I'd never heard of—and judging from all the cars in the lot it wouldn't get much better than this. "Looks like we're home," I said, and turned in.

I was impressed by the structure; the timber and stonework were beautiful. The front of the place was busy so we passed up the bar for a table near the back. Val eyed the gleaming brew vats and copper tabletops, and when the menus came she grabbed one and studied it suspiciously. There are at least a few places in the world that respect vegetarians and as luck would have it we had landed in one.

Val ordered hummus with vegetables and pita bread for an appetizer. I ate left-handed, propping my right hand up so it wouldn't hang and throb. Our meal was worthy of the beer, which was excellent. We each had an oatmeal stout for dessert. Val slurped the head off hers and then reached in her pocket for a cigarette. She lit it, inhaled deeply, leaned back in her chair and blew a thick column of smoke straight toward the ceiling.

"Valerie," I said, "why don't you tell me what's going on?"

She slowly let down her chair and propped her elbows on the table. Massaging her temples she murmured to herself, "Where to start?"

"Why won't you play ping-pong?" I suggested.

She looked across at me, eyes bright with hurt. "Do you have any idea what it's like being the town freak? The dancing bear, the performing seal? Why not just stick a tin cup in my hand and send me out with an organ grinder? How would that make you feel?"

"I never thought about it that way. Some people are good at certain things and they do them because, well, because they're good. Like musicians or athletes, you know?"

"What if you're good at something you don't even like?"

"That could be a problem, I suppose."

"Then suppose you was really good at killing people. You didn't want to kill nobody, you'd rather build houses, but nobody wanted your houses. Would you kill someone just because somebody wanted to pay you for it?"

"I see your point. Although I'm not sure it's as bad as killing someone."

"Oh, Ray, you have no idea!" Her voice wobbled again and her eyes were filling up fast. "I go home every night and feel like I have to scrape shit off me, like roadkill all over a car. Like some old redneck was driving, and the car was me." The tears were spilling over, and she angrily rubbed them away with the heel of her hand. "It helps me understand my uncle Duane better."

"Uncle Duane?"

"Never mind, you wouldn't understand." She dug the wadded paper towel from her pocket and blew her nose.

I never had seen Val cry before today and frankly it gave me pause. She always had seemed too tough for tears, but something, somewhere had turned. "What about Rollin?" I asked.

She tossed her hair back, sipped her beer and pulled a long drag from her cigarette. "Rollie. That poor guy," she said, exhaling smoke. "I got a bad feeling about him. I can't explain it but he's in trouble. It's got to do with the old man somehow."

"You mean you have a premonition of some kind, or do you know something you're not saying?"

"I know it." She spoke flatly. "I don't know how it all hooks up but I know it."

"Like you knew what I was thinking about earlier today?"

"Something like that."

I drank half my beer trying to decide whether I wanted to learn any more about Valerie's suspicions. What level of confidence can be reached before some tacit responsibility exists to deal with what one is learning? In fact this equation had progressed too far already for that to matter. Val knew it and somewhere deep inside I did too. I was struggling to understand my relationship to the whole business when she spoke again.

"I think you're going to help him."

"What makes you think that? What does any of this have to do with me?"

"You had some kind of vision today and I think it's a sign."

"Val, I had the daylights knocked out of me by two hundred forty volts of alternating current and it's a wonder I didn't get electrocuted."

"I think you seen something. I don't know what it was, but once you know something you can't run away from it, you're responsible. Maybe you didn't see nothing but if you did you ought to pay attention. And besides," she took a furious drag on what was left of her cigarette and stabbed it out, "you promised."

We both were quiet for a minute. "I didn't want to quit playing, because of Rollie counting on me and all," she said, "but Ray, it's getting weird in that place. There's been a new bunch coming in and I get a real bad feeling from them. They throw their weight around and they're mean to everyone. They even push Rollie around and you know how nice he is to everyone. It's almost like they think they own the place."

"What about the old man?"

"He's gone crazy. One minute he'll be strutting around like a rooster the way he does, and the next minute he'll be all paranoid and strangled-looking. I seen a couple of them bastards laughing at him last week and he looked awful. I heard him talking to Rollie day before yesterday and it sounded like he was ready to give it all up."

"What do you mean, give it up?"

"He was talking about how people never appreciate nothing, how tired he was. 'Rollie, you got to be strong now,' he said, or something like that. He just kept saying it over and over, like he was washing his hands of everything and dumping it all on young Prince Rollin."

"That doesn't sound like the old man," I said.

"Damn straight it don't."

"Maybe it's a good thing for Rollin to get a little more involved."

"I don't think so, Ray. Something's got the old man rattled and he ain't handling it. It's up to Rollie now but he ain't ready for it neither. You can call me crazy like everyone else does, but something's bad wrong."

"How many other people have you told about this?"

"No one except Rollie. But I couldn't tell him the way I'm telling you. I tried, but I got all tongue-twisted and he just thought I was trying to save my job."

"I believe you, Val," I said. "Maybe I'm crazy too, but after today..."

I sat thinking about the incident at the house, trying to remember what exactly I had seen. A picture would start to form but before I could pull it into focus it would slide to the periphery. Like a dream, it had faded with wakefulness leaving nothing behind but a vague unease.

"How long was I out?" I asked.

"Not but a couple seconds. It was before you fell down that you was really going."

"Going? Like how?"

"You was looking at the ground just like it was a movie—your face was all lit up and your eyes were swirling all around."

"You weren't just reading my mind, then?"

"No, stupid. Anyone would have known you was seeing something. Between me and you I reckon that's what gave Clarence such a case of the heebie-jeebies."

"That's great," I grumbled. What in the world he thought I wouldn't even guess. "Let's get out of here; I've got an early morning."

We drove back most of the way in silence but when we turned into King's parking lot where we started my curiosity got the best of me.

"What about this bottle of cognac?" I eased my truck into an empty space beside Val's beat-up Volkswagen Jetta and killed the engine.

"We gave it to Rollie, like I said."

"Val, I tore that whole place apart and renovated it—if there were some secret compartment in the wine cellar my guys would have found it."

"So mister hotshot architect thinks he knows everything, does he? Are you willing to bet on that?"

"I'm not saying we didn't miss something. I just don't understand how."

"Well, if you wouldn't act so high and mighty you might understand a little more in life."

"I'll humbly accept that as a pearl of wisdom if you'll just fill in some details for me. Where was it? How did you happen to find it? Who else knows about it?"

"Nobody else knows," Val said sharply. "Only Tina. Rollie, he's almost as bad as you for flipping me off."

"I'm not flipping you off. I'm trying to understand something very unusual and you're acting like it's some kind of everyday occurrence. Can you just help me out a little?"

Val rolled her eyes. "Okay, Bwana."

I bit my tongue. She was testing me.

"Like I said, Tina and me went down there. It was slow up on the floor and we wanted to cool off a few minutes, you know, to take a break."

"To catch a buzz, perhaps?"

"I never said that," Val retorted. "Do you want me to go on, or not?"

"Please," I said, inwardly chalking up one point.

"The Bible says not to cast your pearls before swine. You think I don't know how you feel now, mister score-keeper?"

"Oh Valerie, cut the crap! You're too perceptive for your own good; you don't even seem to understand when someone wishes you no ill. You started the story; if you want to finish it, fine. If not,

27

that's fine too. Just don't jerk me around, please; it's been a long day."

Valerie sighed and seemed to shrink a little in the darkness. "All right," she said quietly. "You're right, it's been a long day."

There was a long pause.

"We were in the wine cellar. Yeah, we smoked some weed. I don't even like it much but we just felt like doing something different—it was the middle of the afternoon and nothing was happening upstairs. I was talking about Kentucky and how my grandpa used to work in the coal mines for scrip. She didn't know what scrip was so I showed her a piece."

"Scrip?"

"It's what the miners used to work for instead of money. The coal bosses owned everything and they wanted to own the miners too. So they didn't pay in regular money, they paid in scrip that was only good in the company store. The miners got overcharged for everything but they couldn't do nothing about it. They were slaves, almost as bad as the colored people were.

"I've got a pair of earrings made from scrip. You've seen them—little coins with a hole in the middle. I took one of them off the hook so she could hold it and she dropped it. It's about big as a dime, and it rolled across the floor and just disappeared. We both were watching and saw it drop right out of sight in a crack. Between two of them floor stones."

"Flagstones. Did you get it out?"

"Not at first. It was so tight we could barely see it. We couldn't even get a hairpin beside it. We come back upstairs and waited on some tables, and went down later with a knife from the kitchen. We thought if we busted up some of the cement we could work it out. When we drove the knife in the crack it just opened up—the whole stone slid back and we got the scrip. But the stone was riding up at the back end so we slid it back further and bingo, it popped right out. It was made that way because there was a holler under it. There was another lid with a handle on it that we lifted up and that's where the stuff was."

28

"Amazing," I said, turning the story over in my mind. "Okay, I believe you. What about our friend Rollin? How much of this does he know?"

"He don't pay attention like the old man does and he never even asked any questions. He hardly paid any mind to it till he saw the date on the bottle, and then he sat it up on his fireplace mantel. I kind of thought he should put it away somewhere but he just laughed. The last time I seen it was right up there, pretty as can be."

I turned to face Valerie in the dark. "I don't think either one of us should talk about this to anyone else. I've got to see either Rollin or the old man in the next few days; I'm just wrapping up a little work for them. Maybe I can ask a few questions."

"Thanks, Ray," she murmured, reaching to touch my cheek. "You watch out now, okay?"

I held up my bandaged hand, ghostly white in the darkness. "I'll consider this an omen."

CHAPTER 3

Rollin sat across the desk from me, bursting with vitality but clearly bothered. An uncharacteristic expression of worry knitted his tanned forehead into creases. He pressed up just below his hairline, as if to manually smooth the skin would somehow eradicate what was troubling his mind, but each time he removed his hand the creases stayed. I glanced around the room at his trophies—framed color photographs of Rollin King on Annapurna, on the summit of Kilimanjaro, on a high slope of Everest. More photos of Rollin posing with Sherpas on a glacier, one of him grinning on a makeshift toilet at some godforsaken, windswept mountain camp. Rollin hang-gliding, suspended in sunlight above a lush, green valley with snowy peaks rearing nobly in the distance. Rollin King, the golden child, the old man's only begotten son with whom he was well pleased. At the moment Rollin himself, though, looked anything but pleased.

"Ray, I don't know what's going on. Nobody is more careful than Dad with money but this morning I got a call from the bank saying our account is overdrawn. Just a few dollars, but we had nearly eighteen thousand in there last week to cover payroll and our end-of-month expenses. Suddenly we've got no cash and until I get a handle on things I'm afraid I can't pay you. Or anyone else." He drummed his fingertips on the desktop and frowned even more deeply.

"Have you talked to your father?"

"He's gone." Rollin looked up at me. "He called last night to say he'd be away for a week or two but he never said a word about money. The damned thing is..." He bit his lip and gazed out the window. "They said he withdrew it all. Dad's gone, the money's gone and I'm more in the dark than anyone."

I whistled quietly. "How are you going to operate the business?"

"I've got enough savings to keep things going—just a matter of transferring some funds, but..." He drew a deep breath. "As long as there are no more surprises we'll be okay."

"You're afraid it might happen again?"

Rollin looked anguished. "Not really. But…" He lifted his hands in a helpless gesture.

"Rollin," I said, "What's been going on with your dad?"

"I don't know. He's been really preoccupied about something but he never said what it was. I just chalked it up to problems with Liz. She moved away all of a sudden and that hit him pretty hard."

"Liz?"

"You know—the, ah, older redhead who used to sit down at the end of the bar every night after we opened?"

I could picture her, sitting there with the glow from the wall sconce kindling highlights in her hair. Always alone, quiet but charming, drinking expensive cognac and exuding sensuality. Drinking cognac. I glanced across to the old brick fireplace behind Rollin and saw a heavy flask sitting on the mantel.

"Have you noticed anything different around the bar lately? Any strange people, any unusual activity?"

"Well, now that you mention it there have been some people I've never seen before. A couple of them are real bruisers. Not from around here by the looks of them—they wear suits and like to push people around. One night last week I thought I was going to have to call the cops to get them to leave. Do you think there might be a connection?"

Now don't get me wrong, Rollin is a prince of a guy. He'd give anyone the shirt off his back; he once climbed halfway up Everest without oxygen to help carry a man with a broken hip down. But all that camaraderie and team effort seemed at times to have left him without an awareness of the darker side of human nature, of the greed and slime that thrive at lower altitudes—in the wrinkles and folds of the earth, in the shadows below the glistening heights. Rollin trusted everyone; right at that moment it seemed to be the greatest curse of his privileged life.

"All I can say is don't rule anything out. Do you have any idea where Liz went?"

"Nope. I heard her say once that she lived in Toronto and then in Philadelphia. She didn't talk much to anyone except Dad."

"Did she have a last name?"

"Travino. It was on a Visa card she used here a few times."

Something in the back of my mind clicked subtly, like the tumblers of a lock moving into place, but nothing opened.

"Hmm." I studied the flask on the mantel. "That's an interesting bottle up there."

He brightened, stood and took it down with both hands. "Yes, it is. Two of the waitresses found it down in the wine cellar a couple weeks ago. A really unusual find." He held it so I could read the label: Pour Louis, Rémy Martin 1769, beautifully handwritten on a delicate, parchment-like material whose edges were brown and lifting. The wax seal at the top was stamped with an intricate boss.

"It might be a good idea to keep that somewhere under lock and key," I suggested.

"That's what Valerie said," he laughed. "She's one of the girls who found it."

"I'd take that advice and thank her for it, Rollin. You never can tell what you've got there, and with things the way they are right now I'd get that bottle as far away from here as possible and not tell anyone else about it."

"Really?" He looked surprised.

"Really. Look, it's none of my business. But not everyone is as trustworthy as you are. Put that away for a rainy day; don't show it around."

"Yeah, maybe you're right," he said quietly.

"Give me a call if you need anything else done, and don't worry about the money just yet. Your dad's off licking his wounds—he'll be back."

"Thanks, Ray." Rollin stood up and flashed his million-dollar smile. "Everyone really loves the work you've done. That bar sure made the old man happy. I can't see him ever leaving this place any other way but feet first."

I left Rollin trying to convince myself it was foolish to read anything into his last words, feeling dumb for even thinking it possible that they had any significance. I finally gave up, angry at

Rollin for his choice of words, for his backslapping, high-fiving bonhomie even in its absence on this particular day, for his hopeless innocence of human greed and its perils. Another fish out of water, I thought. And then I began feeling a little sorry, wondering what all this must feel like to him. The poor guy never wanted to run a bar anyway.

~

King's Tavern was the old man's dream come true, his intended legacy to his son. Rollin was the apple of his eye; the old man was immeasurably proud of him and wanted to give him the finest inheritance possible. The problem was, they inhabited worlds so far apart that neither one really understood the other.

The old man was a sly fox who had grown up hard on the streets of Scranton. He had clawed his way up to this place through decades of real estate wheeling and dealing. Rollin, the Eagle Scout, model student, now the ultimate outdoors freak and nicest guy in town, knew nothing of running a business, of wheeling or of dealing. His degree was in environmental studies; he lived to climb actual mountains and came down to earth only often enough to keep the old man happy. Mrs. King had died of illness when Rollin was still a child, and I saw between father and son a fierce, protective and idealistic kind of love. It was a bond forged from mutual adversity, strong as steel even while binding them forever facing in different directions.

For some time I had been afraid the old man might become a victim of his own success. His forte always had been the transaction, not the management of his acquisitions. In evolutionary terms he was a hunter, a stalker—not a husbandman of flocks or planter of crops. Now his assets were growing a bit too unwieldy for him to govern without a working partner. He was balancing an enterprise that loomed over him like a juggernaut. Had Rollin missed that altogether, I wondered?

Gladburg, Pennsylvania had spurned the opportunity to become a resort town earlier in the century. As the steel rail manufacturing industry that ruled Scranton began dwindling in the years before the great Depression, a few restless capitalists began to think about diversifying their holdings. Beyond the grime and smoke of their smelting plants the Pocono Mountains beckoned. Nestled in the hills not far from their factories were charming small towns which appeared to them as peaches for the plucking. Among these Gladburg was one of the most beautiful. It occupied a picturesque high valley that first had been used as a camp meeting retreat for churches in the region. The town was kept sparkling and must have seemed like a little piece of heaven to the industrialists who drove down from their smog-filled lairs on weekend excursions to the country.

A group of investors conceived a plan to make Gladburg a vacation destination for rich New Yorkers and Philadelphians. They bought up property, created a man-made lake with a lodge and began seeking other investors to bring their dream to fruition. They failed to reckon with the conservatism of the town fathers, however— hardworking Dutchmen who saw nothing to be desired in catering to the whims of the leisure class. After several years of financial setbacks and unsuccessful negotiations for still more land a fire of suspicious origin destroyed the lakeside lodge, taking the life of one of the principle investors. The developers withdrew, seeking easier conquests.

Gladburg still retained an unspoiled, traditional character distinct from its neighbors to the east, which had embraced the tourist trade more enthusiastically. The lake had been bought back for a song by the town and turned into a public park. A once-grand downtown hotel, still bearing that unlikely name, was the only other visible relic of the development fiasco. For decades it had been a white elephant to a string of owners. The Grand Hotel itself had been defunct since the late seventies but the restaurant downstairs had hung on by a thread, deteriorating a little more each year, barely making enough to pay the help.

For years the Grand Hotel restaurant had been a place where

working men in faded denim and wool hunched over the stained counter on early mornings, warming their hands around mugs of coffee. At dinnertime widowers and pensioners straggled in to take nourishment from the fare offered up by its meager kitchen. Some local historian claimed the dining room had been rendered years before in a painting by Edward Hopper, but the picture, like the hotel, had been a failure and was later painted over by the artist. I thought the story probably untrue, but not entirely unbelievable.

In the early 1990s there were whispers about a new ski resort being planned a few miles outside of town. Old man King, whose eyes and ears missed little, heard those whispers early and began sizing up the situation. After liquidating a few other properties he made an exploratory offer to the owners of the old hotel, who had heard nothing, and was amazed to have it accepted on the spot.

The ease with which he acquired the property made the old man's head spin. At first he had only remodeled the dreary restaurant but after the ski resort opened it became clear there was more potential in the place than he had expected. He called in consultants who drew up a plan that put him smack in the middle of a development league he had only dreamed of penetrating a few years before.

For phase one the old restaurant was gutted and gloriously made over as King's Tavern—the crown jewel of his new realm. It had been my first major building project up here. I loved the historical aspect of the renovation, and loved even more that King spared no expense in making the place a period piece, a tribute to the roaring twenties. It was fun working with the old man; he was feisty and profane but seemed to have a clear sense of honor, and he knew the difference between glitz and quality. From the moment its doors opened King's Tavern had been a success.

After the first few months of operation King's clientele defined itself as a young crowd, more rowdy and sports-oriented than the old man had envisioned. But they spent money and filled the place with energy, from which he seemed to draw a new lease on life. The ping-pong tables were an anomaly I couldn't understand, since the tavern seemed to cry out for a billiard room. But the old man was adamant:

no pool would be played here, and in time it became another defining quirk of the place, something inexplicable which ultimately, at least while Valerie had been there, turned to King's advantage.

Phase two had just begun; now the hotel was being renovated by a different contractor. The old man had offered me the job but I never seriously considered it. The tavern had been a project entailing real craftsmanship but the hotel didn't square with my reasons for being up here; it was too big and commercial. It did show promise of being a winner, with every amenity and luxury suites that would surpass all other accommodations in the region. The street-level exterior had been transformed during phase one, and the new Grand Hotel facade sparkled with even more class than the original had.

King's project was being hailed as the new paradigm for saving the Poconos. It had been trumpeted on television and nattered about in newspapers. Gladburg was happening, and its energy was sending picture-perfect ripples across the region. King's renovation had inspired countless smaller restorations and established the motif for a promising new development boom. Tourism had boosted business; the downtown now had a night life. There were jobs in Gladburg, and more young people were opting to stay instead of moving to bigger towns as many had done only a few years ago. The demographic changes were in turn feeding the new downtown and King's great enterprise stood at the middle of it all. But something was wrong; the old man was AWOL. I envisioned a ship at sea, slicing through uncharted waters in sun-bright fog, with a child at the helm.

~

It was months since I had been to King's Tavern for anything other than minor repairs so I'd had little opportunity to notice any change in the place. Now my curiosity was aroused, not to mention the fear that one of my greatest professional achievements might fall into unworthy hands.

Wrestling King's Tavern into reality had been radically different

36

from building the lawyer's house but between the two projects I felt my true potential finally was being tapped. King's Tavern had demanded extraordinary creativity within narrow constraints. The lawyer's house, on the other hand, had been like an architectural stage upon which my imagination could freely act. Never before had I been given so much liberty on such costly projects. Between those two jobs I had pushed through all prior accomplishments to a new plateau. It was natural to feel a proprietary interest in the fate of my most important work, was it not?

Ah, the pride of man! The only animal that seeks to justify its own existence, the human builds monuments to himself and worships them, unmindful of his folly. Valerie was one of the few who saw right through such delusions. No monuments for her, thank you—a shaken fist and primal scream were her emblems. Though it cost her dearly she called things as she saw them, in the hard clear light of the morning after—while for most everyone else it was still the night before.

My injury hadn't been such a handicap as I had feared and after two days it was healing well. A nasty pit remained in the middle of my palm where the wires had arced, but the blisters had drained and didn't hurt much now. The lawyer's house was nearly finished; most of the remaining work consisted of cleanup and detailing. Our next job would be less demanding so it seemed fitting to turn my attention to Rollin and his dilemma, and to my own investment in the King portfolio. After work I took counsel with the person to whom I felt most indebted for my recent success.

"Hey, Mike. You been to King's lately?"

"Not since," he said.

"You're kidding! That's history now."

"I was barred." He shrugged.

"You know that was a bad call. Nobody would have enforced it then and they sure as hell wouldn't now."

I remembered the evening well. Mike had been working with me less than a year. We had just finished building that exquisite bar and King's Tavern was the hottest nightspot around. Valerie was still a novelty, not yet despised but openly lusted after by half the guys in town. Naturally that sat poorly with a number of young ladies, who didn't take long to respond in the spirit of the game their culture loves so well. The best defense is a good offense, as they say. Those heady weeks after King's opened had been too much fun to last. After every diversion human behavior always reverts to default mode.

As fate would have it Mike was in the middle of the only fight that had happened at King's Tavern. Some idiot pulled out a knife and stabbed it into the bar as an exclamation point to whatever he was saying—several times in one sentence. Mike nearly choked on his beer. Mike, who had carved, sanded and polished that beautiful wood for weeks on end, walked over to the guy and very quietly told him to put his knife away. The guy laughed in his face and again plunged the blade into the bar. Mike picked him up by his shirt to throw him out the door and the fat was in the fire. The guy's buddy tried to cold-cock Mike, and of course several other guys from my crew jumped in when they saw what was going down.

I literally dragged Mike out of there as the steroid-pumped young goon the old man had hired for a bouncer hollered behind us for Mike to never come back. Of course he hadn't seen what happened and barely knew who Mike was. When the old man heard about it all he wanted was to punch the guy with the knife.

Since that time I'd heard my crew talk about two other fights Mike had been in years before. Both times he had come to the defense of someone who was being bullied, and both times the bully had required medical attention when it was over. I saw Mike as a gentle soul who took no pleasure in violence but wasn't afraid of it either. Later I would find I was only partly right. Mike greatly feared the violence in himself, and generally stayed far away from any situation where it might arise.

Maybe if I had understood that I wouldn't have pressed the point, but I didn't want him to feel any dispossession from the work we had done together at King's Tavern. Building that bar had been a labor of love for Mike. Its beauty was his own handiwork even more than mine, and the idea that he should feel in any sense unwelcome as a customer in front of it was ludicrous to me.

"I'm going over there later this evening—care to join me?" I asked.

"I was wondering when I'd collect that beer you owe me."

"Tonight, Ace." I slapped his shoulder. "But there's something you should know."

"What, you lost your wallet and can I spot you twenty?"

"No, it's a rumor I've been hearing. Seems there may be some kind of trouble going on. I thought to just go have a quiet look around, listen a little. Maybe pick up a vibe."

Mike frowned. "Does this have anything to do with Val?"

"I don't think so. You know the old man canned her?"

"The day she came out here?"

"Yeah. She was tired of being the local tourist attraction. Quit playing ping-pong, and I guess she wasn't much use to him after that."

He shook his head. "So what's the trouble?"

"Val felt positive there was something bad brewing before she left, but she couldn't tell what. I talked to Rollin yesterday and it seems the old man's taken an unscheduled vacation. There's some missing money, possibly some outside forces at work. He's kind of floundering at the moment, so I thought about dropping in for a visit. Strictly reconnaissance."

Mike raised his eyebrows. "Strictly reconnaissance?"

"Absolutely. Mike, I'm way out of my element here. But Rollin is a good guy, and if there's a problem it would be nice to find some way to help him. On the other hand it could be nothing at all. In fact, that would be the best news. You still want to come?"

"Life is rarely the best news, you know."

"I know."

"If Rollie needs help, I'm there. What time?"

"After the yups finish their dinners and go home. The evening crowd doesn't show up till later."

"Nine-thirty okay?"

"Yeah." I grinned at Mike. "It's been a while, you know. It might be nice to kick back for an evening."

My primary mission began receding to the back of my mind almost immediately as I contemplated the pleasures of a night on the town. We would have a few drinks and get a chance to talk about work away from the rest of the guys. We'd probably see a few acquaintances, and might even flirt with some tourists. I really didn't expect to learn much about Rollin's problems or the old man's disappearance in one night, but at least I could tell Val I'd been there. Maybe then she'd lighten up a little.

CHAPTER 4

Passing through the vestibule and big glass doors of King's Tavern was like plunging out of the ordinary world into a lush atmosphere of indulgence. The profusion of greenery, the polished brass and beveled glass all amazed me now, as did the ornate high ceilings, rare wood paneling, luxurious carpeting, leather upholstery, and that magnificent bar. There had been umpteen photographs of it in as many newspapers and magazines, but not one of them prepared a person for the actual experience of it. How the light played on the grain of that old wood! What richness and depth there was in the extraordinary finish Mike had put on it! It was his own secret formula, involving exotic ingredients, masking, heat from a blowtorch and uncounted hours of hand rubbing. The beauty of that bar top testified to the soulful superiority of hand workmanship over anything any machine could make.

Strange how different it felt in here now from when we were working on this place. Back then every step in the process was invested with pride, even jubilation by my crew as we watched the finished product emerge from the chaos of our beginning. We were a new company, still getting to know each other as team members. King's Tavern was a personal proving ground for each of us—most of all for me. I was the outsider but captain of the team, and there were a thousand ways I could have screwed up. Or been screwed. Somehow it had worked out, as if all the hard luck of past years had been tallied and declared sufficient dues for the time being.

Now that process was history; our former proving ground had fixed its own identity. For all its period pretensions it was an identity without a trace of sentimentality, but I didn't understand that yet. I sauntered up to the bar and looked around for Mike. Several familiar faces smiled in my direction and I nodded back. It wasn't yet nine-thirty; Mike would be here shortly. I didn't see Rollin anywhere. I signaled Agnes, the compact, spunky bartender everyone called Aggie, and ordered a Newcastle.

41

Rollin was a bit of a music fanatic and he had made the sound system for King's Tavern his project. Though at first I thought it was overkill to have a rack of amplifiers with six subwoofers hidden through the place, not to mention several pairs of studio monitors and nearly a dozen tiny satellite speakers, the proof was in the hearing. Even at low levels the music had a clarity that was astonishing, and no matter where you sat in the house you got the full effect of stereo. How he managed that I don't know, but Rollin had done his homework. At party volume King's Tavern rocked like no other place, and for sporting events the four giant screens and surround sound were the next best thing to being there. At the moment an old Lou Reed live album was playing.

The crowd seemed boisterous but mannerly. I smiled again at how the old man had expected a more genteel clientele, and how much he'd invested to attract just such a crowd. Now everyone from dot-com tyros to college kids and bikers were reveling in the elegance of his establishment, and who knows how much difference it made to them? In any case, their business was just as good as that of the professionals who enjoyed dinner and drinks early in the posh dining room and then left the evening to the scruffier crowd. As long as the liquor flowed the money rolled. And when the hotel opened everything could change again. This little experiment is just beginning, I thought. Whichever way it goes it stands to make money.

A slender girl who looked scarcely 18 was waiting tables in the front. Valerie's replacement? It had been too long since I'd been here to know the staff any more except by their white shirts and dark green vests. Who was doing bounce duty? I picked up my glass and strolled back to the ping-pong parlor where a grudge match was in progress. Another waitress I didn't know was collecting bottles and emptying ashtrays from the ledge that ran around the room. There was the bouncer, a good-looking young iron pumper I'd never seen, watching the game with a group of spectators. Nothing unusual in here, though it was a marked contrast to the glory days when Val had first unveiled her talent. What a scene that had been! Old man King felt so vindicated he almost got religion over her gift. People came from miles around to watch her play and business soared.

Does anything so good ever last? Alas, the old man had to eat the bitter as well as the sweet. It is probably safe to say Val had not been cut from the cloth of life in the pattern of a waitress. When exasperated beyond her fail-safe point, she simply would drop whatever she was holding, throw her hands into the air and shoot flames from her eyes at her tormentors, who often as not were innocent of any bad intent. Lots of dishes died that way.

Worse still, the old man suffered loss upon loss as angry patrons bolted from the premises to escape Val's vegetarian lectures. It didn't seem to occur to her that a person craving a steak does not care a whit for the sanctity of life, nor would even consider ordering the pasta primavera with pesto sauce instead. The old man forgave her time and again, but as her reputation plummeted so did his patience. Finally the fly had been plucked from the ointment, the squeaky wheel was gone, the aching tooth had been yanked out. Was it better now, I wondered? Had anything been gained?

I wandered back to the bar and took my seat, lost in thought. Suddenly it seemed the good old days in this place had been nothing more than a brief and heady wind that precedes a violent storm; now the blackened sky had ruptured. Except it wasn't rain that was falling, it was time. Where was the old man tonight? I had the sorrowful feeling he was getting very wet—or getting older very fast, depending on which end of the metaphor you wagged.

"What's up, Bwana?" I felt a nudge behind me and turned with a start. Mike stood there grinning at my morose expression.

"When did you get here?" I said.

"A little before you. Been over by the wall, scoping."

I couldn't believe I hadn't seen him.

"I think we may have special guests." His voice was amiable but there was no levity in his eyes. "You might want to take a look to your left when you get a chance."

Glancing around the room I let my gaze sweep across the end of the bar. The two men I saw seated just past where the bar began to

43

curve into the back wall removed all doubt from my mind that Val had been right. One was tall, smooth-skinned and tan, with a high forehead and long blond hair pulled back into a tight ponytail. He wore a blue muscle shirt under a black suit jacket. The other was barrel-chested, with close-cropped dark hair and a carefully trimmed four-day beard. He was dressed in a black suit, white shirt and bolo tie. It's not just that they were massively built—bruisers, as Rollin had said—these guys were predators, with intelligent eyes that locked onto mine in gazes so cold and bloodless it made the hair on my neck stand up. I feigned a bored expression and turned back to my glass. Egad, I thought. I might quit too if I had to wait on the likes of those two.

Mike eased onto the stool to my left and I noticed his hands were empty. "What's your pleasure? It's on me."

"Rolling Rock's fine."

I caught Aggie's eye and ordered Mike's beer. When she brought it I leaned forward and asked what she knew about the big guys. She rolled her eyes and said, "You better save that one for Rollie. Let me know if there's anything else I can get you." She wheeled around and bustled away.

"You've got to start somewhere," I mumbled.

"Some things don't need any starting, Bwana," Mike quietly corrected me. "The way I see it these gentlemen are here on their own recon mission. They aren't missing a thing. I believe they were here earlier and came back in right after you left for the back room. Drinks were on the counter already. They noticed me, they saw you come back in, they know exactly who's here and who's not. It's almost like they're casing the place." He carefully sipped the head off his beer.

"They're from the big city," I blurted without thinking. "Someone's trying to muscle in on the old man and these guys are the bad news."

"From the big city, huh?" Mike mimicked. We burst out laughing.

It was a good belly laugh that sent a calming little ripple out into the room. Nobody knew why we were laughing but it did pop the

44

knot of tension that had started to tighten in my gut. It felt safer now, as if we'd been talking about cars or girls, or sports. Rusted Root was playing on the sound system. Their hypnotic drumming filled my head, giving my jumpy nerves a groove to ride in. Easy does it, I thought. Everybody here is minding their own business; we will simply do the same. Bruisers or no, I will enjoy myself tonight. The only problem was, I seemed to feel the old man's ghost everywhere around me.

~

I looked down at my glass and it was empty. Scanning the bar for Aggie I saw she had been nabbed by one of the bruisers. It was the blond. His voice wasn't loud, but it cut through the ambient noise enough for me to make out a few words: "get in here" and "not fucking around." He leaned at her and punched the bar with his finger. "Now do it!" he snapped, the cables of his thick neck bulging. Where is our young bouncer now, I wondered?

By now a few faces had turned in their direction. Aggie backed away from the men looking both angry and scared. The dark one grinned at her—a broad leer abrupt and full as if a switch had been thrown. She spun around and stalked away shaking her head. Her face was beet red as she whisked past us to the waiters' station where there was a cordless phone. She grabbed it and strode back the length of the bar. She punched in a series of numbers and placed it in front of the blond. "You deliver your own message, sir. I have a job to do." She spoke curtly and turned on her heel.

Good for you girl, I thought. The dark one seemed delighted—smiling and nodding as if to the music. The blond remained expressionless as he put the telephone to his ear. Then abruptly the dark one turned to stare down the faces gawking at them. His smile vanished. Not a spark flickered in his eyes, and just as quickly everyone else turned away. Nobody wanted to be registered in that stare.

Our view was blocked suddenly by Aggie's arrival. "Now,

45

gentlemen, may I get you something?" she asked.

"Bravo," I said quietly. "I'd like an O'Doul's, please. Mike?"

"Same for me."

"Nice to see someone keeping their wits about them," she said.

When she returned with the bottles I asked, "Are we expecting Rollin this evening?"

"I guess we'll find out, won't we?" She turned away and bustled down to the end of the bar, scooped the phone up and returned it to the waiter's station.

Mike chuckled softly and said, "That's quite a woman, Bwana. Sort of reminded me of Val there for a minute."

"If Val had that kind of self-control," I said, "she'd be invincible."

The hubbub in the tavern slowly returned to normal but the crowd melted away from the end of the bar. At the left edge of my vision I could see the two black suits sitting calmly, taking in every detail. They weren't drinking now.

A ruckus from the ping-pong parlor signaled the end of the match and a tide of new faces washed up to the bar. Looking to my right I saw Aggie and the bouncer arguing at the waiters' station. Someone must have reminded him of his purpose in life. Uh-oh. Now Aggie was grabbing his arms; it looked like she was pleading with him. The bruisers couldn't see them from where they sat, but as Mike and I watched it appeared that soon it wouldn't matter. Sure enough, that young fool shook Aggie's hands off him, turned around and headed down the bar. I groaned. Was there any way to stop this kid from walking into a meat grinder?

"Hey, man," I improvised as he walked by. "Did you hear the one about the Christian and the lions?"

He stopped in his tracks and faced me. "I'm a Christian, sir. You got any problem with that?"

I could hardly believe my ears. "You're missing the picture, friend. I'm just trying to save you," I said quietly. The bruisers' eyes were on us now.

"You?" He looked incredulous. "I'm already saved." He turned

46

away stiffly and marched right on out to the end of his plank. I swear, it was like watching a train wreck.

He walked up to those guys all full of starch and said something I couldn't hear. They both smiled at him, engaging, disarming smiles. I saw his shoulders relax a little, and then the blond man leaned forward as if to say something confidential. The kid leaned closer to hear, and as he leaned the man's left arm came up and hooked him around the neck. With one explosive motion the man slammed his face into the bar. The man brought his right arm into play and using both hands smashed his face again into the bar. He yanked the kid up by his vest and standing, shoved him backward. I saw a ribbon of blood arc from the kid's face, backlit briefly by the same elegant light fixture that had lent such a beautiful glow to Liz's hair on so many other evenings.

The music was finished and a stunned silence filled the tavern. Every eye was hostage to the young bouncer's humiliation. He landed like a sack of garbage flung onto a curb. The bruiser shook his sleeves down, flicked at his lapel and took his seat. With a gesture of disgust at the bloody bar he muttered, "Somebody take care of this shit."

Aggie had watched the spectacle grim-faced and helpless. Now she hurried to fetch two towels and dropped one onto the bar, shooting a look of pure hate at the blond man. She stooped with the other one to the fallen bouncer, who was moaning pitifully. People were edging for the door.

The dark bruiser faced the room and said, "This is a private matter. You can leave or stay, but if the police are called someone in this room will have an unfortunate accident. I never forget faces." His smile was reptilian.

"It could be you," he said to a pretty woman I had seen in the ping-pong parlor. She gasped, and her hand flew to her mouth. "Or you. Or you," he said, glancing about the crowd at random. "This is not a matter the police have any interest in." He turned back to the bar and folded his hands. There was a surge for the door.

Aggie's voice cut through the clamor. "Those who have a tab

47

please see me at the register before leaving, thank you."

The crowd at the door roiled. People waited anxiously outside for their companions to settle up and join them. The line of faces at the register reminded me of a photograph by Henri Cartier-Bresson I once had seen. In that image people were crushing one another in their panic to swap currency for gold after news of their government's fall. Here the panicked patrons were swapping their currency for a quick escape from any further unpleasantness—but the brief violence they already had witnessed was as indelibly etched in their memories as the shadows were in Cartier-Bresson's photograph. And the fear: Was I noticed? Could I be the unlucky one? Did anyone call the cops? would hang dark and unmentioned like a bat in the rafters of each uneasy mind.

I couldn't shake the feeling of being somehow responsible but didn't understand why. Val's words echoed in my mind: "Once you know something you can't run away from it—you're responsible." It didn't make any sense; why shouldn't we just leave?

I turned to Mike. "Want to go?"

"Too late, Bwana. Rollie's our friend."

"This feels like the 'b' side of a bad dream."

"Yeah, well it sure beats turning tail."

I looked down at my hands. My bandage was dirty; I had forgotten to change it after work. It looked incongruous against the softly glowing wood of the bar top. I had hardly noticed the bar this evening. How many times before had it obsessed my vision! I ran my fingertips slowly over the sleek finish as a radical new thought began forming in my mind: this workmanship was too good for a place like this. Or was it?

The bar, after all, was only a complex arrangement of atoms arising from an improbable chain of circumstances. It served a passive utilitarian role. Most recently it had served someone's impulse to flatten the face and demolish the dignity of another person. The bar itself was blameless, of course. Were the individuals who had imposed their will on its parts, who had brought it into being, equally blameless?

48

Mike was blameless, I believed. He loved that wood for its inherent qualities. I, on the other hand, loved the status that beautiful wood conferred on us; yes, especially on me.

Perhaps if the wood had had any say in the matter it would have laughed in my face. But the truth is, I felt enlarged by its beauty, swollen with pride as if I were somehow responsible for that attribute, which actually was beyond my comprehension. Maybe that was why I felt responsible for this ugly turn of events. I had regarded all of King's Tavern as my own creation; now I would be held accountable for all its potentialities, whether good or ill. The thought unnerved me.

Aggie had put ice in a plastic bag that she held to the bouncer's face. His shirt was soaked with blood and the floor around him was slick with it. The young waitress, pale with fright, was cleaning the bar in front of the blond man, who sat examining his fingernails and occasionally glancing at his watch. A few people remained in the tavern but they kept their distance from the end of the bar and conversed in low tones. Mike and I alone had not moved. As the bouncer started to pull himself together the blond addressed him in a soft voice. "I do hope you're not going to leave us before your boss gets here."

"I'm just going to the bathroom," the kid croaked.

For the first time I saw a flicker of a smile cross the blond's face. I tried unsuccessfully to squash the thought that this evening could get even worse before it was over. Mike hadn't made a sound, but I could feel the outrage radiating from him. He was hot enough to blister paint.

I was nursing the dregs of my O'Doul's when Aggie appeared with two more bottles. "Compliments of the house," she whispered and hurried away. Obviously she didn't want us leaving yet. That fact was also registered at the end of the bar. I didn't return their flat stares, but from the corner of my eye I saw Mike turn his face straight toward the pair of bruisers.

Finally I forced myself to look, and when I did the face of the dark one opened into a broad smile. He stood and started in our direction. The room suddenly felt very small. My heart was banging so hard I could feel it in my teeth. Mike swiveled to face the man as he approached. But he ignored Mike altogether; his eyes were on me.

"Mr. Brauner, is that right?" he said.

"That's right." For some crazy reason Clarence came to mind, standing in the lawyer's driveway with fear glistening in his eyes. The image did not encourage me.

"Your reputation goes before you, sir," he beamed.

"How's that?"

"No need to be modest, you handsome thing," he oozed, resting a powerful hand on my arm. "The whole world knows what marvelous work you do." He squeezed my arm and moved closer until I felt his breath on me. It reeked of almonds. "You have a bright future," he said. "A fabulous future—as long as your prejudice doesn't get in the way." He stared at me as his smile dwindled to nothing.

He withdrew his hand and tilted his head at Mike. "Your friend here is so butch, but don't you think he could use a sense of humor?" He winked at me, then reached over and tousled Mike's blond hair. My skin crawled as he turned around and walked away. I thought Mike would explode but he didn't move a muscle.

~

One of the big glass doors opened and we turned to see Rollin's entrance. He was dressed in khakis and polo shirt with an old denim jacket instead of the white shirt and tie he usually wore behind the bar. He looked fragile to me. Nobody had reloaded the CD player; the place was spookily quiet and sparsely occupied for a Wednesday night and not even eleven o'clock. Rollin looked around at the faces staring at him, then saw Aggie mopping up behind the bar. She nodded toward the end of the bar and Rollin's eyes finally engaged with those of the bruisers. Under their force he seemed to grow even smaller. After the dominance ritual was completed the dark bruiser smiled disarmingly and beckoned Rollin with a slight motion of his head. The blond still stared, his face blank and unreadable as stone.

Rollin shifted uneasily and slowly approached the pair. "I'm Rollin King. Is there something I can do for you?"

The dark one clasped his hands together, nodding and beaming back and forth between Rollin and his own brooding partner. The blond swiveled to face Rollin and continued staring at him like a specimen. Happy face slowly settled down. The blond turned to Aggie and grunted, "Vodka. With ice." He returned his stare to Rollin.

When Aggie brought the drink he drained it with one tilt of his head, then turned back to Rollin. "Where is your father?"

"I don't know," Rollin said.

"The people I represent may find that hard to accept." The blond sounded bored.

"I'm sorry, I..." Rollin stammered. "Right now I'm finding it a little hard, myself."

"You poor boy," the blond said in a silky voice. "Unfortunately, in the absence of your father we will have to deal with you. We have been instructed to close an account with your father, who owes certain individuals a sum of money. Do you have access to his funds?"

"His funds are all invested in this place." Rollin sounded stunned.

"Well now, that complicates things, doesn't it?"

"Ah, well—I suppose it could." Rollin swallowed and looked at the two men. "How much does he owe?"

"Two hundred to start with. Of course with interest that amount will be increasing rapidly, and his creditors wish to resolve the matter now before it gets out of hand."

"Two hundred dollars?" Rollin was incredulous.

"No, no, no, dear boy," the blond laughed, "that would hardly require our services. Hundreds of thousands, I should have said. My, we are really innocent, aren't we?"

"Oh, he's just the sweetest thing," the dark one said.

Rollin looked like a lost little boy.

"Debtors sometimes disappear," the blond continued, "so we

were given an alternative plan to implement with you in case your father could not be reached." He frowned at Rollin. "Are you with me here?"

Rollin was shaking his head and groping for a stool. He didn't seem too steady. Before I knew it Mike was out of his seat. He pulled a stool over to Rollin and gestured at Aggie for some water. She quickly brought a glass and Mike put it into Rollin's hand, backed off and took his seat again.

The blond looked over at Mike. "You're a real nice guy," he said. "You pay close attention."

Mike returned his stare without a word.

The blond turned back to Rollin and said, "I see you've got friends here. That's nice, because you're going to need some friends. In fact we're going to be your friends. We may even bring some other friends around to help you get through this problem."

Rollin found his voice again. "I've never seen you before. Why should I want to meet any of your friends?"

"But you already have, dear boy."

"So those were your friends in here helping me, as you say, over the past few weeks?"

The blond chuckled. "Did some of them forget their manners? Well then, we'll have to keep them happy, won't we?"

"Just what do you have in mind, mister? And if you're supposed to be my friend why don't I even know your name?"

Rollin's impertinence seemed too childlike to elicit a hostile response from the pair. In fact they seemed amused by it.

"You may call me Smith, and my associate here is Jones," the blond said with a faint smile. "You have two weeks to settle this account. If you default a lien will be attached to King's Tavern. Our clients will require fifteen percent of your gross daily in cash, against the interest accruing on your father's debt. Until either of you are able to satisfy it, we will have certain recommendations regarding your employees, beginning with security personnel. Your own, I'm afraid, are not quite ready for prime time." He turned toward the bar. "Where is that young man?"

52

I looked toward the waiters' station and saw Aggie hurrying to where the bouncer sat hunched with his face in a towel. She touched his shoulder and gestured down the bar. He stood, and much more slowly than he had made the last trip, lumbered toward the bruisers. His nose was smashed sideways. Both lips were split and lumpy; one cheek had turned purple and his eye was swollen shut. His face bore no resemblance to the one he had arrived with. He walked by us like a somnambulist.

Rollin was aghast. "Jason, what did they do to you?" he cried.

"It seems your former bouncer has decided he's not really up to the job. I'm afraid we can't trust your judgment on this; obviously you weren't investing enough to have the proper talent in place. We will be sending you some more experienced help."

Rollin shook his head and said, "This is not right. You can't just walk in here and take over my father's business. You can't tell me who to hire and fire—you don't know anything about this place. This is not right." He was getting wound up. "Somebody take Jason to the emergency room. Aggie?" he called, looking around.

Aggie scooted up, wiping her hands on a towel. The blond man leaned at Rollin and said, "One of the other waitresses may take the young man wherever he wishes to go. This one stays on duty. Understand this: there will be no police report. That would be most foolish. It was an unfortunate accident, but not a bad one. Things could be much worse. I won't remind you again." He gestured to Aggie. "Get that girl; get this piece of shit out of here."

He turned back to Rollin. "Now as for what we can and cannot do. We have a promissory note from your father for two hundred thousand dollars, notarized and payable two weeks from tomorrow. You can satisfy that debt and drive your father's business wherever you will. If you're not able to do that our clients will have a piece of your pretty ass. They have done their homework; I'm quite sure they know as much about this place as you do. We will be here to protect their interest, and about that, dear boy, you have no choice." He turned dismissively back to the bar and raised his empty glass.

The dark bruiser called Jones followed every nuance of this with an astonishing repertoire of smiles, frowns, nods, pouts and eye-popping, accompanied by much hand wringing and silent clapping. If the crisis hadn't cut so close to home it might have been more entertaining to watch that display. I couldn't tell if it was compulsive, like some bizarre manifestation of Tourette's syndrome, or acting. Jones now had Rollin locked in a pouty gaze, and with no warning his face began flipping through the channels. At least a half dozen went by. I have no idea how he did that, or why he stopped with crossed eyes and his long tongue pointing straight out. But as we watched the tip of it slowly curled up until it touched his nose. Rollin's face was ashen.

The blond bruiser calling himself Smith tossed back his final vodka and stood up. He was nearly a head taller than me and I'm six feet. The size and shape of his jacket left no doubt he could rip open a Subaru as easily as a sardine tin. His movements were graceful and feline. He turned to Rollin, towering over him with a strange glow in his eyes. "We'll be back in a few days to see how you're doing, love," he said in a husky voice.

Rollin's head tilted back as he looked up at the huge man. His eyes were wide and helpless; he was trapped on his barstool. Smith's face filled his vision and before he knew it powerful hands were behind his head pulling him up. Suddenly the man's lips were pressed to his, the man's tongue was inside his mouth.

I watched Rollin writhe and could see the force with which he was being held. Smith abandoned all restraint, ravishing his victim until, like a rabbit kicking in a tiger's mouth, Rollin stopped fighting and just yielded. I felt sick to my stomach.

~

There was a sudden crash of glass breaking in the back of the room and then a familiar voice, only louder and filled with more indignation than anyone had heard it before. "Let that man go!"

Smith released Rollin and stood flushed with passion. Rollin dropped into his barstool, crimson-faced and trembling uncontrollably. Jones's face had run out of channels; he sat expressionless.

There was a crackling new energy in the room that felt like lightning about to strike. Every eye stared in amazement as Valerie stood from the corner booth. What was left of her beer was splattered everywhere with shards of glass. She was wearing an old army jacket and her hair was stuffed up under a Pirates cap. Until that moment not one person had been aware of her presence. Even Mike's face registered disbelief.

Val stormed down that bar like a hurricane from hell. When she stood in front of Smith she ripped the cap off her head and threw it to the floor, enraged. All that hair tumbled out and his eyes opened a little wider. She put her face right up in his and blew her top wide open.

"You BASTARD!" she roared. "What gives you the right to treat this man that way? What gives you the right? And you!" She spun around and gestured to everyone else in the room. "What kind of people are you to let this filth get away with that? Look at you!" she sneered. "Chicken shit, every one of you!" Her hard mountain accent cut the air like a blade.

Jones was getting animated again but his vertical hold seemed a little jumpy. Smith looked flustered and amused, as if he had landed in the middle of an opera without a libretto. Moral force apparently was not a quality he had encountered before, but Val was getting ready to fix that. She stuck her finger in his face and went on like a boiler coming apart.

"I seen good people get abused all my life but what you just did to this man is the lowest, vilest thing I ever saw. I don't know who you are, mister, or who you think you are, but I know this man here and he don't deserve what you done."

Smith smiled mirthlessly at her.

"You think rape is funny? Some kind of way to feel superior?" All her rivets were popping now. "Well, let me tell you since no one else here seems to have the guts—you ain't good enough to even be in this place. I don't give a hoot if you're gay or straight or if you

55

fuck watermelons, mister, you ain't nothing but a big pile of shit."

Smith's palm caught Val in the face and knocked her against the bar. She stood back up and wiped blood from her mouth. "My daddy used to hit me harder than that."

Jones's face started flipping through the channels again. "What is your problem?" Val snarled at him, and he stopped on channel zero.

I was afraid this might be the end for Val. After insulting the entire room she stood alone against these two animals—entirely by choice and seemingly unafraid. What could she be thinking? It was not until much later that I realized some things are best accomplished by not thinking.

Smith's face was unreadable, his eyes opaque. Valerie stood there shooting sparks into them. After a long interval his lips peeled back and he laughed soundlessly. "You are a brave one," he finally hissed. "Such a pity for all that testosterone to be wasted on a cunt like you."

I never saw Val's foot in motion; suddenly it was buried in Smith's groin, and then it moved deliberately back to the floor under her. His last syllable got yanked into the next octave and he doubled over, reeling between the barstools.

Jones moved in sideways on Val. He took her right hand between both of his palms, twisting it on a vertical axis until her palm faced outwards, her elbow at a right angle to her body. She yelped as he twisted, the extreme torsion threatening to break her wrist.

"Let her go!" Mike's voice boomed.

Jones's eyes lit up. "My, what it takes to get a rise out of you."

Val was on her tiptoes contorting to take pressure off her wrist. Jones twisted savagely and a guttural sound came from her. Mike began dismounting from his stool. All the sounds in the room were beginning to roar inside my head when Jones looked at me, grinning.

"Let her go." My voice sounded dry and flat. I don't even remember willing myself to speak.

"Mr. Brauner?" Jones said.

"Let her go." This time I spoke with conviction.

Jones released her. She came down from her tiptoes, cradling her wrist to her chest and grimacing. In a flash I saw an image in my mind of three people slowly rotating around an unfocused point. One of them cradled something to her chest.

As quickly as it came the image disappeared and was replaced by more immediate concerns. Smith had regained his stance and was bearing down on Valerie with a malevolent expression. Everything he had done before assaulting Rollin had been marked with cold detachment. Now a line had been crossed; he was coming undone. Val's hijacking of the show had thrown fuel on everything, creating an explosive atmosphere that could blow this place apart. But before he could reach her Jones murmured, "Mr. Brauner says let her go."

Smith turned to me. "Mr. Brauner says?" he sneered.

"Let her go." I don't know how I spoke with such authority but Smith stopped. His nostrils flared and his teeth clicked and he backed off like an unrepentant dog.

"Mr. Brauner should tell this cunt she is lucky for his presence here tonight," he seethed, barely able to control himself. "As for Mr. King," he said, turning back to Rollin, "We'll be looking in on you. I hope you enjoyed this little show of support. Next time we'll find out what kind of man you really are." He smiled that thin, mirthless smile again and it chilled me to the core. Then the two men calling themselves Smith and Jones walked through the big glass doors into the night.

The silence in the tavern was profound. Rollin sat in his stool, still shaking and wiping his mouth with the back of his hand. Valerie stood cradling her wrist with tears streaming down her face. Mike sat, grim and pale, staring through those doors. My eyes strained to see some detail in the darkness outside. As we watched a dark Corvette pulled from the parking lot and passed under the street lamp. The sound of its acceleration was muted by heavy glass, by luxurious carpeting and greenery, by the womb-like atmosphere in which we were suspended. But any illusions of sanctuary in this place were shattered beyond repair.

Looking around it seemed nothing had changed but everything was different. It was as if things before had appeared in only two

57

dimensions and now they had depth, solidity. I realized there were hidden realities—layer upon layer, all neatly concealed behind that which was seen. Was this reality only a stage-set upon which was being acted out some larger drama? Were we players, or just pocket change in someone else's game?

An atmosphere of dread hung in the room, making it hard to move or speak. When the soul has been stripped naked by terror or humiliation people don't rush back into interpersonal contact. There are assessments to be made—delicate internal probings, and tentative external measurements to find what remnants of composure remain. We pondered the wounds to our pride, gauging their depth and tracing their ragged edges. Each of us had smelled our own fear and wished in vain to purge the memory of it. We had been rendered impotent by it, and reduced to spectators at an outrage. We felt each other's shame and oh, how we felt Rollin's humiliation, his utter confusion and helplessness.

There was one person among us who suffered no shame that night. Valerie had thrown everything on the line for Rollin; not only for Rollin, but for decency and humanity. When everyone else had been paralyzed by fear she not only damned the torpedoes but fired a few of her own. She now moved to where he sat and put her hands on his shoulders.

"Are you okay, Rollie?" she asked softly.

He looked at her with tears forming in his eyes. He nodded, then shook his head and finally let it go. Val gathered him in her arms and he sat there with his head on her breast, crying like he probably hadn't cried since his mother was buried. Mike and I moved our stools out a little so the rest of the people couldn't see them and just looked down at our bottles. Aggie bustled around wiping down the bar while fighting back her own tears.

CHAPTER 5

I drove home, navigating the many turns and finally the long lane back to my property in a daze. After parking the truck I sat in it a long time listening to the engine tick as it cooled. My old house stood black against the night sky. Finally I had to move. Climbing out and walking into the side door I nearly staggered with depression. I switched on the kitchen light and opened the cabinet by the sink. There was a bottle of Scotch on the shelf and I poured half a glass. I took a swallow, but before its warmth reached my gut my lips curled back in a grimace and I shuddered. I dashed the rest into the sink, belched an obscenity and put the bottle away.

I lay in bed for what seemed an eternity, trying in vain to stop the images spinning through my head. The swarthy face of Jones, frozen in a ludicrous gawk, and Smith's flat, contemptuous stare. The sickening thud of that bouncer's face being broken on the bar, and the arc of his blood, grotesquely illuminated by the wall sconce. Liz's glowing, blood-red hair. Those two separate images were forever joined in my mind now. And Smith's assault on Rollin—what could anyone think about such a thing? All the petty irritation I felt toward Rollin melted in the face of what had happened tonight. What he had endured was beyond my capacity to grasp.

And Valerie! Whether things were better or worse because of her intervention was pointless to argue; the great and immutable fact was that she had been there. Her stand for Rollin, her fearlessness, was the only comfort any of us could carry away from that nightmare. For Rollin in his hour of need it was comfort of a kind nobody else could have given. Like his fluttering, timid mother reincarnated as avenging goddess, Valerie had flung herself between him and his tormentors. She had been bruised for him, and when he broke down on her breast the rest of the world disappeared for him for a good while. Aggie shooed everyone out the door and the place emptied fast. Mike and I helped her clean up as well as we could and left Rollin and Val alone.

By the time Aggie was ready to turn off the lights they were talking quietly, forehead to forehead. When Rollin saw us look their way he walked over and said, "Ray, I'm sorry you had to see this." Pain glowed in his eyes. "Dad really trusts you, and he's never been wrong about people." The face of Liz flashed through my mind and I tried to suppress it as he continued. "Now I need you to trust me that you'll be paid everything you have coming."

I was incredulous. "Rollin," I said, "you've got way bigger problems than me now. Forget about that—right now getting these guys off your back is the only priority you've got."

"I don't think you understand me," he said. "Dad always paid his bills and so will I. Your work is valued in here and you will be taken care of. That would be Dad's way."

Again I was speechless. Valerie was watching Rollin, and then she turned to me. I saw something in her expression, a knowing, almost mocking look.

"Okay, Rollin," I said with a sinking heart. "Whatever you say. If there's anything I can do to help, you've got it."

Rollin reached back toward Valerie. "Just take care of this girl," he said, laying a hand on her shoulder. "Don't let anything happen to her."

Valerie's expression changed abruptly. She stuck out her chin and said, "I'll take care of myself, Rollie. Right now you need us. And we'll be right here, won't we, Mister Brauner?" She glared at me.

"Of course we will," I said.

"Don't you worry about Val," Mike said to Rollin. "We'll be her guardian angels. We've all got to watch out for each other now. You know these guys may try to split us apart. We can't let them do that."

There was agreement around the circle. There were solemn declarations of loyalty and a big group hug as we went our separate ways, but none of it fooled me. It was all whistling in the dark. Val was the one among us with the least to lose, it seemed, so her recklessness could be understood. But I knew none of us had the means to stand up to these people. And unless Rollin could come up with a lot of money fast they would eat him alive.

~

I lay in bed and cursed my luck for getting caught up in this. Why, after leaving everything behind for a new beginning, was I now plunged into such a pit not of my own making? And who was Valerie anyway, that she could determine my role in the affair? How she got the idea to do that I couldn't guess, and the audacity of it astonished me.

Then my self-pity collapsed into shame when I remembered Rollin. How much more innocent was he than all of us! Of course Val was right; we had to help him—but how? For the first time in memory I wished I could ask my father for advice.

Now there was a pointless thought. Dad had been dead nearly ten years, and when he was alive I wanted only to be as different from him as possible. I still checked myself occasionally after making some gesture that called him to mind. He'd been a sergeant on the Montgomery County police force in Rockville, Maryland. He was well respected by his fellow officers. There had been some strong silent types fighting back tears at his funeral, but I wasn't one of them. I had been more concerned for Mom, who was devastated after his heart attack. I couldn't grieve for losing something I never had.

Dad never made any attempt to enter my world, to understand the things I loved. He was a frustrated military cop. After being passed over for promotion three times he opted out of the Army and entered the civilian police force, hoping to become a detective. He never did, and he never got over it.

Dad didn't know how to think outside the lines; in my opinion it was why he never advanced beyond rank and file. Regimentation and order were second nature to him. He didn't understand why I liked working with my hands, carving wood and making things. To him artists were effeminate and laborers were peasants. The only way I could gain his approval was by engaging in his world, a suffocating culture of macho and bureaucracy. Around his fellow officers I felt

61

like an alien, a reminder of the domestic lives many of them had left behind. To Dad I was a dreamer, an introvert, and worst of all in his regimented mind, a non-conformist.

Dad taught me how to shoot when I was thirteen and I was pretty good. In fact I had a better eye than he did, and it drove him crazy that I really didn't like guns. He enrolled me in karate school the next year and that bombed. I took lessons for six months and every time I came home he tried to spar with me out in the yard. He knocked me down again and again, and confused me with his instructions that usually contradicted everything the sensei tried to teach me. I would retreat to my room, to my sculpting and my guitar, and he would retreat to the driving range where he could hit the damned balls as hard as he wanted. Between his job and the driving range he had ample opportunity to vent his frustrations. Mom just kept hoping for the best, loving us both in spite of the gulf between us.

When I took a job after high school working construction rather than enrolling in community college Dad was insulted. As a true believer in the character-building qualities of military service, he'd have been happier if I had gotten drafted. When I finally began studying architecture at University of Maryland he was merely cynical. In four years he never asked how my studies were going. After I graduated he predicted my internship wouldn't last six months. He was right; I was invited to become a full employee at the firm where I was working after three months. Not once did he visit any of my building projects. Though he never came out and said it, I knew it chapped him pretty hard to see me make it in a profession where he could claim no credit for my success.

Back when I started hanging out with long-haired friends in high school he investigated several of them without my knowledge and found that one was selling marijuana. He staked out the guy's house and made a list of every car that came and went at night, and then picked several of those people to shadow. He played cloak and dagger for weeks and eventually hit the jackpot. With his scribbled notes and license tag numbers of half the people I knew at school he

62

helped coordinate the department's biggest pot bust of the year, which boosted his reputation at the precinct and won him a citation from Governor Marvin Mandel. It was the high point of his career.

My whole reputation went down the toilet until long after graduation. No way would I attend community college with the group who had branded me a snitch. As an only child I was used to being alone, but never had I been shunned by anyone until then. Dad never understood why I resented that episode so much, or why I even cared about the lowlifes he put in the detention center.

But all that was long ago, and on this night Dad's relentless obsession for putting bad guys away didn't seem so unreasonable. I remembered the warning both Smith and Jones had given. I didn't doubt for a moment they would make good on it if the police became involved. If they were willing to make such a public example of the bouncer they'd not hesitate to pay someone a private call. But the warning meant someone, somewhere up the line was vulnerable.

I felt certain Liz Travino was part of this. She had kept herself aloof from everyone but the old man; was it because she was shy, or did she have an agenda? Did their breakup just tip him over the edge, or was she more deeply involved? What was the nature of his debt? I'd never seen him take irresponsible risks. It was hard to believe the old man could be involved with underworld characters— he talked too compulsively to keep any dark secrets for long. And for all his swagger he was a small-town conservative with an inbred suspicion of anyone from any city bigger or farther away than Allentown. Apparently he made an exception for Liz. I knew he wasn't above greasing a palm now and then, but certainly his world didn't encompass organized crime. Or did it? What did I really know about anyone around here?

Now Valerie was deep in this mess, deeper than I wanted to think about. When everyone else had been concerned only with preserving their anonymity, she had plunged into battle in a way most calculated to mark her for reprisal. And I was doubly obligated—I had promised my aid to both her and Rollin, but felt even more helpless to affect things now than on the day she was fired.

I groaned out loud, wholeheartedly regretting the first time Val and I left King's Tavern together. That was back in the glory days, and we felt just like two kids sneaking away from the party to make out in the parking lot. Of course it didn't take long to progress to the next level and before I knew it I was spending lunch breaks at her trailer just outside of town. She never seemed to care that I was nearly fifteen years her senior. And after nearly two years of celibacy, for me the chemistry was a lot more compelling than the math.

We carried on like crazy for several weeks and then her schedule changed. And then my crew and I were going full bore at the lawyer's house, and by the time we saw each other again something in the equation had changed. We still flirted and talked easily but that's where it stayed. It wasn't long after that Valerie's star began to fall. It was clear the intimacy we shared back then had tangled our destinies somehow. How I wished I could go back and unmake that mistake! What if I just walked away? How could I abandon a friend? I wallowed in my bed, sweating and begging for sleep to come.

Tomorrow we had to work; there was a new job to begin. I couldn't let this disaster sabotage our schedule, too much was at stake. But there was one matter from the evening I had been avoiding, a question that confounded my imagination: Why did I wield such authority with those terrible men? It was easy to write off Jones' flattery, even his abuse and release of Valerie, as posturing. He was an obvious exhibitionist, but when Smith came unglued that had been no charade. He was enraged, and when his advance on Valerie was blocked he nearly foamed at the mouth. My words had stopped him like a brick wall and there was no explanation for it.

I didn't know if the others were troubled by it as well, but my experience in high school taught me how easily people will believe the worst about others. I hadn't missed Aggie's expression when Jones released Valerie at my word. And when Smith stopped in his tracks she stared like I was Moses parting the Red Sea. I had been just as amazed, but now was afraid this strange miracle might come back to haunt me. I remembered Mike's prediction that they would try to split us apart and it compounded my anxiety. I tossed and turned, unable to find comfort in any position or solace from a single thought.

CHAPTER 6

Thursday's dawn crept in behind gray, clammy skies. I woke feeling like I had been sucked through a tube and spat onto my bed; my sheets were soaked with sweat. Last night's events ate at me like a hangover. The sense of oppression that had kept me awake most of the night hadn't clocked out yet and the thin daylight didn't help much.

The weather radio reported falling barometric pressure and an eighty percent chance of rain. I groaned and shuffled into the bathroom. Pulling a plastic bag over my dirty bandage, I fastened it with a rubber band and stepped into the shower. I cranked the cold water on full blast and clenched my teeth. Gasping and sputtering, I scrubbed myself with an old loofah sponge while counting fast to one hundred. At the end I dropped the sponge and let the water smack me in the face for another few seconds.

After drying I felt somewhat more coherent and forced my thoughts to the day ahead. At seven thirty—twenty minutes from now—Mike and I were to meet the backhoe operator who would be digging the foundation on our new job. It was a two-story addition on a farmhouse a few miles south of Gladburg. The owners were leaving on vacation in three weeks, and I had promised to have the framing closed in before then. Eventually we'd have to open up the old roof to tie in the new one, not to mention a large portion of what was now an outside wall. Rain today would be no fun, but better now than later.

I dressed in a T-shirt and coveralls, pulled on my mud boots and went into the kitchen. I poured the last of yesterday's coffee into a plastic travel mug and slid it into the microwave. I looked in the cupboard to see what I could eat on the way. I dumped the last apple from a bowl on the counter into a nearly empty bag of chips. There were some leftover chicken wings in the refrigerator and I tossed them in. As I was reaching for my rain parka from its hook by the door the microwave beeped. I turned and pulled out my mug, set it on the counter and snapped the lid down. A scalding blob of coffee squirted out, soaking my T-shirt collar and surprising me with pain. I swore under my breath, grabbed the bag and headed out the door, forgetting my parka.

Halfway to my truck I remembered the parka and turned back to the house. Cradling the bag of food in my right arm and hooking the coffee mug with my thumb I fumbled for my keys with my left hand. Of course they were in my right pocket. I contorted to reach them, and as my body twisted hot coffee spilled from the mug onto my bandage and the heat seared into my burns with a pain that was unbelievable. I flung the mug away and howled into the fog, blindly waiting for the agony to subside.

I felt a sense of futility that for some reason did not subdue but enraged me. Was this the way it was going to be—a battle for every step forward? Fine, I can give as good as I get. Just don't let anyone fuck with me today.

Suddenly I saw a picture of myself crouching by the path, cursing into the fog and clutching my hand to my chest, and recalled the image I had seen before passing out at the lawyer's house. There were three figures rotating around an unfocused point. I remembered seeing a similar image flash through my mind last night when that monstrous man had been bearing down on Valerie.

I understood nothing, but the novelty of those images displaced my rage long enough for me to retrieve my keys and unlock the door. I grabbed my parka from its hook and then saw the roll of blueprints for the job standing in the urn by the door. Feeling foolish but suddenly grateful, I stuck them under my arm and headed back out. I picked my sorry breakfast off the ground and found my coffee several paces away with the lid intact, still half full, and walked to the truck in a more subdued frame of mind.

~

It was seven forty and Mike was checking distances between our stakes with a steel tape when I pulled up. He took one look and shook his head. "Damn, I hope the other guy looks half as bad."

"Don't even start," I growled. "Where's everyone?"

"Mack and Spider are in the stake body picking up steel and forms. The rest of the guys are cleaning up the other house."

"If we don't get something going here there's not going to be a hell of a lot for them to do this afternoon."

"It shouldn't take Digger too long to knock this out since we're on grade. You got the transit?"

"It's behind the seat in my truck. It's going to rain."

"I know."

"I feel like shit."

"I know."

We fell silent, and then Mike spoke. "You talk to Val this morning?"

I groaned inside, remembering my new responsibility. "I didn't think she'd appreciate me calling so early."

"I dropped by her place on the way here. I thought she should have a way to get in touch if she needs to, so I left my cell phone with her."

"You mean the company phone."

"Come on, what difference does that make? It's just a precaution. She didn't want to take it; I even had to show her how it worked."

"Whatever," I said.

He shot me a hard look. "You're right, she didn't appreciate me waking her up. Matter of fact, she didn't look a whole lot better than you do."

I left that one alone and spat out a bit of apple peel. "Well, damn, where is that backhoe?" I fumed.

We stretched twine between the stakes, and then Mike worked his way around the perimeter of the foundation, shaking chalk from a coffee can to mark the line. His low stance and fluid movement reminded me of my old karate sensei. He finished and put the can in his van and I began winding up the twine. We waved hello at the kitchen window to Mrs. Frye as she washed her breakfast dishes. Mr. Frye emerged on the back stoop. He lifted his cap to reveal a pale white dome above his tanned face and scratched it with a callused thumb.

"Looks like rain."

"Probably," Mike said.

"You boys be okay?"

"Probably." Mike grinned.

Mr. Frye chuckled a deep chuckle that built on itself until it tumbled out in laughter. "Yeah, you boys'll be just fine." He bent down to stroke a battle-scarred orange cat that was threading between his ankles, and continued laughing as the cat stretched up his leg, presenting its ears and head for scratching.

About that time a diesel engine could be heard laboring up the driveway. Mike and I excused ourselves and walked around the house to see Digger's dump truck emerging from the mist. His backhoe hunkered on a trailer behind it, and we waved him around the house to the edge of the yard.

After killing the engine, Danny Gipe, also known as Digger, eased down from his cab and stood rubbing his hands together. His eyes were puffy and bloodshot and he moved his head slowly— rather like a man who is seeing double, or else a man with a very bad headache. I looked skeptically at him.

"We were starting to get lonely," I said.

"Rough night." Digger spat, and turned his attention to the backhoe.

We waited for him to unload the machine. It was a big Case tractor about ten years old, and Digger was an undisputed artist with it. The first time I saw him he was digging up a gas line on a slope nobody else wanted to touch, and even he was a fool to have gone near. He was getting double his usual fee, and he worked his machine with surgical precision, like an extension of his own fingers, and uncovered that line without a single contact between his bucket and the pipe. He had the touch all right, but I sure didn't like seeing him in this condition.

After backing his rig off the trailer Digger left it warming up while he paced off the foundation with us. He moved the machine into place, set his anchors and was just starting to work when I heard a hissing noise and he let out a string of profanities. I turned and saw a geyser spewing from a hydraulic line on his boom. He shut the engine off, hopped down from the tractor and punched its great tire with his fist. Muttering he stood facing the offending part, which now wept a thin stream of oil, and shook his head.

"I don't have nothing here," he finally announced. "I got to go back to the shop, I got some hose there."

"How long to fix it?" I asked.

"Maybe fifteen, twenty minutes." He shrugged.

"Mike, run him back there in your van, or take my truck if you want—just make it fast. I don't want to waste all day on this bullshit."

"Come on," Mike gestured. Digger turned to me with palms up but I turned away scowling. He caught up with Mike and they hopped in his van and disappeared down the driveway in a swirl of mist.

~

I stood alone by the disabled backhoe in the sudden silence and raged that the day already seemed to be running into the ditch. Digger's rough night, my ass. Couldn't have been any worse than mine, but by God, I was here. Why the hell can't other people hold up their end of the bargain? The longer I stood there the madder I got. It was going to rain, and after Digger finished his work we'd be out here slipping around in the muck for hours. I thought of Val speaking about my "lesser servants" doing all the dirty work, and laughed out loud. It wasn't a rich, friendly laugh like Mr. Frye's.

I'd planned everything to be ready for pouring concrete Friday morning. It should have been easy; it still could work, but I was getting anxious. Problems have unforeseen ways of compounding themselves; anything that brought work to a standstill was bad news. I paced the wet grass muttering curses.

Finally I walked to the trailer and sat down. I found myself squinting at the site and visualizing the addition we were about to build. It was a ritual I'd always had—to sit down before beginning any job and take in every detail of the site. I would build the planned structure in my imagination like a time-lapse movie before breaking ground. Sometimes the process showed me details I hadn't thought of or gave me ideas that helped the job along. I hadn't taken the time to do that with this job, so hectic had the past few weeks been.

The air was absolutely still. In a near-trance I willed the foundation to appear, then watched as the anchor plates were laid and floor joists spanned the area. Plywood sheets fanned out into subflooring and then the outer walls were raised. The second story took form and I watched as the ridge was set. As rafters began lining up, a whisper of a sound touched me from all sides. My emotions were strangely stirred. I forgot about the house and listened. Rain, soft as a kiss, was beginning to fall. After all the stress and anxiety of the past twelve hours the sound was so peaceful that I suddenly found it hard to think of as our enemy today. It just was, with an inevitability that left no room for regret.

As I sat pondering my surrender to the very thing I'd been dreading all morning, several ghostly shapes materialized from the fog. Deer—five, six, now seven of them milled together in the accreting mist, moving from right to left across my field of vision. They stopped just inside the white lines marking the foundation we were about to dig. They were inside the house now, according to the floor plan, and clearly indifferent to my imagined structure. They looked at me one by one until all seven stood motionless, watching. I didn't move a muscle; I just stared back. It was a face-off that might have continued some time longer but for the distant roar of the stake-body truck coming up the drive. They turned and leaped silently, gracefully into the mist.

I sat still watching for the truck. The headlights appeared first, bright dots in the fog. As the roar grew louder I began to make out the shape of the cab. I watched the headlights disappear behind the house as the truck circled the driveway from the other side, then reappear, cutting a path through the falling rain as Mackey pulled in close to the foundation line. The headlights died, the engine coughed to a halt and after a moment Mackey and Spider got out.

I watched Mackey's eyes sweep the site as he stood pulling on a pair of gloves. He missed me altogether. Spider briefly studied the backhoe and then turned to Mackey.

"Well god damn," he said. "Looks like a flying saucer abducted everyone."

"Maybe they're inside having coffee," Mackey said.

"Digger?" Spider laughed.

"Why not? He's a farm boy."

"Precisely. He's not in there. Mike's van's not here, either." Spider fished in his pocket for a cigarette and lit it. He scuffed his heel in the grass and blew out a cloud of smoke that drifted slowly my way.

The moments before had been clean and quiet, but now the spell was broken. I waited for the smoke to hit my nostrils.

"Morning, gentlemen."

Mackey jumped. "Jesus, Ray, where did you come from?"

Spider looked amused.

"Right here, only it's just me." I rose to my feet and ambled toward them.

"Where is everybody? You look like hell."

"Why, thank you. Body A is right here looking like hell. Body B is taking body C back to his shop for parts. Busted a hydraulic line on his rig. Bodies D and E just arrived in the truck with forms and steel to unload, and I believe that's every body. Unless you want to talk about the bodies over at the other house."

"Had a bad night, huh?"

"It's today you better be worried about. Let's get this stuff down."

"Come on, Bwana, what happened last night? We heard you were there."

"I said, let's get this stuff down."

We walked to the end of the truck. I was damned if I would even start thinking about last night, much less talk about it now. Spider

72

jumped up on the bed and started sliding the bundles of rebar to us on the ground. We pulled them off and laid them in the center of the lot. The rough steel rods tore at my bandage like huge rasps. Nothing but an oversized glove would have fit over it, and I didn't have one. We stacked the forms, some lumber and other miscellaneous materials beside the steel, and in about ten minutes the job was done. My bandage was coming apart, and we were getting soaked. I told Mackey to move the truck out of the backhoe's path, and ran back to my pickup to get my parka.

If it didn't get any worse than this, I thought, we'd be okay. At least there wasn't any wind. I knew Digger wouldn't let a little rain stand between him and the money he'd make today. His backhoe had a canopy—he wouldn't get the worst of it. The ground had a gentle slope but it was firm and there were no buried septic or utility lines on the lot. I wasn't sure if the deer's visit had been a benediction or a reproach but wanted to believe the best. I made a conscious effort to relax—every part of me was getting tighter than a banjo string again.

Spider was examining the backhoe with the kind of scrutiny he usually reserved for Harley Davidson motorcycles and women. He'd found the break in the line—not too hard from all the oil around and under it—and was running his finger carefully over the spot when Mike's van came around the house and slid to a stop. Digger jumped from the passenger side wearing a scowl and brandishing a length of heavy black hose like a weapon. He walked to his dump truck, hauled a tool box from the cab and lugged it over to his machine. Spider stood by with a faint smile as Digger sorted through his tools.

"Ain't you got something to do, asshole?" Digger said.

"I'm just trying to learn how to be a great mechanic like you," Spider said.

Suddenly Digger's arm came up with a medium-sized box wrench and sent it flying. Spider threw up an arm and twisted out of its way, then whirled around and kicked the tool box lid down onto Digger's other hand and stomped on it. Digger howled like an animal and Spider lunged down and grabbed him by the neck and said, "If you

73

ever do such a thing again I will hurt you so bad you'll wish you were dead seven times over. You got that, dickhead?" Digger nodded, blinking, and Spider released his neck, shoving him backward.

I glared at both of them. "You girls want to work now, or go home?" I snapped. "I'll dig this foundation with a pick and shovel if I have to, but I will not tolerate idiots on the job."

"You're the boss," Spider shrugged. "I just wanted to see if old dickhead here would figure out somebody cut his line."

"I don't like you calling me that," Digger growled.

Spider laughed, then Mike stepped in his face. "Are you hard of hearing or what, man?" he said.

"I think you're all hard of hearing," Spider sneered. "I'm just trying to tell the man someone's been fucking with his rig, and he doesn't seem to care about that as much as he does being a dickhead."

"What are you talking about?" Digger demanded, scrambling to his feet.

"Look at your split, man. Run your finger down to the end of it but don't press too hard."

Digger stood by the boom and began examining the split in his line. He rubbed his thumb along the gap, suddenly recoiled and whipped it into his mouth, sucking. He pulled it out to examine it. "Shit!" he bellowed through bloody teeth, then spat.

Spider laughed again. "Case closed."

"What the hell!" Mackey exclaimed, and then walked over to the boom. He gingerly felt along the gap and then said, "By golly, someone broke off a blade in that line!"

Sure enough, there was the tip of a utility knife blade buried deep in the steel reinforcing threads of the hose, broken at such an angle that it was all but invisible. Enough of it protruded to have drawn a generous blood sample from Digger, who stood sucking his thumb and frowning at everyone.

Would this day ever get on track? "Mike," I begged, "go get the man a band-aid or something, will you?" Then turning to Digger I said, "Look, Danny, I'm sorry about your rig. That's a hell of a thing

74

to do, but if you quit now whoever did it wins. Just fix the damned thing and let's get this done."

Digger stood in the rain shaking his head slowly. His long straight hair was plastered to his forehead, and drops were beginning to run off his chin and the tip of his nose. Finally he sputtered, "I'm going to kill that bitch, I swear I'm going to kill that bitch!"

Mackey's eyes opened wide. "You think your woman did that?" he asked with awe.

Digger hurled himself at the tractor's huge tire, pummeling it with his fist until his anger was spent. At last he turned around with a hollow expression, opened his tool box and set methodically to work.

By the time the rest of my crew arrived, the machine was repaired and Digger had completed one side of the footer. We laid out the forms and steel beside the trench and turned the corner, barely staying out of the backhoe's long reach. When Digger was finished Mike and I shot levels and staked corners and steps and then we all swarmed that foundation, working like ants. By the end of the day we were slipping around in the mud, covered with it, eating it. We lost tools; we broke the transit. We narrowly averted yet another fight. I knew all the guys had heard about last night's scene at King's Tavern, but mercifully nobody mentioned it for the rest of the day.

By evening my bandage hung in filthy tatters and my hand ached, but the job was perfect. The pour the next morning was perfect too, and after we finished I couldn't resist scrawling stick figures of seven deer into the still-wet concrete where they had crossed the foundation line the day before.

"What's that?" Mike asked.

When I told him about the deer that had appeared in the fog he just grinned, as if he'd been the one to arrange them.

~

The evening after setting the forms I cleaned my hand and put a new bandage on it. All that muddy abuse hadn't helped it one bit. My blisters were peeling and sore, but the pit in the middle of my palm was swelling around the edges and felt worse. By the time we finished pouring concrete the next morning it was sending little drumbeats up my arm.

I sent the guys home early after caving and agreeing to pay them for an extra couple hours. I fumbled out of my cement-spattered coveralls, uncovering jeans and a clean shirt underneath, and exchanged my boots for a clean pair of sneakers. Mike changed too, and we headed out for the lawyer's house. The walk-through there could be over in half an hour or it could take the rest of the day—we would be entirely at the disposition of Mr. and Mrs. Plum. For the money they were spending and the generous if somewhat offbeat way they treated us, I'd have shined their shoes if they asked.

We picked up subs from Campelli's, a pizza joint downtown, and when we arrived at the Plum's house went out onto the deck to eat. Mike finished first. After draining his iced tea he brushed crumbs from the rail, stuffed his trash into a bag and squinted up at the ridge. Yesterday's rain had washed everything clean; it was a glorious day.

"How's the hand?" he said.

"A little sore—probably should have kept it dry yesterday."

"Not getting infected, is it?"

"It'll be fine," I said.

"Any news from the old man?"

"Not that I've heard."

"You talk to Rollin?"

"Nope."

"We can't just leave him twisting in the wind," he said. "Somebody besides Val has to be there when those bastards come back."

"I know." I'd been having the same thought.

"It's Friday, Bwana. You think it might be a good idea to drop in?"

"Yeah. But definitely without Wonder Woman. You talk to her again?"

76

"No—I figured you probably ought to see her next."

I didn't answer for a minute, and then Mike asked, "You guys okay with each other?"

I sighed and finally shrugged. "Yeah, fine."

My feelings were so contradictory I hardly knew what to say. On one hand Val's courage awed me, but another part of me felt she had dragged me into someone else's mess without my consent. I didn't share her temperament and had no inclination to follow her into battle. There would always be heroes and villains. I wished to be neither; I just wanted to do my work.

"I guess I'm still just trying to comprehend where the old man went; hell, this whole thing has me all confused," I said.

"You?" Mike looked at me.

"I'll stop by her place when we're done here," I finally said.

We began a walk-through of the house, and when we reached the master bedroom suite found the floor had not been clean-swept. "God damn it!" I flared. I snatched up several empty cardboard boxes that had been thrown into the corner and ripped up the scuffed paper that protected the wood floor. I punched everything down into one huge wad and carried it out to the dumpster, calling curses down on my derelict crew while Mike quietly swept up behind me. I found a half roll of rosin paper in the garage, took it upstairs and we laid a clean walkway across the floor and taped the edges down. We went back down and walked through the west wing.

We climbed the stairs to the observatory. I pressed a switch on the wall and there was a low hum. A crack of daylight appeared in front of us, yawning wider as the dome port opened to the sky. Sunlight poured in. I pressed another button and the dome began a slow rotation, and as it turned we scanned the horizon. The view to the south was breathtaking. I found myself wondering what Mr. Plum would value most about this place. Would his gain from it be equal to what I was letting go?

Everything upstairs was in order so we closed the observatory and went down to the atrium. We checked the valves from the solar panels, and I knelt to drink from the stream that flowed through the

77

atrium. Its source was a spring we had uncovered while digging the basement. With an average flow of over thirty gallons per minute that spring had been a near disaster at first, but with help from an unexpected source and some careful engineering it turned into a serendipity which charmed Mrs. Plum more than anything else about the house. It was the sweetest water any of us had tasted. After testing it for purity and tapping it for the house's supply we piped it into the atrium. I talked a landscape designer friend of mine into creating a waterfall for it with small boulders and smooth river stones he gathered and trucked at considerable expense from their place of origin upstate. The stream tumbled down the boulders and ran diagonally through the atrium, finally disappearing into a grate at the front wall. From there we had piped it around the foundation back into its original course underground.

There was still plenty of space for Mrs. Plum to do whatever she wanted with the atrium, but I liked it as it was now. It had a stark, uncluttered quality akin to a Japanese rock garden, livened only with the perpetual music of flowing water.

I was calming down slowly from the stress of the past two days, and aside from the mess upstairs found that I was enjoying this quiet walk through the house. It felt like a good-bye—from now on things would change quickly. This place, which from the beginning had been filled with my crew and all our personalities, soon would shut us out of its memory. Our handiwork would remain, but the collective spirit we breathed into it—that intangible motivating force that got the house built—would be obliterated by its new occupants. Like King's Tavern, our product would take on a new character, different from anything I could imagine.

It was a natural process, part of the deal of being a builder. It was the only part I'd never fully come to terms with, but there was no bargaining with the inevitable. With mundane projects it was easy to walk away, but when the job involved my heart as well as my hands, it felt as if I were leaving behind a piece of myself. Ending this job gave me a feeling that bordered on melancholy.

It was nearly two o'clock when we heard the sound of a car.

"Think we ought to charge him time and a half?" Mike grinned.

"He would," I said as a deep blue Porsche Carrera growled up the driveway. Damn right he would. How could anyone spend as extravagantly as Mr. Plum did except by squeezing money from every possible source, and continuing to squeeze with every ounce of his will until there was nothing left to squeeze? More than once while building this house I'd found myself gloating that I was making money from a lawyer, instead of things being the other way around. But I also knew we were giving him a magnificent piece of work. There were no losers in this deal, I thought—we both stood on equal ground.

If only I could have seen through Valerie's eyes I might have known what a dangerous assumption that was. But I couldn't, and now it was show time.

CHAPTER 7

Mr. Joseph Plum, senior partner in the firm Manning, Lazar, Goldberg and Plum, strode across the ground to the entry of his new home. Thick, iron-gray hair stood above his lined face. Dark, brooding eyes darted beneath his brow. A gold and navy tie erupted from a perfect knot between the points of his impeccably starched collar, and his suit was bespoke. Hand-made Italian shoes that cost more than all the shoes I've owned in the past five years gleamed on his feet. Mr. Plum wasn't a tall man, but he was athletically built and carried himself with the gait of a prizefighter. A smile of unmistakable pride played around the corners of his mouth.

His wife, the silver-haired and perfectly stunning Mrs. Gloria Plum, followed several paces behind. Balancing on heels and looking slightly tipsy, she wore a black frock that ended well above her knees. I wondered what social function she had recently been rescued from, or whether she just carried her own fun with her everywhere. I glanced at Mike as he tried to hide a self-conscious grin. The last time they were here she had flirted skillfully and shamelessly with him, and her husband only seemed vaguely amused. I wondered what kind of arrangement they had, and whether she was ever completely sober. When Mike and I stepped onto the terrace to greet them their faces opened into smiles.

"Raymond! Michael! What a pleasure to see you." Mr. Plum extended his hand. I apologetically held my bandaged right hand to my chest and offered my left for him to grasp, and we shook awkwardly. He shook Mike's hand and Mrs. Plum twinkled at us both. "Nothing serious with the hand, I hope?" Mr. Plum asked.

"Just a little burn—it's healing," I said.

He looked intently at me. "Let's hope so. So many things to do, and so few who can. You need your hands, Raymond—the world needs your hands."

I didn't know how to respond, so just gestured to the open door and said, "Welcome home."

Mrs. Plum touched my arm on the way in and breathed, "It's beautiful, just beautiful." She smiled and winked at Mike, who smiled back, blushing.

Quiet as Mike was, with anyone else he'd have held his own ground. He might flirt back or not, but he never acted dumb. This woman made him as close to dumb as I'd seen him get, and it seemed quite beyond his control. Something about Gloria Plum set more than just Mike's ears burning, and I knew his sense of propriety well enough to realize how it embarrassed him. Another curious wrinkle in the fabric of life, I smiled to myself, and entered behind the three.

Mrs. Plum turned and walked into the atrium where she stopped and cocked her head, listening. Her body swayed almost imperceptibly, and even from behind I knew her eyes were closing. I understood what she was feeling. The water's music did the same thing to me, and I was glad to see that even in her present state its magic wasn't lost on her. Mr. Plum followed his wife into the atrium while Mike and I stayed at the door.

Mr. Plum stood beside his wife and spoke quietly to her. She reached a hand to his and pulled him close. They stood for a short minute like two dolls atop a wedding cake, and Mr. Plum spoke again to her. She turned her face to his and I was surprised to see it streaked with tears. She murmured something we couldn't hear, and he walked back to us.

"She'll catch up," he said.

Good, I thought. Let her take all the time in the world. As long as someone here waters her soul in the beauty of this place I can let it go in peace. Mrs. Plum might be a little nutty but I felt she saw beyond the timbers and stone to the essence of this place. For all Mr. Plum's intelligence, the house to him was a trophy, a material asset he coveted and now owned. But I knew it was neither workmanship nor any genius of design that made it so extraordinary. It was the convergence of craft and design with something more—the profound rhythm that beats through all nature, a timeless, powerful essence the very earth here possessed. It was something beyond any of us that we'd been given the opportunity to dance with for a while. Now it was theirs. For Gloria Plum to be the one to understand that, rather than her husband, was fine with me.

We walked slowly through the west wing, taking time to answer all Mr. Plum's questions and acquaint him with every switch, keypad, thermostat and valve along the way. Every function of the house, from climate control to the security system, incorporated microprocessors that could be accessed by computer. The house could be run from anywhere.

Several of my older guys thought it was fanatical but to me it made sense. A few years down the road personal computers would be used by everybody—even technophobes like Mackey. If Mr. Plum wanted his new house to be a cyber-controlled paradise I was happy to accommodate him. It subtracted nothing from the beauty of the place for him to be able to switch on a security camera from his desk in Philadelphia and scan his driveway here, or turn up the heat pump via cell phone from his car a couple hours before arriving on a winter weekend, or monitor the soil moisture and switch on his lawn sprinklers from a beach in the Seychelles. Mrs. Plum would hold the real cards while Mr. Plum played with his toys.

When we arrived at the steps leading up into the observatory Mr. Plum flipped the light switch at the landing, smiled at Mike and me and clambered up like an excited kid. He paced impatiently around the room as Mike and I trudged up behind him, then stood chin in hand frowning at the spot where the telescope would be mounted.

The joists beneath us were massive oak beams anchored into masonry and buttressed to make the platform impervious to vibration. Mike and I already had discussed options of getting the scope in and decided if it couldn't be carried up the staircase we'd unbolt the dome, get Digger to lift it off with a crane and then lower the scope in. A few hours of hassle for us and a few hundred bucks for Digger—no big deal. I really didn't expect it to be necessary though. I explained all this to Mr. Plum and his frown melted. "You've thought of everything," he said.

"Actually it was Mike's idea," I said, and he chuckled.

"Splendid, the two of you are like Romulus and Remus. Keep it up and someday you'll build a city." He looked intently at us and then laughed again as our expressions sobered to match his. "Just don't forget your benefactors when you reach the top."

He examined the dome controls, and pressed the button to open the port. The cover glided back and daylight again flooded the room. We gazed out to the top of the hill behind the house and I caught a fleeting glimpse of a figure, head and shoulders a tiny speck, disappearing over the ridge. Somewhere out of sight a mockingbird was singing and its voice pierced me with sweetness. The air smelled like trees, grass, rocks and sky. The northern sky itself was a startling blue. I was transfixed. The figure was gone—had it been there at all? Mr. Plum's angle of view hadn't allowed him to see the spot, but when I caught Mike's eye knew he'd seen it.

Mr. Plum pressed another switch and the dome began its slow rotation. A sliver of sunlight broadened on the floor as it turned, and when the port at last faced the valley Mr. Plum stood fully illuminated, like a figurehead on a ship's prow. In the distance was the neighboring farm, its stone barn planted solidly into a little green rise. The old house stood nearby surrounded by hickories and maples, sunlight glinting off its slate shingles. Farther beyond a stream threaded through the valley, partly hidden by hillocks and trees, flashing silver here and there. The mockingbird continued pouring his heart out into the afternoon. I was spellbound by his repertoire—each riff was unique, he never repeated himself.

"One might wait a lifetime for a moment like this but never hold it in his hand," Mr. Plum murmured.

"You better hold tight, Mr. Plum, because tomorrow's another day," Mike returned in his soft voice. I was shocked.

"As usual, Michael, you speak the truth," Mr. Plum said, turning to face him. "But let's not let what happens tomorrow spoil what we have here."

Mike blushed. Blindsided, I searched for something to say, anything at all to change the subject. "What we have here is a first-class way to celebrate the Leonid meteor shower," I blurted. "It'll be in November, after you've had a chance to settle in—why don't we plan for it?" I don't know where it came from and couldn't seem to stop it.

Mr. Plum turned to me. "Ah, the Leonids," he said, half smiling. "They should be spectacular this year, with comet Tempel-Tuttle passing so close to the sun. But I was hoping for more than that." He paused, and then his eyes locked with mine.

"You built this place, Raymond. If you want a party here you'll not have to ask twice. But if we aren't friends first, then all such occasions become quid pro quos. If you want to proceed on that basis I can reciprocate, but I should warn you that I hold the position of greater strength, and I did not arrive where I am by making concessions to weakness."

His bluntness hit me like a bullet and I stood gaping. His expression softened. "Friends, then," he said, offering his hand.

"Of course," I stammered, grasping it with my bandaged right hand. Pain shot up my arm.

"Michael?" Mr. Plum inquired, extending his hand.

"Yes sir. I misspoke."

"I understood you well, Michael, and you needn't apologize. The important thing is that we understand each other. I'm here for both of you if you're here for me."

"Yes sir," Mike said as they shook hands. The lawyer's last line sounded a lot like a quid pro quo to me but I let it pass, grateful and amazed not to have plunged any deeper into the conversational abyss we had stumbled upon. Suddenly I was beginning to reevaluate my assumption about equal ground. I didn't want Joseph Plum for an adversary—life was complicated enough already. What in the world possessed Mike to say what he did? Had his infatuation with Gloria Plum caused him to surrender all discretion?

When we finished in the observatory we didn't get farther than the computer lab below it without stopping again. A sinuous metal track was suspended from the beams above us. From it hung tiny halogen lamps on delicate wires, lending not only illumination but resonance to the room—a fragile, high-tech echo of the starry

84

heavens. But it wasn't the lighting that fascinated Mr. Plum this time; it was the windows, which were made of smart glass. Operating on the principle of a liquid crystal display, each pane had a layer that darkened instantly at the application of an electrical charge. He switched each window on and off again and again, laughing like a child playing with a toy, while Mike watched quizzically. My mind was a million miles away, wanting to ride that mockingbird's song into oblivion. I had a feeling I wasn't going to be that lucky. Sure enough, when we made it back downstairs Mrs. Plum was nowhere to be found.

~

"Jesus, she doesn't just disappear like this," Mr. Plum said. We already had split into three and searched the whole house again. Mr. Plum looked in his car and then walked around the house from one direction while Mike and I circled it from the other. We met in back and walked onto the deck, where we found Mrs. Plum's high-heeled shoes just outside the glass door. Mr. Plum set them inside, shaking his head. He seemed more annoyed than worried. Mike and I looked at each other. I knew we were thinking the same thing.

"Someone should check down the drive to the road," I said. "I'll go up the hill in back and see if there's any sign of her. And someone ought to stay here too, in case she comes back first."

"I'll check the drive, " Mr. Plum said, and abruptly walked out the front door.

I heard the staccato growl of the Porsche being started and turned around in the driveway as I went back out to the deck. Mike followed me and stopped at the rail. I walked to the perimeter of the yard, picked the spot where I thought I'd seen the figure and looked back at Mike. He motioned a bit to the left and I headed up the hill.

It had been many weeks since I'd been up on the ridge; now summer was well advanced and every way up was obstructed by a tangle of undergrowth for at least a short distance. Could Gloria Plum have navigated this in bare feet and a cocktail dress? It didn't seem possible but who else could the figure have been? Nettles welted my arms; nothing made sense as I picked my way through a thicket of blackberry canes.

When I emerged in the clear the going was steep but much easier. The hill was mostly rocks and tall grass strewn with wildflowers and small clumps of weed trees. I was approaching the ridge when suddenly a thrashing sound came from behind me. I felt the hair on my body rise as I whirled around. Too spooked to move and unsure where to go, I stood rooted to the spot. Then a wild movement caught my eye and I saw a thing I had never seen before.

A young buck, a four-pointer, was pushing an old buck with an impressive rack of antlers out of a clump of locust and sumac I'd just passed on my right. The old buck looked lean and too weak to fight back. He was retreating as the young buck advanced with head lowered. The young buck clearly knew what antlers were for, while the older animal seemed unaware of his own. For half a minute neither of them noticed me even though I stood upwind of them. Every time the old buck moved forward the young one pawed the ground and lowered his head, aggressively tossing his antlers. It was too early for mating season; the young buck's behavior seemed illogical to me.

The old buck looked nearly spent; he stood with his head drooping. I could see his sides heaving as he breathed and felt a wave of pity for the beast. The young buck stood its ground, coughing softly but not advancing. I stirred, and in an instant both animals were gone. The young buck leaped into the thicket of trees and bounded out the other side. The older one loped eastward down the slope and disappeared almost as quickly.

Marveling at what I had just seen I continued up the hill. No matter what direction I turned my assumptions were being shattered. Only a few days ago I had believed myself master of my destiny; now I was beginning to feel powerless and insubstantial as a ping-pong ball. In the space of a few hours King's Tavern had fallen in my estimation from a great accomplishment into infamy. The old man, whom I had regarded as indestructible, was now very much in

86

question. Mike, my presumed rock of stability, had shown himself to be unpredictable and reckless, which led to my lawyer client baring just enough of his teeth to let me know who was top dog between us. I was still smarting from that revelation, and now his wife was lost somewhere on this mountain in bare feet and a party dress. Even the deer were showing me my ignorance. And my lessons were only beginning.

My arm hurt like the dickens and I curled it to my chest to lessen the throbbing. The pain reminded me of Valerie and I groaned again at the circumstances I believed had led me into this mess. It was tempting to blame it all on her. But wasn't that what so many others had done? Find a scapegoat, heap all your own hurts on her and drive her into exile by scorn and derision? No, I couldn't do that. Valerie had never been anything but honest with me and for that I could not punish her.

The wind lifted my hair and grabbed at my shirt as I gained the ridge. A succession of rolling hills stretched north to the horizon. The view from here reminded me of the ocean the first time I saw it. This was as close to virgin land as one could find anywhere in the region; there was little but forest as far as the eye could see. Outcroppings of rock splotched with moss dotted the northern slope near the ridge, but the woods began abruptly a hundred feet below me.

I turned back to the house. Mike was still standing on the deck, a tiny figure raising an arm in the air. I threw up my arm to acknowledge him. The house stood dark and solid in the landscape, its graceful symmetry backlit by the lowering sun that illuminated the valley beyond. A fiery highlight glanced off the observatory dome like an exclamation point. An ache rose in my throat and I said a silent thank you to whatever powers had allowed me to build it. God, mother earth, karma or sheer luck—I didn't want to leave a base untouched. Would this accomplishment turn sour on me as well? The ache in my throat wouldn't go away. With a sick feeling growing inside I turned my back on the house and looked again to the north.

The forest below now seemed more foreboding than beautiful; so huge it could swallow a person as irretrievably as the ocean might. It didn't care; it simply existed—oblivious to pride, sorrow or any other plea of human folly. A person lost in that vastness would be untraceable as a minnow in the sea. I thought of Gloria Plum in her little black dress and bare feet and shivered. What in the world was she thinking about, scaling this hill and disappearing into such a wild place? Had that figure been her at all? My head was beginning to feel light and my whole body ached.

I started scrambling down the rocky slope, calling her name.

"Mrs. Plum!" I yelled, cupping my hands to my mouth. My voice sounded puny against the distance yawning on every side of me. After a few more bellows somehow "Mrs. Plum" seemed too formal. "Gloria!" I called desperately, and then stopped to listen.

Suddenly I felt cold all over. A chorus chanting "Gloria" echoed inside my head and the horizon was oscillating. My peripheral vision was going black; I needed to sit now, but it was too late. The ground was rocky at the edge of the woods and I tripped headlong over a boulder and smashed my face into it as I fell. My bad arm was trapped under me and the pain and dizziness were so overwhelming it was all I could do to raise my head before throwing up.

The convulsions of my stomach drew me to my knees and I knelt on that boulder, curling my ballooning right arm to my chest, and puked my guts out. When I was too weak to retch any more I collapsed in a ball, shivering with unreasonable cold. I don't know how long I lay there unable to move. The only thing I remember thinking was that I was dying, and wondering if anyone would ever find Gloria.

~

As it turned out left untreated in that condition I would have died; at least that's what the doctor told me later. But I was lucky, Gloria found me. I remember it like a dream. I was curled up on that rock and there was a gentle hand on my shoulder and a kind female voice saying, "Mister? Are you okay?"

I started up, and was amazed to see Gloria Plum bending over me. I couldn't stand and ended up falling down again at her feet. She didn't know it was me—my nose was broken, my lip was split open and there was blood all over my face. Kneeling at her feet I looked up and croaked "Gloria," and she gasped.

"My hand," I moaned, and then she saw my bandaged hand curled to my chest and let out a little shriek.

"Raymond, what happened to you?" Tears sprang to her eyes as she bent down and propped me up against the boulder. I was surprised at her strength.

"I fell down." I tried to laugh but couldn't. "I've fallen and I…can't…get up." Waves of dizziness swept over me.

"You crazy man!" She was laughing and crying all at once, but then she got serious.

"Your arm is grotesque. Come on, we're going to get you back to the house right now," she said with quiet authority that startled me, even in my delirium. She stooped at my left side, pulled my good arm around her shoulder and stood me up like a soldier. I don't remember much of that walk back to the top but I know Gloria Plum supported most of my weight, and I outweigh her by more than half. She was like a little tractor towing me up that hill.

By the time we crested the ridge my head had cleared enough for me to see again. I was wobbly though, and needed her support all the way down the other side. When we got to the brambles she threaded our way through a nearly invisible deer run that left our legs unscathed, as naturally as if she'd been that way a hundred times. I was dumb with astonishment. I looked at her feet when we emerged and saw they were strong, with high arches. They bore a few little scratches but she seemed oblivious to them. Her calves were lean and muscular; I had no idea she was in such athletic condition.

"Y'gah great legs," I think I slurred at one point, because I remember her response. She looked up into my bloody mug and smiled. "You're hallucinating," she said and continued tugging me along.

By the time we reached the yard my respect for Gloria Plum had grown to heroic proportions but my self-esteem had shriveled into loathing. Somehow I had soiled myself along the way. I was almost too sick to care, but not quite. I longed for something noble to say that would elevate us above the wretchedness of the situation, but it just wasn't happening.

My mind was none too clear at that point but when nobody was on the deck to meet us, it did seem strange. Hadn't anybody seen us staggering down the hill? Where was Mike? As we approached the rear of the house it occurred to me that I was in no shape to tangle with even the few steps onto the deck. "Go round front," I said and we veered left around the east end of the house. I was hanging on to her sagging like a drunk. There in the driveway was the Plums' Porsche with a gray sedan parked behind it. Mr. Plum and Mike stood talking to a man out on the drive, and as they turned I realized who the third man was. What the hell was Clarence, of all people, doing here?

All three of them rushed up as we approached. "Good God, what happened to him?" Mr. Plum shouted.

"Why did you let this man go up that mountain in this condition?" Mrs. Plum snapped back. "Look at his arm—he has blood poisoning. He needs help now." I admired her spunk, and in a hazy way now comprehended something of Mike's fascination with her.

Clarence was staring at everyone with his eyes bugging out of his head. I caught his look and glared back. "I'm fine," I growled, and then felt a swoon coming. "Just lemme siddown." I collapsed into a heap.

Mike knelt and put a hand on my shoulder. "You okay, man?" he asked.

I was shivering and too weak to respond.

Mrs. Plum disappeared and Mike said, "I think this is a nine-one-one—do you have a phone?" He looked up at Mr. Plum.

"She's got it," he said, nodding over Mike's shoulder. Gloria Plum was by the car talking into a tiny cell phone.

90

Mike turned back to me and said, "Where'd you get the face, Bwana?"

"Fellna rock," I slurred, then toppled over and curled up on the grass.

"Hang in there, man, help's on the way," he said, patting my back.

When Mrs. Plum finished the call she brought a wrap from the car and laid it over me. I didn't see Clarence exit, but heard his car starting and pulling away. I groaned in consternation, and Mr. and Mrs. Plum and Mike all started in alarm.

"Clarence," I snarled as indignantly as I could.

"He came to see the house, Ray," Mike said in that soft voice he gets when he's really serious. "He just wanted to look at it one more time. He said it's the most beautiful house he's ever seen. Doesn't that beat all?"

"Beautiful," I murmured, and shivered once more. It seemed like it was getting dark awfully early, but it had been a long day and I was really tired, so I just went to sleep.

CHAPTER 8

When I woke it was the next morning and I was in a bright room all bandaged up with tubes coming and going from me. Mike sat by my bed reading a newspaper. When he saw me stirring he laid the paper aside and stood, grinning down at me. "Get a good sleep?"

"Where are we?" I mumbled. My body felt like it was floating but I could barely move. An electronic monitoring device stood at the bedside. My right arm was shiny pink from the elbow down. My hand was swathed in a bandage and had no sensation at all. "I want to see my hand."

Mike leaned over the bed. "This is Lehigh Valley Hospital in Allentown. They flew you here. You're lucky you still have a hand, Bwana. They said another hour and you might have lost it." I couldn't speak, and he kept on. "This may come as a surprise to you, but there are these things called bacteria that live in the dirt—"

"So I got a little infection."

"No, you had a massive infection that could have killed you. We didn't know how bad you were hurting, man. You didn't let us know."

"I had no idea." I was dazed.

"Neither did anyone else," Mike said.

"What about the Plums?"

"They're worried sick. Mrs. Plum was picking flowers; she said she wanted to see what was over the ridge so she hiked up. I didn't know she was that tough."

"Me neither. Did you see her legs?"

Mike narrowed his eyes and looked sideways at me. I thought I'd pissed him off but then laughter burst from him, and then I started and suddenly we were laughing our fool heads off again for no good reason except the relief of having survived another close one. I was lying there with tears running off my face and Mike was wiping his eyes when a nurse came in. Thinking she had interrupted a private moment, she stammered an apology. The look on her face started us

92

again. Then she began laughing at her own mistake. By the time the doctor walked in all three of us were nearly helpless.

"Must have been a good one," he boomed in a friendly voice.

"Good morning, Doctor," the nurse said, "I was just stopping by to check IVs when these gentlemen caught me off guard. I think Mr. Brauner may be coming around. I'll drop back in when you're done." She was still flushed with laughter, and her brown eyes danced as she stepped aside.

"So I see," said the doctor. He was a big man, jovial and bearlike in his movements. "I'm Dr. Panos and I'll be your physician for your little stay. Would you care to hear about our specials today?"

"Do I have a choice?"

"Not if you'd taken any longer getting here. You'd have lost a hand for sure, possibly your arm. Another day and we might not have saved your life." He paused, scribbling something on a clipboard, then looked up. "You ever hear of toxic shock syndrome?"

"Is that something women get from tampons?"

"That's one kind, caused by staph. There's another kind, caused by strep. That's what you've got—streptococcal toxic shock. TSS happens when certain kinds of bacteria start multiplying in your body and pumping out waste. Pretty soon the poison overwhelms your system, and organs start shutting down. It dissolves tissue; you can bleed to death from the inside. And you know how easy it is to avoid?"

I stared blankly at him.

"Common sense!" he thundered. "You had a little boo-boo on your hand. You were working in the dirt and didn't protect it. All sorts of nasty things live around us, but we get along with them because we've got skin to keep our insides clean. You get an open wound, you protect it. Basic first aid." He leaned in close and frowned. "You got that, Boy Scout?"

He stood up tall. "You didn't know it, but that little hike you took pumped poison all through your body—that's why you got sick so fast."

"How long am I going to be here?" I asked.

"You're going to be laid up for a few days, and you're going to be on antibiotics for a lot longer. But you're going to take them like it's your new religion, because that's why you're still alive. Capiche?"

I was beginning to like this guy, but I didn't have a few days to be laid up. "Isn't there some way I can just take the medicine and get back to my job Monday?" I asked.

"No!" he boomed. "You think you're a cat with nine lives? You can't even walk, man. You're on intravenous fluids. You're stuck here until your blood chemistry is normal and all your functions are stabilized. You want to add renal failure to your list of new experiences?"

I shook my head.

"By all the odds you should be on dialysis now. Anyone with as much poison as you had in your body usually ends up with kidney or liver damage. If they hadn't flown you in here we wouldn't even be having this conversation. You're one lucky guy, so don't start complaining. And besides, you still need some attention on that pretty face. Get used to your new life." He leaned in close again, and winked. "But there are some fine nurses on this floor and they'll be taking great care of you, I promise. Ah, here comes Jackie now." Another nurse bustled in and I perked up. She was a tall redhead. Dr. Panos backed out the door as Jackie approached my bed, sizing me up with a smile and a huge hypodermic syringe.

"Want to roll over, Mr. Brauner?" she said cheerfully.

~

On Saturday Mike was the only visitor allowed to see me, but by Sunday I had turned a corner. I was able to sit up, and my mouth felt parched. There was a bottle of water on the bed table, which I pulled close with considerable effort. I found a small hand mirror on the table. When I picked it up I hardly recognized myself. There were stitches in my upper lip, my nose was bandaged and my right cheek had a bruise that extended up to my eye.

94

Remembering the bouncer at King's I felt more empathy for him now. He might have been humiliated in front of a crowd, but at least he hadn't lain in his own vomit or soiled himself while being rescued by a beautiful woman. That was a whole different level of mortification —more exquisite, and in its own way perhaps more richly deserved.

I had been so condescending in my attitude to him, and now I was in even worse shape than he. And last but not least I had seriously underestimated Gloria Plum—then ended up not only being seen at my rock bottom worst by her, but rescued by her own raw strength. After all the times I'd met with the Plums that was a quality I never had associated with her. I shook my head and laughed out loud. There was nothing to do about it except laugh.

Life was so fragile—now it seemed more of an accident that we survived at all. There were more ways to be taken than any of us could realize. I looked at my bandaged hand, trying to imagine life without it. No more carpentry, no more playing guitar, no more of a million other things. If Gloria Plum hadn't found me… I didn't even want to think about it. Suddenly my control over my own life seemed provisional, alarmingly subject to whim and chance.

Now even Clarence had seen me wobble into the yard propped up by Gloria Plum, getting an eyeful of my humiliation like it was the eighth wonder of the world. But what was it Mike had said—that Clarence stopped by just to look at the house? That astonished me. Mike said he called it the most beautiful house he'd ever seen. Had I misjudged Clarence as well? At least his aesthetic sensibilities weren't dead, whatever else he might think of me.

Why did it matter what anyone thought of me? The question had perplexed me before—it seemed like a secret deficiency, a craven sort of inadequacy that had its roots in some unidentified place and permeated my life like a fungus. It wasn't a thing that threatened life or livelihood, but it fostered a perpetual unease, a sense that I might not be as good as I thought, so continually had to prove my worth by feats of grandeur. Mike didn't seem to be saddled with such baggage—he disliked fanfare and worked for the simple joy of it.

Valerie didn't seem to care much what others thought about her. Why should I?

I thought of my ex-wife, whom I'd met in graduate school. Jillian was an architect too, but public buildings and monumental structures fascinated her while I wanted to build for shelter and comfort. I liked the idea of people living in my buildings, not just passing through them. She loved big events, crowds, parties, and I loved quiet places. Jillian had entered national competitions while I was working with developers; she thought my goals were small and pedestrian. I never was able to articulate why the big stuff left me cold, and she often interpreted my silence as hostility. Lots of times we'd had one-sided arguments, arguments I could never win, so I just kept quiet and that's the way things had fallen apart.

Now I had built something monumental—at least by my standards—but she wasn't here to see it. The last time I'd heard from her she was in California designing shopping malls. It was doubtful she would ever know what I had done here. Nor would my father, who never thought I would accomplish anything worthwhile with my hands. Could they be the ones I was still trying to impress?

My reflections were cut short by the return of the nurse who had walked in on Mike and me the day before. She smiled at my serious face and asked how I was feeling.

"Not much at all. How long before my hand comes back?"

"You'll have to ask Dr. Panos about that," she said. "I think right now you don't want to be feeling too much. He's got you on a pretty strong pain killer until your infection clears up."

"It was pretty bad, huh?"

"About as bad as it gets before you start losing tissue. You're a very lucky man, Mr. Brauner." She smiled again. "You're also somewhat of a celebrity, you know."

"For what? Being the worst mess that ever got dumped into your unit?"

She laid a hand on my shoulder. "They cleaned you up in shock trauma before you came onto this floor. But we heard you're the architect who built King's Tavern up in Gladburg."

96

I felt a rush of ego, but it got choked off before I could savor it. "Yeah, I built it. For whatever that's worth."

"Well, I think it's wonderful. Some of my girlfriends and I were there early this summer, and we thought it was the coolest place. I don't see why you wouldn't be proud of that."

"That's history," I said. "No matter what anyone thinks, there's the next job to do, and the one after that. If you get too attached to something you've already done, you might not make much progress."

"Is that so?" she said, tilting her head and regarding me with amusement. "From what I hear you've not done too badly."

I pushed myself up with my good arm and looked at her. "People say all kinds of things, Miss—what is your name?"

"Anita," she said.

"And I'm Ray. People say all kinds of things, Anita. Tell me what makes you think that."

"Well," she hesitated, tilting her head even further, "let me put it this way. We're under strict orders to make sure everything is done by the book, to spare nothing to insure your—um, well—full recovery."

"Isn't that what a hospital's all about?"

"Sure. But we heard you're working on an important job, and someone's taken a special interest in your recovery. And it seems to be a well-connected person nobody wants to disappoint. And now I've probably said more than I should." Suddenly she seemed nervous, and began bustling around the room. She stooped down to check my catheter bag, and when she started up hit her head hard on the bedside table I had pulled over earlier.

She stayed down sucking in her breath; I could tell it hurt. I dangled my left hand down to her.

"You okay?" I said.

"In a minute," she said. She didn't recoil from my hand so I left it covering hers; then without thinking I dropped it down to the side of her head and stroked her hair. It felt cool and smooth against my palm. She moved her hand over mine and pulled it down against her

97

cheek where it stayed for about one second before the whole morning ran into the ditch.

There was a commotion at the door, and a familiar voice hammered the silence into shards: "What the hay-ull is going on in there?"

Anita stood bolt upright, knocking the table again with her head and sending the mirror clattering to the floor where it shattered. Grimacing and blushing deeply, she said "I'm so sorry, Mr. Brauner." She stooped once again to scoop up the pieces of broken glass and dropped them into the pocket of her scrubs. This time she backed carefully away from the table before standing. "I'll be out of your way now," she said and wheeled around, nearly knocking Valerie over in her haste to leave the room.

"Whoa!" Val stood open-mouthed, staring. "Some kind of pickle you got yourself in, huh, Bwana?"

I stared back at her. She was wearing a faded cotton sundress, bright red socks and her Doc Martens boots. Her hair tumbled down in ringlets nearly to her elbows. A paper bag was cradled in her right arm, and a canvas book bag hung from her left. Her face was a curious swirl of hurt and astonishment.

"You always did have a way with ladies. I just never seen nobody move so fast," she finally said in a shaky voice. "Maybe I better be on my way." She turned and rushed out the door.

"Wait, Val, for God's sake!" I called. "Please come back!"

The doorway stood empty; all I could hear were fuzzy fragments of hospital sounds from up and down the floor, and the reedy rattle of the air conditioning unit under the window. A great sob was beginning to well up inside me. I buried my face in the pillow until it passed.

~

When I got my composure back only one thing seemed clear. I was losing control of my life. The longer I lay supine in the arms of fate the worse things were going to get. Picturing Val standing there

98

with that surprised look all over her face made my eyes fill with tears, and I've never been one to cry. What was happening to me? What was happening with Valerie and Rollin? What was happening to the little paradise I thought I'd found up in the mountains of Pennsylvania?

There was a light tap at the door and my heart skipped a beat. I pushed myself up hoping to see Val again, but instead a man in formal attire wheeled a metal trolley to my bed. He lifted a domed cover from the top with a flourish and a delicious aroma filled the air.

"Mr. Brauner, my name is Travis and I'll be serving your lunch. Today we have blackened tuna with pasta, tomato chutney, buttered asparagus shoots and a summer salad. I'm sorry we weren't able to give you a menu earlier, but you were indisposed." He was quietly deferential, and presented everything with the poise of a maitre d'.

I was stunned. "This is hospital food?"

"No, sir, this meal is from Armands. In addition to our downtown restaurant we provide catering for a few clients in the area. As excellent as they may be, we understand the hospital meals might not meet your standards; again let me apologize for not providing you a menu earlier." He pulled an elegant leather folder from a holder on the side of the trolley and handed it to me, bowing slightly. "For your dinner, sir. You can give me your order when you finish here, or phone it in any time before 3 o'clock. May I serve you now?"

"Not so fast," I said. "I never ordered fancy meals and I'm not about to start living large from a hospital bed. Take it to the next room, and I'll eat the house food."

Travis seemed puzzled. "You are Mr. Raymond Brauner?" he asked.

"Yeah. Where'd you get my name, anyway?"

"It's in my order, sir," he said. "The billing is of no concern; we don't cater for anyone we don't have an account with. If the meal is not satisfactory tell me what you would prefer, and we'll try not to disappoint you again."

99

"The billing is of no concern?" I rasped. "I did not order outside food and I'm not about to pay for something I never asked for. You've got a lot of nerve coming in here with that—that—gourmet meal at a time like this, when I haven't eaten in two days."

"Sir, I'm sorry if I didn't make myself clear." Travis bowed again slightly. "There will be no bill, your meals are being provided as a courtesy from one of our regular accounts." He was so sincere, so unbearably polite that I began to soften. And to tell the truth, I was ravenously hungry.

"Look, I don't mean to take it out on you," I said, "but this has been a bad couple of days for me, and I'm confused. Who is paying for this?"

It seemed all but beneath his dignity to discuss arrangements, but I had asked a reasonable question. "I believe your order came from the law firm of Manning, Lazar, Goldberg and Plum—maybe you're a client of theirs?"

"Christ—why didn't you say so, man? One of them is my client." Now some pieces were falling into place. Good old Mr. Plum had come through for me, and here I was balking like a mule at a gift being handed me on a silver platter.

"Your client?" Travis said. "That's unusual... Then you will be eating, sir?"

"What the hell, it smells really great," I grunted, pushing myself up.

"Here, let me," Travis said, back in control as he reached for the remote switch and pressed a button. The bed hummed and lifted me into a sitting position. He pulled the table over and began laying out the service—linen napkin, real silver, fine china and crystal. I could hardly believe my eyes.

The food was incredible. It was divine. After tasting it I told Travis to come back in fifteen minutes and set to work. It was getting easier to use my left hand, and I was so hungry I abandoned all manners. The asparagus was dispatched with my fingers. I was cleaning up my plate with a spoon when there was a sound at the door, and I looked up to see Valerie standing there.

I dropped the spoon and looked at her with my mouth full of penne pasta. She looked back at me with huge eyes and said, "I always seem to show up at the wrong time."

I covered my mouth with a napkin and swallowed everything at once. It was too much and it hurt going down, but finally I could speak. "I'm glad you came back. That little, uh, incident—it wasn't what you thought it was."

"You don't have to apologize for nothing."

"I'm not apologizing. I'm just trying to explain what you saw wasn't what you thought."

"And what do you think that was?"

"I just reached down to pat her head after she banged it on the table. It was an accident."

"Pretty lucky accident, huh?"

"That's what happened, Valerie. I was just as surprised as you were."

"I bet you were."

"Won't you come in? I wanted to see you but things got out of control."

"Things always are out of control. All anybody can do is control his own self."

Where was this coming from, anyway? Valerie wasn't even my girlfriend! But I swallowed my pride. "Okay, you're right. But is there anybody who doesn't screw up now and then?"

"I guess not," she sighed, and slowly approached my bed. "You look real banged up."

"Yeah. I had a little fall."

"I heard."

We each were trying to think of something more productive to say when Travis reentered. "Would you care for dessert, Mr. Brauner?" he said.

"No, I'm done. I haven't looked at the menu; I'll call later."

"Of course." He bowed slightly. "May I?" He gestured at the table.

"Please," I said, and rolled it away from the bed. Valerie watched as Travis efficiently transferred the dishes onto his trolley, covered them and wheeled everything out the door.

"Pretty fancy for hospital food," she remarked.

"It was catered. My client had it sent over."

"Looks like someone's trying to fatten you up for the kill," she said.

"What do you mean?"

"Don't you know there ain't no such thing as a free lunch?"

"I wouldn't exactly call it free, Val. I've been building the man's house for over a year and a half, and I got sick looking for his wife."

"I heard you got infected from working in the dirt."

"And your point is?"

"Just don't sell your soul for a mess of pottage."

"What the hell is that supposed to mean?"

"It's from the Bible. There was two twin brothers who both wanted the birthright, but only one of them could have it. The second-born was cooking up a meal when his brother come in from hunting. He was so hungry he sold his birthright for a bowl of pottage. The second-born got it by deception, but the firstborn lost it because he was in too much of a hurry to fill his belly."

"I went to Sunday school but I've never heard that before."

"Well, maybe you ought to try reading what the Bible says for yourself. You might learn a thing or two they didn't teach you in Sunday school, or college neither."

"When did you become an expert on the Bible?"

"I never was any expert. My daddy's a preacher and I read it growing up. I still do sometimes."

"Your daddy who used to hit you?" I said.

Valerie's jaw tightened. "Yeah. He never learnt that in the Bible though."

"I'm sorry." I laid back and closed my eyes. "There was no reason for me to say that."

"It's better than pretending it didn't happen," Val said. "His daddy was mean, so that's what he learnt. It's hard to grow up nice when there ain't much nice around you."

"How about your mother—isn't she nice?"

She didn't answer, and I saw she was on the verge of tears again.

"You don't have to talk about it, Val—it's none of my business."

Her eyes met mine with such intensity that I wanted to look away but I couldn't. "Daddy hit Mama too and one time he hurt her real bad. She got nerve damage and went blind. He never touched her after that, but she got all balled up inside and now she don't talk neither." Val sat motionless except for the tiny convulsions that moved at her throat. "Except to me, but I ain't there."

She rubbed tears away with the heel of her palm. "She never was one to stand up for herself." Her last words were barely a whisper.

"Jesus Christ, Val, I had no idea," I said in a shaky voice. I felt my own eyes filling up again.

"You better watch your tongue, mister," Val said.

"What?"

"The Bible says not to take the Lord's name in vain, or you will not be held guiltless." She fished through her pockets for something to blow her nose on.

There was a box of tissues on the nightstand, and I reached over and handed it to her. "Since when did you start crusading against profanity?"

"You never heard me take the Lord's name in vain, did you?" she challenged.

"I can't remember."

"You can't remember because it never happened. I might have what some people call a foul mouth, but mister, you will never hear me take the Lord's name in vain. Some things are common and some things are holy, and you ought to know the difference." She blew her nose long and loudly.

"You never cease to amaze me," I said, shaking my head.

"I better be going now," she said, standing abruptly. "I brought you some falafels and pita bread, but you probably don't want it after all that fancy food."

"You know I love falafels. I'll have them for supper. You don't have to go yet, do you?"

103

"I told you I ain't nothing but trouble for you." A tear glistened on her cheek. "Besides, that pretty nurse might be back in here and I'm sure she don't want to see me again."

"Valerie, I don't even know that nurse. You're the one I'm worried about."

"Well don't you bother yourself, Bwana," she said. "You got more on your own plate than you can shake a stick at."

Her expression softened and she touched my arm. "You know I did tell you to see a doctor about that hand. You got to start taking care of yourself, too. I'd be real careful about taking gifts from strangers." She laid her paper bag on my table and walked to the door.

"Will you come back again?" I called after her. "Please?"

She turned around and smiled. "Okay," she said shyly.

CHAPTER 9

Later that afternoon Dr. Panos dropped by and I asked him about my prognosis. He warned me of dire consequences if I frustrated any part of my treatment. My kidneys weren't yet out of danger and my face still needed work, but that had to wait for my infection to subside. My hand was going to take a while to come back; there was tissue damage and possibly some muscle loss. I might need physical therapy.

"Thanks a lot, Doc," I said morosely after he finished. "How about this catheter—is that how you intend to keep me captive?"

"I think we can take that out in a day or two." He smiled at my long face. "Just remember how much worse things could have been."

Anita came in to check my IVs and I tried to make conversation with her, but all I could get from her were curt responses and a mechanical smile. I was beginning to feel sorry for myself when Mike stopped in. After I filled him in on my day he hung his head. "It's all my fault," he said. "If I had just disconnected that line—"

"Bullshit!" I exploded. "It's nobody's fault; it's just luck. Every time you get up it's a gamble. A mother gets killed by a drunk driver and some asshole wins the lottery. The next day it's another roll of the dice. We just had a bad roll, that's all."

I truly didn't give a damn whose fault it was, but being out of control of my life was becoming intolerable. I needed to be doing something. We had a critical decision to make—whether the Frye job should go on, or wait. Once the roof was opened it would be essential to keep moving until everything was under cover. Mike and I mulled that over. He seemed reluctant to take on the responsibility, but said he'd leave it up to me.

I had seen the way he solved problems on the Plum house and had no doubt he could handle the Fryes' addition. Spider and Mackey were fine carpenters, but Mike's skill went beyond reading blueprints—he knew how to deal with people.

105

I was still upset about what he'd said to Mr. Plum up in the observatory, but that was an extraordinary situation. The Fryes weren't sophisticated folks and I knew Mike could answer any questions they might have. The guys needed to keep working; several of them had families to support. The decision really rested with the Fryes so I gave them a call. After explaining to Mr. Frye what their options were, he said he'd talk it over with his wife. Minutes later he called back to say if I was comfortable with Mike handling things they had no worries. After hanging up the phone I looked at Mike.

"It's all yours, Ace. You'll get your regular wage plus fifty percent, if that's okay with you."

"Time and a half? Isn't that too much?"

"Not a bit. Just think—you get to run interference with Mr. Plum, besides busting up any fights. See if you think it's too much two weeks from now."

"Okey-doke," he said, "just don't forget to answer the phone in case I need some mojo from the mountaintop."

"You're the one with the mojo now. Just keep things moving and don't let Spider get started on the Fryes with any of his alien abduction crap."

"It's back to Rush these days, Bwana. You know Spider."

"Well, then no more talk radio on the job. We'll make it a condition of employment."

"And that would include NPR?"

I knew he was trying to lighten me up. "No exceptions," I growled.

~

Scarcely five minutes after Mike left there was another tap at the door.

"Yes?" I said.

There was a light rustle and a mass of foliage entered the room supported by a pair of shapely legs. I couldn't see who was carrying the plant until the cargo turned and a pair of bright eyes peeped

106

from behind it. Gloria Plum had her arms around a big clay pot—the whole business must have weighed at least thirty pounds. She wore a short denim skirt and a sleeveless black silk blouse. I tried not to stare as she carried the plant easily and bent to set it on the floor by the window. Brushing her hands together, she straightened and flashed a cheerful smile. "How're the old war wounds, soldier?"

"Fine, thanks," I said. "I just can't believe there wasn't someone to help you in here with that thing."

"I wouldn't let them," she laughed. "This 'thing' is my baby—I grew him from a cutting and I've had him nearly three years now. I thought you could use a little fresh oxygen in here. You will say a kind word to him now and then, won't you?"

"Mrs. Plum, I'll read it a bedtime story every night if you want me to. You really shouldn't have. What is it?"

"Just a philodendron, but isn't he handsome?"

"He's beautiful. You sure you trust me with him?"

"Of course. And please call me Gloria. Joseph is the one with all the complexities."

"And you have none of your own?" I was feeling reckless.

"Well, let's just say, none that aren't common to most women."

It was the first time I could remember seeing her without her husband, and she took my breath away. Her silver hair was pulled back and laced into a short French braid. I didn't see any makeup, yet even dressed casually she looked elegant. She stood hands on hips, with little smile wrinkles deepening at the corners of her eyes. Some people call them crows' feet, but they only made her seem more alive. I finally found my voice.

"Okay Gloria, but please call me Ray."

"I thought your fellows called you Bwana."

I laughed. "Yeah, that was Mike's little joke at first, but it seemed to stick. Brauner, Bwana, whatever. Won't you sit down?"

She dragged a chair over, plopped into it and crossed her legs. "And what is Michael's nickname?"

"I call him Ace, but only in self-defense."

"Ace of what? Hearts or diamonds?"

"Good question—I'll have to poll the rest of my guys about that. Why, are you doing research on nicknames?"

Gloria laughed, then looked down at her lap and got serious. "No, nothing like that. It just feels, I don't know—fun, I guess, to relax and be myself with someone who doesn't have an agenda and isn't so full of himself. Or herself." She sighed. "Silly, isn't it?"

"I don't think so at all. But I've been called pretty full of myself on occasion."

"Well, just watch yourself then, buddy, and don't be that way with me." She made a stern face.

"I promise. I owe you an apology, you know."

"What on earth for?"

"For what I said coming down the mountain. I wasn't hallucinating."

She looked puzzled, and then it dawned on her. She smiled once more and again I felt myself melting. "Ray, that was the sweetest thing. For you to notice something like that in the condition you were in—do you realize I am fifty-two years old? When a woman my age receives a compliment like that from a gentleman, it doesn't become her to take offense."

"Well, it was uncharacteristic of me."

"But why? You meant no harm, did you?"

"Of course not."

"Do you know how suffocating it is to be around nothing but terminally polite people, knowing half of them would stick a knife in your back if they could? I welcome a little spice now and then. And you know something else? I love your crew. That Michael is such a sweetheart. Even that motorcycle fellow, what's his name?"

"Spider."

"Spider, bless his heart. They get so polite every time we come around it just about makes me crazy. I really would rather they just be themselves. They're real people, Ray, and sometimes it seems like my whole world is full of nothing but fakes and flakes. It's refreshing to be around regular folks once in a while." She uncrossed her legs and tucked them sideways under her.

108

"That's kind of you," I said, "but to show some manners is not a bad exercise for them. Besides, I'm not sure Mr. Plum shares your attitude."

"Oh, Joseph is a hopeless control freak, but as long as you're straight with him he'll respect you. Anyway, he believes you're a genius."

"Yeah, right. I'm just a working stiff, you know?"

"Well, I come from a family of working stiffs. When I entered Joseph's world everyone thought it was such a step up for me. It was exciting at first, seeing him fly through law school and help build the practice. But so much of it's built on brute force, on thousands of hours of billing and bullying and butting heads. He's a litigator, you know."

I just watched her. She sighed and went on. "For so many years he's been married more to his work than anything else. Sometimes I just don't know. I've wanted so long for him get away from the office, to have a place for his telescope and wash his soul clean in nature. I've been hoping this house would be a new start for him. Gosh, it was so beautiful up on that ridge." Her eyes were dreamy.

"I know—it always reminds me of the ocean up there," I said. "You are one remarkable lady, do you know that?"

"Why do you say that?" She seemed amused.

"How you managed to get up there in your bare feet and then haul me down without a scratch—I never imagined you were so tough."

"Did you think I was just a pretty little party girl?"

"Did I say that?"

"You didn't need to," she said, laughing gently. "That's the side of me that appeals to Joseph. He can display it and use it to his own advantage. But we all have more sides than most people see, don't you think?"

A picture of Valerie came to mind and I laughed too. "No doubt."

The phone rang, and I picked it up to find Travis on the other end.

"Mr. Brauner, would you care to order dinner?"

I looked over and saw Valerie's brown bag sitting where she had left it. "Actually I'm not hungry now, Travis."

"But you might be later. Have you read our menu?"

"To be honest, I haven't had the chance."

"Maybe I can make a few suggestions, Mr. Brauner, and you can tell me if something strikes your fancy."

I felt trapped. "Hold that thought," I said, and covered the mouthpiece.

"Did you know the law firm is sending me catered meals up here?" I asked Gloria.

"No, but I'm not surprised. Why?"

"It just seems a little extravagant, that's all."

She shrugged. "Go for it. You should see how they indulge themselves."

I uncovered the phone. "Okay, Travis—do you know how to make tabouli?"

"Tabouli?" He sounded puzzled.

"Yeah, middle eastern salad with parsley and mint. And some hummus, baba ganouj and a side order of steamed couscous. That should do it."

"But Mr. Brauner—"

"That's my order. With spring water. Thanks." I dropped the phone in its cradle and smiled at Gloria. "I couldn't resist."

"Always consider who you're dealing with," she murmured. "People at the top aren't easily intimidated. But people on the bottom get pushed around all the time." Her eyes dropped into her lap.

"Well, most of us are somewhere in the middle, and that guy doesn't seem to be able to take 'no' for an answer."

"I'm sorry, Ray. Everyone deserves to get their way once in a while. And after what you've been through, you've got it coming in spades. I really do need to be going now though—I promised Joseph I'd meet him for dinner." She smiled that radiant smile once more, unfolded her legs and stood up.

"I'm glad you came. You know, if it hadn't been for you I might have lost my hand," I said.

She touched my shoulder. "You came looking for me, remember? You're the one who went the extra mile. Joseph and I both know that. If there's anything you need please give me a call."

"Thanks. But all I need now is to be out of here and back to work, really."

After she walked out I lay there a long time thinking. I now understood Mike's fascination with Gloria Plum. Once again he had seen the essence of a thing before I had.

I napped and before I knew it Travis was at the door. Gone was the trolley and fancy place setting; instead he carried a basket with a thermal cover. "Your middle eastern food has arrived, Mr. Brauner," he said indifferently.

"Thanks," I said. "Just set everything on the table. Give me about fifteen minutes."

I rubbed the sleep from my eyes and once fully awake found the food wonderful. I had no idea how Travis drummed up my order, but all of it was perfect. And even cold, Valerie's falafels were great. While eating I pondered what she had said to me a few hours before. I wasn't exactly taking gifts from strangers, but neither did I want to be obligated to Mr. Plum. I knew these meals weren't coming out of his pocket; the law firm wrote stuff like this off to the tune of thousands of dollars every quarter—hell, probably every month. What difference could it make?

When Travis came back for the dishes I tried to apologize. "Hey, I didn't mean to put you out with my order," I said.

"We aren't put out," he replied coolly. "If you want something that's not on the menu, all we need is enough time to prepare it. Would you care to order your breakfast now?"

"Look, I'm sorry. Why don't you take tomorrow off and I'll have the house food. If it's really bad I'll order by phone. And don't worry, it'll be from the menu."

"Mr. Brauner, tomorrow is my day off. It's no skin off my ass whatever you decide." With that he turned around and walked out.

111

~

The days began blurring into each other. My face got worked over by a plastic surgeon who said he could make my broken nose prettier than it had been. I told him not to do me any favors, just restore me to my original specs. My hand was healing, but as Dr. Panos had warned it had some problems. My whole right forearm was shrunken, atrophied and weaker. Those little bacteria had done their work with a vengeance. A physical therapist showed me exercises that would encourage muscle growth, and said in six months or so I might be as good as ever. Might be. Meanwhile, increased use of my left hand would make it more dexterous, so theoretically it was possible for me to end up even better than before. I didn't take much comfort from that, but determined to make the best of whatever hand fate dealt me. At least I was alive.

My mother drove up from Maryland and stayed two days. We talked about her garden, about old neighbors and friends, and I took sweet refuge in her oblivion to the complexities of my own world. I told her a little about Valerie, and her interest seemed disproportionate to Val's place in my life.

I continued to take catered meals, but made it a point to be nice to Travis. I had him dump the "mister" as soon as I was able to patch things up with him. He turned out to be a regular guy and had that rare integrity, which Mike also possessed, to want to do everything as well as it could possibly be done. He was in fact the maitre d' at Armands, and when he told me this on my fourth day in the hospital I was incredulous.

"Why in the world wouldn't they let a waiter do this—don't they need the maitre d' for more important things?" I asked.

"You're a VIP," he answered simply. "It happens once in a while."

"Who are your other VIPs?"

"I served Hillary Clinton a few years ago, sometimes some businessmen from New York. People from your law firm, when

112

they're in town. Anyone who needs security."

"Why, are you a cop?"

"No sir," he laughed. "But I did have to go through a security screening before serving the First Lady. Since then the management uses me only for important clients, so it doesn't happen that often."

"And I'm an important client?"

"Maybe difficult would be a better word." He smiled slightly.

"You know what I mean. Why am I important?"

"I don't ask those kind of questions."

I knew Mr. Plum was behind this, and although it made me a little uneasy to remember what Val had said about free lunch, Gloria Plum's visit trumped that in my mind. I never had been a high roller but I worked hard for my clients. If one of them wanted to extend a red carpet for me, so be it. But in the back of my mind I couldn't stop wondering what the hell pottage was. It didn't sound nearly as good as what I was eating.

Inevitably Mr. Plum stopped by, and when I thanked him for the meals he brushed them aside as if they were nothing. He referred to my situation in heroic terms, at one point comparing me to the architect Howard Roark from Ayn Rand's novel The Fountainhead. After enduring several references to my illustrious future and my indomitable spirit my patience wore thin. I told him I felt neither illustrious nor indomitable, that I just wanted to be out of the hospital and back to work.

"You're a natural objectivist, Raymond," he laughed.

"I don't really know anything about that," I said.

"Don't you consider productive achievement to be your highest activity?" he asked.

"I guess so."

"And isn't reason the only absolute there is?"

"I don't know, Mr. Plum. There are times when it seems that way."

He leaned over my bed and looked intently at me. "You have greatness in you, Raymond," he confided. "The world has no end of common folk, but there aren't many like us. We make the world into

113

what we dream. That's why you should learn to dream big dreams. Great dreams."

He laughed again, and exited back into his world of litigation, legal matters and dubious dreams I couldn't begin to fathom. How he and Gloria fit together was beyond me. One of them must have changed a great deal over the years.

~

On Wednesday morning Rollin visited me. He kept apologizing for not coming sooner until I cut him off.

"It's okay, Rollin," I assured him. "The best thing you can do for me now is to keep your own ship afloat. You hear anything from your dad?"

"Not yet. He said a couple weeks, so I'm not going to jump to any conclusions."

I didn't have the heart to comment on that, and asked how things were at the tavern.

Rollin looked glum. "Well, we haven't seen any more of Smith or Jones, but there's a big stone-faced guy named Angelo who showed up to be our bouncer."

"What's he like?"

"Not so bad," Rollin said. "He's all business and reasonably polite. I doubt anyone will give him any trouble—you know how word gets around that town. Except he won't fill out any employment forms and demands his pay in cash every night. Thirty dollars an hour, can you imagine that?"

"Unfortunately, yes. How's business?"

"It was pretty bad Friday night, but Saturday was bigger than ever. I think people were curious. And there were some new people—including several of the troublemakers who came in before Smith and Jones showed up."

"Did everyone behave?"

"It got a little pushy a few times but there wasn't much behind it; anyway the regular crowd seems to leave the new folks alone. But

114

Angelo insists on doing the revenue report at the end of the night."

"The revenue report?"

"He knows our computer system inside and out. He takes a printout of the day's business with him when he leaves every night."

"Ouch. They want to know what you're grossing, I guess. You got any ideas about how to deal with these guys?"

"I'm not going to move on that until I hear from Dad."

Somewhere in the back of my mind it seemed I heard the wind roaring, and I felt like grabbing Rollin by the collar and shaking him until his teeth rattled. Instead I sank back into my pillow and said nothing. His problem is mutating into a monster, I thought, and he still doesn't get it.

We made idle talk for another few minutes. There seemed to be something bothering him but I didn't feel like drawing it out. Finally we had exhausted our conversation and I could sense him preparing for his exit. At the last moment, pretending a nonchalance I knew he didn't feel, Rollin mentioned that there was one more thing.

"What's that?" I asked warily.

"You remember that bottle of cognac?"

"Yeah?"

"It's gone."

"Gone? Just like that?" I was incredulous.

"It, uh, disappeared the night you were there. You know, when we had our visitors."

"You didn't take it home?"

Rollin looked stricken. "I forgot about it until that night, and then—well, I looked for it the next morning and it was gone."

I groaned out loud. "Man, did you ask your employees about it? Who opened the next morning?"

"I've talked discreetly to every person who worked those two days and nobody knows anything. Nobody even knew about it except you and me and the girls who found it."

"Did you say what you were looking for?"

"Only a bottle of cognac. I'm sure they all thought I was looking for something from our inventory."

115

"Do you realize that bottle might have helped you out of the mess you're in?" I didn't actually believe it, but couldn't help saying it.

"I've thought about that, yes. But who knows if it was even real?"

"Nobody," I admitted. "It wasn't appraised, wasn't insured—ah, what's the use?" I lifted my hands and let them fall back onto the sheet. "Could have, would have, should have—it doesn't matter. I'm sorry, Rollin. Really sorry to hear it."

I was sorrier than he could possibly know. Not for the cognac—for we truly didn't know a thing about it—but sorry beyond words for his naiveté, his carelessness, his complete cluelessness. Now I knew there was nothing to stop King's Tavern from being taken cleanly out of Rollin's hands and delivered to the powers of darkness. I could see it already, a done deal. The sharks had somehow gotten rid of the old man; now the boy was just a plaything for their amusement. He was unable to administer the least aspect of his father's business—Christ, he couldn't even keep a bottle of liquor safe. Rollin finally took his leave and I lay there drained, struggling with no success to forget it all.

~

Valerie came to see me the next day, and when I told her Rollin's news she fell apart. "I told him to put it away, Ray," she cried over and over. "Nobody takes me serious, nobody ever understands." I expected her to be disappointed but she seemed devastated.

"I take you seriously, Val," I said, and opened my arms to her. She finally let me hold her while she wept, but there was something deep inside that nothing would comfort. Anita came in to check my IV and when she saw Valerie quickly whirled out. I let Val exhaust herself, and when she was finished she just sat on my bed looking dazed.

I was afraid to speak for fear of saying the wrong thing. Images from my past haunted me. Regardless of what Val had said a few days earlier I never felt I had a way with ladies. She didn't even know

116

I had been married. How could she know it had gone bad in four short years—probably because I never knew the right thing to say?

My outspoken wife had so often interpreted my silence as hostility, when it was nearly always the result of too many thoughts colliding, becoming too twisted together to sort out on the spot. I'd pull one strand out in desperation and it would be the wrong one, or be tangled up with several others that seemed irrelevant or said only a tiny part of what I was thinking. Unfortunately a tiny part of a complicated thing can appear to be something quite different from what it really is, so I often retreated into silence to avoid making things worse. There were so many times Jillian completely misunderstood me that when at last she filed for divorce I never contested it. I loved her, at least I believed I did, but with her everything required too much explanation and finally it just seemed easier to let go.

Now Valerie was sitting on my bed, looking at me with questioning eyes, and a strange thing started happening. Long-buried feelings of inadequacy I hadn't felt since my marriage were surfacing, and they disoriented me. Val was no longer my lover; she was hardly convenient as a friend, yet at that moment I felt certain she held something of great importance to me. I had no idea what it was, and felt an overwhelming sense of dread I might lose her before finding out.

I sat there looking at her with all my thoughts and feelings bumping into each other, and suddenly tears sprang to my eyes. I was embarrassed and tried to stop them, but the more I fought them the faster they came.

In an instant the tears triggered a humiliating childhood memory. I'd been riding my bicycle in my old neighborhood, and pulled up alongside some bigger boys on the corner. With no warning one of them kicked me over, bike and all. I landed on the asphalt tangled in my bike and only found after getting home that my collarbone was broken. But when dad saw me he seemed angrier with me for crying than he was at the boys who had pushed me down. I could still hear the contempt in his voice as he ordered me to suck it up and be a

117

man.

I never cried after that. I didn't presume anyone's sympathy and kept my emotions well hidden. Now they were getting out of hand, and I felt ashamed. I couldn't look at Val; I covered my face with my hands and felt my body shaking. Dad would have no mercy, I kept thinking.

I was spinning way out of control when I felt Valerie's hands on my wrists, pulling me toward her. I was too far gone to resist, and when her arms went around me I buried my face in her shoulder. I was furious, nearly choking with rage at my lack of control when I heard her voice in my ear. "He ain't here, Ray, do you hear me? He ain't here!"

Her words hit me like a slap. I reared back and demanded, "Who? What are you talking about?"

"You know who," she said softly. "You ain't got to worry about him now. You got to worry about the living, not the dead."

"But how do you know?" I insisted.

"Because you know. I'm just telling you what you already know."

In that moment I felt confusion unlike anything I had experienced. And just as quickly it was swept away by the look in Valerie's eyes. There was a pain there, a shadow I couldn't put a name on. "Val, how could you know what you just said?" I asked.

"Sometimes you see things you wished you never did," she said, looking sadly at me. "I never meant no harm."

"There was no harm done," I said, opening my arms to her. This time she met me more than halfway and held me desperately, as if I were the last warm body on earth.

CHAPTER 10

My forced vacation at Lehigh Valley Hospital Center was marked
by the classic steps of grieving: I experienced denial and anger,
skipped bargaining since I had no chips to bargain with, and ended
stuck on depression. I never made it to acceptance. Mike stayed in
touch every day by phone, keeping me posted on the Frye job, which
was progressing just fine without me. Part of me felt great relief but
another part of me felt unneeded and irrelevant. I hated being out of
the picture and fretted endlessly over details he was handling capably
in my absence. He was always patient, and humored me with little
anecdotes of the guys' spats and accomplishments.

Getting out of the hospital felt like being born again,
accompanied by the shock of birth as well. I'd been laid up for
twelve days and knew I wasn't going to hit the ground running. I was
wearing an IV pump on my belt, a device about the size of a portable
CD player that metered clindamycin, a powerful antibiotic, through a
tube that snaked up under my shirt and entered a vein near my
shoulder.   Dr. Panos sent me home with two weeks' worth of
clindamycin for the pump and made it clear that I wasn't to do any
manual work until the tube was removed and my burn completely
covered with new skin. Although my food in the hospital had been
excellent my appetite was diminished and I'd lost weight. I wandered
out into the world again feeling like a survivor of some war, fragile
and a bit overwhelmed by the reality I'd craved so restlessly to
reenter.

When Mike picked me up at the hospital on Wednesday I asked
him to take me out to the Frye job. Coming up the drive everything
looked as it had before but when we pulled around to the rear of the
house the addition blew me away. I hadn't watched the
transformation of the site; I'd only seen the house as it had been two
weeks ago and now it was a different thing. The new framing rose
impressively over the yard. The gable peaked nearly thirty feet above
the ground. Spider and Mackey peered down at me from the rafters

and faces appeared in the windows.

By the time Mike cut his engine the cheers of my crew were filling the air. The guys leaned out windows and popped up between rafters chanting "Bwa-na!" and pumping their hammers. It put a grin on my face and even though I couldn't pick up my tools I stayed most of the afternoon admiring their work. They'd been slamming; the job was ahead of schedule and it all looked great. Mike had handled things so well it was a small shock to realize how disposable I had been. In the hospital the thought had depressed me, but now that I was back on my feet it gave me a secret feeling of freedom to know that my crew could carry on like a well-oiled machine in my absence.

Before driving out to my place I asked Mike to swing by the post office so I could pick up my mail. We came into town via Second Avenue past the dairy plant, the old shoe factory that now housed craft shops, boutiques and a gourmet eatery, and finally the neatly kept row houses that lined the avenue into the downtown district. We drove by the brownstone courthouse and I squinted at the late afternoon sun reflected from its tall windows. We turned left onto Hancock Street and parked by the post office facing Main Avenue. Neither of us had change for the parking meter so Mike waited in the van for me.

I walked around the corner, up the granite steps and ambled through the glass door into the lobby. It was crowded and as I threaded my way past the boxes toward the main counter I pivoted to avoid a woman hurrying past me. In doing so I bumped the backside of a man who was taking mail from a box, and he dropped several letters. I backed off with an apology, but not before he wheeled around and gave me a stare that would have frozen a rattlesnake.

"I'm sorry," I repeated, and bent to pick up his mail.

Instantly his foot shot out to block me and he said, "No you don't." His eyes never left mine.

I straightened and lifted my hands. "Excuse me," I said and started to turn away, but a movement in his eyes stopped me.

120

He looked at my bandaged hand and then at my face with recognition in his eyes, and his mouth twisted into a smile. It took me a split second to realize it wasn't friendly at all; it was something quite else. It was malevolent and slightly crazed. His eyes bulged and he stood there like a cocked trigger, radiating violence and daring me to say a word. I felt anger rise up hot inside, but giving him a cold stare I turned around and walked away.

Talk about not worth it—that was the most pointless provocation I'd seen in a long time. The guy wasn't some young punk either; he was as old as me and built like a wrestler. I wouldn't take him on my best day, let alone the shape I was in now. What the hell was that about? I was still flustered when I arrived at the counter and only after speaking with the clerk did I begin to cool off. When my mail came I preoccupied myself sorting it and then headed out through the lobby. When I got to the door I saw the man standing outside to the right of the entry, waiting. I went out on the left and didn't even glance over as I headed down the steps.

I made it to street level before I heard him calling, "Hey! Hey you, Brauner!" I never broke my stride, but kept walking until I rounded the corner at Hancock, listening for footsteps. My heart was pounding when I opened the door to Mike's van.

"Let's go," I said.

"You alright?" Mike asked.

"Let's go, " I repeated, looking straight ahead.

"Okay, Bwana," he said, pulling out from the curb.

"Look up there," I said, nodding to the corner. The man stood staring as we approached the intersection. I locked the door but he did nothing except continue to stare as we rounded the corner a few feet away.

"You know that guy?" Mike asked.

"I was going to ask you the same thing," I said.

"Never seen him before. What's his problem?"

"I don't know. I bumped into him in the lobby and he went off."

"What did he say?"

"Nothing. It was just the way he looked at me. I knew it and he

121

knew it. He was waiting for me outside, but I got past him."

"So you got past him, that's good." Mike looked at me. "End of story, right?"

"Funny thing about it," I said, "he knew who I was. He looked at my bandage and called my name."

"So you bump into a guy. He looks at your bandage and calls your name. That's it?"

"I guess you had to be there." I began flipping through my mail.

Mike burst out laughing and poked my arm. "Come on, man. He's a creep. Don't let it get to you. Lots of people know who you are in this town. You're gold here, Bwana. Anyone forgets that, you've always got backup."

He grinned and I knew he meant it. But I didn't want to worry about backup; I just wanted to be about my business. What was going on here? With the familiar sights of Gladburg around me again I'd been feeling good until a few minutes ago but now my peaceful easy feeling was gone.

I recalled the night in King's Tavern when all my illusions about this place had been shattered. Lying in the hospital I had willed that memory into the farthest corner of consciousness. The images from that night were receding; I wanted to shrink them down to nothing. But now my senses were tingling, and as we approached Market Street the sight of the Grand Hotel looming over the block brought everything flooding back. The plate glass facade of King's Tavern looked elegant, even important with its gold leaf and canopied entrance. But all I could think now was that behind every facade lurked unseen realities. I suddenly felt great empathy for Rollin.

"Any word from the old man?" I asked Mike.

"Funny you should ask," he said. "You feel like stopping in to see Rollie?" He turned the corner onto Market Street. The entrance to the parking lot was just ahead.

"Sure, why not?"

~

Passing through the vestibule and big glass doors of King's Tavern switched all my senses to high alert. The last time I'd walked in here naively believing I had stock in the place. Now it felt like we were entering no man's land, and I wondered how it felt to Rollin. There was little time to ponder the question for there he stood drawing a glass of ale from the tap. His face opened into a huge smile when he saw us. Wiping his hands on a towel he came around the bar like an excited kid.

"Hey Mike!" he exclaimed, and then he grabbed me by the shoulders and beamed, "Ray, you look great! Great to have you back, man, just great!" A few happy hour patrons turned their heads, and although it was still early I noticed the dining room was bustling.

"What can I get you guys?" Rollin asked. "This one's on me."

"Hold that thought," Mike said, then he turned to me. "You got anything to eat at home?"

"I guess not much," I said. How long since I'd been grocery shopping—a month? I hated to think what my kitchen looked like.

Mike turned to Rollin. "Show us a table, old buddy, and we'll order from there."

Rollin motioned for the hostess to seat us and said he'd be back later. We landed in a booth near the end of the bar. We weren't there a minute before I heard a squeal from across the room and glanced up to see Valerie's friend Tina headed our way.

"Well, look who's here!" she exclaimed, giving Mike a big hug. "I haven't seen you guys in ages. And look at you!" she declared, peering closely at my face and taking my bandaged hand in both of hers. "Are you all better now, or what?"

"I think I just started to get a whole lot better," I said.

"I busted him out a couple hours ago, " Mike said. "Best not tell anyone you saw us until we get a head start out of here."

"So now you've got the law on your tail, have you?" Tina laughed.

"No, just a bunch of good-looking nurses. I told him not to play more than one at a time, but he never listens to me so we had to sneak him out when it all hit the fan. He made a real mess over

123

there—had 'em scratching each other's eyes out just to change his catheter bag."

Tina looked dubiously at me. "I don't know—he is kinda cute, but you think with all those rich doctors over there they'd be fighting over his skinny butt?"

"Hey!" I interrupted. "All I ever did was be a nice guy. Is it my fault nobody knows how to treat a lady? I just elevated their standards a little, you know?"

Both of them fell out at that. "I can guess what got elevated," Tina laughed, "and it wasn't anybody's standards, either. Now may I get you gentlemen something to drink?"

After a superb dinner of grilled salmon and a fine Gevrey-Chambertin I was feeling almost normal again. Tina was an attentive server, and kept us laughing with every visit to the table. Mike had his cheeseburger platter with a couple of Rolling Rocks, and as we enjoyed our meal it seemed almost like the calendar had been turned back. The soft clink of glass and silver, the air of conviviality, the quiet hum of conversation with muted jazz woven through it, all wrapped in the luxurious ambience our own hands had wrought, seemed to perfectly fulfill the old man's best expectations for this place.

I must have smiled to myself as I sat, half expecting to hear Valerie's incongruous accent pealing from some nearby table, and pictured her balancing trays of food and drinks as she strode like a warrior from the kitchen to her tables and back again. Mike, ever observant, remarked, "When it's good, it's very, very good."

"Yeah." I didn't need to hear the next line; neither of us wanted to think about that now. We were contemplating our pleasant condition when Rollin appeared with another Rolling Rock for Mike and the bottle of Gevrey-Chambertin for me.

"Where's Tina—don't tell me we wore her out?" I said. "We still have the matter of our check to discuss."

"There will be no check today, fellows, dinner is on the house. If you want to tip your server however, there would be no objections," Rollin smiled as he poured my wine.

"Now wait just a minute," I protested. "That's not—"

"That's the way it is," Rollin said, holding up a hand. "Work out your guilt on Tina, I'm sure she'll appreciate it. I'm just glad to see you both here and well. If you have time before leaving though, I'd like a word with you back in my office."

"Sure thing, Rollie," Mike said.

The bar was beginning to load up with the usual evening crowd. The noise was getting louder and the music had been turned up a notch or two; now a Dave Matthews disc was playing. Mike sat there drumming on the edge of the table and I was even getting into the rhythm when Tina reappeared.

"Is there anything else I can get you guys?" she asked.

"Yeah, a doggie bag for the rest of my beer," Mike slurred.

"Get outta here with your doggie bag!" she laughed, shoving him on the shoulder. He pretended to topple over, and she slid in beside him.

"I think we're good to go," I said, "but since Rollin took away the pleasure of paying our check the least we can do is make sure the help is taken care of." I folded a twenty into her hand. "Does he do that sort of thing often?"

"No way. You guys are really special around here—you know that, Ray. Both of you know it. You made his day coming in here like this."

"How are things?" I asked.

She looked around darkly and sighed. "We're in trouble."

"Bad, huh?"

"I'm surprised Angelo isn't here yet. You haven't seen the bouncer they sent, have you?"

"Nope. But if my last visit was any indication I'm in no hurry."

"He's not quite so dramatic. But Rollie needs help in a big way right now, and I don't see it coming. That damned old man…"

We sat silently a few seconds and then she stood up. "You're going to talk with him, aren't you?"

"That's why we're here," Mike said.

"Good," she said, laying a hand on his arm. "It was so good to

125

see you both—please don't be strangers from now on, okay?"

"Wait, there's something in your ear," Mike said as he reached for the side of Tina's head. He withdrew his hand and there was a bill folded between his fingers. "You ought to keep that in a better place," he scolded.

"You clown!" she laughed, and swiped it out of his hand. She hugged his neck, and as he pretended to strangle she laughed again and smacked him. "Goofball!"

Then she came over and hugged me tight. "Thanks, Ray. You both are so sweet." She pulled back. "Now don't forget there's someone else you need to see when you're all done here." I didn't answer, but she kept drilling me in the eyes until she whirled around and walked away.

~

Rollin followed us into the office and breathed a sigh as he closed the door, whether of relief or dread I wasn't sure. I glanced across the room at the fireplace mantel where on my last visit here a bottle of cognac over 200 years old had sat unguarded as a dime store vase. I felt a brief stab of resentment but shook it off. Mike walked around looking at the pictures on the wall, shaking his head and chuckling at one in particular. "This you, Rollie?" he asked.

We walked over to the photo and Rollin laughed sheepishly. "Yeah—but it wasn't my fault." There was a crumpled sailplane on the ground surrounded by curious cows, with a wild-eyed kid climbing out of the cockpit, barely recognizable as our favorite bartender.

"How did that happen?"

"I was set to land when a Lear jet that hadn't been cleared for landing came in right over me. I got tossed around in his wake turbulence, lost my lift and never made the runway."

Mike turned around. "No kidding?"

"No kidding. Turned out he had an electrical failure, no instruments and no radio. He was so rattled he didn't notice me until

126

his last turn. It was pretty close."

"When did this happen?"

"Eighty-five."

Mike whistled. "Man, you must have nine lives."

"We were both lucky," Rollin said.

I'd never noticed that picture before, and stepped up for a closer look. It was actually a framed clipping from a newspaper in Frederick, Maryland. A very young, very frightened teenager peered out from it. At least it hadn't scared him away from the sport, I thought. Maybe there was more resilience in Rollin than I gave him credit for. Something about his demeanor tonight seemed more purposeful than I had expected. Dared I hope he would have good news for us?

After little further talk he got to the point. "Look, I don't know where Angelo is tonight—he's usually here by now. I can't leave the bar for long but I want you to hear this." He pulled a cassette out of his pocket. "It's from my answering machine two nights ago."

Rollin opened his desk drawer and took out a tape player. He slid the cassette in and pressed the play button. It was the old man, and he sounded bad. He was distraught and barely coherent, a condition I could hardly associate with him. There was automobile traffic in the background; now and again other voices could be heard. He was calling from a pay phone somewhere in New Jersey—that's all the information Rollin had been able to glean from caller ID. I had a pretty good idea of the city.

"Rollie? You there? Listen, Rollie, this is your old man. I'm sorry, I really fucked up. I really fucked up Rollie; I hope you can forgive me. Oh, God, oh Jesus..." His voice trailed off.

"You know, I promised your mother I'd never gamble again. God rest her, you've never seen me gamble, have you, Rollie? You know that's why I wouldn't have billiards in my place; I don't want anybody gambling in there. I used to gamble so bad your mother almost left me, but after you were born I swore I'd never make another bet. And I never did, until that redhead came along. God help me, I never would have but she—ah, Rollie..." We waited as

127

cars whizzed by in the background.

"I loved that woman, Rollie, I thought she loved me. I thought I was helping her—ah, what's the use? She set me up, Rollie, it's like that was the whole reason she came to town." He hawked and spat and when his voice came back it sounded even more resigned.

"I lost a bundle. There were some high rollers, some real gangster types she hooked me up with. At first I was just playing for her and we were winning, and then I thought if we could pay down the construction loan how far ahead we'd be... Ah Jesus..." Again his voice trailed off.

"They took me, Rollie. They had me sign papers I don't even know what they said, and Liz was already gone and they got me drunk, Rollie. Those bastards had me drunk, like some fuckin' little puke!" His voice shook with anger, even in his state.

I didn't want to hear any more, but there wasn't much after that anyway. Too far down the slope to even think about stopping, he had cleaned out the bank account and gone to Atlantic City, I guessed, desperately hoping to make a killing and regain some of what he'd lost, but it was a doomed trip. Now he was on the street, homeless and paranoid.

"They'll kill me, Rollie. These guys don't fuck around. They won't hurt you but they'll kill me if they find me. I can't come home, Rollie, they turned me into a goddamn fugitive."

He never said who the people were, how much he lost, or any more about Liz. His call ended with more pitiful apologies, begging Rollin to forgive him and to try and keep the tavern afloat. And to think I had really believed there was nothing the old man could do to surprise me. Even though Valerie had tried to prepare me for something like this, actually hearing the tape was almost more than I could bear.

Rollin switched the player off, slid the cassette out and pocketed it. None of us looked at each other. After a long silence Rollin spoke.

"I played it for Buddy Sykes yesterday," he said. "Dad's lawyer. I believe you've met, Ray."

I nodded.

"He filled me in on a few things I didn't know. Dad gambled a lot. He lost badly a couple times. The last time was right after I was born. I never understood why Dad wouldn't have pool tables here." He looked grim. "Buddy thinks Liz was working for someone who knew about Dad's past. Maybe someone with an old score to settle."

At least Rollin was coming around to facts now. The tape made them unavoidable, although it left many questions unanswered. Who really was Liz? More importantly, who was behind her? Was it just a sore loser from the old man's past? He never mentioned how much he lost during his rambling call; had the amount been pumped up? Couldn't he raise a couple hundred grand using the hotel as collateral? Then I groaned inside, realizing he'd probably signed it over to the debtors as collateral, which was why they were walking in with such impunity.

"Buddy thinks we should demand to see all papers that Dad signed; even have them analyzed by a handwriting expert. We need to confirm the legality of this debt—right now we have nothing but the word of these people. What do you think?"

"I don't think a handwriting expert is going to help anything," Mike said. "You should ask to see the papers though. If the debt is legit maybe Buddy can talk with these people and buy you some time."

"Time for what?"

"To raise the money, if that's what it comes down to."

"How can I raise that much, Mike? I don't even have a trust fund any more; we put everything into the hotel."

"You sunk your trust fund in this place?" I was incredulous.

"Don't you think it was a good investment?" Rollin looked up wide-eyed.

"What I think is irrelevant now," I said. "You don't have the luxury of second-guessing anything, right now getting these people gone is all you can afford to think about. And if your dad really owes them they'll have to be paid or you'll never see the end of them."

My words were still hanging in the air when we heard angry voices in the hall. Rollin walked quickly to the door but it was

129

pushed open before he got there. A man with an arrogant manner walked in with Tina behind him, looking exasperated. The skin at the back of my neck prickled as I recognized the very man I had encountered at the post office that afternoon. A scornful expression spread across his face.

"Can I help you?" Rollin asked.

But the man laughed coarsely and ignored Rollin. Looking at me with disdain he said, "Mister Brauner! So this is the little hidey-hole you were running away to, eh? Did nobody ever teach you manners, or what?"

I stared. He threw back his head and laughed again, and it was a sound like nothing I had heard—completely demented, yet supercharged with virility. This guy was afraid of nothing. I remembered what Valerie had said about a couple of troublemakers laughing the old man down and wondered if he had been one of them.

"I don't believe I caught your name," Rollin tried again, and the man gave him a look as if a dog had just pissed down his leg.

"When I want any shit out of you, junior, I will pop your head off and squeeze it out. I was talking to Mister Brauner here, but he doesn't seem to have his wits about him." He turned back to me and folded his arms.

"Look pal," I said coldly, "I don't know what your problem is, but it was crowded in that post office. I bumped into you by accident and I apologized. Now if that hurt your feelings badly enough to track me down, I apologize again. I'm sorry; it really was an accident."

The man's expression changed from one of irritation to pure malice, and he responded in a voice that made my skin crawl. "Mister Brauner, I am not your pal. Don't ever call me that again. There are witnesses who saw you assault me today with no provocation. The problem is yours, not mine. If you don't climb down from your high horse before you get knocked down things will be very unpleasant for you. And once you find out how unpleasant, that little hospital stay will seem like a memory of paradise."

130

He seemed to forget me altogether as he turned to Rollin. "Okay, junior, since you're so big on formalities you can call me Tony. Your other security person had obligations tonight so I'm here instead. I see you have your little friends here for support and I'm touched. But unless you pay your debt by tomorrow night we're going to have to get a little more involved in the business, and your interest rate may go up. I'd hate to see your credit ruined before you have a chance to make things right."

With no warning the man turned and drove his fist into Mike's solar plexus. I heard the wind go out of him, and as he doubled over the man brought his knee up into Mike's gut with such force it lifted him off the floor. He went down like a rag doll. Seconds passed, and then he gasped horribly as he pulled himself to his knees.

"He'll be fine," the man said, "but maybe with a little better attitude now. Somebody should tell that hillbilly bitch there are no second chances from here on. Now everyone back to work. Brauner can help the tough guy home. Get him out of here, Brauner; go on, beat it!"

~

We took the rear exit, the same door Valerie used the day she had been fired. There were no last words with Rollin or Tina. I held Mike up all the way out and when we got to the parking lot he lost his hamburger platter. My grilled salmon ended on the ground beside it and then Mike started laughing. I failed to see the humor of it and told him so.

"But you didn't even get hit," he wheezed. Again he doubled over, from pain as much as from laughter, "and you wasted that salmon!"

"That's right," I said angrily. I didn't want to talk; there was nothing to say.

"Come on, Bwana, lighten up," he said.

"Mike, I couldn't lighten up right now if my life depended on it. You go right ahead though and laugh all you want, don't let me stop

131

you."

Mike straightened up as well as he could and laid an arm over my shoulder. "Ray, we're not going to let these pricks destroy Rollie." He winced. "It's been a while, but I've been sucker-punched before. My fault for not seeing it coming. But that's not the end, Bwana. It's not over yet, and don't you forget it."

"Whatever you say."

"Okay, here's what I say. We're going to the grocery store to get you stocked up, and then we're going to see Valerie. And we're not going to tell her about this. She'll find out from Tina eventually, but right now she needs to cool it. The last thing we want is for her to go on another mission, right?"

"Right."

"So we're going to cheer her up. Don't make this into something bigger than it was. That guy thinks he's scared us off and we'll let him think that for now. But don't believe it for a minute. We can't pay the old man's debt, but we're going to take care of Rollie. They're not going to destroy his manhood for something the old man did."

I studied Mike's face in the hard light of the parking lot. His jaw was set and his eyes were determined; he meant what he said. "Come on, let's go to the IGA and get you some provisions." He slapped my shoulder. "You're getting way too skinny for anyone to believe my story about you and those nurses."

~

Our visit with Valerie began on a light note; she seemed delighted to see us. Mike appeared fully recovered; he stood tall and showed no sign of pain. He knew better than to regale Val with jokes about the nurses, but he did make her giggle several times with his patently ridiculous stories. He showed her my IV pump and claimed it actually was filled with vodka. When he told her "Bwana wouldn't even let them give him a shot in the bum for fear it would put a mark on his perfect ass," she whooped with laughter. After we'd

132

been there about ten minutes he asked to use the cell phone he had left with her and ducked out the door.

Valerie lived in an old Airstream trailer. She had bought it cheaply at auction after arriving in the area, rented a spot for it with utility hookups on a dairy farm just outside Gladburg and said it was nicer than living in town. I couldn't argue with that, preferring the country myself; but frankly expected squalor when I first saw that thing sitting there under the trees by the old springhouse. Instead I found everything inside neat as a pin. Val had few belongings but still managed to create a homey environment in that tin can. A hand-braided rug covered the floor, a beautiful quilt made by her grandma dressed up the back of her daybed and curtains framed each window. An old Washburn guitar sat in a battered case against the wall. It wasn't until the following spring that I noticed the jonquils and grape hyacinths she had planted beside the stones lining the walk to her door, and the fragrance from lilies of the valley that surrounded the springhouse in profusion.

There was a built-in pine bookshelf over Valerie's daybed and I found its contents fascinating. It held a well-worn King James Bible, a dictionary, two old volumes of Shakespeare and several collections of poetry. There was Edward Steichen's *The Family of Man* and a book of paintings by Georgia O'Keefe. There were biographies of Gandhi and Martin Luther King. There was a small, well-worn paperback titled *The Problem of Pain* by someone named Lewis. There was a dog-eared medical encyclopedia that looked like a college textbook and a repair manual for a 1987 Volkswagen Jetta. There were a few other things I don't recall, but just two novels— Dostoyevsky's *Crime and Punishment* and *The Color Purple*. I also knew Val kept a double-barreled shotgun under her daybed, and even though it hadn't been discussed I felt pretty sure she was a crack shot with it.

I once asked Val why there was nothing on her bookshelf besides reference or repair books that had been written in her lifetime. She corrected me with *The Color Purple* and then opined that as prophets have no honor in their own country, genius is not often recognized

133

in one's own lifetime.

Indeed, there were sides to Valerie that no one in town dreamed of. Even with my privileged view there was much I didn't understand. All I knew right now was that she needed friends and I'd pledged to be there for her. I had no idea where that might require me to bleed from next, and dreaded finding out.

When Mike stepped out the door with the phone Val turned to me and demanded, "So what kind of trouble are you in now?"

"What do you mean?"

"Don't you go playing me for a dummy, Bwana—something's got you both all eat up and Mike can't hide it neither. I guaran-damn-tee you he ain't up to no good on that phone now."

"I have no idea what Mike is doing; it's none of my business. I just got out of the hospital and haven't even been home yet, for Chrissake."

"You better watch what you say, mister. It's a sin to tell a lie and even worse to swear it on the name of the Lord."

"I'm not swearing and I'm not lying. I just want to go home and put my life back to something resembling normal. Can you please cut me a little slack?"

She looked at me suspiciously, and then softened a tiny bit. "Okay," she said, "but I know something's not right. You better be careful now before you get yourself in some kind of trouble."

"I've had enough trouble the past few weeks to last a lifetime— I'm not about to make more for myself or anyone else."

She looked skeptical. "Mighty sure of yourself, aren't you?"

"Valerie, what is it with you?" I flared, suddenly angry. "You don't let up for one minute! I really try to be your friend but everything I say ends up being challenged."

She looked hurt. Her dark eyebrows furrowed and then drew up in the middle. "Sometimes you see things you wished you never did. I just don't want nobody else to get hurt, Ray. I guess I don't have much social graces." She seemed deflated, as if I'd punched all the wind out of her.

"Aw, Val—" I started to apologize, but just then the door

opened and Mike appeared on the step.

"Umm—maybe I should take a walk," he said, looking back and forth between us. "I think I need to see a man about a horse."

"There ain't nobody with a horse out there, you lummox," Valerie said. "Now I want you both to promise you're not going off to do something stupid, alright?"

"Stupid? Moi?" Mike grinned like an overgrown kid. "You've never seen me do anything like that, have you, Bwana?"

I remembered the scene in the observatory with Mr. Plum but pushed it back. "Nah," I said. "This man keeps us all on an even keel."

After looking back and forth between us Val dropped her head. "You be careful, Mike," she finally said.

His face looked like it had been slapped. "I promise," he said.

After we left he asked, "What did you tell her?"

"Nothing." I was irritated. "You don't have to tell her anything; she already knows."

"Knows what? Now she can read minds?"

"She's probably been that way forever. It's one of her biggest handicaps." To be honest I hadn't noticed it until recently, but seeing it now seemed to put a few other things in perspective.

"Handicaps?" Mike looked puzzled.

"Sometimes she knows exactly what people are thinking, but the problem is she doesn't understand why they're thinking it. She knew something was wrong tonight—she said so as soon as you went out the door. I didn't say a word and she told me you were up to no good on the phone. She thought we were in together on something but I finally convinced her I had no idea what you were doing. I guess I was a little hard on her."

Mike didn't answer but I could tell he was really chewing on that.

~

The next morning I went back to the Frye job. I didn't pick up a tool all day except for a measuring tape. I walked around and made

135

myself familiar with everything that had been done in my absence, and spent some time talking with the Fryes. Mike was tight-lipped; in fact the whole crew seemed to be uncommonly preoccupied with working. There was no horsing around, no joking or sarcasm; everyone was quiet as sawdust. Several times I caught a couple of the guys looking at each other with a strange expression. I couldn't quite nail down what it was but they seemed to know something I didn't.

At the end of the day I reminded Mike that tonight was the two-week deadline at King's Tavern and asked what time he thought we should be there. He stopped gathering his tools and looked me in the eye.

"Bwana, the thing you're needed for tonight is not at King's."

"What do you mean?"

"You know the one person who most needs to stay away from there, don't you?"

Ah, shit.

"Go and visit Valerie. Take her out to eat, go see a movie, do anything she wants but whatever happens don't let her come near King's Tavern tonight."

I took a deep breath and blew it out.

"Just pretend like it's two years ago," Mike suggested.

"I can't do that," I said. "But I'll go see her. If we can spend fifteen minutes together without a quarrel it'll be a miracle, but I'll try. What are you going to do?"

"Be there. I think most of the guys are planning to show up. All separately, all quiet. If we're lucky that's the way the whole evening will go."

"You really think there's a chance of that?"

Mike gave an inscrutable little smile.

"You know something you're not telling me, Ace? Like how come nobody made a peep today, and everybody was sneaking glances around like there's some sort of conspiracy?"

"There are some things you may be better off not knowing. Let's just say everyone is doing what they can to help Rollie."

"Now you've really got my attention," I said. "This involves my

136

crew, which is the backbone of my business and the means to finish the addition on these folks' home, and you're telling me I don't need to know what's going on? Am I going to wake up tomorrow and find half my employees in jail or hospital or worse?"

"Anything is possible, but we intend to avoid that. Like I said, we can't pay the old man's debt, but we can encourage these cretins to show Rollie some respect."

"Just how do you expect to do that this late in the game?"

Mike smiled slightly. "We've already sent them a message."

"A message? Like, dominate us, humiliate us, walk all over us? That was some kind of message, Ace—I'm sure they're really impressed now."

"Remember what I told you last night? It's not over yet, Bwana. Our pal Tony was feeling pretty cocky when we left, and I knew he wasn't expecting any further complications for the evening. After he had a chance to get relaxed me and a couple of the guys went over for a visit."

"Don't tell me this. You went back to King's last night?"

"It was a good visit. By the time we left he was being really nice to us."

"Oh, no!" I groaned. "He'll come back and eat you for lunch—man, what have you done?"

"All we did was ask him to treat Rollie with respect. Nothing personal, we just asked him to let Rollie and his lawyer see whatever papers the old man signed, and work out a realistic payment plan."

"That's it?"

"Yeah, basically."

"So everyone just sat around Rollin's office and had a nice civilized talk, right?"

"Well, that would have been the best way to go. He—well, it took a little persuasion before he'd listen to us."

"What kind of persuasion? The same kind he used on you?" Little fingers of nausea were starting to creep up my throat.

"No," Mike said, "we never once hit him even though it would have been fair if we had. We got him to listen, and that's the important thing."

"I don't like this at all. You're not telling me the whole story here and these guys are hard-core. They specialize in hurting people, whereas you're a carpenter, for God's sake. You can't out-bad them and you don't want to try."

Mike pondered for a few seconds, and then looked up. "You're right, we can't out-bad them. But what we did wasn't bad; it was necessary. People like that live by intimidation; it's the only language they understand. We got his attention. We didn't challenge the debt, only their way of dealing with Rollie. We told him everything would work out if everyone acts civilized. We could have slapped him around pretty good but we didn't, and I think he appreciated that by the time it was over."

"He appreciated that, huh? How could you tell?"

"Look, Ray, are we supposed to sit on our hands while these guys tear Rollie to pieces? Maybe what we did was wrong, maybe not. But if we do nothing then don't we become responsible for whatever happens?"

Suddenly Valerie's words echoed in my mind: Once you know something you can't run away from it, you're responsible. I couldn't help but wonder which knowledge carried the greatest liability—the terrible fix Rollin was in, or the information Mike had just laid on me.

"I don't know," I said, "but I guess it doesn't matter what I think anyway, does it? You're already involved and now you've got the whole crew in this thing. What if I said forget it, leave my employees out of it? It looks to me like everybody already has their minds made up."

"You'd never say that," Mike replied. "You're the one who got me involved in the first place—because you don't want to abandon Rollie to those bastards any more than I do."

"I guess you're right. So now instead of one or two people having to watch their backs every one of us has to."

"The way I see it their problem got bigger, not ours. They thought it would be a cakewalk to come in and scare Rollie into

138

giving them whatever they want. I don't think they counted on anyone standing up to them."

"Or escalating things into a war."

"Don't you wonder why those first two clowns haven't been back? I think it's because Val stood up to them and spoiled their act. Enough of those goons go home with their tails between their legs and whoever's behind them will want to just settle up and get the hell out. I don't think they've got an unlimited supply."

"I hope you're right."

"Think positive, bro," Mike said with a grin. "It's going to be alright because it has to be. Now it's time for you to be a hero and keep our heroine charmed for the evening." He actually looked cheerful.

CHAPTER 11

I went home and spent more time than usual trying to make myself look presentable. I shaved, put on my best denim shirt and a pair of khakis and even polished my shoes. I put a fresh antibiotic pack in the IV pump, checked all the tubing and clipped it to my belt. When I arrived at Valerie's she was working underneath her Jetta. The front end was up on metal ramps and there were tools and parts scattered around her.

"Got yourself a job?" I said.

She crawled from under the car, her hands black with grease and her face dark with frustration. Her hair was gathered up under a bandana. She sat on the ground with her arms on her knees and regarded me critically.

"Just look at you now. Ain't there some pretty nurse somewhere pining for your perfect ass?"

"I've been thinking about you, Val. I wanted to see how you're doing."

"Well I'm doing just fine, thank you."

"Kind of hard to tell from the look of things."

"Busted my timing belt," she scowled. She pulled the bandanna from her head and shook out her hair. She wiped her hands on the bandanna, balled it up and threw it at me and finally climbed to her feet.

"You know how to fix a timing belt?" I was impressed.

"I never done it before, but the book shows how." She nodded at the repair manual open on the ground. "It's nothing but a bunch of stuff to take off and on," she shrugged, "except it's a greasy mess in there, and some of them bolts are stuck on pretty tight. You got time to give me a ride?"

"Depends on where," I said.

"In town." Val seemed dejected. "I thought I might get this done today, but it was kind of a bigger job than I thought." She looked uneasily at me. "I need to clean up a little, if you can wait."

140

"Where are you headed?" I asked again.

"You know good and well where I'm headed."

"Valerie, you're not going in there tonight. That's the last place you need to be, believe me. You get cleaned up and I'll take you anywhere outside of town you want. I'll even buy you dinner, but you're not going to King's tonight."

I was prepared for fireworks but instead Valerie just sagged. Her head drooped and heavy black hair fell like a curtain across her face. After several seconds a small voice came from behind it. "Who's going to stand up for Rollie?"

"You already have," I said. "Now it's somebody else's turn."

She tossed her hair back and looked up at me. "And who would that be? It don't look like you're planning to take your importance over there."

"What do you mean, my importance?"

"Who was it they listened to last time, stupid? Or do you think everyone else is stupid too?"

"Stupid? What do you mean?"

She shook her head impatiently. "Sometimes you act like you've got old-timer's disease. If I didn't know you any better I'd swear you was dumb as a rock."

"Well, since I'm hopefully smarter than a rock, maybe you'll do me the favor of explaining what you mean over dinner."

Val put her hands on her hips and eyed me up and down. "Well now, that depends. Are you asking me for a date, or just trying to hustle me out of town?"

The IV line tugged at my skin and I shrugged, trying to gain a little slack in the loop of tubing taped to my shoulder. Valerie was watching me closely. "Feeling kind of twitchy?" She walked slowly to where I stood, slid a hand around my waist and turned her face up to mine. "Answer the question right and win the prize," she breathed, pressing against me. Fragrance from her hair mingled with the faint aroma of motor oil, shutting down my good sense, and suddenly I found myself aroused.

"What's the matter?" she taunted. "Cat got your tongue?" She closed the last gap between us and kissed me hard. Her tongue found mine but I was taken by surprise, and before I could respond she pulled away. "There ain't no such thing as a free lunch, is there, Bwana?" she said softly.

She turned abruptly and disappeared through the door into her metal cocoon, leaving me standing like a wooden Indian alone with an erection instead of a cigar. After collecting my wits I sat down at the picnic table under the big ginkgo tree that towered over her trailer.

I thought about those few weeks we spent together, how we'd eaten lunch here under the changing leaves after debauching her little daybed in ways the manufacturer never intended. I would race back to King's Tavern and always walked in with building materials or tools in hand to keep people from thinking anything was up. I marveled now at my naiveté—most of my crew had known exactly what was going on but thankfully kept their mouths shut. That was our ritual until one day we found the ginkgo suddenly bare. All the leaves had dropped within the space of a morning and the ground was covered with them, but by then it was too cold to eat outdoors anyway. And after Val's star began to fall it was one of those things nobody dared mention.

Now nearly two years later I was sitting here with a hard-on like an awkward suitor, all dressed up and waiting for Valerie, and who could know what she was feeling? The poignancy of my own emotions surprised me, caught somewhere between memory and loss. I wasn't even sure what was lost and what remained between us but felt something precious was gone.

As for Val, she had come up here with little to lose—or so it seemed to me—but somehow I felt her loss had been greater. Now she had no income, few friends and little sympathy from the town she had tried to make her home. At least she had Tina for an ally, as well as Mike and me. Now Rollin was among Valerie's champions but with things the way they were at King's Tavern he couldn't give her job back. Her options seemed to be dwindling fast. I had no idea what she might do next.

142

My thoughts wandered and I was starting to wish for something to read, and even thought of asking Val to hand out her old guitar for me to thump on when the door to her trailer opened and she stepped down.

There should have been music, but like nothing I could have played. She was wearing a long, flowing dress that appeared to be an evening gown that had been altered with a Bowie knife. The sleeves had been cut out and the armholes left unhemmed. The top would have been too small had it not been similarly hacked down the middle front and back and the bodice laced together with rawhide, which allowed a generous amount of skin to show. I didn't see a bra. The whole thing was elaborately tie-dyed a remarkable shade of deep purplish brown.

Valerie preserved her modesty by draping a lacy black shawl over her shoulders, complemented by elbow-length black gloves with silver and gold stars painted on them. As she clomped down the trailer step I could see the tips of her Doc Martens peeping from beneath her hem. Her hair was a glorious tangle of curls that bounced nearly to her elbows and her skin looked freshly kissed by dewdrops and light. She smiled shyly as I stared at her. "Do I look okay?"

"If you looked any better I'd be afraid to take you out." I was awestruck.

"Is that good?" A tiny shadow flitted over her face.

"Very. I doubt there's another person north of the Mason-Dixon line who could wear that, Val, but you look absolutely orgasmic. Don't even question it, just believe."

Valerie grinned. "You must believe, brothers and sisters; casting away all your doubts and fears," she orated, her cadence and lifted hands the perfect impression of a Pentecostal revivalist. I laughed out loud at the same Val I'd known back in the glory days, back in that brief, magical time when she had been funny, bold and exotic; before anybody had seen the doubts, fears and awkwardness hiding just behind her strange beauty.

143

~

Since we both had enjoyed our first visit to the Millstone brew pub I thought it might be the perfect venue for tonight. It seemed a world away from Gladburg and the troubles at King's Tavern. Valerie agreed; she actually had liked their menu. I was hungry but my nerves kept me on edge and the drive seemed much longer this time. When we finally walked through the old oak doors and passed the copper-trimmed bar every head turned to stare at Val. She seemed oblivious to the turbulence in her wake and I ignored it.

We were nearly to the dining area when something made me turn and look back. I had a fleeting glance of the bartender's face staring at us before a waitress carrying a tray of empty pitchers intervened, and my heart sank. Would this dinner also be a lost cause?

We found a table near the back. After studying the menu both of us started with gazpacho soup and India pale ale. The gazpacho was pungent with cilantro and garlic and would have been perfect for the late summer evening if my appetite hadn't been so rudely choked off. My beer tasted bitter and I kept seeing the bartender's face over and over, knowing but not knowing for sure that it was Tony—the very son of a bitch from the post office who had ambushed Mike in Rollin's office door.

It's good, I kept telling myself, because if it's him that means he's not at King's tonight. And also it means he's a working stiff, which I tried to believe made him less intimidating than a full-time professional leg-breaker or whatever they were called. But how incredible that of all people we might encounter while trying to stay away from Gladburg's troubles, it would be him! Why is he here, of all places? Maybe it wasn't him. Fat chance. None of these thoughts were helping me be the sparkling dinner companion I had hoped to be. Not that Val wouldn't have seen through it anyway, but I had at least expected to breeze through the evening. Now already I was struggling.

If Valerie suspected anything she didn't show it. She took her gloves off and attacked her meal with gusto. I had roasted chicken

144

and she didn't say a vegetarian word. The food was outstanding but I couldn't get my mind off the bartender who was pulling our drinks, and thinking about Rollin and the guys back at King's Tavern brought a knot to my belly that pretty much killed the rest of my appetite. I toyed with my meal and wouldn't touch my beer.

We ate in silence until the waiter brought a tray of dessert samples to the table. After much deliberation Val ordered tiramisu. When I just asked for water she looked at me like I'd sprouted another head.

"Is something wrong?" she asked after the waiter left.

"Wrong?" I smiled. "What could possibly be wrong? My whole crew is putting themselves on the line trying to prevent a hostile takeover of King's Tavern while I sit here dining with a beautiful woman. I can't figure out if I'm lucky or irresponsible."

"Maybe you're both."

I looked back at her with a big question mark curling around in my mind until she laid a hand on my arm.

"It's alright, Ray," she said. "You were right, I didn't need to be there tonight." A smile touched her face like sunlight and was gone.

It wasn't like Val to say reassuring things to me out of the blue; it was almost as if she'd burst into song or begun speaking perfect French. A dubious relief slowly settled over me. I looked at her again but the moment had passed; she was busy cleaning up her plate and seemed unconcerned with whatever I was thinking.

The waiter returned with my water and Val's tiramisu, and she began carving the top away as I watched. She plopped the first bite into her mouth and slowly pulled the spoon out with a rapturous look. "Here, try it," she said, handing the spoon to me.

I took a bite and it was very good. I handed the spoon back.

"Don't you want one?" she asked.

"Nope."

"The bartender don't make the desserts, you know." She busied herself sculpting her whipped cream while the hairs on the back of my neck stood up.

"What made you say that?"

145

"It's not like you think; you put your feelings right out where everybody can see them."

"Don't turn this around, Val. I never said a word about the bartender; how could you possibly know what I was thinking?"

"I got eyes, Ray. You might think I'm just a hick chick but I pay attention and you ought to give me credit for that. All I do is look and put two and two together."

"That's all?" I was angry. It felt like an invasion of privacy and I didn't want to let her off easy. But how could I blame her for seeing what she saw?

"Never mind, sorry I mentioned it," she said, digging into her boot for a cigarette. She lit it and inhaled deeply, regarding me with her eyes like steel.

Something broke inside me as I looked back at her and struggled for words. Her eyes softened and she touched my hand. "Ray, you know we can't do nothing for Rollie if we're fighting all the time."

I took her hand and nodded.

"Do you know that man from somewhere?"

"I'm not sure. I only saw him for a second but he looks like the goon that came to King's Tavern last night. He took Mike down like a sap and pretty much ruined everybody's evening. But it might not be him."

"It's him alright," she said. "He seemed pretty surprised to see you too. If you was the kind of person that wanted to, you could make him squirm a little, don't you reckon?" She sat there looking innocent as a lamb.

"Maybe I don't give you enough credit," I finally said. "Are you going to finish that dessert or will I have to do it for you?"

"I'll split it with you," she said, mashing her cigarette out.

After finishing the tiramisu we ordered a chocolate mousse and split that too, sharing the same spoon. I paid our waiter and we stood to leave. Val picked up her gloves, wrapped the shawl around her shoulders and we made our way to the front of the pub.

As luck would have it the bartender was unoccupied when we walked by and I grinned at him. "Nice to see you making an honest buck, Tony." I noticed a long, fresh scratch along his jaw and a knot on his forehead that hadn't been there yesterday.

"Nice bitch," he shot back, leering at Valerie. She turned away with her nose in the air and he laughed. "She ought to come in here more often; I could fix her up with a real man." Several bar patrons looked up in shock while others buried their faces in their mugs.

"Great job," I said, tossing a dollar bill onto the bar. "That last glass of water was perfect. You like water, don't you, Tony? It works wonders to clear your head."

He looked stricken for a few seconds, and then his eyes bulged. "Get out of here!" he snarled.

"We were just leaving. You take care now, Tony," I breezed as Valerie took my arm and steered me away.

"No, you take care, Brauner. You both better take care," he yelled as we walked out the door.

~

"Whoo-whee!" Valerie said when we got back to my truck. "You sure put a stick in his eye. What made you say that?"

"Say what?"

"About the water."

"I didn't trust that bastard pouring me anything but water, Val. There wasn't much to talk about otherwise." I started the engine.

We rode without speaking for a few miles and then Valerie said, "You know what Mike was up to last night?"

"More than I want to."

"It had something to do with mister personality back there, huh?"

"I'm afraid so."

"He must have scored some points cause that man's definitely got a fractured ego."

"I'd say he had it coming. I think you would too if you'd been there."

"I ain't arguing with you, but you better know where to stop.

147

Some people just get meaner when they get riled. I seen it all my life."

"So that's why you went after the big guy at King's?"

"Somebody had to do something. I didn't see you using none of your influence, mister high and mighty."

"Well, I can't see how anyone else would have done any better." I almost smiled at the picture of Valerie's towering rage and Smith reeling between the barstools clutching his groin.

"That was then and this is now," she said.

We rode in silence for a while and then my curiosity got the best of me. "You keep talking about my influence; what's that supposed to mean?"

Val stared at me. "You're kidding, right?"

"No, I'm not kidding. Why would you think a thing like that?"

Valerie started laughing a deep belly laugh that ended on a note of scorn. "Mister importance spends his whole life trying to get people to take him serious and when they finally do he goes, 'That didn't happen, did it?'"

"Look, everyone knows I'm the guy who built King's Tavern; so what? It was just my job."

"Just your job?" Val scoffed. "How about that fancy house you built? Was that just your job? Was carving David just a job for Michelangelo?"

"Come on, Valerie, you wouldn't flatter me like that. King's Tavern is just another bar and you know it."

"Not to Rollie it ain't. Not to the old man and not to them bastards that are trying to get hold of it, neither. I tell you, Ray, to them people you're some kind of hero. I think it's a shame myself. But you got all this importance to them and you don't even see it, when you could be using it to help things."

"I'm no hero to Tony back there," I said.

"Yeah, well he's an exception. That don't mean it's not true about the others."

"They're wrong. I'm just a regular guy. People can think whatever they want but that doesn't make it true."

148

"Listen to you, Bwana! You sat there in that hospital eating fancy food and getting fussed over by pretty nurses like you was some kind of king. Who was paying your meal ticket? Don't tell me it was Geico."

"No, Val, it was my client. You know that."

"That's the kind of thing rich hot-shot lawyers do for folks, is it?"

"No, but most folks didn't just build a house for them either."

"Ray, it don't matter why, it just matters what. You might not be jack shit actually but to them you have some kind of importance. Them bastards at King's wouldn't listen to nobody, but they listened to you."

"Those bastards were criminal thugs. They were full of shit. And thank you very much for your opinion of me."

"You know better than that. They never stopped until you told them to. Now why do you think that was?"

"I don't know. I really don't know."

"Who did you say was paying for your fancy food, mister genius?"

"Mr. Plum. No way, Val. He's all tied up in his work up in Philadelphia; he's an outsider. His time is way too expensive for him to get mixed up in some local vendetta."

"Looks to me like he just made a mighty big local investment."

"So now he's got his trophy house; what else does he need?"

"Maybe his wife knows."

"Did you ever meet her?"

"No, but I heard all about how she rescued you."

"If you met her you might understand. She's sort of innocent, like you."

Valerie snorted. "Like me? Then she ain't innocent at all."

"Nobody's completely innocent, Val. But some people are more innocent than others—they do things for the right reasons and care more about other people than themselves."

"Well, you could be one of them too if you weren't so wrapped up in your own self. But unfortunately you don't see that." She turned her head away.

149

"I wish I knew what to do," I said. "Unfortunately I have no magic abilities."

She turned back to me. "Ray, nobody's got magical abilities. You use what you've got. And you don't even see that; you're so busy trying to make yourself look good. Maybe your lawyer friend is an upstanding citizen, but if he wasn't would you even want to know it? Or would you rather pretend he's great, so you could wash your hands of everything and be mister above-it-all?"

"Okay, suppose Mr. Plum was the scum of the earth and I knew it. What good would that information do anybody?"

"Nothing, if you didn't do nothing. But if he thinks you're special enough to do favors for you there's something to work with. Maybe you've got more pull than you think."

"I'm just a working stiff, Val. I do my job and move on. Nobody made me Mr. Plum's advisor and I don't think my opinions would impress him one bit."

"Don't you ever take responsibility for nothing?"

"Only for what I do and say. Not for what others do or say."

"Or for the good you could do if you was willing."

"We seem to be talking in circles now."

She rolled down her window, turned her face into the night and didn't speak again until we were back at her place. I pulled up beside her crippled Jetta and turned off the engine.

"Well thank you for the dinner, Mr. Brauner," she said, staring straight ahead.

I sat watching her.

"Is there something bothering you?" she finally asked, looking sideways at me.

"Nah, I was just wondering if you've got strings on that old Washburn in there."

She softened. "You know there's always strings on my guitar. You come on in and play if you want; I'll make you some coffee."

"I don't want any coffee."

She waited for me to walk around and open her door. Where is this going, I wondered as she took my arm for the few short steps to

150

her trailer.

~

The night was cool and hinted of autumn. When we got inside Valerie lit a pair of candles and set them on the counter, opened her windows, then disappeared into the back of her trailer. I sat on the rug and took her guitar from its case. Sure enough, there were fresh strings on it and when I strummed a few chords it even sounded in tune.

Val was a pretty fair player and she knew a lot of traditional songs, and some beautiful early American hymns. Her singing voice was rich and sorrowful, with none of the hard edge that came through in her speech. More than once it had raised goose bumps on me. The idea once occurred to me that nobody could sing like that without having passed through some unimaginable suffering, some awful furnace of the soul. I had dismissed it as a romantic notion but now I wasn't sure.

Val padded back wearing faded flannel pajamas. She pulled a pillow from the daybed and flopped down on the floor across from me. I was trying to pick out the melody to "Wave", a song by Antonio Carlos Jobim, but my fingers were nervous and the bandage around my palm felt clumsy. "Here, you play something," I said, handing the guitar to her.

"No, you keep right on there," she insisted.

I segued into more familiar chords of "The Girl from Ipanema" and Val began singing along. She never had heard of Jobim before meeting me but when I made a tape for her she became a believer. She even had learned lyrics to several of his songs. Although she couldn't mimic the Brazilian accent she didn't sound bad. By the end of the song my fingers were warming to the task. I pulled a fat unnamable chord out of my head for the finale that stretched my left-hand fingers all over the guitar neck. Val whooped after it faded to silence, and I grinned.

"Will you do 'Corcovado'?" she asked.

151

"I don't play that song," I said.

"You told me that once but you never said why."

"It makes me sad."

"You're not the sentimental type," she scoffed. "Why would a pretty song like that make you sad?"

"It's something that's over now."

"If it's over why does it still bother you?"

"There was a time of sadness, Val, and that song just reminds me of it."

"Oh." She seemed surprised.

My fingers found the first chord and plucked it softly. Its moody intervals expanded into a melancholy space with the second chord, but God, what beautiful chords they were. That was the joy of Jobim. Before I knew it I was seduced by the sound coming out of Val's old Washburn. My fingers moved like shadows over the fretboard as I fell into the song's rhythm, slow and intimate as a heartbeat. The bandage over my palm was forgotten. The flames of Valerie's candles flickered and swayed in the breeze that came through her window.

I started singing about quiet nights and quiet stars, not knowing why I was attempting this. I rarely sang; my voice had such a limited range there wasn't much I could get through without cracking on the high notes. But this song had other perils for me.

Valerie had her head cocked and was listening raptly; she hadn't expected me to cave in so easily. The truth was, I loved that song and just listening to those chords coming out of that old mahogany soundbox would go a long way to compensate for anything else it might do to me. I got through the first verse without effort but the second would be the test.

I sang the first three lines with my eyes closed. The high notes were coming and I could feel the back of my eyelids burning. When I got to the part about finding the meaning of life my voice nearly broke—but I averted that and angrily struck a dissonant chord. Val looked up, startled.

"I told you I don't play that song," I growled.

She came over and put her face up to mine, the guitar large and clunky between us. "Hey," she said, gently shaking me. "I didn't mean to make you mad." She kissed me on the forehead and then pulled back. "Are you okay?"

"Yeah." I felt embarrassed now. "I thought I could do it, but..."

Finally with a wistful voice Val said, "She really must have been something."

"She was my wife."

"You? You had a wife?"

"Is that so hard to imagine?"

"No." Val studied me. "Not any more, anyway."

I didn't say anything.

"How come you never told me?"

"It never came up."

More silence.

"That's an awful pretty song," Val finally said. "She must have loved it."

"She never heard it."

"Don't say you wouldn't play it for her neither."

I laid the guitar down. "You want to know what happened? I'll tell you, Val. But don't say I tried to keep you in the dark, because I'd have told you about her any time if you had asked."

"I never said you kept me in the dark."

"Yeah, but you thought it, didn't you?"

"So now you're a mind reader?"

"No, I just pay attention and put two and two together."

"Ha ha. So what was her name?"

"Jillian."

"Jillian." Val seemed to turn the name over in her mind. "Was she classy?"

"Yeah, I guess you'd call her that. She sure worked hard enough at it."

"How come she never heard you play 'Corcovado'?"

"We were both so busy back then. We had gotten kind of distant and I was looking for a way to change that." I had tried to bury that night so deep in my memory it would never rise again. Talking about it was against all my instincts but now it was too late to stop.

"I learned it for her Valentine present. We had a dinner date. When I got home I sat there practicing that song, waiting to play it for her. I hadn't even been upstairs yet. After two hours I started walking through the house and found everything of hers was gone. Cleaned out. When I looked in her closet and saw everything gone, it—well, all the feelings I had right then are all mixed up with that song in my head."

"Wow," Valerie murmured slowly, "that's just awful."

"Yeah. Well, like I said it's over."

"I'm real sorry. If I knew that I never would of pushed you."

"It's okay, Val. Now we're even."

"What do you mean even?"

"I felt pretty bad after making you talk about your parents at the hospital."

"I didn't mind telling you that. I'm not proud of it but I can't change it."

"Then you understand. And the thing is, I'm really over her. It's just that song, you know?"

"Mmmm. I think so."

"Here, you take this and play something sweet." I handed her the guitar and this time she took it.

She strummed a chord and pulled the case over, took out a capo and clamped it on the second fret. After fine-tuning the strings a bit she started finger picking a simple pattern. When she started singing a small shiver went up my spine:

"There is beauty all around, when there's love at home.
There is joy in every sound, when there's love at home.
Peace and plenty there abide, smiling fair on every side.
Time doth softly, sweetly glide, when there's love at home."

The tune was simple but beautiful in the manner of a Shaker chair—honest, refined and sturdy enough to hold weight. With an

154

ache in her voice and perfect control of every note, Valerie made it all her own. She sang a chorus with a short turnaround and began another verse.

"In the cottage there is joy, when there's love at home.
Hate and envy ne'er annoy, when there's love at home.
Sweetly sings the brooklet by, brighter beams the azure sky.
Oh, there's one who smiles on high, when there's love at home."

Valerie's eyes were filling but she kept going all the way through the refrain and finished the song properly.

I was spellbound. "I've never heard anything so beautiful. Where did that come from?"

"It's my mama's favorite song," Val said. "It's from an old hymn book; it's what she always wished for."

I tried to picture her mother, locked into a closet of darkness so dense she couldn't reach out to anyone except Valerie. I groped for a reference point but couldn't come up with anything. It seemed for a moment that we were stranded in sorrow like two insects in amber, and suddenly Val began banging out chords and belting out Pete Seeger's song about the foolish frog. She was attacking her strings with such gusto I was afraid she'd break one. I laughed and joined in singing, and we didn't get through the first verse before there was a loud snap and the D string gave it up. We both fell out laughing.

"Well, it was good while it lasted," Val sighed. "I used to have some spares but they're all gone." She pouted, and then a mischievous grin spread across her face. "So I guess we'll have to find something else to do."

She started toward me and just then a picture flashed in my mind of a pack of guitar strings. They were lying, of all places, in the bottom of my tool box. How they got there I couldn't remember; they'd been there for months. "Hold that thought," I said, and started to get up.

"Where are you going?" Val's eyebrows arched and then lowered ominously.

"Out to get something," I said. "I'll be right back."

She sat back and folded her arms, frowning.

I stood and opened the door. After stepping down to the oak pallet that served as her porch I took a deep breath of night air and thought I heard a rustling sound. I paused and there was nothing, but when I began walking the few steps to my truck I heard footsteps running on grass. Startled, I caught a glimpse of a figure running behind Val's car and up the drive. Whoever it was skirted the cone of illumination from the security light by the farmhouse and turned out toward the road. I stood quietly listening and after a minute or so heard the faint sound of a car accelerating away.

I opened my truck and found a flashlight under the seat. I unlocked the tool box behind the cab and after rummaging for a few seconds found the strings and pocketed them. I locked everything up and went back into the trailer.

Valerie was sitting where I had left her, but her attitude had changed. She looked coolly at me as I pulled the strings from my pocket and handed them to her.

"What is that?"

"Strings. For your guitar."

"I just need a D."

"Yeah, well the way you play you'll probably need another E before long. Go ahead and take them; they've been in my tool box forever."

"Thank you Mr. Brauner," she said, taking the pack and putting it up on the counter. "It was a very nice evening."

"Yeah, for me too," I said. Normally I would have been happy to make my getaway like this, but things were anything but normal now. "Why don't you let me put that string on for you?"

"It's late. I'm sure you have to be at work in the morning," she said.

"I want to do it, Val. I'm not even allowed to work yet anyway."

"Since when did you become mister suave and smooth?"

"I'm not suave and smooth; I never have been."

"You're telling me?" She rolled her eyes.

156

"I'm sorry if I offended you; I just wanted to give you some strings for your guitar. Do you want me to leave for that?"

"The only reason you're here is to keep me out of trouble and I can take care of myself, thank you very much."

"This isn't a good time for you to be alone," I said. "You may not think I do anything to help anyone but I'm trying now."

She sat on her knees looking up at me and finally slumped. "Go home, Ray," she said tiredly.

"Valerie, please," I implored.

"Begging don't become you," she said, looking away.

"This isn't what you think it is."

"And what would that be, mister mind reader?"

If I told her about the prowler outside she probably wouldn't believe me now. My brain was doing gymnastics trying to think of a way to mend the impasse. Finally I just sat down and reached over to pick up her guitar. She put her hand on it and said, "You don't have to treat me like a baby. I know how to change a string, you know."

"I know that, Val. You can take care of yourself without anybody's help, but nobody can live without friends. Do you think I like being alone all the time?"

She looked over at me. "I don't know. Do you?"

"Sometimes. But sometimes it gets terribly lonely."

She didn't answer so I pressed on. "I'm an outsider up here, Valerie, just like you. I could live here ten years and it wouldn't make a bit of difference to anybody, I'd still be an outsider. You're the first person, well, maybe besides Mike, that I've been able to talk to in years. I know we don't always see things the same way but I care about you more than anyone else up here."

Val softened. "That's sweet." She crawled over and hugged me, and then said, "I need to be alone now, Ray, but you can come back and put that string on tomorrow. I just need to think for awhile, okay?"

There was nothing left to do. I stood to go, and she hugged me again at her door. Just before stepping out I said, "You've got some shells for that shotgun under your bed, don't you?"

157

"Why?" She seemed surprised.

"With things the way they've been around this town lately—well, it's probably good to have some kind of protection." I shrugged, as if it were a small matter.

"I had strings on my guitar, didn't I?" she asked.

"You did."

"Then don't you worry about me, Bwana. I'm a big girl."

CHAPTER 12

I drove into town with my thoughts in a jumble. I wanted to be angry with Valerie but couldn't. The night felt ominous and blacker than usual, and when the lights of Gladburg appeared through my windshield they brought little comfort.

Driving by King's Tavern nothing looked unusual. Two couples stood on the sidewalk talking and laughing and a glimmer of hope began to grow in me. I passed the parking lot and found a spot on the street halfway down the block. Walking back to the tavern I noticed Spider's vintage white Harley police cruiser parked in the lot with several other big bikes. As I approached the main entrance one of the men in the group talking called my name and stuck out his hand. No bad vibes happening here. My glimmer of hope grew brighter. I shook and smiled a quick hello, then plunged through the vestibule and big glass doors into King's Tavern like a man on a mission.

It was like a party inside. I knew Rollin must be tending bar, with classic blues rocking on the sound system. At the moment Taj Mahal was singing "You're Going to Need Somebody On Your Bond" and I briefly wondered if anything could be signified by the lyric.

I saw two of my guys sitting at the bar chatting up some ladies and clearly enjoying themselves. Familiar faces with names I didn't quite know, people from the early days, were all over the place. Among them were some big fellows, local boys from dairy farms with wholesome faces, broad shoulders and thick arms that now hoisted heavy pints of ale. Mackey's friends? A cluster of Rollin's pilot buddies stood talking with some women. There in a booth sat Mackey with two girls who looked barely old enough to be legal, beaming at whatever was being said by one of them. Wouldn't his wife love to see that, I thought. Was I being paranoid, or did it matter that nobody in the room seemed vigilant, or even to have a care in the world? I looked around for Mike and finally spotted him alone at the end of the bar surveying the room. He had seen me already and nodded when my eye met his. At least one person was holding the fort.

I looked down the bar and saw Rollin working the tap. Behind him a big guy whom I took to be Angelo stood at the waiters' station, watching the crowd with a bored expression. He looked capable enough of handling any man in the room, but not any two or three. But that looked like a moot issue now. Nothing in the air suggested trouble, in fact the atmosphere seemed downright festive. Still I couldn't shake the feeling that something wasn't right.

I worked my way back to the ping-pong parlor where whoops and shouts were ringing out. Spider and another biker named Gus were engaged in a match. The second table was idle; everyone in the room had been drawn into their game. Both men were aggressive players and they were in the middle of a spectacular volley. I watched, fascination slowly displacing my unease. Though Valerie had beaten him as easily and indifferently as all the rest, Spider was one of the champions. He had an uncanny way of spinning the ball any way he wanted, which usually won him the game. Val's intuition had busted him right there, and after that it was all over but the motions. Gus appeared to be nearly Spider's equal though, and since the score was eighteen-all I decided to stick around for the conclusion.

I was so taken by the game that I didn't notice Tina until she stood right in front of me, concern all over her face. "Ray, are you okay?"

"Any reason I shouldn't be?" I asked.

"You look so serious. And after last night I was so worried."

"It wasn't me that got hit."

"I know." Her voice was sad but then she brightened up. "Well, don't you look handsome! Let me guess where you've been."

"Okay, shoot."

"I'd say you've been out on a date with some pretty lady. Am I warm?"

"You're making me hot just standing next to you."

"You goof!" She laughed and then hugged me. "Anybody we

160

might know?"

"My, aren't we inquisitive?"

"Inquiring minds want to know."

I laughed. "It was probably someone we all know and love."

A roar came from the crowd and someone called 20-18, game point. We turned to watch the finale. Spider was down by two points and Gus was serving. The serve barely touched Spider's corner of the table but he had fallen back already and with a smooth flick curled the ball just over the net where it bounced sideways before the big biker could reach it. Another cheer went up.

Gus made his last serve. The return went high leaving Spider wide open for a slam, but he was ready for that and another volley began. The staccato rhythm drew us all in, and the duration of it soon had the room at fever pitch. Finally the big biker moved in with a devastating overhand and scorched the ball down the middle so hard I was sure the return would go wild. It did, a high pop-up headed east, but somehow Spider managed to get it across the net. They both stared in disbelief as the ball clipped the table on Gus's side and bounced sideways to the floor. The room went crazy again.

It was tied up at twenty, advantage to Spider now. He served with no flourish; a low, fast one aimed at Gus's right corner, and on his return put the ball on the left edge of the table. Gus couldn't move quite fast enough and it was 21-20, game point. When Spider served a spin next Gus's paddle sent it into the crowd and the game was over. The room erupted in cheers and Spider and Gus laughed and hugged, slapping each other on the back.

"Can I bring you something to drink?" Tina asked.

"I was headed back to the bar, I haven't talked to Mike yet," I said. "You wouldn't know anything about his activities last night, would you?"

"Oh, God." Tina blanched. "I don't want to talk about it. All I can say is I had no part of it. I've got to get back to work, but I want to hear all about your date before you leave now, Mr. Brauner."

I was headed toward the bar when Spider saw me. "S'up, boss," he said with a grin.

"Hoo-rah," I grinned back and we bumped arms.

He put an arm across my shoulders and appraised me. "You're looking peaked, man," he said. "We've got to get you on a hydration program."

"I was headed in that direction."

We walked back to the front and found Mike in the same spot at the bar. There were two empty seats beside him now and we took them. I greeted Mike and then turned back to the ping-pong champ.

"So," I asked, "everyone just decided to go out for a late one?"

"Evidently."

"Everyone having a good time?"

"Everything's cool." Spider's grin didn't make me feel any easier.

I looked at Mike. "You two didn't happen to see each other last night, did you?" He didn't answer, so I turned back to Spider.

"I guess that all depends on what you mean by 'see each other'," he said.

"What? From the one who was so offended by the President's legal hairsplitting that you wanted to build a gallows for him on the Plum's front lawn? Talking as a simple-minded ass, did you see each other last night?"

Spider looked across me to Mike. "Did you see me last night, man?" he asked.

I felt a flash of irritation. "Hell, you don't need to say anything if you don't feel like it, Spider, but that's not exactly your style. I guess you told me anyway. Who else was with you? Lopez? John? Mackey?"

Spider kept looking helplessly at Mike, and finally Mike leaned toward me. "Not the time or place right now, Bwana," he said.

Lovely. I ran my fingertips over the burnished wood of the bar top, unable to think of a good thing to say, and then Rollin appeared.

"Newcastle, on the house," he said, setting a glass in front of me. "Last call, gentlemen, is there anything else I can get you?"

"Another Grolsch and a Rock for Mike," said Spider.

"You got it." He looked at me. "You okay, Ray?"

"Yeah, fine."

He patted my hand with a sympathetic smile and turned back to his duties.

In fact I was disoriented as hell. I'd walked in expecting a catastrophe and found a party. I hadn't the slightest idea why when it was a night we all had dreaded. In the present atmosphere my indiscretion seemed minor, but I regretted being here already. I couldn't tell what was wrong, but my mind kept replaying the sound of footsteps running on grass. I kept thinking about Valerie alone in her flimsy trailer and felt a terrible anxiety. My only comfort was that I wouldn't want to be the one who tried to tangle with her.

Rollin brought Mike and Spider's beer and disappeared again.

"Val doing okay?" Mike asked.

"I guess that depends on what you mean by 'doing okay'," I said. Spider guffawed, spewing Grolsch.

"When I left she was okay. There are complications."

"Complications?" Mike raised an eyebrow.

"Not the time or place right now, Ace," I said.

"That was very adroit, boss." Spider never missed a beat.

"Thank you, I thought it up all by myself," I said, and then we all laughed. That broke the tension for me. Finally I started to relax, realizing that other matters required only the right time and place. How near that time and place would be was out of my control so I just drank my beer and waited.

Mackey saw us at the bar and came over to introduce Hilda and Amy, his new friends. Spider made them giggle and blush at first with his openly suggestive remarks. Closing time came and we moved it out to the sidewalk where Mackey and Spider stood swapping jokes with the girls. The rest of the bar crowd dissipated in a stream of laughter, conversation and cars while we stood there being silly. I kept stealing glances inside and noticed Mike doing the same.

We saw Angelo standing at the main register with Rollin watching from behind him. The big man continued punching keys until finally he tore off a long printout. He studied it in the light and then opened the register drawer. He pulled out several stacks of bills and began

163

counting out a quantity of cash. He turned and looked straight out at us, then put the money into a slim briefcase on the bar. Rollin hovered at his elbow saying nothing. The man seemed oblivious to him. He turned and picked up the phone as Tina swept the floor.

Hilda and Amy were showing no signs of boredom. I was beginning to wonder where this little scenario was headed when Spider started talking. "Well you know, that reminds me of the old hillbilly who was out on a Sunday drive with his young son."

Here we go, I thought.

"They're out in the old pickup bumping down the road, when they pass a flock of sheep. One of the ewes has its neck caught in the fence and when he sees that the old man says, 'Hot damn! Looks like we got ourselves a treat, boy!'"

Amy made a face.

"He pulls the truck over, drops his trousers and takes his pleasure on the poor beast for a while, then he remembers his kid. 'Come on over here, boy, and get yourself some of this good stuff!' the old man hollers. So the kid drags himself out of the truck, goes over to the fence and kneels down with his head between the wires."

"That is so gross," Hilda said.

"What's the matter?" Spider shot back. "Don't you know that when you're all grown up sex with a minor is one of the most sublime pleasures that await you?"

Mackey laughed nervously, and the girls eyed Spider with distaste.

Spider laughed. "Just wait until you're thirty-five and fat, with a strapping young fourteen-year-old in the house. You might even find you don't mind taking it in the back door."

"You're disgusting," Hilda said, edging away from Spider. I saw Angelo through the plate glass, sitting on the cooler nearest the waiter's station looking in our direction.

"You're just young," Spider confided, "but I won't hold that against you. Hell, I'll bet you've got a nice little grommet there yourself."

"Come on, Spider," Mackey protested weakly.

"Aw, what the hell," Spider said. "I'd say they're both a little tight right now, but we could fix that, couldn't we, buddy?"

"You are just awful," Hilda said, taking the arm of her friend. "Come on, Amy, we've got to go."

Mackey stood there with his mouth working but no sound coming out. The two girls stalked off while Spider laughed.

"Man, what did you do that for?" Mackey asked as they disappeared around the corner into the parking lot.

"Easy, Mack. We don't need them right now, do we?"

"Yeah, but—"

"But you're a happily married man, remember?" Spider was enjoying himself.

Mike shook his head grinning and I suppressed a smile. It was true, and Mackey knew it best of all.

The girls' car squealed out of the lot just as a cab pulled up at the curb and honked. Looking inside we saw Angelo stand up. He exited through the kitchen and a few seconds later came around the corner of the building with his briefcase. "Evening, gentlemen," he said as he walked by us; then he climbed into the cab.

"Son of a bitch," Mike muttered as the cab drove away.

"G'bye Hilda. Night night, Amy," Mackey said sadly. Spider just laughed.

~

We stood awkwardly for a moment. Then Mike asked, "What do you think, boys? Did we do the right thing?"

Spider spoke up first. "Hell yes. Those fags came in here like fucking altar boys."

"Aye," agreed Mackey. "We did the right thing."

"And what was that, Mackey?" I asked.

"You don't know?" His big face was full of surprise.

"I have no idea."

He looked at Spider and Mike, bewildered.

"Go ahead, tell him," Mike said.

"Well," Mackey began, "we came in last night and caught an old

165

boy off guard. In the men's room, while he was taking a leak." He glanced around nervously.

"Go on."

Mackey looked embarrassed. "We, uh, dunked him."

"Dunked him?"

"Actually, we darn near had to drown him."

"Don't tell me. In the toilet?" My heart was sinking.

"In the handicap stall."

"I can just picture it."

"No sir, I don't think you can." Mackey was blushing now. "No offense, Bwana, but…" and then his voice just ran out.

I looked at Spider and Mike and both of them were staring straight at me.

"And the result of this?" I asked.

Mike spoke. "Our friends Smith and Jones came in tonight with a process server. Buddy Sykes was here with Rollie, and they just gave them some papers and walked out like lambs."

"Lambs?"

"Yeah."

"You don't know what was in the papers?"

"No, Buddy took them with him when he left."

"And then everyone just partied?"

"What else was there to do? A bunch of good people were here to show support, and they would have turned this place into a car wash before anyone could have laid a hand on Rollie. I think the bastards knew that. It was a lot better than what happened two weeks ago."

"This isn't the end of anything."

"Nobody expects it to be."

Tina and Rollin were turning out the lights now, and as they disappeared into the kitchen Mike turned back to me. "What was Valerie's complication?"

"There was somebody outside her trailer tonight."

"Any idea who?"

"It was dark. I startled whoever it was and he ran; I didn't see his

166

face."

"And you didn't stay there with her?"

"She wouldn't let me. I tried."

"You need to get your testosterone back up, boss," said Spider, dead serious.

"She didn't want a babysitter."

"Then don't act like one," he said. "Start taking andro and eat more red meat, man. You won't have that problem any more, I guarantee."

"The problem is elsewhere, Spider." I could feel my hackles rising.

"That's what they all say," said Spider. "I tell you, it's easy to fix."

"I don't think that's really the issue here," said Mike. "Did you tell me once that Val keeps a shotgun under her bed?"

"Loaded."

"No shit?" said Mackey, his eyes wide. Spider laughed again.

"Does she still have the phone?"

"I guess. It never came up."

Rollin's Subaru rolled out of the parking lot. He smiled and waved at us, then in a shifting of gears disappeared up Market Street.

Tina followed Rollin out of the parking lot in her little Mazda sports coupe. She rolled down her window and we walked over.

"I still want to hear about your date, Ray," she said.

"Next time, I promise," I said.

"You okay, Tina?" Mike asked.

"Yup, it's sleepytime. It's been a long night."

"You take care, young lady," Spider said.

"Thanks so much for coming, you guys," Tina said as she blew us a kiss. She pulled onto the street, turned left at the corner onto Main Avenue and was gone.

Suddenly I was aware of being fatigued nearly to the point of collapsing. "Well, boys," I said, "that's it for me tonight."

"You really think Val's going to be okay?" Mike asked.

"I think anyone who tries to get close to her is going to be shot full of holes."

"Ha!" Spider exclaimed.

"You ought to check on her in the morning, Bwana," Mike said. "We can keep moving on the house but right now she needs a big brother. I think you're the man."

"You the man," Spider and Mackey echoed loudly.

"I'll take care of it," I said.

We shook and bumped arms and then took our leave. I heard the fat sound of Spider's Harley coming to life in the parking lot as I climbed into my truck. I drove home mercifully void of any complex thoughts, a weary animal loping home to its den.

CHAPTER 13

I was deep under the ocean when the alarm sounded. It was so dark I couldn't see the sky; I didn't even know which direction it was. I started for what I thought was the surface but got tangled up in nets. Someone had strung nets all through the area and my lungs were bursting. I held my breath as long as I could but finally let it out in panic, and the sound of my own voice crying out woke me. I was tangled in my sheet gasping for air and the phone was ringing off the hook.

I grappled with the sheet muttering curses and when I finally got free and took a step across the floor the IV pump fell out of bed alongside me, swinging from my shoulder by surgical tubing. I grabbed it up and stumbled across the room to where the cordless phone sat in its charger. The digital clock blinked 4:37.

When I picked up the phone someone was crying on the other end. The voice didn't register at first but then recognition clicked in. "Valerie? I can hear you, I'm right here," I said. "Tell me what's happening."

After a few seconds she managed to say, "It's Tina."

"What about Tina?"

"Someone beat her up real bad." Her voice was shaking.

I went numb all over. "How bad?"

"I don't know, they said they flew her to the hospital."

"'They' who, Val?"

"The police. Oh lordy, Ray, they said she was crying for me!" Valerie broke down again, and it took a few more minutes to get the rest of the story out of her.

A neighbor had found Tina in the parking lot behind her apartment. By the time the police arrived she was trying to sit up and crying hysterically for Valerie. Of course they had come to Val's trailer with a lot of questions.

"Why was she calling for you?"

"I don't know, Ray, how could I know?" Her voice trailed off in

169

a soft, keening wail.

"What did the police ask you?"

"They thought we were out together and I might have seen who done it. Why would anybody hurt Tina, Ray?"

"I don't know, Val. Doesn't she have a jealous boyfriend?"

"Curtis?" she snorted. "He can't even find his own dick. He's just a drunk; he don't have it in him to beat her up like that. It was those bastards from the tavern, wasn't it?"

"I don't know, Val." My heart felt like lead.

"I want to go to the hospital, Ray. I've got to see her."

"You think they'll let you?"

"I don't know, but I've got to go. Will you take me?"

"It's four-thirty in the morning, Val. No one is going to let you near her now."

"No," she cried, "I've got to go now."

"Valerie—" I started, but she cut me off.

"You son of a bitch," she cried. "You said you'd help me and now you're bailing out. Well thank you very much, Bwana, I'll find my own way." The line went dead.

I sat down in a daze, trying to think. Then I got up and paced, muttering curses and feeling more frightened by the second. I walked into the kitchen with my stomach in a knot and dumped two-week-old grounds from the coffee maker. I started a fresh pot and took the Scotch from the shelf and poured some into a mug. I had a swig, and when the coffee was done I filled the mug, took another swallow and fooled myself into believing I was thinking more clearly.

I punched Mike's number into the phone. It rang three times, four times. Just when I expected his voice mail to intercept a woman answered with a voice so surly it made my skin prickle. "Whaddayou want?" she growled. My mind reeled; I had completely forgotten Val had Mike's phone.

"Val, it's me, Ray. I'm coming. How soon—"

"You bastard!" she cried.

"Valerie, I'm more awake now. I'll be there in fifteen minutes."

"You take as long as you want, Bwana, because I don't need your help. The first motherfucker who comes around here is going to get their face blowed off." She clicked off. I took a huge gulp from my mug and hit the redial button gasping.

When she picked up I didn't let her start. "Val, I'm coming. I'll honk my horn to let you know it's me. You can shoot anyone else but don't you dare shoot me. I'll see you in fifteen minutes."

I tossed the phone down and grabbed a pair of jeans from my closet. I hopped around the room pulling them on, scooping keys, wallet and a wad of bills off the dresser and cramming them into my pockets. I pulled on a sweatshirt and fumbled with the IV pump like a madman, unable to find rank enough words to curse it with. I finally got it attached, grabbed another pack of meds to refill it later, jammed my feet into sneakers, yanked my jacket off the chair and headed out the door.

I careened into Val's yard with my horn blaring. I cut the engine and ran to her trailer calling her name. Nobody answered and I banged on the door.

"Val, open up, it's Ray."

No answer.

"Are you okay, Valerie?"

A footfall came from somewhere to my right, and my heart nearly jumped out of my mouth. I whirled around to see a shape stepping from behind the ginkgo tree, and in the moonlight saw a shotgun leveled at me.

"Jesus Christ, Val, you scared me to death," I gasped.

"Thou shalt not take the name of the Lord thy God in vain. Get in the truck."

"I'm sorry, I forgot. I really didn't mean it. Jes—I mean, gee whiz, Val, will you put that gun down?"

"Get in the truck."

I began walking backwards. "Okay. I'm getting in the truck, see? Here, now I'm in the truck. Now will you put that thing down?"

"Open the other door."

I reached over and opened it. Valerie circled the truck to the passenger side keeping the gun leveled at me. I could barely see her

171

now with the interior light filling the cab. She stood outside the passenger door staring in at me. Finally she climbed into the seat beside me, keeping the gun on her lap pointed at me. She pulled the door closed, and I felt safer in the darkness.

"Drive."

"Drive where?"

"To the hospital, stupid."

"Valerie, we need to talk. We don't even know what hospital she's in."

"The shock trauma hospital, stupid. I think you was there once. If you don't start your truck now you won't have a window no more."

I started the truck, and turned to Valerie. "Look, Val, I'll take you. Right now, no problem, we're going. But you've got to put that thing away. If someone sees you with that going through town we'll be in trouble, and we've got three lights plus the toll plaza to deal with."

She stared coldly at me in the dim light from the dashboard.

"Please, Valerie," I said. "You don't need that; I'm with you and I'm going to stick with you. Honest."

I saw her shoulders relax just a bit.

"Just put it behind the seat. That way it's there if you need it but it won't get us in any trouble. Right now we've got enough trouble already."

She sighed and seemed to give a little. "I ain't putting this away until we're up the road," she said. "I don't like the way it feels around here."

"That's what I was trying to tell you a while ago," I said, backing around her broken car.

"What are you talking about?"

"Somebody was outside your trailer tonight."

"I don't believe you."

"I didn't think you would." I headed up the drive toward the road.

"How do you know?"

172

"I saw him, Val. I scared him and he ran like the dickens out to the road. I waited until I heard his car start up and drive away."

"Is that why you was trying to stay?"

"That was one reason."

She seemed stunned as we turned out onto the main road. Finally she said, "What made you go outside?"

"I had some strings for you in my tool box."

As we approached town I reminded her about the gun again, and without a word she broke it open, slid two shells out, pocketed them and then twisted around and laid it on the floor behind the seat. We made two green lights out of three, cleared the other end of town and sped through more miles of state road without incident. When we finally hit the turnpike I put the pedal down and prayed there would be no speed traps. Muddy brown color was spreading across the eastern sky even before the lights of Allentown came into view, and by the time we arrived at the hospital the sun was almost up.

~

When we found the emergency room entrance I parked the truck and we ran into the building. At the first counter we came to Valerie asked if a Kristina Utterbach had been admitted, but the harried woman behind the desk seemed barely aware of our presence. Even at this hour there were at least a half dozen people with acute medical needs sitting in the waiting area behind us.

"I'm sorry, you'll have to take a seat over there," the woman said to Valerie, motioning toward the waiting area.

"Can't you just tell us where Tina is?" said Val, a tiny edge of hysteria creeping into her voice.

Maybe it had been a long shift or maybe the desk was understaffed, but for whatever reason, the woman didn't get it. "Please have a seat," she repeated. "You may notice there are other people here before you."

I saw a change come over Valerie's face. Her eyebrows arched and then furrowed together and I knew I had to do something fast,

173

or else security would be called and we'd have a much steeper hill to climb. I stepped forward and said, "Ma'am, we don't want to trouble you but we're here because the police asked us to come. Kristina Utterbach was flown to shock trauma a few hours ago and we'll be happy to be out of your way if you'll just direct us to her." Now Valerie was crying again and my own temper was nearly at the snapping point.

"Are you family members?" the woman asked.

"My name is Ray Brauner and this is Valerie Tolliver," I said. "When Miss Utterbach was flown here she was crying for Miss Tolliver, and the police seemed to think it was important for us to be here. Could you please help us?"

"Mr. Brauner—" Suddenly the woman looked sharply at me. "Were you a patient here recently?"

"Yes ma'am, I was."

Her demeanor changed. "Just one moment," she said, and typed a flurry of keystrokes into her computer. She studied the screen for a few seconds and picked up a phone. Turning away she spoke in a voice too low for us to hear, but when she turned back around everything was sweetness and light. "Dr. Hallock will see you, Mr. Brauner; I believe he can answer all your questions. Would either of you care for coffee while you wait?"

"Thank you," I said. "I believe coffee would help."

"Come around there," she said, gesturing to a door beyond the counter. She met us on the other side and led us down a short corridor to a carpeted doctors' lounge with soft lighting and comfortable furniture. There was a table with coffee already made and beside it a basket of fruit and fresh pastries. In the corner stood a glass-fronted refrigerator with bottled water and juices. "Help yourself to anything," she said sympathetically. "When Dr. Hallock comes I'll bring him in." She left the room.

Valerie stared around in a daze. Tears glistened on her cheeks as she looked up at the recessed lighting, down at the carpet and around at the drapes and furnishings. "Welcome to Bwana's world," she murmured in a voice all wet from crying.

174

"What's that supposed to mean?"

"All it takes is your name," she said in wonderment, "and now instead of out there, we're in here. Just like—!" and she snapped her fingers. "And you tell me you don't think you got importance?" She shook her head in disbelief.

"Valerie, I provided that woman with information, that's all. I even stretched the truth a little just to hurry things along."

She looked at me through her tears and actually laughed. "Ray Brauner," she said, "you are the blindest man I ever knew. You better wake up and appreciate what you got before it's too late."

I didn't dare argue with her. My real fear was that the news would be the worst, and we'd been brought back here so our grief would be hidden from the people in the waiting room. I was sure that's what places like this were used for but couldn't tell Valerie that now. I tried not to think about it for fear she would pick up on the panic that was growing inside me.

Until this moment I had been so preoccupied with getting us here that there was no time to think about anything else, but now I was at the end of doing—waiting with Valerie in dread of the unknown, in a waking nightmare of terrible possibilities. I kept hearing Tina laughing at Mike and calling him a goofball, Tina reminding me there was one more person I needed to see, and the idea that Tina might not make it uncoiled in me. It grew like a horror, and the next thing I knew Valerie had her arms around me and we sank onto the sofa. We held each other while she cried silently.

We heard steps, and both of us stood as a man entered. "Mr. Brauner?" he said. "I'm Dr. Ken Hallock."

"Ray Brauner," I said, extending my bandaged hand, which he shook gently.

"And you must be Kristina's friend, Valerie." He took her hand in both of his and smiled at her. She nodded and tried to smile back.

"How is Tina?" Val asked in a voice barely above a whisper.

"I think she's stable for the time being," Dr. Hallock said. "Sit down, please. I'm going to have coffee; would you care for some?"

"Yes, thanks," I said.

"Valerie?"

"Thank you," she whispered.

"Cream and sugar?"

She nodded, her eyes wide as saucers.

We waited awkwardly while he poured us coffee. "How is she, Doctor?" I finally asked.

"I won't lie to you," he said. "Kristina is badly hurt. How anyone could do such a thing to another person is something I'll never understand, but I believe she has a good chance of pulling through. Right now we're worried most about her head injuries. She's had a severe concussion, which often is followed by swelling. Swelling inside the skull causes dangerous complications, so we're doing all we can to control that. The rest is just structural damage, which we're pretty good at fixing."

"Can I see her?" Valerie whispered.

"She's in a very deep sleep now, Valerie. She needs to stay that way for a few days because it helps keep the swelling down. We'll let her wake up when that danger is past, and see how soon she's ready for visitors."

"What were her injuries?" I asked.

"Kristina has a broken nose, a blow-out fracture of her left orbit with some possible damage to the eye itself. She has a broken clavicle and three broken ribs. The police believe she tried to fight back; we found tissue under her nails that may be from her attacker. She also has two broken fingers and some internal bleeding. She wasn't raped or sexually molested; she appears to have been beaten up by somebody who just wanted to hurt her." I saw rage behind his eyes, and felt grateful for Tina's sake that he took her injuries personally.

"Is her family here?" I asked.

"Her parents arrived about an hour ago."

"Was Tina conscious when she came in?"

"She was semi-conscious."

"Did she say anything?"

"She wasn't coherent enough to answer any questions. But she

176

kept calling Valerie's name." There was sorrow in his eyes as he looked at her. "She was afraid for you; she wanted you to go somewhere safe."

Val covered her face, and her body heaved silently. When she took her hands down her expression was one I hope to never see again. "They wanted me," she cried in a stricken voice, "but they got her instead. Oh, lordy, it's all my fault!" I put my arms around her and she buried her face in my shoulder like she never wanted to see daylight again.

I let her cry for a while and then Dr. Hallock came over and touched her shoulder. She looked up with her face bewildered, and he knelt in front of her. "Valerie, this wasn't your fault," he said. "Someone else did this to your friend. We're doing everything we can to make her better; you're going to have to trust us now. Can you do that?"

She nodded, big tears spilling.

"Meanwhile if there is any danger to yourself, please do what Tina was trying to say. Go somewhere safe. Give the police time to find whoever did this." She looked down and wiped her eyes but didn't respond. I saw that he wanted an answer from her. "They've done enough damage already, don't you think?" He kept his focus on her until at last she nodded. He took both her hands in his and gently squeezed them.

Finally Dr. Hallock stood and shook my hand again. "I wish I could tell you more, but right now we all need to be patient. If you believe in prayer, now would be a good time to pray for your friend. Once she's through this crisis the rest should be easier." He smiled at Val. "Have faith, Valerie," he said. "God is a great healer."

She nodded again, and tried to smile.

~

We drove home in silence. I kept seeing Tina's face as she pulled out of the parking lot, and kept hearing her laughter from the night before. It was a dazzling morning but the sun made everything

177

worse. I wanted to send it away; I wanted the sky to cave in and pour darkness all over us. I wanted something so dire to happen that all this would be forgotten, for something to plunge us so completely into the necessities of the moment that nothing mattered except the next step, and then the one after that. I pictured Rollin making his way up the spine of some icy mountain and envied him in that place for a moment, and then realized no matter where I was, nothing could change what happened last night. This was our own mountain and we had to climb it.

Valerie was dry-eyed but she seemed unaware of me, of the truck, the road or anything else. If we'd left the turnpike and headed out across the hills it probably would have been the same to her. When we passed through Gladburg there was no recognition on her face. We stopped at two lights and she never blinked. But when we passed the "Registered Holstein Cattle" sign just before her driveway she came alive. Unfastening her seat belt she twisted around, hung over the seat back and retrieved her shotgun. She dug into her pocket and pulled out two shells, rammed them into the breach and closed it. This time she had it pointing toward the door.

When I pulled up beside her Jetta nothing looked different. Tools and parts were scattered about and the repair manual still lay open on the ground. We got out and since my side of the truck was closest I reached the trailer first.

"Move," Val said from behind me.

I stepped aside and Val crouched close to the door examining something. Then she stood up and began circling the trailer slowly, holding her gun like the point man on a patrol. She stopped at every window looking at something I didn't see, and when she was back at her door she unlocked it and pulled it open. Still holding the gun at her waist she poked her head in, looked both ways and then stepped up inside. She walked to the rear and in a few seconds she was back. "All clear," she said, stepping down to the pallet.

"What were you looking at?" I asked.

"Clay mud," she said. "If anyone opened the door it would be busted off and I would know it."

178

"I thought that only worked in movies."

She gave me a withering look. "I learnt that from my uncle Duane. He was a sniper in Vietnam and he taught me how to take care when one of the boys up the holler was laying to rape me. He didn't want to have to kill nobody else."

I wanted to ask her something but when I opened my mouth whatever it was went away. I stood there for a long moment with my mind wiped clean. Val seemed to be moving in slow motion as she leaned in her trailer door and stood the shotgun against the wall. She turned back to me. "It's time to go," she finally said. "I seen all the hurt I can stand."

"What are you saying?" All of a sudden I felt queasy.

"I want to go home."

"Home? You mean to Kentucky?"

She tilted her head at the trailer. "Can your truck pull this down yonder?"

"Well—gee, I guess it could. Are you serious?"

"I'm tired of fighting and I'm not doing any good now. Take me home and I won't ask you for nothing again."

"Valerie, I—"

"You heard that doctor, Ray. I can't stay here no more. If you take me home I can keep my trailer. I'll pay whatever you want."

"Don't even mention paying me. What if I don't want you to go?"

"Please, Ray. Now I'm begging you, okay? Just take me home and then you can forget about me." She sounded desperate.

Suddenly it seemed the ground under me was crumbling and if I didn't move quickly everything would be lost.

"I'll take you on one condition."

"Say it."

"You have to come back. When things calm down, whenever it's right, but you have to come back at least once more."

"Why?"

"Just promise you will."

"Maybe," she said uncertainly. "I want to see Tina."

179

"Then think about it. Because that's my price."

I didn't quite understand why I was so adamant. Right then I might have said it was because I hated to see her give up. But something was supposed to happen between us, and I didn't even know what it was. All I knew was that it hadn't happened yet.

~

It didn't take Valerie long to agree with my terms, but we had to move quickly. I thought if we left tomorrow I could be back by the middle of next week. Valerie said she could have the inside of her trailer ready by morning.

I checked her tires and they looked good enough for the trip. There was no way yet to tell about the trailer brakes but the wiring harness looked intact. By some serendipity Val had gotten an equalizer hitch along with her trailer that fit the receiver on my pickup. My truck was a workhorse factory equipped for towing, so I paid little mind to it.

Valerie sat on the picnic table watching me as I examined the running gear on her trailer. She looked so melancholy I wanted to put my arms around her and tell her everything would be okay, but something held me back. After deciding the trailer was roadworthy I was about to leave.

"What about my car?" Val asked.

"Gee." I scratched my head. "Can you finish it today?"

"I don't know," she said, and then tears were welling in her eyes. "It turned into a bigger job than I thought, and now with Tina and the trailer and all…" Her voice faltered and I realized she was altogether overwhelmed. Had it been only yesterday that I had come over here to ask her out for dinner? So much had happened since then there hadn't been time to adjust; we were just reacting to events as fast as they were thrown at us.

Without thinking I opened my arms and she moved into them. We held each other close under the great ginkgo tree, a thing we hadn't done in many months. For the first time since I'd known her

180

Valerie seemed completely defenseless.

What happened next was something I may never understand, but the memory of it will be with me always. I turned her face up to kiss her and when our lips touched my normal world was upended. The familiar erotic undertow was there and I knew it could sweep us away in a heartbeat if we allowed it, but then it was transformed into something much more powerful, maybe even transcendent. There was an exchange of emotion between us unlike anything I imagined possible. It was almost as if our bodies melted and we felt for an instant everything the other was feeling. It was beyond sexual; it came from the center of each of us and flowed to the center of the other. It was visceral yet it consisted of knowledge beyond thought. It was so overwhelming that both of us recoiled in astonishment.

"What—?" I started to say, and she laid her hand over my mouth.

"Sshh."

"What—"

"Don't, Ray," she whispered.

"Don't what?"

"Don't try to understand; you can't. Just don't forget."

"Was it you or me?" I was completely bewildered.

"It wasn't neither of us. It's a gift and you just have to bear it."

"How do you know?"

"The same way you know."

I felt like shaking her shoulders until she made sense, but instead took her face in my hands, gently kissed it and held her close. She pressed against me and I buried my face in her hair. There was no urgency this time, only the sweet awareness of sexual attraction. The pleasure lingered briefly and once again we were dropped back into the real world with a Ford pickup, an Airstream trailer, a broken car and many pressing matters to attend to.

181

CHAPTER 14

When I pulled into the Fryes' yard everything looked normal. Guys were working on the roof, hammer blows and saw cuts were ringing and it felt almost like I had woken from a dream into the real world. My body knew better—I had barely slept and eaten nothing since last night's uneasy meal with Valerie. When Mike came out to my truck he said, "You all right?"

"It's not me."

"What's up?"

"It's Tina."

"What about Tina?" His eyes widened.

"She's in the hospital, all busted up. Someone got her in her parking lot last night."

"Jesus." I saw the color drain from his face. "What did they do?"

"Broke a bunch of bones, for starters. The worst part is her head injuries; I think the doctor said everything else was just structural."

"Just structural?" He leaned on my door with both hands, and as he turned his face up to the sun I saw his throat contract several times. "Jesus God, what did we do?"

"Don't even go there," I said. "Val did the same thing and it's nothing but a bottomless hole in there. Somebody did it, but it sure as hell wasn't you."

"Yeah, but—"

"Yeah but nothing. The police are handling it and right now that's the best thing for everyone."

"Ah, Jesus..." Mike just stood there shaking his head. I could see him struggling.

"Save your energy for damage control, Ace. You better get Spider and Mackey down here because I need your help. Things are going to be a little complicated for a few days."

"Ah Jeez..." He stood there a few more seconds and finally said, "Okay, you've got it," and turned back to the house.

I got out and then remembered my IV pump. I'd turned the

182

beeper off hours ago; it was long past time to refill it. I dug in my jacket for the antibiotic pack and was standing at the door reloading when the three of them emerged from the house.

"What the blazes is that?" Mackey asked over my shoulder.

"That's my drugs," I said, closing the cover. "Goes into a needle up here," I pointed to my shoulder, "and kills the bacteria that tried to kill me."

"No shit?" Mackey's eyes were wide.

"What's up, boss?" Spider asked warily.

I finished with the pump, clipped it to my belt and turned to face them. "Tina's in the hospital."

"What for?" Mackey said.

"Someone harmed her last night after she left us. Right now she's in a coma with possible brain damage and many broken bones."

"Oh gosh," Mackey said in a wavering voice. "Oh my God."

Spider looked at me tight-lipped and I watched the color drain from his face too.

"She was crying for Valerie when they found her," I said. "Whoever did it probably went after Val first. I believe it was the person I flushed outside her trailer. Val is considered to be in danger, and she asked me to tow her rig home to Kentucky. We're leaving in the morning."

"Valerie's leaving?" Mackey gulped.

"Well, I think this was kind of the last straw, Mackey. I mean, imagine if you were her."

He didn't respond, but finally Spider found his voice. "We should have killed that son of a bitch," he said grimly.

"It wasn't him," I said. "If you had killed him Tina would probably be dead now too."

"What makes you so sure?"

"Valerie and I saw him last night. He was tending bar at the brew pub where we had dinner, over near Stroudsburg."

"What?" Mike was incredulous.

"I'm way beyond kidding. He had a knot on his head and a nasty attitude and I had no idea why until I met up with you. And it's my guess those other guys will have an alibi too. I think they used someone else for this."

"You should have gotten that bastard outside of Val's and fucked him up," Spider said.

"Should have, could have, would have," I said. "It doesn't change anything now."

"Is—is she going to make it?" Mackey's face was working painfully.

"The doctor said her head injuries are pretty bad. I think right now it could go either way."

Spider was like a stone wall.

"What can we do?" Mike said.

"I was hoping someone would ask," I said. "There's not much we can do for Tina except wait. But Val and I could use some help right now."

"Whatever it is, you got it," Mackey said, his big face earnest as I'd ever seen it.

"Spider?" I said.

"You name it."

"Val was trying to change the timing belt on her car yesterday before all this hit the fan. She's got her hands full now getting her trailer ready, and I thought maybe you boys could finish the job for her."

"Val was doing that?" Mackey said.

"I have no idea how far along she is," I said. "I thought maybe you could handle it over the next few days. She'll come back for it later."

"Hell yes, we can do that," Spider said. "We'll tune that little fucker up tight as a drum."

"Fuckin' aye," said Mackey.

"Can you all keep things moving on the house here for the next few days?" I asked.

"Count on it," Mike said.

"You look beat," Spider said.

"I've been up all night and I've got to get some sleep before heading out tomorrow. See you all before quitting time."

~

When I stopped back by Val's she was nowhere to be seen, but after a moment she rose up from the bushes behind her trailer again holding the shotgun at waist level. This time I felt better about her vigilance. When I told her my guys would take care of her car she was skeptical. "How do I know they won't make it worse?" she demanded.

"Val, Spider could probably rebuild your whole engine blindfolded and with one hand. He's not going to make it worse."

"Spider?" She was indignant. "I don't want him coming near my car."

"You're not exactly in a spot to pick and choose. He said they'd do it and I trust him."

"You trust him," Val retorted. "He never calls me anything but 'Tree' and I hate that."

"That's just because you're tall. It doesn't sound so bad."

"That's a lie and you know it."

She was right. It was derived from "Country", which had been used derisively to begin with, and even more regrettably had been split into two separate words, of which "Tree" was the second and least offensive. But to her it still carried all the connotations of both words together. Unfortunately some nicknames keep being used long after people forget where they came from.

"Look, Val, right now my guys are feeling pretty bad about Tina and they really are trying to help. If there ever was a time you could trust them to do the right thing, this is it."

Somehow that persuaded her and she handed me her key. I went home, set the alarm for three and slept.

When I woke up and fastened my IV pump to my belt I noticed my jeans were nearly falling off me. I cinched my belt tighter and made a mental note to eat as soon as things were finished at the job.

I had an appointment with Dr. Panos in two days, so called the

185

number on his card and was surprised to find he wanted to speak with me. After filling him in on my situation I discovered he already knew about Tina through the hospital grapevine. When he realized she was a friend of mine he was immediately sympathetic. He wasn't at all happy about me going out of town, but grasping the urgency of the situation said he'd allow it as long as I kept up my meds. "No exceptions, no missed days—you got that?"

"Got it."

"You got spare batteries for that gizmo?"

"Do I need them?"

"Young man, you treat that machine like it's your second heart until you're done with your prescription. Yes, you need them. How's your weight?"

"I haven't weighed lately but I think I'm staying trim."

"Staying trim?" he boomed through the phone. "Are you gaining or losing?"

"Probably lost a pound or two," I said.

"Not good, not good at all!" he fumed. "Are you eating?"

"Well, somewhat."

"Mr. Brauner, do you realize your whole system has suffered a huge assault and you still have enemy troops inside your body? If you don't do everything in your power to get well they will start multiplying again, and if that happens it will be worse than before. Did you hear me—I said worse."

"What should I do?" I was confounded.

"Eat, man! Eat more red meat, eat more fresh food, eat more everything. Your whole immune system is compromised now; among other things we need to get your testosterone level back to normal."

"You don't know a guy named Spider, do you?"

"Spider?"

"Never mind; okay, I promise to eat."

I arrived at the Frye job just as the guys were wrapping things up. I gave Spider the key to Val's Jetta and Mike's cell phone back to him, and then went over the schedule with Mike and Mr. Frye. The

186

three of us walked through the addition and I noted again with relief that Mike had given priority to the roof. In a few days everything would be under cover; the house would be okay. I hated leaving everything on his shoulders but once again he was ahead of the curve.

I stopped by an ATM and withdrew five hundred dollars and then went home and ate a big supper from my freezer. I tried watching some news on TV but it was too taxing, so went to bed early and slept like a stone.

~

Early Saturday morning was damp and gray but I felt rested. When I backed my truck up to Valerie's trailer and plugged in the wiring harness I felt like kissing the sky. Everything worked. Her running lights glowed like Christmas decorations in the thin mist, her trailer brakes grabbed enough to keep us from jackknifing coming down some steep grade and the equalizer hitch would transfer enough of the Airstream's weight to my front wheels that snaking through the mountains would be safe.

So many things had gone wrong in the past few weeks; how we got this lucky with the trailer I couldn't say. Val already had detached her hookups, drained her holding tank, duct-taped her cupboards and stowed all her loose things. I watched as she collected her tools into an old steel box and put it in the trailer. She gathered the parts from her car onto a plastic tarp, folded it up from the corners and locked it in the trunk of the car. She took down the clothesline that ran from the utility pole by her trailer to the ginkgo tree.

I looked up at the old ginkgo and then down at her flowers and stone-lined walk with a pang of regret. My eyes were seeing things with a new clarity, and I realized this place really was beautiful. If it seemed so after the little time I'd spent here, after nearly two years how hard was it for Val to leave? I looked at her but she was all taut muscles and nervous energy. She finished winding up the clothesline and pressed it into a drawer inside the trailer. She picked up her welcome mat from the oak pallet, laid it inside and closed the door. She folded the metal step under the trailer, picked up one edge of the pallet, dragged it to the ginkgo and heaved it up against the trunk. Slapping her hands on her jeans she approached me.

"Well, that about does it." There was no emotion on her face, only a flat stoicism I couldn't penetrate.

"Let's see how this thing rolls," I said. We climbed into the truck and I carefully backed the trailer into the tall grass. Valerie hung out the window and peered back.

I dropped the transmission into drive and turned hard to the right and then left to avoid the Jetta, slowly pulling out of what had been Val's front yard. I had missed the car by several feet when she let out a screech. I jammed on the brakes. "What?" I said.

"My flowers," she moaned. "You just ran over my flowers."

I looked in the mirror and it was true.

"I'm sorry. I was trying to miss your car and didn't see the flowers."

She slumped down with an empty expression.

"You're leaving, Val," I said. "Why worry about the flowers if you're not here to enjoy them?"

She gave me a baleful look. "You don't understand nothing."

"Enlighten me." I steered down the driveway, feeling the inertia of the trailer behind me.

"I guess you wouldn't mind if your hotshot lawyer run a bulldozer through that fancy house now that you're done with it."

I started to say that was different but realized my folly in time to keep my mouth shut, and then we were at the road. After looking twice both ways I eased onto the blacktop, watching carefully in my side mirror as the trailer followed. I felt Val watching me.

"I'm sorry about your flowers," I said. "If you want I'll fix them when I get back."

"It's okay," she said sadly. "Mr. and Mrs. Streidl liked all I done to their place. When I told them I had to go they thanked me for making it pretty. They said I was a good tenant."

"I know you were," I said. "They'll never get another one like

188

you."

I maneuvered through town feeling unwieldy and conspicuous. After the lights I gained more confidence. About twenty minutes later we passed under the turnpike, and finally saw the sign for Interstate 81. Now there was a single road to take us nearly all the way home. Most of it was one long ride down the state of Virginia. Just like laying brick, it would be a matter of taking one mile at a time. It was only that last 100 miles or so into the hills of Kentucky that concerned me.

~

The fog burned off and the morning turned beautiful as we rolled through the Blue Mountains and then Harrisburg. Valerie's mood seemed to brighten with the day. Crossing the Susquehanna River she peered out at the expanse and declared, "That's the biggest river I ever saw. Where do you reckon all that water comes from?"

"I think it starts somewhere in New York."

"Where does it go?"

"It empties into the Chesapeake Bay, and the Atlantic Ocean after that."

"How come there's no boats on it?"

"Lots of people go boating on the Susquehanna."

"I mean big boats. Like for carrying coal and stuff."

"It's too shallow for shipping. It's a wide river but not deep."

She pondered that and then asked, "Did you ever go on a big boat?"

"You mean a ship?"

"I mean like on the ocean."

"I was on a cruise ship once."

"Was it like 'The Love Boat'?"

"I thought you didn't have a TV growing up."

"We didn't, but my cousins up in Hazard had one of them satellite bowls in their yard. Mama and I went up there and seen that show. And some others." It sounded almost like a confession.

189

"And what did your daddy think of that?"

"He didn't like it much." She fell silent for a few seconds. "So where did you go on your cruise boat?"

"We sailed from San Diego down around the Baja Peninsula to several Mexican ports. San Lucas, Mazatlan, Puerto Vallarta."

"We who?"

"That was when Jillian and I were together."

"Oh." She seemed deflated and didn't inquire further.

We rolled by Hagerstown, Maryland and then across the Potomac River and the tip of West Virginia. The day was windy and cool for August and the sky was electric blue, scattered with clouds that changed like smoke. By the time we made Virginia my legs needed a stretch so I pulled into a truck stop near Winchester. I fueled up, checked the oil and found it three quarts low. I went in and bought a case and threw it behind the seat with my duffel bag.

It was one o'clock and still I wasn't hungry, but knew I had to eat. Dr. Panos hadn't been kidding about my condition and several of my crew were troubled by my gaunt appearance too. Those bacteria were still viable inside me and I needed to make serious business of getting well. The thought of a relapse scared me, but the problem was everything else. It all took away my appetite. I was running on pure nervous energy. "Not good, not good at all," I kept hearing Dr. Panos mutter. I parked in a row of trucks that stood idling and we went into the restaurant.

I ordered steak and mashed potatoes and Val had salad with cornbread and a glass of milk. The meat was tough and I had trouble with it. Val saw me struggling and never said a vegetarian word.

When we got back on the interstate I put the pedal down and started passing slower traffic. It had been over three years since I'd driven down 81 and the only thing I remembered about that trip was the rain. Now we could see the hills around us and appreciate the slowly fading colors of late summer.

We passed a farm with a huge flock of sheep grazing in the distance and Valerie sighed. "I used to want a little lamb more than anything in the world."

"Did you want a sheep also?" I laughed.

"Ain't that what a lamb is?"

"Yeah, but the lamb is temporary, the sheep is what you end up with."

"Everything you have is temporary anyway."

"In a sense, I guess it is."

"In what kind of sense would it not be, mister professor?"

"I'll have to think about that."

"You let me know when you figure it out."

We rolled through Harrisonburg and Staunton babbling about the scenery and enjoying the sunshine. I pulled my sun visor down while Val fiddled with the radio. She flipped past several country stations and listened for a minute as a radio preacher ranted about the second death and everlasting torment in the lake of fire. He consigned liberals, abortion doctors and homosexuals to the flames and I could almost see the spittle flying from his face. She kept hitting the seek button until she found an NPR station from Roanoke. Two brothers with a syndicated car repair talk show were lambasting a hapless caller for letting his engine run hot for so long that his head warped. She found their slapstick humor greatly amusing.

By the time we hit Roanoke the auxiliary tank was getting low so I stopped to refuel and check the oil. A quart low this time, and when I did the math found we were getting 7.9 miles per gallon of gas. By now the mountains were on all sides of us.

Somewhere down around Wytheville Valerie squealed and pointed up through the windshield. There not a hundred yards above us was a tiny airplane. Its wings were bright yellow and orange, sunlit against the blue sky like a thing on fire. I could make out a little framework under the wings and the silhouette of the pilot reclining in a seat, with the engine and propeller behind him.

Valerie rolled down her window and stuck half her body out, waving her arms and hollering. I was about to pull her in and tell her he would never hear her when she started yahooing and laughing hysterically. I gawked up through the windshield and saw the plane

191

wagging its wings up and down in acknowledgement. We paced it for a few more miles, then it banked off to the right and the last I saw of it was a golden speck against the sky in the side mirror. Val plopped back in her seat with a sigh, put a bare foot up on the dash and laughed again to herself.

~

We were down in the foot of Virginia driving into the setting sun when Valerie broke a long silence. "How long do you think it will be before Tina wakes up?" she asked.

"I don't know," I said. "From what her doctor said it's not safe yet. Probably no news is good news, at least for the time being."

"I like that doctor," she said. "He's a Christian, you know."

"I liked him too," I said. "Although I'm not sure what the Christian part means."

"It means he has faith in God, Ray. It means he don't think he's doing it all by himself."

"A little humility is a good thing in a doctor, I guess."

"Don't you reckon it's a good thing in everyone?"

"Well, sure. But if it arises from a person's superstitions I'm not sure how good that is."

"You think believing in God is superstitious?" She seemed taken aback.

"Why is it so hard to accept that nobody can live forever, Val? Why do people have to believe someone up there will make an exception just for them? Look at all the absolute fools who claim to speak for God. Take that preacher on the radio. I mean, listen to what some of them say."

"The fool sayeth in his heart there is no God."

"Is that some Bible quote again?"

"So what if it is? You ought to be careful what you say about fools; you might be talking about yourself, mister."

"There are lots of kinds of fools, Valerie. Do you think every self-appointed Bible thumper out there speaks for God?"

192

"Of course not. And nobody takes it for real because of the fakes."

"So you admit they're fakes?

"There's all kinds. But if there's a lot of dumb asses calling their self a genius there must be a few actual geniuses too, wouldn't you reckon? Although I ain't met too many."

"What does that have to do with anything?"

"What do people make a counterfeit out of most, Ray? One dollar bills or hundreds?"

"Hundreds, I'm sure. What's your point?"

"People don't fake something that's worthless. If there's fake Christians out there there's real ones too. I've known some."

The sky had turned a deep indigo. Soft, pearl-colored lenticular clouds rose like cartoon bubbles from behind a ragged band of darker clouds that hung across the horizon in a boiling, twisted mass. I sat behind the wheel marveling at the sight and shaking my head. How could I argue with her?

"You said you went to Sunday school when you were little," she went on. "But did you ever pray and then really listen for the Lord with all your heart?"

"No," I admitted.

"Then I reckon you don't have much knowledge to put your opinions on."

"I don't have to join a cult to know they're going to try and steal me blind."

"That ain't the same. Being a Christian means following the Lord, not some other person. You can't look at a house from the outside and say what it's like on the inside, but that's what you're doing. You're pretending to know something when all you got is a notion."

"I have eyes and ears, Valerie. Look at your father. You said he used to hit you, and your mother too. He's a Christian and a preacher, for God's sake. Don't you see something wrong with that picture?"

Valerie stared at me but when she spoke again her voice was calm.

193

"There was something bad wrong with that. But you don't remember all of it. I told you he never learnt that in the Bible. That didn't have nothing to do with God; it was the way he was brought up. My grandpa was real mean, and Daddy learnt a lot of bad from him." She looked down at her lap.

"After he hurt Mama I hated him," she said softly.

"And now?"

"I feel sorry for him. After that something inside him turned. I think he's all eat up inside now, and can't hardly forgive himself."

We rode in silence for a few minutes and then she spoke again.

"If it wasn't for God I probably would have killed him. I was living down in Hurt and planned different ways to do it, but I knew it would be a sin. I prayed for the Lord to take away my hate, cause I didn't want to be like that. And the Lord showed me I needed to go away. So I did."

"The Lord showed you? How did he do that?" I really was curious.

"Oh Ray, it don't matter how! Everybody's looking for some glorious revelation when they don't even use plain good sense. Sometimes the best thing the Lord does is open our eyes to things we ought to see already. I was all balled up in anger and the Lord sent me away to burn it out."

"Did it work?"

"My daddy didn't want to be bad. He was wrong, but he's not wicked. There's others that really are. When I seen that difference I couldn't hate him no more. I can't even hate old man King." Her eyes narrowed. "I'd rather put it on someone who deserves it, like that bastard that went on Rollie."

Transference, I thought. Textbook example; psych 101.

"You're not as smart as you think, you know." She looked at me with her eyes like steel.

"Life wouldn't be the same without you to keep me humble."

"Don't you patronize me, Bwana," she said. "I don't see you giving me no credit neither." She turned away from me, toward the darkening hills slipping by her window.

The sun was gone. The cartoon clouds turned pink overhead and then dissolved as the landscape blended into monochrome. Long after it seemed possible a shaft of coral light pierced the band of clouds on the horizon like a beacon. It lingered for seconds and then was swallowed up as the day gathered itself down toward the hills, and things that lay beyond our sight.

~

It rained overnight; the next day dawned clear, hotter and more humid. We had stopped at the Hampton Inn in Bristol but Valerie insisted on sleeping in her trailer. She came up to my room to shower in the morning while I studied the map and reloaded my IV pump. Yesterday's antibiotic pack wasn't depleted, but I replaced it with a new one anyway.

We ate at Shoney's where I loaded up with sausage and fried potatoes. Valerie had grits and waffles with fruit. She made a face and shuddered when I put the first bite of sausage in my mouth. I shrugged; it was the best breakfast I'd had since getting out of the hospital. While we were finishing I asked Val a question I had wondered about ever since meeting her.

"What was it that made you come up to Pennsylvania? Of all the places you could have gone, why there?"

"I looked on a map," she said, "and I seen the Appalachian Mountains run on up there. When I heard there was coal mining I thought maybe it would be easy to fit in." Her brow furrowed. "But the only way it was like home was there was no way to make money. So when I heard there was resorts in the Poconos I come over there."

"The Poconos are poor, Val. Did you think it would be like the Hamptons?"

"I don't know nothing about the Hamptons but I know people ain't much different wherever you go."

"Well, at least you ended up in Gladburg."

"At least?"

195

An obese waitress with bleached hair refilled our coffee while I watched Val. "There are worse places, you know," I said.

"You think Gladburg was the first place I landed?" Her expression was cynical.

"I don't know," I said. "You never told me anything about before."

She didn't answer.

"Was it that bad?"

"Two times people tried to make me a whore, Ray," she said. I saw the hurt look in her eyes again, the same one she had when she told me about quitting ping-pong. "Two times."

"I'm sorry," I said. "I guess people really are the same everywhere."

She stared into her coffee. "One time I was so broke I went with a man who was going to give me a job. Then I found out what he wanted. "

"And?"

"I left him."

"You're lucky."

"Is that what you think?" She looked up at me.

"Well, at least you got away, didn't you?"

"Why do you keep saying 'at least'? I ain't never going to get away from that man, Ray. I still have dreams about what all happened that night."

"I'm sorry, Val."

"You want 'at least'? Well at least he'll think twice before he ever tries what he done with me again. At least I made sure of that." Her voice was turning husky with rage.

"What happened?"

"He liked to hurt women. He made videos of it." Her eyes flashed fire. "He come on all nice like he wanted to help me, but it was a big act. When he saw I knew it got real ugly."

"Did you report him to the police?"

"The police?" she scoffed. "People like that always got some way to get off, I seen it all my life. Besides, I was in a place I never should

196

have gone. The only good that come out of it was he had a lot of cash on him."

I nearly choked on my coffee. "And you took it?"

"It was my life he was aiming to take, Ray! How do you think I could own a trailer? I had nothing. After the way he done me he didn't deserve to walk away clean." Her eyes still smoldered.

"You weren't afraid of him coming after you?"

"Not the way I left him. I didn't care no more anyway; I was just tired of everything."

"I can't blame you for that."

"I was set to come home after that, but then someone told me about Gladburg and I had a feeling I ought to go there."

"You had a feeling?"

"Real strong. Like there was something I was supposed to do there."

The waitress brought our check and left before I spoke again. "I think I've had that kind of feeling too."

"I guess it all come to nothing anyway." Val's anger was spent. "Now Tina's hurt bad, and poor Rollie…" She sat shaking her head, her eyes welling.

I didn't know what to say. "You never know, Val. Maybe you did more good than you know."

She snorted. "Yeah. Maybe."

I paid up and we went out to the truck.

CHAPTER 15

After leaving the interstate above Kingsport the route into the hills was better than I'd expected. Again I had a surge of hope that for once things were going to work out smoothly but I felt worse than ever for Val. The only thing she had gotten for all her suffering up north was the trailer I was towing, and with its tarnished skin and creaky parts it didn't seem like much.

"Did you let your folks know you're coming?" I asked.

"Sufficient to the day is the evil thereof."

It made me uncomfortable when she spouted Biblical phrases like that. "Do you know if there will be a place for the trailer?"

"There's a place."

She said it with such certainty I didn't push it. I wondered what kind of accommodation her father would make for his wayward daughter but I wasn't about to touch that. We'd just have to deal with the moment when it arrived.

As we approached Kentucky on Route 421 the hills got steeper and the curves tighter. Even with a smooth road it was taking all my concentration to handle the trailer. If I had looked at my dash sooner I might have noticed the temperature gauge climbing, but by the time I saw it we were well into the danger zone. There was no place to stop, not even a shoulder. I cut the air conditioner and rolled down my window, and the dread essence of engine coolant hit me in the face.

"I smell antifreeze!" Val exclaimed.

"We've got trouble," I said. I looked in the side mirror and saw a small procession of cars behind us, and we were climbing a hill with no end in sight. Driving any farther was presumptuous but what else was there? I looked at Val and her eyes were squeezed shut and her lips were moving. Just great, I thought. Of all possible times, she picks now to go native on me.

There was nothing to do but keep going. The odor of radiator spew filled the cab and I watched the gauge climb higher. My stomach was in a knot by the time we crested the hill, but there on the other side of the road was a ramshackle tourist shop with a sign advertising handmade quilts and furniture. I hit the turn signal.

There was a turnout just big enough for our rig, and as we slowed for oncoming traffic I saw steam swirling from under the hood. When we finally rolled to a stop an assortment of sputtering, ticking and growling sounds continued from the engine compartment. They sounded huge in the sudden silence. My heart was somewhere down in my shoes.

A billow of steam enveloped me as I lifted the hood. After it cleared it didn't take long to spot the problem. One of the radiator hoses had burst and still was softly belching steam. There was no telling how much damage had been done.

I banged on the door of the shop. There was a sign in the window, and the words "Closed Sunday" jumped out at me. I walked around the building looking for a faucet or a pump but saw nothing except trash and a row of empty chicken coops. Kudzu vines covered every tree in sight and gave the place an eerie feeling of desolation.

I kicked an old tire and recoiled in horror as a huge black snake slid from inside, over my shoe and sped away like a thing possessed. The hair on my neck was still standing up when Valerie walked around the corner of the building with a glass of water in her hand. I was speechless.

"You look like you seen a ghost. Here, I thought you might be thirsty." She handed me the water.

"Where did that come from?" I stared at the cold glass in my hand.

"There's a spring across the road. You don't have to be afraid; the glass is from my trailer."

I took a sip. "I'm not afraid."

Val looked like she was about to giggle, but she didn't. "You really ought to have more faith, Bwana."

"In what?" I asked.

"Obviously not in yourself," she said, and then burst out

199

laughing.

~

Valerie had several plastic jugs in her trailer that we used to fill the radiator from the spring. We topped them off and put them behind the seat with the oil. I started the truck and the engine seemed undamaged, although we had a regular geyser blowing from the radiator hose. I pulled back out onto Route 421 trailing water.

A few miles up the road there was a place called Biggers' Garage with several giant dump trucks parked outside but it was closed too. The building had living quarters behind it so I walked around and up a flight of rickety steps and banged on the screen door. I heard sounds from inside, and after a long wait a huge man with no shirt came to the door and stared down at me.

"I've got a split radiator hose and I was hoping you might be able to help me," I said.

"Garage is closed Sundays, bud," he replied in an accent even thicker than Val's.

"Would you sell me a couple hose clamps and a piece of radiator hose?"

He stood scratching himself. "What you got?" he finally asked.

"Ninety-five Ford pickup."

"What kind of motor?"

"Four sixty."

"They won't be nothing with the right bends in it. You need a Ford part for that, buddy boy."

"I just need to clamp something over it to get me to Harlan."

"You just need to clamp something over it." He seemed reluctant, but finally pushed open the door. I stood aside and then followed him down the steps. When we rounded the corner there stood Valerie by the truck smoking a cigarette. "Well I'll be damned," the man muttered.

I lifted the hood, and waving away steam the man peered in at the hose. "It's wore out," he said. "She's going to keep on till she's wide open."

"You got anything I can put around it?"

He turned around and headed back to the garage. Taking a big key ring from his belt he unlocked the side door and pushed it open. There in the semi-darkness I could see a dump truck with its engine partly dismantled. Beside it was parked a huge diesel tow rig.

We walked to the back where an assortment of formed hoses, belts and gaskets hung from the wall. He ignored those and digging around in a trash barrel beneath them pulled out a length of hose that had been cut from a larger piece. He rummaged further in a drawer and came up with a can, a piece of sandpaper and a handful of hose clamps.

We walked back out to my truck and he unscrewed the radiator cap with a rag. The split hose quit sputtering and he wiped it dry, and then he drew a knife from his pocket. He held the scrap of hose next to my radiator hose and squinted, then carved one end and made a cut down the length of it. When he slipped it over my radiator hose I was astonished to see that it almost looked made to fit. He pulled it off and whittled a little more until he seemed satisfied. He handed me the clamps. "Open 'em up," he said.

I got a screw gun from my tool box and zipped all four clamps open while he sanded the split on my hose. He unscrewed the lid from the can and spread a gob of tire patch cement around the split. After slipping the new piece on he popped the clamps around it. I handed him the gun and the clamps were on in thirty seconds. "I'd pull 'em down with a regular screwdriver," he grunted. I already had one in my hand. Eyeing my bandage he took it and in another minute the job was done.

"No guarantees on that one, bud," he said.

"You got water?"

He went back into the garage and returned with a five-gallon can. "Start her up," he said, and I did. He poured water into the radiator until it spilled over. We waited for the thermostat to open, and he topped off the radiator again and screwed the cap on. The three of us stood watching for leaks and saw none.

201

I reached up and closed the hood. "How much do I owe you?" I asked.

"Twenty dollar ought to do it."

I handed him a twenty. "Thank you—Mr. Biggers, is that your name?"

"That's my cousin."

"You work for him?"

"Naw, I just live on up there."

"Well, thank you anyway."

"Y'all be careful now," he said. "I wouldn't be pulling no load like that less'n you get some new hoses."

"Yeah, well, thanks. We kind of had to leave in a hurry."

"I guess you did." His eyes slid over to Val and he openly looked her up and down. "Bye," he said.

~

We stopped in a place called Cranks where I filled up with gas and oil and bought five more gallons of water to stow behind the seat. When we got back underway I noticed a stooped woman lugging a big plastic bag down the shoulder of the road. Several children scampered ahead of her, rummaging through the weeds. I wondered out loud what they were doing.

"Collecting cans for the recycle plant," Val said. "It's the one job most people down here can do if they've got a mind to work."

"I thought coal was the backbone of the economy here."

"Well, the economy got a broken back. Most mines are owned by big companies far away, and they don't hardly need people any more."

"How do they operate?"

"They do everything with machines now."

"So that leaves more time for fiddling and drinking moonshine, right?" I was only kidding but she didn't find it funny.

"Ray, do you know before I come up north there was six openings at the Coalbright mine where I grew up and over forty men

202

showed up? There ain't that many able-bodied men left in the whole town. They come from all over the county, just looking to feed their families. In the end they shut the mine down a few months later anyhow."

"Why?"

"Because the easy coal was played out and there's more profitable mines somewhere else. The companies never give a hoot for the people; they just take the coal and leave nothing but a big mess behind."

"Don't the people object?"

"The people don't have a say. The land agents come through a long time ago and stole all the mineral rights, then folks got throwed off their own land and nobody had to pay them nothing. Now there's hardly a way for them to fight it."

"And you were there to see all this?"

"No, stupid. It happened to my granddaddy and the folks before him. Nowadays the lucky ones might own a truck and drive coal, like them big trucks back yonder at that garage."

"I thought the federal government had a war on poverty down here back in the sixties."

"Ha!" Val sounded bitter. "They gave breaks to the operators so they could make more jobs but then machines come in and put everybody out of work. Now they're taking the top off the mountains and dumping them in the valleys cause it's the cheapest way to get coal. The streams and woods don't even matter. The only reason there ain't a war is because the people can't fight back."

"There's usually two sides to every story, Val."

"You think I'm lying?" Her eyes threw sparks.

"I know you better than that. But sometimes things are more complicated than they look. I don't doubt some people may have been unfairly compensated for their land, but the fact is without coal we wouldn't even have had electricity for most of the last century, and—"

"Bullshit!" Val exploded. "'Unfairly compensated', my ass! Did you ever hear of broad form deeds?"

203

"I've heard of them."

"Did you know the crooks and swindlers come through here a hundred years ago and gave people money for signing a 'X' on a paper most of them couldn't even read? They paid chicken feed to come dig a few holes; at least that's what they said. They made it sound like they was doing people a favor, and then later companies come in with bulldozers and run families off their own land. Everything the people worked for got took away from them. There wasn't a thing they could do about it because the paper their great-granddaddy signed was a broad form deed that gave up all their rights to the mining companies."

"That may have happened in some cases, Val, but you're talking like it was the rule, not the exception. We have laws about that sort of thing."

She looked contemptuously at me. "You truly don't know nothing, Bwana. I been here all my life and you can't tell me how it was. They even got college students up in Gladburg that know what happened here. You go on and think whatever makes you feel smart, though."

We rode in silence. I wasn't feeling smart, and the cab of my truck felt smaller by the minute. Finally I said, "You're right, Val. I don't know much about down here. I'm sorry."

She looked reproachfully at me but the chill melted just a little.

"So does your uncle Duane work in a coal mine?"

"He was a roof bolter over in Letcher County until about ten years ago. There was a collapse and three men on his shift got killed." She looked pensive. "After the tunnels in Vietnam and that he didn't want to work under the ground no more."

"I can't blame him. What's a roof bolter?"

"They screw big old bolts up into the roof of the mine to hold it from falling. Except in that part of the mine there was nothing but dirt over the coal seam and the bolts didn't have nothing to grab."

"What does he do now?"

"The government tried to get him to come back and work for them but he wouldn't. So now he just does a little farming, a little

204

handy work."

"What did they want him for?"

"What he done before, only more specialized."

"Maybe he could make a new life for himself."

"Ray, so many times I wished you would actually listen to what I say. But maybe it's better you didn't. It don't really matter any more anyway, at least not to you."

"What do you mean? I listen to you, Val."

"Then maybe there's something wrong with my understanding. But it don't matter anyhow, because your world ain't down here. Duane's is."

"And how about you? Is your world down here?"

She looked out the window and twisted her hands in her lap and then for the second time in as many days my rational world was turned inside out. I felt a terrible anxiety in the pit of my stomach, a nervous churning I couldn't account for until she turned back to me. Seeing her face unnerved me; there was no mistaking what was happening. For some reason I was experiencing Valerie's emotion viscerally, in my own body. I felt invaded and overwhelmed, and hadn't a clue how to stop it. Like the pealing of a faraway bell her strange remark from two days ago echoed: "It's a gift and you just have to bear it."

~

Now I knew coming home was not something Valerie looked forward to, in fact she dreaded it. It was a thought I hadn't considered. But overshadowing that was the disturbing experience of becoming a receptacle for another person's feelings. It repulsed me; even more it frightened me. I wanted it to be a fluke, a coincidence caused by indigestion or maybe something in the air. From the corner of my eye I saw Val studying me and realized she knew what I was thinking.

"So is this something I can blank out, or is it like a curse that never goes away?" I said.

"Did you ever think what it would be like to be born deaf and all of a sudden be able to hear?" she said.

"Never."

"There's more than one way to look at most things, you know."

"This is not a thing I want at all," I said.

"Sometimes you learn things you don't want to know, and in the end it don't really matter how," Val said. "It's just the way life is."

I could have sworn I heard her say "it's what you do with it that counts," but she didn't. She thought it, and I heard her think it. And once again it occurred to me how small the cab of this pickup really was. Right now I wanted nothing more than to put a great distance between myself and this person whose thoughts were beginning to make noise in my brain. And then I turned to face Valerie only to see her crying out the window.

"I never asked for this" was all I could think, but then realized it wasn't coming just from me; it was Val too.

My mind seemed to be slipping out of my own control so I forced it to other things. I pictured the Frye house, and mentally walked through the new addition looking for my crew. The visualization helped focus my thoughts and for the next half hour it was like a veil had dropped between us. Valerie was deep in her own reverie; to my relief I had no clue what she was thinking. I hoped the boundary between us would remain intact.

As we approached Harlan I began to feel a tickle of interest in our surroundings. Even as an outsider I wasn't completely unaware of the history of this region. I knew there had been bloody battles between the coal industry and union organizers, but I thought all that stuff had been hammered out decades ago. Val seemed to think the coal companies had gotten the upper hand, but I would reserve judgment on that. Poor people always seemed to feel they were that way because someone had taken advantage of them, and big corporations were easy targets for their discontent.

Maybe it was true or maybe not, but right now what seemed most important was to discharge my obligation and get the hell out with as little damage as possible. We weren't far off schedule; with luck I could be out of here tomorrow free of Val's trailer and back in my own world by tomorrow night. There were problems enough to think about at home.

In the outskirts of Harlan I pulled into a nearly deserted shopping center. My heart jumped when I spotted a Western Auto store but when I drove closer saw the "Out of Business" sign in the window. Looking around I saw half the stores shared the same status. There seemed to be little point in hunting for an auto supply store that would be open on Sunday so I decided to press on.

Valerie directed me off the highway onto Route 38, which doglegged through part of downtown Harlan. I swung too wide at one corner and the trailer nearly sideswiped a shiny Mercedes sports coupe parked in front of Jenny Lea's academy of cosmetology. The bright new car seemed incongruous in the drab town. In the distance a great brick warehouse with a faded sign that read KY MINING SUPPLY CO loomed over lesser buildings. The sidewalks and storefronts looked tired. They reminded me of an old person not quite ugly, who no longer had the motivation to tend to appearances. No suitors would be calling; no takers would smile back, so why bother?

Up a side street I caught a glimpse of an old courthouse, still commanding in its appearance, and wondered at the dramas that had unfolded behind its walls through the decades. There were trees and benches out front but not a soul to enjoy them. As we passed out of downtown an old man on the sidewalk pulled a blue Popsicle from his mouth and gaped at our rig as it lumbered by. Valerie was somewhere far away, inert and expressionless as the buildings around us.

We drove east out of Harlan along the Clover Fork of the Cumberland River, by depressing strips of houses that appeared to be built from scrounged materials. Permanence, along with any sense of grace or style, seemed far down the list of priorities here. Most were simple bungalows covered with aluminum or vinyl siding. Some were trailers so decrepit with age that beside them Val's Airstream looked like a palace.

207

We drove through a tiny place named Ages. There was a brand new convenience store not much different from the ones around Gladburg, except in Gladburg there were also several large supermarkets nearby. Here and there timber bridges spanned the Clover Fork, leading to hardscrabble neighborhoods that ran up against the flanks of mountains beyond. Children scampered through yards and on one bridge a group of teenagers smoked and dangled fishing lines in the water. The valley broadened into bottomland in places and occasionally the crazy quilt of a garden could be seen going to seed. We passed the entrance to a mine, bristling with fences and signs warning trespassers of armed guards.

Outside of Evarts, where Valerie had attended high school, in the sycamore shade between the river and the road a young man polished a souped-up Camaro. He turned to stare as we passed. I looked at Val and she was alert now but pensive, walled away. After the gut-twisting intimacy we had just shared it was like a stranger was riding in my truck.

"We almost there?" I asked.

"'Bout ten more miles on this road."

"Have things changed much?"

"Couple new stores back up the way."

"How do you feel about coming home?"

"How do you feel about just driving, mister question man?"

"I'd feel better if I knew where we turn."

"Left up Bent Fork. After Hurt."

"Is that a road?"

"Hurt's a town. Bent Fork is a creek but also a road." She turned her face away.

I remembered her talking yesterday about living in Hurt, but hadn't understood it was an actual place. Now that made more sense. Maybe there were other things that would make more sense in time as well. Time was one thing we didn't seem to have much left of, but I didn't want our communication to break down yet. This wasn't Norman Rockwell's America; to my senses it felt more foreign and less forgiving by the mile. Valerie was my only guide to this place and

208

I wanted her with me now.

"Do your folks live on Bent Fork?"

"My mama and daddy's place is five miles up Bent Fork, by the Coalbright mine. Duane is past the mine just over the ridge. There's room for the trailer there."

"Sounds kind of far off the main drag."

"You take what you got."

"Is it pretty there?"

She let out a short laugh. "A coal camp never was made for pretty. But Duane's place is nice."

"Do you have brothers and sisters?"

"One each."

We hadn't talked much about our families. All she knew of mine was that I was an only child and my dad had been a cop. "What are your brother and sister like?" I asked.

"Violet is two years older; she married just to move away from home. She's married twice now. Victor is youngest; he moved up to Hazard to be a welder."

"Have you been in touch with any of them?"

She looked down at her hands and again I felt a tug in my stomach, like the time before but not so strong.

"Well, I was the black sheep of the family; I think they were just glad to be shed of me," she finally said. "Except for Mama, and Duane. But he always was different too."

I took that as a no.

CHAPTER 16

The farther we got from Harlan the more rugged the terrain became. We passed entrances to several mines but everything about them looked deserted. The road left the Clover Fork and twisted between rocky outcroppings that occasionally gave way to woods. We were climbing, and pulling the trailer was slow business. I kept a close watch on the temperature gauge. Here and there a spectacular view would present itself and just as quickly be hidden by the next curve. In one densely wooded area we passed under a high bridge that wasn't a road, but a gigantic tube connecting one mountainside to another. I guessed that it was a conveyor of some sort for coal.

After navigating that stretch we were in a valley once more. A creek plunged through a gorge to the left of the roadway, but it was of a different character from the languid Clover Fork. Val said it was the Bent Fork, which flowed from the mouth of a cave somewhere in the next county. Railroad tracks paralleled our route on the far side of the creek, but the woods mostly hid them from view. We twisted by dilapidated clapboard shacks and dark veins in the striated outcroppings of shale and granite. Mountains hemmed us in again, steep ragged slopes patched with pines and scrappy hardwoods.

Approaching the town of Hurt more houses came into view, and then we passed a breathtaking anomaly. There between the creek and the road sat a huge new home. It rose like a taunt, like a scornful finger in the face of its abject neighbors. A hulking four-wheel drive truck with nearly man-sized tires was parked in the driveway with another smaller four-wheeler beside it on the grass. A big above-ground pool could be seen at the far end of the lot before the lawn thinned into gray dirt and rocks. A scattering of homes more typical to the region could be seen beyond the broad lot on either side, and despite their beggarly proportions somehow they looked more tasteful to me. Valerie turned away when we passed like she didn't want to see it.

Hurt was a neater town than most we had been through but there was something disquieting about the place. I drove slowly, taking in details. Most of the buildings were on the right side of the road, facing the creek. We passed a gas station with a convenience store, and a plain corrugated metal building set back from the road with a sign that said "Church of the Risen Savior." A few children played around the entrance. There was a red brick post office with a flag and a beauty salon with a neon sign boasting of video rentals and a tanning bed, all along the main drag. Several side streets ran back into a ramshackle neighborhood. Aside from the beauty shop I didn't see much evidence of affluence here except for the fancy house just outside of town. Valerie stared intently at everything now. I sensed an alertness that bordered on apprehension coming from her.

Across from the post office, beyond the creek and through a stand of young trees, I saw a rail yard overgrown with weeds. A massive timber structure loomed over the tracks. There was no bridge connecting the town to the yard but a dirt road led into the area from the woods on the far side. Through the trees everything appeared derelict and abandoned.

And then the town ended abruptly. After passing what should have been the middle of it, suddenly there was nothing. Between the road and the creek I noticed remains of several stone foundations. To my right there was a scattering of concrete slabs, now cracked and overgrown with weeds, where houses once had stood. A poplar was growing from under the edge of one, which had been pushed up and now appeared to be casually leaning against the tree. I'd break that slab apart with a jackhammer before some kid crawls under it and gets killed, I thought.

There was no development at all beyond the town. No outskirts, no sign of life except for old foundations, the railroad tracks beyond the creek and the mountains beyond everything. A traveler coming from the opposite direction would seem to be miles from nowhere and suddenly find himself smack in the middle of Hurt, Kentucky. Val, lost in her own thoughts, provided no clue.

When we got to Bent Fork Road I saw that it followed a crease in

211

the mountains that looked impenetrable from the main road. I was apprehensive about going farther with Val's trailer until I remembered there was a mine up there. If coal trucks could make this trip many times a day we could certainly do it once. I dropped the transmission into low and stole a glance at the temperature gauge. It held steady as we climbed.

The road was nearly worn out, with asphalt patches giving way to potholes here and there, but it was wide enough for big trucks to pass each other. After crossing the railroad tracks we passed a barricaded turnoff that bridged the creek and led back into the woods. That must be the access road to the rail yard I'd seen through the trees back in town.

It didn't take long to reach the crease in the mountain, and then I saw the crease was actually a canyon. It rose abruptly on each side of the road and we were plunged into twilight. Although the sky was blue overhead no sunlight reached the roadway. So jagged were the walls on either side of us that it seemed this chasm must have resulted from a seismic event in some earlier time. I could see drill marks in the rock beside us from the widening of the roadbed and knew that making it had been no small undertaking. Bent Fork didn't even appear on my map so I assumed the road had been privately built. There must have been a hell of a lot of coal coming out of this place at some time to justify such expense.

After ascending through the gloom for more than a mile the grade leveled somewhat and the road took a hard right turn. There was clear light ahead and as we rounded another curve I looked left and what I saw took my breath away. We had emerged into a natural bowl surrounded by mountains. I could see the road ahead divide, with the left branch winding down to the center, where a gigantic industrial complex dominated everything in sight. It looked like a small city. There were immense concrete buildings; huge corrugated metal structures towered grotesquely atop one another until you could hardly tell where one ended and another began. Massive conveyors, some covered with tubes like the one we had driven under earlier, ran across the complex. I saw tunnels leading into the mountain in half a dozen places, great man-made mountains of scorched-looking black waste and sludge ponds large as lakes. Huge towers bristling with power lines marched down the opposite side of the bowl, maybe a mile and a half distant. Everything was black and gray. It was ugly as anything I've ever laid eyes on, ugly in an aggressive and pitiless way. It looked almost medieval, like a penal colony in some advanced state of decay.

"Welcome to coal country," Val murmured.

~

I was so staggered by the enormity of what I was seeing that I couldn't even speak at first. I stopped the truck and sat there with my mouth gone slack. The thought occurred to me that the entire town of Gladburg might fit into this bowl; that this place might even be Gladburg's negative image in some parallel universe. I'd never been given much to mathematical or cosmological theories, but what I was seeing now required some kind of philosophy to digest.

"It ain't nothing but filthy lucre," Val said.

"What?"

"Lucre, like riches. Money, you know?"

"Lucre, like in lucrative?"

"Like that."

"So this would be the Coalbright mine?"

"Coalbright Number Two."

"I don't think I could bear to see Number One."

"Oh, it's lots smaller than this. It was just the first one, before they started all this. Do you know my great-granddaddy used to own half that mountain over yonder?" She pointed to the slope where the steel towers carried their burden of electricity down to the dismal dystopia below us.

"No kidding?"

"Nope. It used to be real pretty here, but I never saw it like that. My granddaddy's old house was still up there when I was little but they tore it down putting in bigger power lines. Everything old is

213

gone now."

"Does your father work for the company?"

"He worked here fifteen years, but the mine closed before I went away. Most folks who could left after that. Daddy stayed on to minister to the ones that didn't have nowhere to go."

An absurd question occurred to me. "Did he study for the ministry, like at a seminary?"

Val rolled her eyes. "You think someone who went to a fancy school is going to be a preacher up here? He was a miner, just like his daddy and his granddaddy."

Oh. I was careful not to follow my thoughts any further for fear they'd find their way into Valerie's head. I was still new at this but now realized I had to move on with no reflection, at least until I was somewhere alone. I put the truck in gear.

"Where do we go—left or right?"

"Stay right and you'll see the company houses up yonder."

At the fork a shot-up, rusted sign arched over the road saying COALBRIGHT MINING CO., HEART, KY. Below in smaller letters were the words LIGHTING THE CUMBERLAND VALLEY. Someone long ago had spray-painted the letter B in front of the word LIGHTING, and it seemed to me a reasonable correction. I wondered who had misspelled the name of the place— the mining company or the folks back in town.

After the fork the road narrowed considerably. Another quarter mile and we rounded a small knee in the mountain and there to the right, hard against the rocky slope, was a development with tight rows of houses. What it made me think of was a failed Levittown. That was the first community of mass-produced housing, built in New York after the Second World War, but that was made for people who had a choice. This place clearly was not.

As we got closer I saw the houses were hardly more than cabins, identical in structure; some were clad with aluminum siding but many were unpainted clapboard. Some had tarpaper and some had shingle roofs. Most had covered porches, but the lots were too small to accommodate anything more. Nearly the whole row back by the mountain had burned down. Several houses were completely derelict and falling over. A few yards boasted grass and even a flower here and there, but the overwhelming impression was one of decay. It was not unlike some urban neighborhoods I'd seen in industrial cities, blasted by time and neglect.

"Your folks live here?"

"I reckon," Val said, and I could feel the tightness down in my gut again. "The second street."

"Is there a place to turn around?"

"You don't need to, it comes out the other end."

As we turned the corner several children who had been running between houses stopped to stare as if a flying saucer was landing in their midst. And there may as well have been—plain as it was, my white truck and Val's faded aluminum trailer were probably the brightest things that had rolled up that street in years. I felt more conspicuous than I ever had in my life.

"Stop up there," Val said, and I pulled over behind a battered black Lincoln. "Wait for me, but if I call will you come?"

Something in the air between us made my skin prickle like lightning about to strike. "Whatever you want. Are you sure you're okay with this?"

She grabbed my hand and squeezed it. "I'm okay," she said, and leaned over and kissed me hard on the mouth. Then she reached for the door.

Valerie walked by the Lincoln and up into the yard, and I saw little eyes peeping over a windowsill from inside the house. Someone opened the door before she had a chance to knock. It was a man but I couldn't see his face. After a moment he extended a hand to her, but she ignored it and hugged him around the neck. He came onto the porch and I could see her talking, then looking toward the street. They exchanged a few more words and then started down the steps, Valerie first. The man was a striking figure, powerfully built, and when his features came into the light there was no mistaking his identity. She made a small, fierce gesture at me that looked like "come here." I slowly got out of the truck and met them halfway.

215

"Daddy, this is Mr. Ray Brauner," Val said. "He done me a big favor bringing my trailer all the way down here from Pennsylvania. Ray, this is my daddy, Mr. Vance Tolliver." She seemed a little out of breath.

Mr. Tolliver just stood there looking back and forth between us, then over at the trailer, stunned.

"Daddy?" Val said.

Mr. Tolliver blinked as if waking from a dream, and then pulled it together. "Mr. Brauner," he said gravely as he stuck out his hand. "Much obliged." His voice was deep and sonorous, with a thick Kentucky accent. Like Valerie's his hair was coal black and swept up from a peak in front. He was handsome in a severe way, with penetrating blue eyes that almost made me want to look away. I was struck by the resemblance between father and daughter. We shook and his grip was like a vise around my weakened hand. When he noticed my bandage he asked, "Are you all right?"

"He just come out of the hospital," Valerie offered. "He got a real bad infection that could a kilt him, but it's a-gettin better, ain't it, Ray?" Val's speech seemed to be regressing rapidly.

"Yes, it's much better," I said.

"You ain't got the AIDS now, do you mister?" Mr. Tolliver asked, a suspicious look creasing his brow.

I almost laughed at that, but managed to say, "No sir. I got burned on my job."

"He builds houses, Daddy," Val said. I don't think she realized how desperate she sounded for some sign of approval.

"Well, you take care of that hand, young feller. The Lord needs good hands; there's a mighty work to do for his name's sake."

I was saved from further admonition when the door opened and two women appeared on the porch. Val cried, "Mama!" as she flew to the steps, where the younger woman guided Val's mother down. A wordless cry came from her mother as they fell on each other's necks.

"Oh, Mama!" cried Valerie, while her mother laughed and cried all at once. Her face turned up to Val's, who stood half a head taller, and she ran her hands over the contours of Val's face while tears flowed down her cheeks. And then they put their faces together and cried and communed in a language that neither I nor anyone else there was privy to. I backed off a little and stole a glance at Mr. Tolliver. He stood there watching his wife and his daughter with the saddest, loneliest look I've ever seen on a man's face.

The younger woman stood to the side and now I knew she had to be Valerie's sister. She was almost as tall as Valerie, with dark red hair thick and curly as Val's, but not as long. She wore a shapeless dress that ended below her knees. I saw that she too had been beautiful. She watched her sister with a skeptical expression, and when a pair of children burst out of the house and raced down the steps she called them sharply. "Samantha! Cody! You come back here right now!"

But it was a lost cause. They raced around and around the little yard, making circles around Valerie and her mother until Samantha overcame her shyness. She ran over to Val and hugged her legs, and Val bent down to the little girl and hugged her back and then took her hands and said, "Just look at you, Sammy! I thought you was another girl, you look so growed up!" And Samantha's face shone like a hundred-watt bulb, and Cody began playing hide-and-seek from behind his sister until he, too, overcame his shyness and hugged Valerie.

All this heartened me, and then Valerie stood to greet her sister, whose face was turned away. "Vi, this here is—" she started, and then she saw what I had already seen. An ugly bruise covered the right side of Violet's face; even the white of her eye was blood red.

"Oh, Vi, what happened to you?" Val cried, but even as she tried to hug Violet her battered sister put her arms up and pushed Val away.

"I am just fine, thank you. No need for you to waltz back in here like you was some kind of angel, neither," Violet hissed.

"I know I ain't no angel, but I love you," Val cried. "Who done that to you?" She whirled around. "Daddy, did you—"

"It weren't Daddy. And it ain't none a your affair so you just

217

don't worry about nothin. And if you're fixin to go put that fancy trailer up at Duwayne's you best be gettin on."

"Vi." Mr. Tolliver looked pained. "Mr. Brauner just had a long drive and he done our family a marvelous work by bringing the lost sheep back to the fold. I was a-hoping you could think of something more gracious to say."

Mrs. Tolliver stood crying silently while Valerie struggled to control herself. I was wondering how I might get out of this and back into my truck when Violet finally said, "I thank you, Mr. Brauner. Now you can take my sister on up the road and leave us poor folks be."

I started back around to the driver's side of the truck but Valerie said, "Ray, wait!" Then she turned and put her hands on Violet's shoulders and said "Vi, I know I done different from you but I ain't no better than you. You're the only sister I got and I love you, you hear?" Violet shrugged Val's hands off her, turned around and went back in the house crying. Her children followed.

Val put her arm around her mother and gently guided her toward me saying, "Mama, there's someone I want you to meet. He drove me all the way here from up north, a-pullin my trailer behind his truck. This here is Ray Brauner."

"Mrs. Tolliver," I said. I put my hand out and she found it, seeming surprised at my bandage. Then she put her hands to my face and touched it lightly all over. She felt the shape of my brow, the scars on my nose and chin, even my lips. The sensitivity in her touch made me think of an artist. She had an expressive face, with delicate features and soft brown hair.

When she had finished her examination her hands dropped, and she sagged a little. Val took her hands and said, "Mama, we're going up to Duane's now but I'll be back to see you real soon, maybe even tomorrow." Her mother put her hands to Val's face again, and Val took them and kissed them both again and again. Mr. Tolliver and I shook hands, both of us too uncomfortable to say a word.

~

218

We made our way around the rest of the bowl on the poorest road we'd been on yet. The left side was a sheer drop in places, in others pieces of rock and dirt lay fallen across the roadway from the mountain above. After we passed under the high-tension lines Val directed me onto a narrow unpaved lane that twisted up the slope like a rattlesnake. I had serious misgivings about taking the trailer up such a grade. If we met another vehicle there'd be no passing room, and I sure as hell wasn't going to back this rig down the mountain.

"Duane made this road. There ain't nobody uses it but him," Val said. I must have looked annoyed because she quickly added, "And you won't have me bugging you no more, so you can get your privacy back."

"Did I say you were bugging me?" I asked.

"You ain't got to say it. But it ain't like you think; sometimes you're just too obvious."

"So are you going to quit using proper English for good once you move back here?"

Her mouth dropped and she actually blushed. I laughed harshly and said, "Bet you didn't see that one."

"What difference does it make to you anyway?"

"Val, you're smart enough to read literature. A little bit of country is not a bad thing, but you're starting to sound like you're giving up on yourself."

"I am not."

"That's good. Because you're not going to stay here forever, you know. I don't think you'll want to be completely out of practice by the time you decide to venture back into the world again."

"Well don't you worry about me, mister smart pants. I can make myself understood good enough."

"Well enough."

"What ever. You better worry about your own self, because pride goeth before a fall, you know."

"Is that another pearl from your oracle of ancient wisdom?"

She looked at me like I was crazy. By now we were a good ways up the mountain and the road had become so narrow branches were scraping the trailer. Some curves were so tight I could hardly get around them without dropping the trailer wheels off the roadbed. At least the truck was doing better than I had hoped. I was beginning to feel a little relief that soon the trailer would be cut loose. The drive home would be so much easier, I thought, when a subtle odor wafted through the open window.

"I smell antifreeze," Val exclaimed for the second time on this trip. I raged inwardly and looked down at the temperature gauge. It was still in the safe zone but it wouldn't stay there long.

"How much farther do we have?" I asked.

"About a mile and a half."

"Is it all like this?"

"The last part goes over the top."

"Well, let's see how far we can get." My jaw clenched as the gauge crept higher. The trailer twisted and groaned behind us as we slowly climbed through the woods. After the next switchback the engine was too hot to risk going farther so I found a spot clear of tree branches to stop. I put the transmission in park, turned off the ignition and opened my door. When I lifted the hood a spray was fanning from the end of the patched hose closest the radiator and the underside of the hood was dripping. The antifreeze was so diluted with water I was thankful we had noticed the odor at all.

I was debating whether to try and fill the radiator right away or sit and let everything cool first. I gave the hose an idle, experimental nudge and there was an explosive gush and all I knew next was pain. It knocked me backward and closed around my hand like a steel trap.

"She's going to keep on till she's wide open," the man at Biggers' Garage had said, and sure enough it was wide open now. The old hose had come apart above the patch, right at the junction with the radiator. The spray temporarily blinded me, my face had superficial burns, but my hand took the brunt of it. All my bandage did was hold boiling water against the new, tender skin underneath. I must have cried out because the next thing I remember Valerie was standing in front of me in her jeans and bra, using her T-shirt to pat

220

radiator water from my face and hair. She didn't realize yet that my hand was in the most excruciating pain.

There are very few things that can take one's mind off pain like that; even Valerie's breasts spilling over her bra inches from my face barely registered. But when I saw what was happening behind her my hand was forgotten. "The truck!" I yelled, shoving her aside.

I made a desperate lunge, managed to reach the open door and scrambled into the window. I grabbed the roof, pulling the door closer to the cab, and tumbled in. The door swung wide and caught on a tree. It took all of two seconds to fold completely back over the front wheel well, but that slowed things enough for me to get my foot on the brake before all was lost. The whole rig slid to a stop with the right trailer wheels completely off the road, buried to the axles in leaves and loose dirt. In the passenger side mirror I saw the trailer tilted at a crazy angle; the back end was hidden in foliage. All I could see ahead was the raised hood. I sat there in the sudden quiet with my heart hammering out of my chest. I set the emergency brake hard, took several deep breaths, leaned back on the headrest and shut my eyes.

The adrenaline began dissipating and my hand felt like fire. I denied the pain. I withdrew into a dark place and groped for a mantra but all I could find was an enigma. What was I being punished for? Was there any way to pay the account all at once instead of doing it on the installment plan? I felt like a dog having its tail docked an inch at a time.

All Valerie's religious talk reminded me of being taught in Sunday school that God sent trials to help build our characters. But in time I learned something I never understood as a boy: character growth is by no means guaranteed in trials. How one handles trouble and what is learned are wild cards. I've watched trials turn into train wrecks because all the wrong things were done or said, with no saving grace salvaged from the aftermath. Just another day down the toilet, and everything else that could be sucked down with it.

In some trials the right path was impossibly narrow and convoluted and at times completely hidden from view. These seemed like diabolical trials—with no possible good outcome, only bad or worse and not even a way to know them apart until it was too late. I was closer to wisdom than I realized at that point, but would have none of it. I wanted to wake up and find myself somewhere else, if only I could let go. Just let go of everything. I was drifting, but my hand was like a red-hot anchor that wouldn't let me go far enough.

"Ray!"

I jumped and opened my eyes. Valerie was leaning in my door pale and trembling. "Are you okay?" she asked, clutching her T-shirt to her chest.

"I was getting my breath back."

"You scared me. I kept calling but you never would say nothing."

I studied her through a fog. "I was just meditating on the folly of all human endeavor. Wasn't it one of your prophets who said everything is vanity, nothing but a big joke?"

"He never called it a joke." Her lip was trembling and suddenly I felt a crushing wave of sorrow for my insensitivity. My own slack emotions filled and then staggered under the weight of Valerie's anguish.

"I'm sorry," I said.

She fell onto my shoulder. "No, I'm sorry," she wept. "All my life all I wanted was to do good for someone, and everywhere I go nothing but bad things happen. I'm sorry about your truck, Ray, I am so sorry." She kept trying to apologize until I hushed her. I held her, stroked her amazing, fragrant hair and let her cry, and each sob was like a knife through my heart.

~

Valerie didn't realize my hand had been burned. Keeping even the smallest secret from her felt like a victory now, but I was intuitively learning how to turn my mind to other things. There was nothing to do about my hand so there seemed to be no point in dwelling on it. And ignoring it seemed to lessen the pain somewhat.

I refilled the radiator while Val put her shirt back on. We had

222

such a short distance left to cover; the problem now was getting the trailer back onto the road. My door wouldn't close but I didn't care. I just wanted Val's trailer delivered to wherever we were going and then to be cut loose from all further responsibility. If I could have taken one clear look through her eyes I might have seen that nobody is cut loose from all further responsibility. But I still had a few things to learn.

When I started the truck and dropped it into low the rear end seemed for a moment to grip but then started sliding farther off the road. I pounded the steering wheel in frustration while Valerie cringed. I set the brake again, hard.

"Rocks," I said, "We need rocks." Val jumped out like she'd been whipped. I looked behind the seat for a container and saw the case of oil. I dumped the remaining quarts from the box and we scouted up the grassy lane. Val scrambled up the slope on the left side and began gathering rocks into the front of her T-shirt. I picked from the lane, muttering curses at my stupidity for not owning a four-wheel drive truck. Back when I had bought it four-wheel drive didn't seem necessary. How could I have known that five years later I'd be pulling a 25-foot trailer up the side of a mountain? Before I knew it Val had dumped a shirt full of rocks into the box. We kept going until the box was over half full and both of us dragged it back to the truck.

I unlocked my toolbox and looked inside for something to dig with, and the best thing I could find was my framing square. I began hacking away at the soft ground beneath the rear tires and we crammed rocks into the space. I got my hammer and pounded rocks tight into the crevice. My hand was screaming, but we made another trip, and then another, until finally we had a solid rocky lane a foot wide and about four feet long ahead of each rear tire. We were sweat-streaked and filthy. Val's T-shirt looked like some misshapen rag found along the road and my bandage was in tatters.

We climbed back in the truck and once again Valerie began doing her closed-eyed mumbo jumbo. Whatever works, I thought. Just let me discharge my obligation and get the hell out of this place. Once

223

again I started the engine and dropped it into low. After releasing the brake I lightly pressed the accelerator. I felt the rear end bear down and slowly, miraculously we began inching forward. I watched in the right-hand mirror as the trailer rocked and slipped, trying to climb back onto the roadbed. We came to the end of the rocks and the trailer wasn't all the way upright, but we were still moving forward. I stole a glance at Val and her eyes were still squeezed shut and her lips were still moving. I accelerated a little more, felt a slight bump and looked back at the trailer. Finally I blew out the breath I'd been holding—we were going to make it.

A palpable relief filled the cab but we were locked in silence. Val had gathered a veil around her thoughts, to guard her privacy, I suppose, although by now her composure was too frayed for complete coverage. She sat so stiffly I was afraid the rocking of the truck would knock her head on the doorpost. Her pride couldn't conceal her dismay for all the trouble she felt she'd caused. I knew damned well that nearly losing the truck was my own fault but it was getting really hard to be nice about things.

Two more switchbacks and we were in the sun again, nearing a saddle in the mountains. The trees thinned out and I caught glimpses of the Coalbright pit below us on the left. The grade leveled and a grassy meadow opened on our right, and then I saw two big dogs coming toward us in the lane at a fast trot. Valerie let out a little shriek.

"Stop," she cried, "it's Nimrod and Jehu!"

They were Dobermans, large and intimidating enough to give anyone pause about coming closer, but Val had her door open before the truck stopped.

"Nimmy! Jayboo!" she called, and both dogs flew to where she stood. They leaped up on her and knocked her to the ground, where she hugged both, laughing to high heaven as the three of them rolled around like puppies. The dogs wagged their rumps, woofing and squealing until I thought they'd jump out of their skins. Val got to her feet. "Ten hut," she called out, and they both froze, their eyes riveted on her face. "Sit," she said, and they sank to their haunches.

224

"You want to come meet my buddies?"

I climbed from the truck and the dogs turned their attention to me. "This is Ray," Valerie said to the dogs. "Nimrod, meet Ray." Nimrod extended a paw. I took it in my left hand but Nimrod growled and I recoiled, the hair on my neck standing up. "Your right hand, stupid," Val whispered. By now my fingers were bright pink and swelling, but I gingerly took Nimrod's paw and he carefully smelled my dirty bandage, then licked my fingers. Jehu sat like a statue until Val introduced him, and when I took his paw he also examined my bandage and licked my fingers gently.

"At ease," Val said, and immediately the dogs were up and frisking. She caressed them both and then said, "Go on home, tell Duane we're a-comin." They streaked up the road like comets and were out of sight in five seconds. I stood looking up the lane, amazed.

When we got back in the truck I asked Val what would have happened if I'd been a stranger alone.

"They'd a kept you inside your truck, and if you didn't leave they'd raise all hell until Duane come to see what was going on."

"How long have you known those dogs?"

"Since they was pups, seven years ago." She was quiet for a few seconds and then said meekly, "You never said nothing about your hand."

"It doesn't hurt much now."

"You're lying."

"Well, if I don't think about it, it doesn't hurt so much."

She looked reproachfully at me.

We bounced on down the lane but the going was easy now. The encounter with the dogs had a healing effect on Valerie's spirits and now I even detected some anticipation behind her composure. At the end of the meadow the lane followed the perimeter of it to the right and began climbing again, and then we were looking east over a succession of Appalachian ridges similar to the ones behind the Plum house, only more ragged and irregular. Val pointed southeast beyond the power lines now about a half-mile distant and said, "See up yonder? That's Black Mountain; it's the highest spot in Kentucky."

It looked more like a lump than a peak, but it was the highest point in view. I scanned the horizon. To the left, just before more woods obscured our view, was a bleak sight. A huge chunk of land was barren of trees. Not only that, the mountains themselves had been shorn off and what should have been valleys between were filled in until they were no more than shallow troughs. It looked to me like vast piles of debris had been dumped over square miles and then crudely leveled, preparatory to a final landscaping job. It stood out so starkly I asked Valerie if a new interstate was coming through.

"That's your basic mountaintop removal," she said. "Cheapest way there is to get coal."

"When are they going to finish it?" I asked, puzzled.

"Finish it?" Val looked strangely at me and then laughed when she saw I was serious. "That's it, Bwana. Stick a fork in it."

"You mean they just leave it like that?" I was appalled.

"They take the coal any which way they want; nowadays the cheapest way wins."

All through my career I had been so constrained by environmental regulations it was unthinkable to destroy the geography of a place. We were supposed to work with the land, not against it. To obliterate not just mountains but valleys and streams, with no regard for restoring them ever again, flew in the face of reason. I thought these things happened in other countries, not here. And then I remembered reading about protests over mountaintop removal, but it had been just another item in the newspaper. Seeing it with my own eyes jolted me to the core. Things happened differently here than in the world I knew; the same moral imperatives didn't seem to apply.

We followed the lane along the edge of the meadow. The scene was in my mirror, but from the corner of my eye I noticed Valerie studying me. "What?" I demanded.

"Don't you think you ought to check your water?"

"Ah, shit!" I pounded the steering wheel and looked at the gauge.

226

It was far over the red line.

I shut everything down and pulled the hood release. With no pressure in the radiator I saw no need to wait, so poured water in until it overflowed. A few seconds later the engine regurgitated half of it.

"How far do we have?" I asked Val.

"About a half-mile."

"The motor's too hot to hold anything now. What should we do?"

"Let's walk, and let Duane bring us back." She was practically bouncing up and down.

"I guess a little walk would do us good," I said.

~

The sun had dropped behind the mountain but the series of ridges to the east were still bathed in the late afternoon light. We followed the lane around the meadow, which Val said was usually planted with corn. I asked if Duane owned this land.

"No, but he got him a lifetime lease on it from Mr. Cottrell because he saved his boy's life."

"Who's Mr. Cottrell?"

"One of them who's getting rich tearing up them mountains back yonder." She tossed her hair out of her face.

"When did this happen?"

"Before I was born; they were in Vietnam together."

"It sounds like quite a story."

"They were riding in a convoy that got hit. Duane didn't even know Johnny Cottrell, he just started carrying wounded men down an embankment. He got hit with shrapnel and burnt but he saved sixteen that time. Johnny was one."

"There were other times?"

"Duane got two bronze stars plus two purple hearts, but he don't ever talk about none of it. Folks around here learnt it through the paper when he come home."

227

"Didn't you tell me he was a sniper?"

"Yes. But he done a lot more than that."

"Like what?"

"At first they put him in the tunnels because he was used to working underground, but when they found how good he was they sent him to sniper school. He never got lost in the jungle. He got the most dangerous patrols because he knew where the booby traps were. He always could feel when something wasn't right. Nobody could hide from him, but he knew how to move without nobody seeing him. They said he was better in the jungle than a Viet Cong."

"He must be quite extraordinary."

"He was a legend." Valerie looked at me with her eyes like steel. "Lots of men called him the bravest man they knew."

She took a pause. "After he got burnt they wanted to give him a new face and a undercover job for the CIA, but he wouldn't have it. It bothered him a lot, what he had to do over there. They made him a hero when he come home and he couldn't stand it."

We walked in silence.

"So what did he do?"

"He went up into the mountains and nobody seen him for seven months. It was winter when he left and some folks thought he died from the cold, but Daddy said he knew how to live like an animal. Then when he come back to the holler people kind of took him for crazy. After that they left him alone; I think most everyone's been scared of him ever since."

"How did he end up with this land?"

"After Johnny come home he looked up Duane to thank him for saving him, but Duane said he was just doing his job. Johnny saw where Duane was a-livin then and told him they was going to tear it up for coal. Duane said if he had any pull with his daddy's company could he find him a little piece of mountain he might buy.

"The company said this land would never be tore up because the coal was too deep to strip, but Mr. Cottrell didn't have enough pull to sell him none of it. But when he told the other big shots how Duane saved Johnny's life they give him a lifetime lease up here. I

228

doubt any coal company ever done a thing like that before or since."

"Mr. Cottrell must really love his son," I said.

Val laughed harshly. "Now there's another story," she said. "Johnny ended up being a lawyer for some environmental group and now he's a-workin against his own daddy's company. Sometimes I worried Mr. Cottrell would turn Duane out just from spite of the way things ended up."

"Amazing," I said. "Val, that's a remarkable story. You ought to write about these things."

She snorted. "People don't pay no mind to what goes on down here. You wouldn't even believe it your own self. You reckon they would care if it was in some paper?"

As we walked Val explained that farming had been a way of life here long before coal mining. "I thought bootleg liquor was the traditional product down here," I said.

"That was in the old days. You could make a lot more money from your corn that way, but people have to eat too."

I asked, only half joking, if we might find a still on Duane's property.

"No, stupid, he just grows sweet corn. He plants a big garden and gives most of it to folks that's out of work. He don't like to see people drunk. I think he seen too many lose their self that way."

Something was being left unsaid but I couldn't tell what. After passing a stretch of woods that rose from the end of the meadow we came to a barricade across the lane tied with cans and pieces of metal. Valerie stopped, cupped her hands to her mouth and gave three of the most unearthly cries I've ever heard a human make. In the brief silence that followed I heard a crow call.

"What was that?" To this day I don't know whether I thought it or said it.

She turned and gave a little half-smile and unfastened the barricade. Cans rattled and clanked, and within seconds the dogs were coming toward us again. They circled us noiselessly and then one stayed ahead of us and the other followed; they seemed to be both guarding and herding us along. The lane curved right and when

229

we passed the edge of the woods what I saw ahead stopped me dead in my tracks. Although I had never been here before everything looked old and familiar to me.

We were at the base of a clearing of maybe two acres. A log house of indeterminate age stood at the top of the clearing just below the woods. There was a small barn to the right of the house; to the left was a big garden. The lane curved up to the barn, turned and continued below the house to the garden. A meadow billowing with purple asters, Queen Anne's lace and goldenrod spread down to where we stood. Why was I so stirred? I had no reason to recognize anything and yet there was a familiarity about the scene bordering on inevitability, as if nothing else could exist here except just these things. I felt a quickening in my chest as the realization dawned on me. What I was sensing wasn't just coming from the homestead but from the ground itself; the structures simply resonated with that power. There was a harmony here that I had felt in only one other place—the Plum property.

I realized Valerie was smitten as well; we both stood there for a long moment caught up in our own individual thoughts but somehow bound at the core of our emotions. How such a thing could be possible remains beyond me; all I know is that we were like two strings on a guitar, both vibrating to the same chord and unable to move otherwise.

"That's a right good sight for sore eyes, now, ain't it?" The quiet voice came from so close behind us I felt my heart flip-flop inside my shirt.

Val gasped as she whirled around. "Du-wayne!" She stamped her foot. "I swear if you scare me like that again I'm going to fix you."

Then they fell together, rocking back and forth and laughing until finally Duane pulled back, took both her hands and said, "My lord, girl, look at you. Just look at you." He was grinning with tears at the corners of his eyes and kept shaking his head. "You look like you been dragged through the dirt twice. My lord, what's been a-keepin you?"

CHAPTER 17

I watched from the side as Valerie and Duane greeted each other. He wasn't as tall as me but he was lean and rugged, with wild dark red hair and a beard that was going to gray. I could see that he was her father's brother—the Tolliver stamp was a strong one. He might even have been handsome with a shave and haircut. But when he turned to me I understood why people might be afraid of him. The right side of his face was horribly scarred, with not much beard to it. It looked like his flesh had burned until it ran like wax down his jowl and the side of his neck. When he spoke the portion of his mouth on the burned side barely moved.

When Val introduced us he extended his hand. "Welcome, brother," he said, and for a moment it felt like nobody in the world existed except the two of us. When I put out my bandaged hand he took it in both of his and examined it. "You been hurt."

"It's nothing," I said. And it was partly true; at least the pain had receded to a dull ache.

"Ray just come out of the hospital," Val started once again. I felt a flash of annoyance. This situation was not about me; it was about getting her squared away and me out of here as soon as possible, and no sooner had I thought it than Val stopped herself.

"Is that so?" Duane said, looking at me curiously.

"It's really not much." I felt suddenly self-conscious, as if there were more than just my hand under scrutiny.

"I got me a trailer, Duane; I've been a-livin up in Pennsylvania, and Ray was good enough to pull it back here with his truck."

"Pennsylvania? Lordy, Valry, I wondered where you got to."

At first Duane seemed a little overwhelmed, but then I thought otherwise. There was more to him than met the eye. Something about how he had come up behind Val and me so quietly and invisibly still spooked me.

The conversation was pulling in too many directions already and somehow I knew there was no hope of getting out of here tonight. It would be enough to have the trailer cut loose; fixing the truck would have to wait for tomorrow. I tried to relax and yield to the moment.

"Would you like something to eat?" Duane asked.

Val said yes, and as we walked up to the garden she chattered like a schoolgirl. Duane moved inside a calm that seemed remarkable considering the intrusion we had visited upon him, but there was no hiding his delight at seeing Valerie. He listened quietly, chuckling and shaking his head at her anecdotes of our trip. She didn't omit the final incident either, only now all her stress was gone. She was as relaxed as I'd ever seen her, even funny. Watching the change in her began to loosen my knot of tension and as for the place, it had a strangely tranquilizing effect all its own.

In the garden there were late tomatoes, corn, string beans, squash and enough green things to make a big salad. Val seemed like she was in heaven as she held the growing armful of produce Duane picked. He was a skilled gardener; the neat rows and raised beds could have graced the pages of a horticulture magazine. Every plant looked pampered and walking between the rows I marveled at the volume they yielded.

Duane led the way into the house. It was spare inside as a monastery. The pine floor had mellowed to a golden color, and I noticed the crossed trusses of the open ceiling had been hewn from rough timbers. The inside was mostly one big room, including the kitchen at the rear of the house. There were doors to two other rooms—a bathroom behind the kitchen and what I surmised was Duane's bedroom in the front, with a loft above them overlooking the downstairs.

Furniture consisted of a table with four ladder-back chairs, and two rockers with footstools in the living area. A good cast-iron stove sat at the end of the room on a raised stone hearth. There was a long open cabinet crammed with books, boxes and knickknacks, and hanging on the wall were two hunting bows. I saw no television or radio.

I learned that Duane had built this place in 1979 after acquiring a lease for forty acres at a dollar per acre from the company that leased mineral rights to several large coal operators in the area. The original Tolliver homestead had been just behind us on the other side of the mountain. Here the view was broader and the morning sun came up early. It almost rivaled what one saw from the Plum house; even the power lines and the portion of stripped mountains visible on the horizon couldn't spoil it.

Duane and Valerie puttered around the kitchen while I stood watching. He turned and asked if I would like some meat.

"It's deer," volunteered Val.

"Yes, thank you," I said.

Duane went out the kitchen door to a closed-in back porch and returned with a strip of sirloin, which he laid on the counter and began carving. "This doe was kilt yesterday. I just finished putting her away when the dogs started up a fuss," he said, almost as if to himself. "I knew it was Valry a-comin; I've been feeling it nigh on two weeks." He scooped the trimmings into a bucket, salted and peppered the meat and took out a skillet. "How do you want yours cooked, brother?"

He looked at me and spoke with deliberation, like each sentence was a thing he had to think through. I sensed he didn't often have company. "The same as yours," I said, and he seemed pleased.

Val made biscuits and a big salad while Duane cooked the steaks and boiled corn, and when it was ready we sat down in good spirits. Duane extended a hand to each of us. For a few seconds holding hands around the table it felt like I had fallen into a time warp, a hidden wormhole safe from the uncomfortable tide of events that had been sweeping me along for so many days. Duane bowed his head and said simply, "We give thanks for this bounty, and for bringing Valry safe through many dangers." I kept my head bowed until both hands were released, and wondered how much Duane understood of what he had just spoken.

The venison was tender, with hardly a gamy tinge, and I knew the doe was very young. I could feel my body taking on energy as I ate. Valerie had no meat but did most of the talking, describing the town of Gladburg to Duane in more flattering terms than I would have

233

guessed she felt. She introduced King's Tavern as a restaurant where she had been working, which was true enough. Duane made little comment, but listened closely. I had the feeling Val was laying a foundation for the larger story to follow at a more convenient time. And I had the feeling he understood this as well.

After we finished eating Duane filled a jerry can with water and we followed him to his truck, a heavy-duty heap of mismatched parts that sat up by the barn. It was a four-wheel drive Ford years older than mine, equipped with a winch in the front and a home-welded boom with a hoist in the rear.

We got in and bounced down the drive. By now daylight was fading, but when we passed the woods that hunk of horizon where the mountains had been pillaged for coal stood out like an open wound. And then the truck and trailer appeared ahead.

At first not much could be seen beyond my truck's raised hood, but as we got closer and the dimensions of the trailer became apparent Duane seemed surprised. After stopping he got out and walked around it, looking thoughtfully at it from all sides. He examined my wrecked door. Finally he stood back with us, stroked his beard and began chuckling.

"Look at that trailer. Just look at that. My Lord, girl, I'm guessing there was some mayhem involved." He glanced over at her. "Just a little, maybe?"

I felt myself blushing. I glanced over at Val and saw her looking at the ground. She was kicking a stone around with her hands deep in her pockets, and instinctively I knew what was happening. This had nothing to do with me.

I felt a rush of bravado as Val spoke. "I paid for it. I been working nearly two years, you know."

Duane put his head back and laughed, a sound so genuine and full of mirth it made me laugh. I watched Val's face redden further but now I was on my own, glad to be watching Val spin her wheels for once instead of things being the other way around.

"I bet you did," he finally said, still laughing. "I hope you ain't still paying for it."

234

"It's mine legal, I got the title for it," Val said a bit defensively.

"What do you want to do?"

"Can I put it by the garden?" she asked with pleading eyes.

He looked at her so intently I thought she might quail under his gaze, but she didn't. He seemed to be reading something I couldn't see in her face. At length he seemed satisfied, and turned and lifted the can of water from the back of his truck. I started my engine and got out to watch as he poured water into my radiator until it overflowed.

"By the garden?" I asked.

He nodded. "Take her straight up to the barn and then back her down around the house." He screwed the radiator cap on and lowered the hood.

Nothing pleased me more than a plan of action. I finally could see the shape of my freedom just ahead. Another half mile and Val's trailer would be in place, my duty would be discharged and my life could be put back in order. The stress of the past few days began to recede and my mood lifted even more.

Val and I climbed into my truck, I dropped the transmission into low and we followed Duane up the drive. I held my door closed with my left arm as we passed the barricade and the strip of woods where the drive curved right, and we emerged in the clearing below Duane's house. Looking ahead I realized our final ascent would be steeper than anything we had navigated yet, but it was only a short distance. The trailer groaned gently behind us, and I glanced at the temperature gauge. It was approaching the red line, but in less than a minute we'd be at the top.

The meadow looked ghostly in the twilight. I switched on the parking lights, and Val oohed as her trailer's running lights came alive in the mirrors. Duane parked his truck and hopped out, directing us up just past the barn. When the trailer had room to swing around the front of the house I dropped it into reverse. I steered right to begin backing and as soon as the trailer broke left, cut left to establish a turning radius. Duane ran back to guide us from the rear, and stood motioning us straight back. I centered the

235

wheel but the trailer had turned too far and I had to pull forward again. The second time I got it right, and we straightened out. Duane continued guiding us; by now he was visible only by the meager illumination from the trailer's taillights.

By the time the trailer reached the garden Val's excitement was hard to contain. She hung out her window calling encouragement and it was all I could do to see Duane in my mirror. He had his arms up motioning me to come back just a little farther when suddenly my truck choked. I pressed the accelerator and the engine coughed and nearly died. I saw a cloud of white exhaust hanging between the truck and trailer, illuminated by my backup lights. I tried the accelerator once more but the engine just wheezed and then gave up with a gasping sound. I cranked the starter for about thirty seconds but all that produced was another few puffs of white exhaust. Valerie slumped in her seat and groaned.

The sound had hardly faded away when Duane appeared at my door. "Brother," he said in a voice that sounded almost apologetic, "I believe you blown a head gasket."

~

Of all the guys on my crew Mackey was the one you could count on to try to say something philosophical when things went wrong. Although his sincerity was never in doubt his sayings rarely proved helpful. One of his favorites was "when life shits on you, sometimes you have to make a shit sandwich." I have no idea what he meant by that and don't think he did either, but I wasn't about to be a willing participant in my own degradation. But now events were careening so far out of control that my will itself was being threatened.

Being more a hands-on kind of guy I've never been too interested in theoretical science, but I have studied enough to understand a few things. Quantum mechanics proposes that due to the wave-like properties of matter, no matter how tightly one controls the variables of an experiment all anyone can count on is the probability of a given outcome. A moving electron might end up here or there, and

236

one might predict with some reliability where it will not go at all. By manipulating variables you can influence the probabilities, but the bottom line is, nobody can be certain where it will end up. The corollary of this now hit me like a hammer: if uncertainty was the rule regarding the smallest units of matter, why should my own reality be different? So many forces influenced my path it was impossible for me to imagine all the possibilities, let alone know what particular future would be mine.

Until now I had reckoned with the probabilities I wished for as if they were certainties, taking no thought for how other people's necessities intersected my course. It never occurred to me to calculate anyone else's chosen probabilities into mine. Up to this moment I had considered this trip to be only a temporary inconvenience; I certainly never bargained for a life-changing experience. But three times now I had felt my moorings slip, and suddenly was helplessly watching the shore of my one chosen probability drift away, still within sight but achingly, terrifyingly out of reach.

I don't know whether ten seconds passed or ten minutes. I remembered Duane standing at my door. I turned to look, and had the feeling that if I put my hand out to touch him what I was seeing would be just a dark shape in the trees beyond. I blinked several times and his silhouette finally pulled into focus. "Do you want to come in?" he asked. He stood there like a grizzled statue, inside a stillness that seemed absolute.

"Can you fix it, Duane?" Valerie asked.

"I can."

"Come on, Ray, let's go in."

We climbed out of the truck. I reached behind the seat for my duffel bag and as we trudged up to the house for the first time in my life I felt very old. On the porch Duane paused to turn a light bulb in its fixture by the door until it came on. Laying a hand on my shoulder he said, "Don't worry, brother. You'll be all right." In the hard light his eyes looked honest enough above his ruined face. With no knowledge of my circumstances I had no idea how he could say such a thing but my will was so beaten down all I could do was nod.

Valerie uncovered my hand in the light over the kitchen sink. The bandage was brown with grime, and pieces of dirt fell out as she unwound it. My hand was pink and bloated next to hers and it hurt to flex it. She asked Duane for clean rags, and he returned with a box of sterile gauze. Val ran water over my palm in the sink and then coated it with aloe from a plant in the window. After wrapping it with clean gauze she taped it with duct tape.

I took a fresh pack of clindamycin from my duffel bag and the IV pump from my belt. "That's his medicine," Val explained while Duane watched. When I opened the case my heart nearly stopped. The pack inside was still full and the indicator on the pump was blank. Feeling slightly panicky I went out to my truck. There were fresh batteries in my glove compartment, and after finding them I breathed easier. Back at the kitchen table I installed them, and there was a comforting beep as the indicator flashed. I left the unfinished pack in place, wondering what Dr. Panos would say if he knew how many hours of medication I had missed. I saw Duane shaking his head and figured he'd never seen such a device before.

Duane brought bedding from his room and led me up a narrow staircase into the loft where there was a cot and another rocker. After switching on a lamp and opening a window at the gable end he said I was welcome to settle in there. A comfortable breeze drifted through the window.

"Thanks," I said.

"If you give me your key I can look to your motor," he said.

"Would you like a hand?"

"Valry can kick it over while I look to it. You take it easy now."

"Okay," I said. Why not? Val had trusted Spider with her car; now I was the one not in a position to pick and choose. I handed Duane my keys.

After Duane and Val went outside I dug for my cell phone. I wasn't sure whether there would be a signal up here, but when I switched it on the roaming indicator flashed and I punched in Mike's number. After two rings he answered.

"How's everything back at the ranch?" I asked.

"You want the good news or the bad news?"

"Some good news first, please."

"Val's car is nearly fixed. Mackey has a friend with a body shop who owes him a favor, so they took it there for a facelift. They're not sure what color Val would like."

"You're kidding."

"No, I'm serious."

"I'd go with the original color or something close to it."

"Brown? Mackey will be disappointed. I think he was pulling for a lime green metallic job."

"I'm not sure Val needs that much visibility now, either up there or down here. You know?"

"Yeah, you're right. I'll give them the word. How was your trip?"

"Well, the good part is we made it all the way up the mountain to Val's uncle's place before my head gasket blew. The bad part is I'm stuck here until he can fix it."

"You're bullshitting, right?"

"I don't have that luxury. The engine overheated, split a radiator hose and after that things got complicated. At least she's home safe."

There was a long pause.

"How's Tina?"

"Not good." Mike sounded strained. "She's had some bad swelling and they're kind of worried about her. Brain damage, that kind of stuff. We're all kind of worried."

That punched the wind right out of me. Outside I heard Duane's voice and the sound of my engine cranking, endlessly cranking but not starting.

"How's Rollin holding up?"

"Not well at the moment. He's pretty shattered about Tina, and he just found out from Buddy that all the papers the old man signed are airtight. Whoever drew them up knew what they were doing, I guess. They're watching everyone like a hawk now. There was a bad crowd Saturday night. They drove the band out around eleven. Apparently someone called the police about public lewdness, and it just got worse after that."

"Public lewdness? What the hell are things coming to?"

"I don't know. At one point there were a couple drag queens dancing on the bar."

"My God. You actually saw this?"

"Unfortunately."

"How about who attacked Tina? Do they have any leads?"

"The police have checked and you were right. Everyone we've seen at King's has a solid alibi. Whoever did her was someone else. They questioned all our guys; they wanted to see Val again but I told them she was gone. They'd like to talk with you as soon as you get back."

We talked about the job for a minute or two, I promised to keep in touch and we ended the conversation on a melancholy note.

After switching off the lamp I lay on the cot while Val and Duane sat on the front porch talking deep into the night. Before drifting into a troubled sleep I heard them arguing about something. Not in anger, but several times I heard Val's voice rising passionately before Duane calmed her down. I dreamed they were weaving baskets from their arguments, filling them with stones from the road and dumping them at my feet, while far away Rollin watched, wringing his hands and weeping. I had no idea what any of it meant.

CHAPTER 18

The morning dawned pink. Somewhere a rooster had been crowing and I woke disoriented, not understanding where the light was coming from until I rubbed the sleep from my eyes and found the window above my head. My back ached from the cot and my arm hurt even more. I peered out at the sky and saw a phalanx of clouds spreading down nearly to the horizon. The rising sun painted the underside of it in flaming coral but even as I watched the clouds were starting to devour the sun.

I went downstairs onto the porch and looked out over Duane's domain. The meadow below the house was burnished with gold but the mountain ridges on either side faded into monochrome. The light was rapidly turning gray as the sun rose into the overcast. My dew-covered truck sat forlornly in the yard and I could see Val's trailer bumper nearly even with the edge of the garden. Another twenty feet and a little better angle and we'd have been done, I thought. I could have made it home tonight, if only...

Then I remembered last night's conversation with Mike and a sick feeling washed over me. Tina might not make it. I could hardly bear thinking about that now; I needed some kind of diversion to occupy my mind.

I heard chickens behind the house and walked back toward the barn. Nimrod and Jehu trotted up wagging their butts and sniffing my hands. I didn't see Duane's truck. There were the chickens, at least a half dozen of them pecking in the open doorway of the barn. An old tractor sat inside with an array of farm implements behind it in the shadows. I pissed into a clump of thistles going to seed just outside the door.

There was a faint path leading up into the woods beyond the barn and I followed it for a distance. The dogs kept close and I was glad for their company. After about a hundred yards I saw a clearing ahead, but the dogs were no longer with me. I looked back and saw them both sitting in the path watching me. I called but they wouldn't

241

come. I cajoled a little more, and Jehu rose from his haunches, gave a mournful little woof and sat back down. I didn't feel like playing games with them now. The sky looked like rain and if that happened this might be my only time outdoors today.

I turned and hadn't taken three steps before there was a swishing sound. My body folded at the waist and knees and suddenly I was rocketing up toward the treetops. My head hit something and my chin hit my knees, and before I could comprehend a thing I was wrapped up tight twenty feet above the ground with the dogs raising absolute hell below me. I've never heard such frenzied howling in all my life. The more I struggled the tighter things got and the louder the dogs barked. My heart felt like it was about to burst from my chest.

After many seconds I quit fighting and my panic subsided. I started examining my enclosure and found I was caught in a camouflaged net along with a considerable amount of vegetation. It took a while longer to realize a mounted tire had dropped down over the whole business, cinching the bag shut and squeezing me into a fetal position from which it was impossible to get free. All my thrashing succeeded only in bringing the tire down tighter. I could turn my head sideways just enough to see the dogs howling up at me from below.

I tried to get an arm free to pull some sticks away from my face but it was no use. I was caught fast; there was no way down without human intervention. Duane was gone and Valerie would still be asleep. I tried calling the dogs, which made them bark even louder. Whistling quieted them for an instant, but only for an instant.

I heaved the tire upward with my left shoulder, trying to gain a little wiggle room. I began doing it at intervals, each time attempting to move my body into a more comfortable position. It was slow going; sticks and leaves kept poking me; I felt ants crawling up my legs. I was starting to weary of the dogs' howling when I heard a new sound.

"Ten-hut!"

Suddenly it was quiet.

242

I squirmed to get a view of the ground and caught a glimpse of Valerie in a nightdress looking at the dogs.

"Up here," I said, and the dogs started again.

"Ten-hut!" she called again and they stopped, while she looked incredulously upward. And then she saw the squirming cocoon holding me up and gave a little gasp.

"Ray?"

"I can't get down," I said miserably. I felt something crawling under my shirt and made another pathetic attempt to heave the tire upward.

"You—you can't get down?" Val asked hesitantly, and then she lost it. Her laughter came slowly at first but built on itself until she was helpless. I've never seen anyone laugh like that. She laughed so hard she doubled over, and then went down on her seat, and kept on until she was literally rolling on the ground while the dogs frolicked around her. "Well I'll declare, if I haven't caught myself a man this time I reckon I never will," she finally sighed, reclining and gazing up at me.

"Can you please help me?" I pleaded.

"Don't you know better than to go poking around other people's business?" she demanded, climbing to her feet.

"I was just taking a walk," I said mournfully. "And suddenly I was up here."

"Well I don't know, Bwana. I used to know how to work this thing but it ain't easy. If I can't do it we mought just have to wait for Duane."

She was walking around looking for something and after a few minutes I heard her talking to herself, along with some clanking sounds. I squirmed until my cocoon turned enough to see what she was doing. She was straddling something on the ground, and then she started heaving on a rope. I heard the squeak of a pulley and felt myself descending almost imperceptibly. My cocoon began twisting slowly and with each revolution I could glimpse Valerie working. After a few more revolutions I began to see what was happening. There was an old engine block hanging opposite her about waist

243

high. Some kind of block and tackle arrangement was lifting it as she pulled. I couldn't do a thing except stare out at the trees spinning around me.

After several minutes a pile of rope lay at Val's feet. I was halfway down and could see sweat glistening on her face as she worked. Winding several turns of rope around her forearm she leaned back with all her weight, then hand over hand grabbed a new length and repeated the process. After what seemed like an eternity I was on the ground again and the engine block was somewhere in the treetops. Val walked the rope several times around a stout tree and tied it. I was unable to move until she lifted the spare tire off the net, which freed its corners, and I slowly disentangled myself.

"Well, ain't you a sight!" Val said, hands on her hips. We both were exhausted. I pulled off my shirt, shook it out and checked the IV tubing taped to my shoulder. It looked unscathed.

"What in the world is he trying to catch with that?" I asked.

"Not the likes of you, I reckon."

"Then why would he rig up such a damned thing? You don't go to that kind of trouble for nothing." My temper was beginning to flare now that my feet were on the ground.

"You ought not be poking around in other people's business," Val said again.

"Poking around? I was just taking a walk, for God's sake. I didn't come down here to be a tourist, you know."

"I know." Her eyebrows knitted together and then she softened. "I'm real sorry that happened to you. Come on, let me fix you some breakfast."

I looked suspiciously at her. It wasn't like Val to suddenly become all domestic and cozy.

"What the hell is up that path?"

"It don't matter. Let's go have breakfast."

"I'm not going anywhere until I find out why I had the living shit scared out of me."

"It wasn't meant for you. I'm sorry, Ray, it's my fault for not telling you not to come up here. Come on, let's go eat." She took my

244

arm and tried to turn me toward the house.

"I'm taking a walk," I said, brusquely pulling away.

"Ray, don't. Please?"

"If you want to come, fine. If not I'll be back—unless I fall into a pit or get impaled on a stake next." I abruptly turned and began walking up the path.

"Wait," Val called. She ran up and grabbed my arm. "I'll take you, but not this way. It ain't safe."

I realized she was telling the truth.

"There's a way up from the garden," she said. "Plus I need to pee. The dogs woke me up so sudden I never had the chance."

We made our way back down to the house where Val used the bathroom. She emerged with a shirt of Duane's over her nightdress. Then we headed out the front door and up to the garden. Once again I was struck by the vitality of the plants. I couldn't help remarking on the unusual vigor of everything.

"That's because Duane knows how to pay attention," she said.

"How's that?"

"Most folks just plant things and let them be. He pays attention to every one. He talks to them and listens. They like someone to listen to them, but most folks don't understand that. People don't know how to pay attention."

It sounded naïve, but it was hard to argue with the garden itself. Looking at the plants I didn't understand what they might have to say, but I couldn't help noticing there was something happy about them. If they had voices I thought they would be singing right now, even in the cool humidity of this gray morning. The idea lightened my mood. I heard Valerie humming as we walked between rows of okra and eggplants, and imagined the plants bending close to listen.

When we got to the far corner of the garden Val continued up to the woods on a footpath that was barely discernable. It resembled an animal trace more than anything. Once in the woods we had to duck and dodge tree limbs and I would have lost the trail altogether if not for Val and the dogs, who ran on ahead of us. I thought of Gloria Plum tugging me through that deer run in the brambles behind their house and smiled. My frame of mind had changed so much just from the simple walk through the garden that I nearly forgot my reason for being there, until we emerged into the clearing.

I felt the hair rise on the back of my neck. There must have been a quarter acre of marijuana plants staring me in the face. And these weren't the thin, spindly plants that my friends had cultivated without much success back in high school. They were bushy, dense plants, top-heavy with huge flower clusters. The air was pungent with the smell of them. I was almost afraid to breath for fear it would make me high. High above a nearly transparent net spanned the area with leaves and branches scattered randomly across it.

"Holy Christ." It was all I could think to say.

"Thou shalt not take the name of the Lord thy God in vain." Val's voice suddenly had a hard edge.

"Jesus, Val—" I began and she cut me off again.

"Why is it you have such a hard time respecting sacred things?"

"This isn't sacred, Val; it's—it's illegal," I sputtered.

Her eyes narrowed. "The Bible don't say a word against growing any plant the Lord made. But it says not to take his name in vain."

"Okay, I'm sorry. I guess growing up the son of a cop made me kind of spooky about certain things. Like illegal things, for instance."

"You got no right to judge any man. You had to see what ain't even yours to see, and the first thing you do is drag the Lord's name in the dirt. Sometimes you ain't got the sense of a jackass."

I swallowed my pride. "You're right, Val. I'm sorry I came up here; I should have listened to you."

"So now what are you going to do, mister big shot?"

"What do you mean?"

"One word from you and things here could get turned upside down. With all the good Duane does for folks who don't even know it there would be a lot of people hurt."

"I wouldn't dream of that. What Duane does up here is none of my business in any way."

She looked at me with her eyes like steel. "A little knowledge is a dangerous thing."

246

"Very good. Alexander Pope, from An Essay on Criticism. You're smarter than you know, Val." It was patronizing, and I realized it before the words were even finished.

"He said 'learning', not 'knowledge'. How smart are you?"

I felt like cringing. "Not very."

"Gold star for Bwana." After a few seconds she tilted her head in the direction of the house. "You better have breakfast before you get sick again. If the great Ray Brauner croaks down here we'll never hear the end of it."

Her tone stung but I was too chastened for words. And beyond that I was aghast. What I was seeing here was a felony, an ongoing criminal enterprise. It was knowledge I had no use for yet I had demanded it. Now it was mine, but only as a burden. Why had I been so adamant about coming up here?

"You can't undo it." Val regarded me through half-lidded eyes. "It's time to go." I nodded stupidly and followed her through the woods. I stumbled and branches whipped me in the face but she never looked back.

~

When we got to the house Valerie sent me to the barn to gather eggs. I hunted high and low before finding several hens' roosts, and collected half a dozen eggs. Back in the kitchen Val had made coffee and was slicing vegetables into a cast-iron skillet. I broke the eggs into a bowl and whipped them while she silently grated a pile of cheddar. I made toast while she cooked omelets and we sat down to eat.

The air between us was thick with tension. "I'm really sorry for what happened," I said. "It wasn't my intention to pry."

She didn't reply. We continued taking tiny bites of food and eating with exaggerated politeness. My appetite was gone. I tried one more time. "I hope you don't think I would do anything to hurt Duane."

She dropped her fork with a clatter, pushed her chair away and

247

headed out the back door. I followed her as far as the kitchen sink and then thought better of it. I came back to the table and tried to clean up my plate but couldn't. There was a tightness in my gut that wouldn't go away. I cleared the table and washed the dishes entirely with my left hand just to be doing something useful.

By the time the dishes were done I found myself curling my right arm to my chest. A familiar thudding sensation had crossed my threshold of awareness, causing an alarm to go off in my mind. I climbed to the loft and fished in my duffel for a fresh pack of clindamycin. I unclipped the IV pump from my belt and when I opened it didn't want to believe my eyes. Yesterday's pack was still full. The pump's readout screen was blank again.

I fumbled the batteries out, squeezed the test buttons and watched the indicator strips come alive. Nothing wrong there. I looked more closely at the pump and saw several deep scratches across the face of it—no doubt from spreading rocks under my truck yesterday. Had I broken it? I put the batteries back in and pressed the "on" key. No beeps, no indicator. It was dead as a brick. I sat there for a long time staring at it.

The pain thumping up my arm goaded me into action. I dug in the duffel bag for my cell phone but once it was in my hand wondered who to call. Mike? Dr. Panos? There was nothing they could do to help me. Call 911? An ambulance would have a terrible time climbing over this mountain even if I could describe how to get here. Worse still, it would bring strangers onto Duane's place. A helicopter was completely out of the question. Or was it? Was hiding Duane's secret more important than saving my life? I didn't know what answer would imply the greatest cowardice; I only knew what I could not do.

I fought growing panic and tried to make a plan, but all I could think of was enemy troops inside my body. If they started multiplying again, Dr. Panos said, things would be even worse. I kept hearing him say if I'd taken any longer getting to the hospital I'd have lost my hand, possibly my arm as well. Another day and we might not have saved your life.

For a few terrible minutes I was more afraid than I've ever been. This was no bruiser threatening to whip me in front of a bar crowd, no mugger kicking me to pieces in a parking lot. In either case I might put up some resistance and get in a lucky punch, but my opponent now was formless, depersonalized. And unlike most diseases it would not allow the dignity of a prepared exit. It was a fast killer, multiplying exponentially, raging through living tissue like a fire and dissolving substance at the cellular level. By now I had heard too many horror stories about flesh-eating bacteria—internal organs liquefied, skin sloughing off like a burn victim's and everything taking place in a matter of days, sometimes even hours. A metallic taste roiled in my mouth and I recognized it as fear.

For some reason my mother came to mind. I dialed her number without thinking, and hearing her calm, disembodied voice saying "Hello" through the phone shook me.

"Mom?"

"Well, what a nice surprise! I was beginning to think you might have taken off somewhere."

"Actually, I did. I'm in Kentucky."

"Kentucky? What on earth are you doing down there?"

"I had to pull a friend's trailer down here with my truck."

"With you just out of the hospital? Why couldn't he rent his own truck?"

"It's a long story. I was just thinking about you." I felt choked up.

"What's the matter? You sound stressed out. Are you taking your medicine?"

"I've got a bag full of it with me. Fresh batteries too."

"That's good. Are you eating enough?"

"Yes, Mom. I just had a homemade omelet you wouldn't believe."

"That's good. How long are you going to be down there?"

Just then there was a two-toned chirp from my phone telling me the battery was low; there wasn't more than fifteen seconds of conversation left.

"Maybe a couple of days. My phone's dying; I'll have to call you when I get back."

"You take care of yourself now, Ray. Don't forget to call."

"I won't. I love you, Mom."

"I love you too, sweetie. Whatever happened to that Valerie girl?"

"I'll tell you later. My phone's going to cut off." And then it did.

Her voice echoed in my ears. I sat on the cot, the cell phone in my left hand and the IV pump in my bandaged right. I stared back and forth between them. Now I was stripped of all defenses; reduced to a naked soul scrabbling with destiny on the muddy anvil of creation.

A gentle rain had started to fall, and I was torn between lying down and going outside. Slowing my metabolism might buy me a few extra hours; on the other hand the sweetness of life beckoned irresistibly. The muted colors outside the window seemed impossibly beautiful now. I didn't know how much longer it would be before things got ugly so decided to take what pleasure I could right here, right now. I tossed the pump into my duffel bag. I untaped my tubing, pulled the needle from my shoulder and felt a reckless thrill at being cut loose from all artificial support.

I had just gone downstairs when the front door opened and Valerie walked in with an armful of flowers. She had bathed somewhere outside the house and was dressed in overalls and Duane's faded work shirt. Her hair was damp and braided loosely down her back. We stood facing each other, and finally she spoke in a quavering voice.

"What's going on?"

"My pump's broken and my infection is back. It's been over a day now."

She looked stricken.

"I need to get to a hospital, Valerie. The only thing that can save me is an intravenous antibiotic."

That brought her back in typical style. "That ain't the only thing," she said almost defiantly.

"It's the only thing I know of," I said quietly. "I was just thinking to go outside and enjoy the rain, enjoy the garden for a little while."

I saw she understood everything I was thinking, and although I didn't understand it, I knew what she was thinking too. I really didn't want an argument and tried to preempt it.

"Prayer is like a placebo, Val. It only works if you believe in it. Right now I have a bacterial infection, and those bacteria don't believe in anything except reproducing themselves."

Tears welled in her eyes. "It wouldn't cost you nothing to try it."

"Why should I go out on my knees? Everyone has to die, and I'd rather die a man than a beggar."

"Well, you ain't dead yet, Bwana, so don't go tempting fate. Maybe a little humility would make you more of a man." She sniffed, honking, and angrily wiped her face on her sleeve.

"Maybe you're right," I said. "It's just something I never learned to do."

She went into the kitchen, put the flowers in the sink and opened cupboards until she found a pitcher. She began arranging the flowers in it. "Duane will be back soon. He'll know what to do. Just don't wander off and get yourself in another fix." Her face was stubborn and full of concentration as she peeled leaves from the stems of black-eyed susans.

"I won't go farther than the garden," I promised. "I just hope he won't mind taking me back to Harlan. I really need a hospital, Val."

She gave me a look so full of sorrow it nearly broke my heart. "I can't tell Duane what to do. But he'll think of something." She turned back to her flowers, and I knew it was to hide her face.

I went onto the porch and listened to the rain. Right now it was the most beautiful sound I could imagine. I couldn't fathom the expression I had just seen on Val's face, but she seemed to believe Duane would help. I knew he was a practical man, and didn't figure him to share her blind faith, although he had said a rough grace over our meal last night. Val's father was the one who seemed more fanatical. I wondered if he knew the extent of his brother's horticultural enterprises.

I walked to the garden. Normally I would not prefer to walk uncovered in the rain but everything was different now. Drops of

251

water stood on every leaf and petal, and beaded the skins of tomatoes and peppers. The pitter-patter around me seemed to be the sound of quiet work being done, akin somehow to the hammer of a cobbler or the stitch of a tailor; only this was nature's workshop. Things were growing—it was uncanny, I could actually *feel* it.

Val's claim that Duane paid attention to his plants was plausible to me now. I realized they were aware of me, and giving me permission to be here. Although they were benign there was nothing passive or dormant about them. I picked a small tomato and before putting it to my lips felt an odd compulsion to acknowledge it. My thanks was only a thought, but somehow it was understood. When the fruit burst and its flavor exploded in my mouth all my senses tingled, and I knew the transaction had been an honest one. What would it be like to live a whole life like this? I didn't understand whether my heightened sensitivity was due to this place, or if something inside me was changing. Either way, I decided, if there were a heaven something about it would be like this.

I turned my face up to the rain. My shirt was clinging to my skin and my jeans were getting soaked. The wetness didn't bother me but the growing pain in my arm anchored me to the heaviness of physical reality. I looked over the garden and felt a wave of unspeakable sadness—not for myself and the complications that had brought me here, but because this was the reality we were supposed to know. The garden, even in myth and metaphor, was what we were put here to tend, yet so few would ever approach it. We were too busy making names for ourselves, plowing through the earth's resources and fighting over inconsequentials. However I felt about Duane's illegal activities, he knew more of the garden than most people ever would. I felt the plants telling me it was time to go, not to linger, and reluctantly made my way back to the house.

I took a much-needed shower and changed into dry clothes. By the time Duane's truck rumbled up the drive two hours later I was very sick. I was sitting in the living room rocker, feverish but too proud to lie down. My fingertips were turning blue. Valerie laid cool cloths on my forehead while my shoulders were wrapped in a quilt to keep me from shivering. I was too dizzy to keep my eyes open but afraid to drift off for fear of waking up in some unknown purgatory worse than Lehigh Valley Hospital or worse still, not at all.

When the door opened and Duane walked in it was like watching a movie on a tiny screen. I could see and hear everything except it all seemed far away from me somehow. Duane was carrying a box of peaches that he put on the table, and there was a young woman behind him Valerie greeted with some reserve. I felt nothing from her at all; she seemed flat and almost completely withdrawn. Duane remarked on Val's flowers and when he turned his attention to me I felt a heightened sense of awareness. He walked over, stooped and gently placed a rough hand on the side of my neck.

"You warm enough, brother?"

I nodded.

"He needs a hospital, Duane," Val said. I was relieved that she was pressing my cause; I didn't have the strength to do it myself.

"He needs more than that," said Duane, peering at my eyes. He stood back up and turned to Val. "Your mama needs to see you now."

"Duane! His pump is broke and he needs antibiotics."

"I know about that. And we're going to help him, ain't we?" His voice was kind but I saw he was on another track.

"Duane, let me take him. Please?" Val implored.

"Go on, girl. Your mama's waiting for you." He abruptly turned gruff. "You come on back here for dinner. Let Ardie look to him now."

I realized they had been through this argument already. I remembered hearing Ardie's name spoken last night as I was falling asleep. Nothing made sense but it was pointless to reason; Duane was in control. I saw Val's eyebrows bunch in the middle, but before any tears spilled she whirled around and walked out the door. Moments later I heard Duane's truck start and rumble away down the drive. I felt utterly abandoned.

Duane leaned over the rocker and said, "Come on, brother, let's get you laid out." He pulled my left arm over his shoulder and stood

253

me up, just as Gloria Plum had. He walked me to his room and pushed the door open with his foot. I was too weak to resist and when we got to his bedside he lifted me easily and laid me down like a rag doll. I was sure this was the place I would die, and so disheartened Val had deserted me that I couldn't speak.

~

A fever can be a scary thing. It can squeeze thoughts into strange shapes, distorting perceptions of time, space and even basic facts. When I'd lost it at the Plums I was completely unprepared, but this time I was on guard. I was doggedly hanging onto consciousness for fear of the alternatives. All my senses were still functioning; right now everything around me seemed uncomfortably sharp and bright.

In the directional light from the window I could discern the joints in the sheetrock of the ceiling. I heard low conversation from the kitchen, but couldn't tell what was being said. My arm throbbed while the rain outdoors seemed to be lessening. A fly buzzed somewhere in the room but my eyes couldn't find it. I wanted to open the screen and let it out, to feel the outside air once more, but wasn't strong enough to attempt it. I heard Duane going out the back door, and then for a while I heard kitchen sounds—running water, a pan on the stove. My body ached all over and I began to feel nauseated. My priority began to shift from staying alert to holding on to my guts. Right about the time I would have welcomed almost any anodyne there was a tap at the door.

I turned my head and there stood the woman Duane had brought home. She looked no older than twenty. She was of mixed race, with smooth caramel skin and unruly blond hair pulled straight back. Her features were sensuous and slightly exotic; it was a woman's face, but something about it was so wide open and childlike she looked almost alien. I lifted my head from the bed to stare. She met my gaze and I realized she was waiting to be invited in.

"Come," I said, lying back but still staring.

"I made tea for you," she said in a shy voice, and then I noticed

254

the jar in her hands.

"Could I have some water?" I said. Right now the thought of anything else made my stomach churn.

She put the jar on Duane's nightstand, knelt down and peered at my face. I noticed with a start that her eyes were two different colors—one was brown and the other nearly green. Her scrutiny wasn't intrusive; instead she seemed contemplative. She ran a soft hand over my forehead and then pressed it to her throat, appraising.

"You need some tea," she concluded, sounding like a child trying to mimic an adult. "My name is Ardelene Younger but you can call me Ardie. You better drink this now." I changed my mind about her shyness. I did not want tea but she was insistent, and helped me to a sitting position. When she put the tea to my lips it tasted so hideous I nearly gagged.

"No thanks," I said weakly, pushing it back.

"Go on, mister, you need it," she urged, pushing it back at me. I recoiled from it but she guided it back firmly to my face.

I looked over the jar at her and for a moment felt like weeping. Now I was making a whistle stop at old age on my train to the grave—taking orders from a child, and there wasn't a thing I could do about it. I took another sip and shuddered. She patted me on the shoulder and smiled. "Drink a little more," she encouraged.

I took a mouth-filling gulp, swallowed it and gagged horribly but by some miracle it stayed down. I handed the jar back to her. "Water," I begged. The inside of my mouth had never tasted so foul.

"Take ye another." She looked at me sympathetically but her voice was firm, and she held the jar in front of my face. I turned my head to the side. "Just one more," she insisted.

In despair I grabbed the jar and downed one more gulp, and my diaphragm felt like it had been punched upward from the inside. My shoulders heaved and I retched violently. I felt like I had woken inside a nightmare—it wasn't enough just to die in a strange place; I also would be tormented by a creature so innocent I couldn't fight back. She took the jar and set it on the nightstand.

"Water, please," I rasped. I could hardly breathe without retching

255

and felt another heave coming, but then she laid her hands on my neck. She stared into my face with her strange eyes and the convulsions in my throat simply stopped. I felt my diaphragm slowly unclenching as I leaned back on the headboard. When she finally removed her hands my mouth still tasted awful, but my insides felt stable.

"Is that better?"

"I think so." I felt the rest of me gradually relaxing.

"Good. I'll get some water now."

She stood and left the room, and I began taking cautious inventory of myself. My muscles still ached with fever but my stomach no longer churned. My bowels, which had been highly unsettled until moments ago, felt fine. The throbbing in my arm involved my whole body now but my mind was clear and my peripheral vision had returned. The taste in my mouth was all that remained of whatever had just happened. I was turning it over in my mind when Ardie returned with my water. She sat beside me on the bed while I drank, and after washing the terrible taste from my mouth I asked, "What did you do to me?"

She didn't seem to hear, and took my bandaged hand in both of hers. "How did you hurt your hand?" she asked.

"It was burned."

"Can I see?"

I looked at her closely. Her wide eyes were on me again and for a few seconds they startled me. Was it my imagination, or had I seen their colors change? One was still brown and the other nearly green, but while I watched it seemed a current passed between them, causing tiny fluctuations in their hue. Looking into them was like peering into sun-dappled water; I couldn't see the bottom. One part of my mind kept telling me such things weren't possible, but there was no mistaking what had happened just moments ago while those eyes were on me. I nodded, and she began unwrapping my bandage.

The inner layers of gauze clung to my skin as my hand, swollen and grotesque, began to be exposed. I stared as Ardie's slender fingers rolled the bandage away. I always had taken pride in having strong, rugged hands; now my right hand—a man's very symbol of purpose in the world—was not only useless but had poisoned my whole body. I had been granted a reprieve from that but hadn't valued it properly. Now I would gladly give my hand to save my life, but things weren't that simple any more.

Ardie gasped in surprise as she lifted the last bit of gauze from my palm. She held my hand like a sacred thing. "Look," she cried, "It's like the Lord's!"

I looked, and saw only what I'd been seeing every time—a wound that wouldn't heal, a source of constant aggravation and very probably the cause of my demise. All around the pit in the center of my palm the skin had blackened ominously.

"That's my burn," I said.

"But don't you see? It's just like Jesus' hand!" She held it with a tenderness approaching reverence.

I couldn't imagine such a thing. "I'm nothing like Jesus; my name is Ray."

"But mister Ray—" she stopped and looked plaintively at me "—you're a believer, ain't you?"

"No, I don't think so. Not like you."

She pondered that, and then said in her child-like voice, "Then he brought you here."

I hardly had the heart to respond. "I don't think so," I said. "I'm just a guy whose truck broke down in the wrong place."

"No, if he brought you then you're in the right place."

Suddenly I snapped. "Listen, Ardie, I have a bacterial infection that will kill me if I don't get to a hospital. Nobody seems to understand I'm stuck here; I'm dying, for God's sake. Did Duane tell you that?" I tried to put some rage into it but my strength was nearly gone. I sank back into the pillow, despairing.

Tears spilled from her eyes and I felt my last bit of will dissolving in them. She cradled my hand and I could feel heat coursing down my arm into her cool hands. "Poor mister Ray," she said. "You got a terrible fever but you ain't going to die. The Lord brought you here for a reason."

I tried to think of one good reason—even one half-assed, lame and stupid reason—for being stuck in this place and came up blank. And then, although it opposed every principle of logic in which I believed, I finally just submitted to her. Ardie looked and sounded like someone's bastard stepchild to me, yet who was I but a dead man talking? There was a kindness and pure simplicity about her that made me ashamed to argue any more. And to further confound my logic her touch was making me feel better somehow. It had a soothing quality that eased my fever's aching. I could think of worse people to have around me on my way out the big door.

What happened next completely shredded all that remained of my precious logic. It was stranger by far than anything I could have dreamed in my most fevered imagination. Ardie still cradled my hand in hers but seemed to be growing more listless by the minute, and before long she curled up on the bed beside me. "I never done it like this before," she whispered, "but it needs it." She opened the top of her dress, pulled my hand inside and cupped my palm over her breast. She closed her eyes and seemed to meditate.

Within seconds my arm felt like a conduit carrying heat straight into her breast. There was no pain on my part; instead there was a sensation more like a low electric current. I felt her nipple swell, filling the pit in the center of my palm. Beads of perspiration formed on her forehead. I freed my left arm to touch her, and was alarmed to find her skin hotter than mine. By some means beyond comprehension Ardie was pulling the fever out of my body into hers. I tried to draw my hand away but she clutched it more tightly to her breast. "Don't—it all needs to come," she whispered.

"But how about you?" I was frightened for her.

Her strange eyes opened. "I'll be alright," she murmured.

"Are you sure?"

She nodded, and her eyes closed again.

I felt my hand becoming wet and sticky and realized with a shock her breast was flowing with milk—and then to my confusion I found myself aroused. I moved closer and gently kissed her hot forehead and she groaned. I tasted her salt and smelled her skin and hair and became almost unbearably turned on. I kissed her again and she moaned "No," but kept my palm pressed tightly against her.

By now Ardie's breast was a hand-sized orb of pure heat under my palm. But instead of pain I felt a clean white light coming from deep inside her, rifling up my arm, flushing the enemy troops inside my body and annihilating them on contact. How such a thing could happen was beyond all reason, yet somehow I knew no bacterial infection could stand against it. I realized that I would live, and knew even further that no more antibiotics would be necessary. I lay back, ashamed of my sexual weakness, and finally understood that I was receiving a miracle.

I lost track of time after that and don't know how long it was before Duane came in, or in what configuration he found us. He let me sleep undisturbed. Val later told me he had to carry Ardie out to his truck and back into her family's house in another coal mining community two mountain ridges away.

I didn't waken until after nine the next morning. Sunlight filled the room and I had no idea where I was. Then I looked out the window and saw my truck and Val's trailer and vaguely remembered coming here, but not why I was in Duane's room. I couldn't recall any part of the day before.

CHAPTER 19

I found my duffel bag at the foot of Duane's bed and took it to the bathroom to shave and shower. I relieved myself, and was amazed at the copious stream of dark urine that flowed from my bladder. After an interminable piss it turned clear for the last ten seconds or so. I never had seen such a phenomenon before but felt fine so I flushed it away, somewhat puzzled.

I turned on the hot water, washed my hands and reached in my bag for my shaving materials. I saw the IV pump but paid it no attention. Only when I began applying shaving gel to my face did I realize with a start there was no bandage on my right hand. I stared at it. Not only my hand but also my entire arm appeared perfectly normal. There was no soreness, not even a hint of muscle atrophy. Had I been dreaming that it was hurt? There wasn't any sign of injury until I rinsed my palm and looked at it. There in the center was a smooth, perfectly round depression. The sight of it made my heart race, and I felt a sense of urgency to understand what it signified.

But it was futile as trying to pull a dream from the haze of half-sleep. I was sure I'd been hurt somehow; I thought I remembered being in a hospital recently but couldn't connect the dots. I began to question my wakefulness, and wondered if this was just a vivid dream. I remembered hearing somewhere that you can never control the light in a dream. I looked at the fixture over the sink and reached up to turn the bulb in the socket. My wet hand hissed on the hot glass and I jerked it away; then I found the switch and flipped the light off and on. I looked in the mirror and studied my face under the drying foam. Everything and nothing was familiar.

I shaved and showered in a state of mild confusion. The shower felt wonderful, and when I turned off the hot for the last minute the cold mountain water hammering against my skin made me certain I was awake. After drying I looked in my duffel for clean underwear and again saw the IV pump. I picked it up and saw a deep gouge across the face of it. Whatever the thing was, it was broken. I tossed it back and saw my cell phone. Good—I could find the last person I had called and figure things out. I tried it but the phone was dead. What now? Valerie's face came to mind and I thought she was somewhere here with me but the circumstances of everything were unclear. I was unsure of anything except being wide-awake and uncontrollably thirsty.

I drank deeply from the bathroom tap and then dressed, walked to the kitchen and drank two more glasses of water from the sink. Everything was neat and clean—no sign of breakfast anywhere. I knew this was Duane's house but didn't understand how I knew that. Had we even met? Ah—we must have arrived late last night; Valerie was still in her trailer sleeping. Yes, of course—and the day was getting away from me. I needed to get back to my crew, back to work in Pennsylvania. Time to shake a leg, get ready to go. Valerie's trailer was still hitched to the truck, but that wouldn't take long to remedy. Why was it so late already?

I walked out to the front porch and was astonished to see a man standing on a wooden bench with his head buried in the engine compartment of my truck. My driver's side door was crumpled at the hinge and hung crookedly in the frame. What the blazes was going on?

"Excuse me—" I blurted, and the man's head popped up. I noticed that his face was horribly scarred, but a big grin spread across it as he saw me on the porch.

"Mornin', brother," he said cheerfully, wiping his hands on a rag.

"Is there a problem?" I said.

"It don't look like you got a problem." He hopped down from the bench and regarded me with amusement. "Put her there," he said. I took his hand and we pumped for a good ten seconds, both of us squeezing harder until it felt almost like a contest of wills. He was strong as any man on my crew.

"You got a right good grip there, brother," he finally laughed.

"You must be Duane," I said.

"I am," he replied.

261

"What happened to my truck?" I heard the door to Valerie's trailer open and close on the other side.

"Nothing but a burnt head gasket. Could a been worse, I reckon."

"I'm afraid I don't understand," I said.

Just at that time Valerie walked around the end of the trailer and gave a little gasp.

"Looky here, girl. Don't this man look fine? Why don't you fix him some breakfast?" Duane said.

"Ray, are you all right? Oh my goodness, look at you—just look—" and then she began laughing and crying all at once.

"What, is something the matter?"

"No, there is nothing the matter, you lummox," she laughed in an unsteady voice. "Let me see your hand."

I held it out to her. She felt the depression in my palm and looked up at me. "Does it hurt?"

"No. But I don't understand what's going on—I'm not sure whether I just woke up or I'm having the weirdest dream of my life."

"Are you hungry?"

"I'm starved."

"What are you waiting for, girl?" Duane said, still laughing. "Take that man in there and fix him something to eat. Get him some coffee and some of that good deer sausage—that'll wake him up right quick."

I followed Val into the house. The front door had hardly closed when she threw her arms around me and began kissing me madly. Her face was wet with tears and her hair smelled like exotic wood and spices and before I could comprehend a thing I was enormously turned on. I pulled her hard against me and when she felt my arousal I thought she would devour me right there. We were recklessly approaching the point of no return when she pushed away and said "Not here."

She peeked around the edge of the window and pulled herself together. "I'll put some coffee on while you go up to the barn and get some eggs," she announced, and marched to the kitchen where

262

she banged some pans around in search of the percolator. She was still breathing hard as I went out the back door.

I didn't understand how I knew where to go, but somehow found my way straight to the hens' roosts. I had two eggs in each hand when Valerie appeared in the door of the barn. She snatched them from me, set them on a crossbeam by the door and pulled me behind a partition piled with straw. Her mouth locked onto mine as we tumbled down on the bales.

Both of us were on fire and there was no time to waste. She tugged my jeans loose while I unfastened her overalls, and when we both had kicked off enough clothes she began to guide my entry. As her hand circled me my whole body convulsed with a sensation I never had felt before. It was almost like an orgasm, only instead of being abrupt it was like a wave that slowly receded, leaving my skin prickling with pleasure. It was all the more remarkable in that I was still fully loaded and not even close to coming. A low moan came from Val as I entered her.

As a matter of discretion I've never been inclined to talk about my sexual encounters, but this was unlike anything in my experience. I already knew Valerie to be an unusually passionate lover—she climaxed easily, and once her motor started she had no inhibitions. But this time there was an animal intensity that passed anything I had known. She bucked and clutched me desperately, making sounds like a wounded creature. Before I knew it our heads were jammed into the corner, and when we both came two extraordinary things happened almost at once.

Once again there was an exchange of emotion between us so raw that it transcended the physical. Like before, it seemed to come from the center of each of us and envelop us so completely that nothing could be hidden. It was a nakedness more profound than any exposure of skin could approximate. This time I didn't fight it. The result was as if I'd been watching the reflection of stars on the surface of a lake on a warm night and just fallen in. And suddenly I was soaring among the stars, one with the stars, the stars were part of my being and Valerie was the center of the whole universe. And

263

then I felt our bodies shudder and it seemed the whole barn shook, and there was a metallic clang as something heavy fell to the ground on the other side of the wall.

The crash startled us back to reality and we scrambled madly to get our clothes on. I hurriedly picked pieces of straw from Val's hair as she buttoned her overalls; then she kissed me deeply one more time and we headed back out into the day. I picked up the eggs from the crossbeam and followed her to the house energized, exuberant and as totally void of understanding as I've ever been.

~

Before going through the back door Val turned around and grabbed my shirt with both hands and yanked me close. "Do you realize that was worth waiting all your life for?" she said.

"Will I ever be the same again?"

"Do you ever want to be?" She stared into my eyes and then whirled around and entered the back porch. She picked a tomato, a green pepper and a yellow squash from the windowsill and we walked into the kitchen.

I sliced the vegetables while Valerie broke the eggs into a bowl and began whipping them for an omelet. She was humming to herself, and when she caught me glancing quizzically at her she shook her head and declared, "Mister Brauner, you are something else."

"Else than what?" I asked.

"Whoo-whee!" She threw her head back. "Listen to mister philosopher—he's back already." She shook her head and laughed quietly to herself. "Do you want some sausage? It's deer meat."

"Sure. I can't remember the last time I was this hungry. In fact, I can't remember anything. I'm all confused."

Val dropped her fork into the bowl and turned to look at me. "You're not kidding, are you?"

"No. I woke up this morning and nothing hooks up, Val. I know this is Duane's place but don't even know how I know that. I don't

264

remember coming here."

"What else?"

"Well, while I was shaving the thought struck me that I was hurt, but I feel fine. It feels like I just woke up from the craziest dream. Except I can't remember what it was. Am I going nuts?"

Valerie covered my hand with hers. "No, you're not going nuts," she said thoughtfully. "You were real sick and you're better now. I think you should eat your breakfast and then I'll try to help you out."

"One thing now, if you don't mind."

"What?"

"Will you tell the truth if I ask you a dumb question?"

"I promise."

"Are we married?"

At that Valerie threw her head back and whooped with laughter.

"Never mind," I mumbled.

After eating the best breakfast of my life I helped Val clean up the dishes; then she poured the last of the coffee into my mug, sat down and began quizzing me about the day before. What was the weather like? Did I remember taking a walk? Did I meet anyone new? Every question drew a blank.

Then she went back to the day at the Plum's house when my hand had been burned. Recalling that experience was like pulling back the corner of a shroud, and it wasn't long before lights started coming back on. Each detail triggered another memory. The events at King's Tavern were like a monster waking in my mind. When she recounted our trip up the drive and how the truck had nearly been lost, our arrival here snapped into focus. It was almost like a circuit breaker had been reset; once my mind had been jogged I was relieved to find all my memories intact.

I indulged Valerie's account of finding me trussed up in the treetops after I'd walked into Duane's trap, and was relieved when she told me he hadn't been upset. I was hardly prepared for my recollection of Ardie, though. Val couldn't tell me much about that since she hadn't been there. But when I remembered those strange eyes, and what actually had happened in Duane's bedroom, I felt

265

embarrassed and humbled beyond words. Part of me still battled with disbelief, but the physical evidence was impossible to refute. Now I knew what that broken thing in my duffel bag was. Gratitude welled inside me and brought a lump to my throat. Ardie's milk had bathed my hand only yesterday, and studying it I realized there was not even a callus left on it. The skin was soft, supple and perfect.

Valerie knew something very personal had transpired between Ardie and me and seemed to not want to know any details. But I had a question for her. "Why did you want to take me to the hospital if you knew she could help me?"

She didn't answer right away. Finally she asked, "Do you remember the time you told me how innocent your big-shot lawyer's wife was?"

"Mrs. Plum? Yes, I remember."

"Well, Ardie really is innocent. She's probably the only person I know in the world who is."

"But why would you not want her to help me?"

"Ray, what you don't know is that little girl is going to be sick a long time after yesterday. She don't just miraculously heal people; she takes their sickness in her own body and somehow she always gets better. Don't ask me how. If your medicine was helping you then it would have saved her and her family a lot of trouble."

I didn't know what to say.

"One time she took a woman's rabies out of her, and she like to have died. They had to anoint her and prayed without ceasing a whole week before she could take a drink of water."

"What does anoint mean?"

"They put olive oil on her head like in the Bible times. It's a sign of faith and the Holy Ghost honors their faith."

"The Holy Ghost? What is that, Val?"

"It's the third person of the Godhead. The Father is too glorious for anyone to look upon, and since the Son gave himself to be a man he can't be everywhere, but the Holy Ghost can."

"Ah—how silly of me."

"Don't be getting smart. You want to deny the power of the Lord

266

after what happened to you?"

"No," I said quietly. "I don't deny anything. But how about what happened with you and me up in the barn? Was that the Holy Ghost too?"

Valerie blushed and dropped her eyes, and I felt a terrible anxiety churning inside. I knew that was a question I shouldn't have asked.

"No, that was something else. I don't rightly understand it myself. But I know it's a gift you ought not drag in the dirt." She looked at me again with her eyes like steel. "There ain't nobody I ever had that with in the whole world. After that I don't think it would be right to even try." She kept her eyes locked on mine. "Of course whatever you think is up to you."

~

When we went back out Val asked Duane if she could take his truck to visit her mother.

"I believe that's a right good idea," he said.

She turned to me. "Will you come with me?"

"I don't know; right now I'd probably be in the way." I tried to hide my discomfort at being put on the spot. I sensed Val's disappointment instantly but recoiled at the thought of a second helping of critical scrutiny and awkward conversation with her family. As out of place as I felt, at least up here there seemed to be less chance for unpleasant surprises than in that run-down neighborhood.

"In the way there or here, choose your pick," Val said.

"I'd rather stay and help with my truck, if Duane doesn't mind." I looked at him for encouragement.

"Whatever you want, brother," he shrugged.

Even as I felt Val's hurt and frustration they suddenly were swept away by her own will. She knew the only way of hiding her feelings was shifting gears in her head. It was a neat trick, I thought—too bad she hadn't done it well enough in Gladburg.

"Duane, can I take the dogs with me? Please?" Her eyes were

267

shining and this time I felt she wouldn't be disappointed. But he seemed more reluctant than I had expected.

"I don't know, girl. They ain't been off the place in a long time."

"Oh, come on, Duane – they'll love it. You know we used to ride everywhere together."

"I ain't worried about them—it's other people."

"We won't be anywhere but Daddy and Mamma's. Please?" Val's hands were folded to her chin and she was practically jumping up and down, and I could see Duane melting.

"Well, alright," he finally said. She threw her arms around his neck and kissed his cheek.

She whistled and seconds later the dogs were streaking up the drive. When she said, "Want to go for a ride, boys? In the truck?" they nearly jumped out of their skins. They raced around barking and leaping up at the door of the truck until Val opened it for them. They jumped in, woofing excitedly.

Duane laughed shaking his head and said, "Bring 'em back before dark."

She blew him another kiss as she started the truck, and we watched it rumble away down the drive with their silhouettes swaying from side to side until they turned the corner at the bottom of the meadow and were lost to sight.

We gazed down the empty drive and out over the mountains until we heard the sound of metal clanking as Val opened and closed the barricade. When Duane turned back to my truck I asked how it was going.

"I'd say you was lucky," he said in his deliberate manner. "Your heads ain't been hurt. Your gasket was cooked on one side, but I picked up another'n yesterday while you was a-playin with my bear trap up in the woods." He chuckled softly.

I noticed the ruined hose had been replaced, and when I looked closer saw the other hoses were new as well. "What else did you have to buy?" I asked.

He didn't reply, and I tried again. "What all did you replace?"

"Nothing but what needed it," he said, almost as if to himself.

"I'm grateful for your help," I said. "I never meant to be a burden."

"Ain't a burden at all, brother. I'm much obliged to you looking out for Valry." He kept his face buried in the engine. "It weren't no easy drive down here, I reckon."

"It wasn't bad. Just the last little stretch. Can I do anything to help?"

He didn't reply, and I realized there wasn't much to do except keep out of his way. Methodically he scraped remnants of burned gasket from my engine block with a piece of sharpened bone, then polished the milled surface with a solvent and a rag. After several minutes watching I broke the silence.

"I appreciate what you did for me, Duane."

"It weren't me," he said. I knew he didn't want to talk about it, but I had to ask one thing.

"Why did you bring Ardie to help me instead of taking me to the hospital?"

He waited a long time before answering. "I seen it in your eyes," he said.

"Seen what?"

"Sepsis."

To him it was like that answered everything, but to me it just opened up more questions. Before I could ask anything further he laid his polishing rag down and turned to me.

"You know I was in Vietnam."

"Yes."

"I seen it there. You was well poisoned when ye got here. By morning there was no help for it."

"You saved my life."

"No." He was emphatic. "It was the man upstairs."

It took me a minute to understand what he was saying. "I would like very much to thank that girl's family," I said.

"It wouldn't be no use for that."

"If it weren't for her I wouldn't be here."

"Then thank the Lord, brother. That's what they'd tell ye." His eyes were steady. "They're simple folk. Now they got to look to Ardie, so she can help the next one. You can't do nothing for them." He turned back to the engine.

The head itself had been cleaned and polished; it lay on a tarp covering the other side of the engine. Several cardboard boxes held pushrods, rocker arms and smaller parts. Duane meticulously screwed bolts into the engine block, noting how deeply they penetrated before extracting them and then counting threads. One bolt seemed to stick and turned with difficulty, even with wrench force applied. He unscrewed it and excused himself to the house. I expected him to return quickly, but after ten minutes he was still gone.

I went into the house and found it empty. I walked out the back door and up to the barn, and all was dead silence until a pair of hens darted clucking from their roosts. I looked behind the wall where Valerie and I had heard something fall at the climax of our lovemaking and nothing was there. Had that happened at all? I saw the bales of straw where we had lain. I poked my nose into the straw and sniffed deeply, then abruptly straightened up wondering what Duane would think if he saw me do such a thing. I looked up at the rafters and then all through the barn until I was satisfied nobody had seen me except the chickens and barn swallows swooping through the dusty air.

I was tempted to follow the path up into the woods a little ways, but then thought better of it. There was nothing but silence that way anyway. Where was Duane? I walked back down to the truck and things were still untouched. It was a beautiful afternoon and I had too much energy to hang around doing nothing, so decided to walk down the drive.

~

The meadow below Duane's place was alive with birds and buzzing insects; in the humidity of the afternoon it seemed a natural factory for the production of earthy essences. I tried to identify

270

different aromas, from wild onion to honeysuckle and sassafras to decaying leaves and faint essence of skunk, and finally gave up. So much life was happening, and I realized how often these things escaped my notice. I recalled my walk through the garden yesterday and the awareness I had sensed in the plants around me. I felt a similar awareness here but in a more muted way. The meadow was a garden for other creatures. A small rabbit watched me from its perch atop a weathered stump. When I stopped and said, "tsk tsk" it stood on its hind legs with nose twitching. I laughed and it disappeared into the undergrowth, and I continued my amble.

After the drive curved left around the edge of the woods the house was no longer in view. Several gnarled apple trees appeared below the woods, hung with dimpled, lumpy fruit not quite ripe. I pulled one and bit into it, and it was spicy and delicious as it was ugly. This brief strip of woods was mostly pine, sprinkled with a few locust and sassafras trees. The fruit energized me and when the barricade appeared in the drive ahead I took a running jump and cleared it easily by several inches. I looked eastward out over the succession of mountain ridges to the horizon. Hard to the southeast beyond the power lines the lump of Black Mountain was visible, and as my eyes swung left to the other end of the horizon the disturbing, unnatural sight of former mountains turned upside-down made something catch in my throat.

Before long I was nearing the edge of the meadow where we had left the truck two evenings before. On the high side of the drive tall grass fell on itself in graceful sheaves. Tiny purple asters winked and nodded through the flowing green. On the lower side a thicket of honeysuckle and poison ivy made a barrier to the hardwood growth below. Surprisingly there seemed to be no kudzu on Duane's property. Continuing around the perimeter of the meadow the drive curved left and inclined up as it approached the saddle in the mountain. As I gained the top, the Coalbright pit appeared ahead through the trees.

When the lane twisted away from the meadow I was startled by how steeply it dropped into the woods. It was hard to believe I had

271

attempted to pull Val's trailer up such a grade, and even harder to believe we'd actually made it. I walked to the first switchback and heard the sound of a motor in the distance. I was curious to see the spot where we had almost lost the truck, and was nearly to the second switchback when I realized a vehicle was coming up Duane's drive. I rounded the bend and saw a small four-wheeler barreling up the lane toward me. When it came within hailing distance it slowed, and before I had gotten ten feet past the curve it stopped right in front of me.

The driver was a beefy guy about thirty years old dressed in camouflage pants and a Metallica T-shirt. His sandy hair was cut high and tight, military style, and his skin was stretched taut across a face that looked oddly flat. He stared at me without expression for about ten seconds as his engine idled; then he switched it off.

"Who the fuck are you?" he asked. His voice was dull and hard; he reminded me of one of my father's particularly unpleasant colleagues from long ago, only with an extreme hillbilly accent.

"I'm Ray Brauner," I said. "Who are you?"

He dismounted from his machine and dug into his pocket for a pouch of tobacco. He pinched a big wad and stuffed it up between his cheek and gum. His fat knuckles stretched his mouth into a grotesque shape until it was in place while his eyes never left mine. It was a gross performance that would have been almost comical except for the unfriendliness radiating from him. He ignored my question.

"Whatha fuck are you doin here?" he asked.

"I might ask you the same thing," I said.

"You drive a white pickup?"

"Could be. What's your drift, pal?"

"Whatha fuck is that? You drive a white pickup, or not?"

"Yes, I drive a white pickup," I said, starting to flush with anger. "If you've got some business with Duane I won't stand in your way; otherwise I think you'd better be going."

At that he started to laugh. At first I thought maybe he had loosened up but then he stopped and said, "You think I'm some

272

kinda chump? He's down by the mine; I seen his truck there ten minutes ago with his dogs."

He moved closer. His mouth was working the wad and he had a mean look in his eyes. "Where's Valry?"

"You know so much, why don't you tell me?" Now I was beginning to understand the shape of things.

"You making fun of me?" he asked in an incredulous tone. A dribble of brown appeared at the corner of his mouth.

"No, I'm asking you to leave."

"The fuck you are. You're fuckin her, ain't you?" He advanced another step, and I took a step backward. "That's why you're scared, ain't it?"

"Actually, you stink," I said, "and I think you ought to leave."

"You're fuckin with the wrong man, punk."

"Excuse me?"

"I can take any man in this god damn place, and I think you been fuckin Valry." He exposed teeth like rotting corn. "This ain't your place and it ain't your day. There ain't even nobody around to help you, fuckhead." He leaned forward and spat a brown gob at my feet.

I never even thought about it; when his eyes dropped I hit him. My right arm flashed out and my fist connected with his face so hard it scared me. His head snapped up and he staggered back with one arm flailing; then he tripped over a root in the lane and went down on his seat. He cupped a hand to his face with blood running down his arm. His head wobbled as I stared unbelieving, and then he came back to life.

He wiped the blood on his fatigues and shook his head to clear it. As he scrambled to his feet I saw his nose looked like a rosebud that had been stepped on. The lower half of his face was bright with blood, and there was a strange light in his eyes I had never seen before in anyone so close to me. Suddenly his right hand, which he had used to push off the ground, whipped around and the hair on my neck stood up. In it was a big knife pointed at me.

My old sensei's wisdom leaped in my memory, and the one principle he had drilled into his karate students through all the

273

painful evenings of drills, forms and combinations. Combinations. When you're trapped in a threatening situation you never hit someone just once. You use combinations; you overwhelm them until they are incapacitated. It served no purpose now to think what I might have followed that punch with. Clearly there had been a window of opportunity big enough to steer a truck through, but I had just stood there gaping.

In the dojo we had gone through the motions against empty hands, batons, staves and knives and now, too late, I understood the value of doing a thing over and over until you are too exhausted to think. Because that's the point when action becomes internalized, and so automatic that execution no longer requires thought. Thought just slows you down; in a fight there's little time to think—only to act. I thought about getting inside his arc, I thought about trapping his arm and going for his throat, but all the thinking paralyzed me; I wasn't trained. I was just staring this animal in the face while all his lights came back on.

"You just signed your own death warrant, fuckhead," he said in a soft voice. "Only now I'm going to hurt you first." His mouth was purple and the logo on his shirt was turning that way. "You want to try that trick again? Come on, fuckhead."

He advanced slowly, gesturing with his left hand for me to come on. I tried to use my peripheral vision to find anything I could use for a weapon or a shield. A stick, a rock—anything at all. I dared not take my eyes off his. That was the last scrap of wisdom I had from my training, and I was damned if I'd give that up. As my feet sensed the ground under me I had one idea. It was flaky but right now there was nothing else.

"You're losing your ride," I said.

"What are you talking about?" he sneered.

"Your little toy truck." I pointed behind him. "You must have left it out of gear."

I saw a flicker of doubt in his eyes, but then he turned to look back at the four-wheeler. It was all I needed; as his eyes left mine I quickly stooped and grabbed a rock in each hand. Too late he realized his mistake but now I had an equalizer. Two of them, in fact.

I hefted the rock in my right hand and we stared at each other for several seconds and then a change came over his face. His eyes got wide and his mouth fell open. He seemed to be focusing on something behind me. A tremor began in his hands and the fire behind his eyes went out.

"Wh—why, Duwayne," he said, "I thought you was over at the mine." He began backing up and fumbled to put the knife away, but his hands were shaking and it rattled to the ground behind him. I whipped around and saw Duane walking slowly toward us, hands loose, expressionless. I looked back at the man.

"Me and mister, ah, the mister, here, we was just having a little talk. Just a little talk, that's all." His hands were empty now and he looked pale around the eyes. I backed off to the side of the lane and watched.

"You remember what I told you about comin round here?" Duane's voice was clipped and tight.

"Ah—yes sir, I do." The man looked stricken. "I ain't never been up here neither, Duwayne, have I? You know I ain't."

"Go away, Hadley. Don't you never come on this place again."

"Yessir." Hadley was nearly hyperventilating. "Yessir, I promise."

He began walking backward again, and when Duane said "Git!" he turned like he'd been stung and ran for his four-wheeler.

Duane stooped to pick up the knife. He took the blade between his thumb and forefinger and I saw an odd, faraway look in his eyes. He drew back and just before releasing it turned on the ball of his foot. The knife disappeared into the woods; I never heard it land. I saw just enough of its flight to understand Duane could have put that knife anywhere in Hadley's body he chose—with a velocity that would have shattered bone.

Hadley jumped on his machine and looked like a cartoon as he backed it around and careened down the lane. I felt my shoulders relax, then remembered the rocks in my hands and let them fall to the ground. We listened to the sound of the four-wheeler as it disappeared around the curve and down the mountain. I looked at

275

Duane and saw a tired, ancient look on his face. He seemed lost in thought, but as we began trudging up the drive he said, "You done good."

Not many words passed between us the rest of the afternoon but somehow a barrier had melted. There was an ease that transcended any kind of talk, and by simple gestures he let me know exactly what to do to speed the work on my truck along. By the time we heard Valerie rumbling up the drive the head was back on my engine. Many smaller things remained to finish the job, but they would wait until tomorrow.

CHAPTER 20

After a simple supper we went onto the porch to enjoy the breeze. Duane and Valerie sat in an old metal glider up by the wall and I took an empty rocker. Nimrod and Jehu paced circles on the floor and collapsed into languid, sighing lumps at our feet. By now the mountains had turned from green to blue and evening was coming on. A wood thrush was singing his heart out in the meadow while a chunk of moon the color of chalk rode up the deepening sky. Tiny lights were winking on here and there across the horizon by the time we were settled. The glider creaked gently as Val pushed against a piece of log upended for a footstool.

"Whoo-whee," she sighed.

"Where was the explosion?" Duane asked. At first I had no idea what he was talking about.

"In the number four hole," Val said. "The company said it was methane but Daddy was talking like someone set it on purpose."

"Lordy, lordy." Duane shook his head.

"They never sent nobody down to look. They just dumped a big gob pile in front so nobody could get in."

Duane said nothing.

"Daddy said they wanted it to blow so they could collect insurance on it."

"They ain't going to collect squat." Duane's voice was hard. "They want to close it all down so they can turn everyone out. You mark my words."

Now the conversation began to pull into focus. I didn't know whether to feel relieved or disappointed that our earthshaking experience that morning had been partly the result of an underground explosion. At least I hadn't been imagining things.

"Can I ask a naïve question?" I said.

"Sure," Duane answered.

"What's the name of this place?"

"You know that already," Val said.

"I saw 'Hurt' in town, and 'Heart' on the sign at the mine."

A look passed between them, and then Val said to Duane, "You tell him. He won't believe nothing I say about down here."

"I believe you," I said. "It just took a while to understand."

"Well, brother," Duane said thoughtfully, "that goes back a ways. Do you know about the union troubles here?"

"Not much. I've heard things were bad."

"The first of it was long before my time," said Duane. "A man named Applebaum started the Coalbright Mining Company in nineteen and twenty-four, and he named the town Heart, when they found all the coal in the heart of these here mountains. There was some terrible times when the unions come in. Back then the coal bosses would rather kill a man than give him any rights. But after Applebaum died his son struck a deal with the United Mine Workers and things got better for a spell.

"Then the big companies started buying up mines with the most coal. Duke Power got Coalbright, and the new management signed a contract with a different union. When times got rough they wouldn't stand with the miners.

"Now Coalbright owned half the town, right down the mountain to the middle of it, and they controlled everything on their side. Nobody that lived in their houses could say a word against the company. They couldn't buy anywhere but in the company store. They had spies a-watchin. If a man or woman bought even a pair of shoelaces from the five and dime they could be turned right out of their homes. And oncet a man got the black lung he couldn't work, nor get enough benefits to live on. The company turned them out as well. Said their houses was for working men, not for retirement.

"In nineteen and sixty-six the miners started a petition to go back to the UMWA, and there was talk about new strikes. I seen nothing but trouble ahead and signed up the next year for Vietnam. I went away for nigh on six years."

Duane's voice was slow and deliberate, almost hypnotic. By now it was nearly dark, but I could see his brooding shadow. He was bent forward with his hands extended before him, like a man in prayer, except they moved outward occasionally to accent what he was saying. Valerie was rapt, listening with her head cocked slightly. She pushed on the upended log, rocking the glider gently as the dogs dozed at our feet.

"When I come back to Heart it was the fall of nineteen and seventy-three. Lord, I was happy to be done with that war. I didn't care to be fighting another'n back at home, but the company was a-diggin in against the miners, and it was like a kettle that was bound to boil over. You could feel it in the air, plain as wind before a storm. With everything that was a-goin on I wasn't much fit for society nohow. I found me a little place up on the mountain yonder past the town. I had a lean-to and a cave with a spring, and a little thicket of mountain laurel around me, and I hunkered down.

"Come April there was a big strike and the company took it bad. They said if the men wasn't working they had no rights, and they evicted ever blessed one off their land. Gave 'em two weeks notice.

"When two weeks passed not half the people had left. They had no place, you see. They just had no place at all to go. When the strike went on and nothing happened, some who left even come back. And then the third week there come a big rain, and it rained nigh on three days. The second night of the rain is when they sent the bulldozers down. I heard them a-comin; I was layin up the hill watching.

"They had men pound on the door of every house and pull the people out. Gave 'em five minutes to gather their belongings and get out. Lordy, it was terrible. Women and babies crying, the men so surprised they had no fight in them. And the men from the company had carbines; they was shooting up the houses even while they was a-pullin the people out. Brother, even with all I done in Vietnam it was a shameful thing I seen that night."

Duane went quiet for a long time. Valerie stopped rocking the glider and we sat in stillness as crickets and cicadas thrummed in the meadow. One of the dogs moaned; then the other jerked awake and nibbled at an itch. Val reached down to stroke them and they fell still. When Duane began speaking again his voice was cold.

"After that the dozers went to work. They was lined up at the

279

end of town, and when they come through they just scraped everything on their side of it to the ground. They pushed all the cars that was left into the creek, and half the houses too.

"The sound of it was awful. I could hear the men driving them a-whoopin and a-hollerin and knew most of them was drunk. I reckoned in the dark I could pull most of them off their machines and drive them into the creek afore they got me, but it was too late to save a blessed thing. And I knew I had kilt enough already. By God, that was the hardest thing I ever did not do."

I sat stunned. Those old foundations had haunted me the moment I saw them.

"You never told me you was there," Val said.

"Lord, there's many a thing I never told you, girl. And there's many a thing I'd never tell another soul."

After another long silence he answered the question I was thinking.

"Not a blessed thing happened to them that destroyed the town. After the strike was over the UMWA come back in to represent the miners. The company agreed to build new homes for them, but they said the town seceded when they changed their name. They never would have a thing to do with it after that. They built all them ricky-tick houses up by the mine and that was that. It was just their way to keep the workers down. There ain't a one that ever called this place Heart since then but the company itself."

After a long silence Duane asked Val, "You still got that old guitar?"

"You still got that old mandolin?" she said.

"I do," he said. "Would you like to play some?"

"Whoo-whee!" she exclaimed, throwing her head back. "We might even get old Bwana here to favor us with a tune."

"You play music?" Duane asked me.

"That's probably a matter of opinion," I said. "One man's music may be another man's noise."

"Well, if it ain't mister philosopher, back again," Val said.

I could feel Duane's eyes through the darkness. "Well said,

brother," he remarked. "I would like to hear anything you play." He stood to go inside.

After he left Val said, "You really must have made an impression on him."

"What makes you think that?"

"He don't take to just anybody."

Valerie headed down the steps and around the truck to her trailer, and in a minute she was back with her guitar and several candles. She put the candles along the railing and lit them. Duane returned with not only a mandolin but also a violin and bow.

The next few minutes were spent tuning up, and then Duane picked up the mandolin and he and Valerie launched into a surprising, nearly flawless rendition of "Blue Moon of Kentucky." When Val finished with a long howl at the moon the dogs pulled up with a start and joined her, and we all fell out laughing.

"Do you remember 'Fair and Tender Ladies'?" Duane asked.

Valerie shifted tempo and began playing a slow intro. Duane's mandolin picked up the high notes and when she began singing I couldn't help wishing all the people who had laughed at her at King's Tavern could hear her now. It was as if there had been just too much sorrow and beauty in the world, and when it all spilled over it happened to land on Valerie, and became her singing voice.

When the song was finished Val handed me her guitar and took the mandolin from Duane. All I could think to play was "Fox On the Run." My voice wasn't much and Val's mandolin skills were sketchy, but Duane's fiddling more than made up for us, and when their harmonies came in on the chorus I couldn't keep the grin off my face. To be playing bluegrass music with Valerie and Duane on a clear Kentucky night on a mountain above a coal mine was one of those improbable, incomparable experiences I could never have foreseen any more than being nearly electrocuted at the Plum house, or feeling the earth shake at the climax of lovemaking. And above every other thing it felt wonderful to be well and strong again.

But my surprises for the night were not finished. At the end of the song Duane laid his fiddle across his knee. He pulled a small

281

pouch from his pocket and asked me, "Would you like to smoke some marijuana?"

I should have seen it coming but I hadn't and felt completely blindsided. "Duane, I haven't done that in many years," I said.

"His daddy was a policeman," Val volunteered. "Bwana's a law-abiding citizen."

Duane's earnest face was searching mine. "It's all right, brother," he said. "There ain't no harm a-goin to come to you here."

He drew a hand-rolled cigarette from the pouch and lit it with an ancient Zippo lighter. He didn't smoke hungrily, as I had seen marijuana smokers do in my youth, but drew one single puff from it and then passed it to me. The pungent smoke curled between us and I followed his example. It took all my self-control to exhale without exploding in a fit of coughing. I passed it to Valerie, who took an indifferent toke and handed it back to Duane. He pulled on it once more, but when he handed it to me again I declined.

Duane picked up his fiddle and began playing a reel that I soon recognized as "Sally Goodin." I came in on the guitar the second time around while Val worked her way through the chords on the mandolin, and by the third time we were locked in. To be honest, although I had played bluegrass before it never had been my favorite thing. But that night it was like every barrier had fallen down and the essence of music itself descended on us. I never have felt such pure joy in playing anything.

By the end of the song I realized Duane's marijuana was also unlike anything I had smoked before. Back when I was a teenager we would sear our lungs with huge amounts of harsh, woody smoke to get half this high. What I remembered most about those times was the feeling of unease that often accompanied the experience. Just one puff of Duane's fragrant herb tucked all my anxieties under a warm fuzzy blanket and loosened the music in my brain in a way I hadn't felt for years. It made my crew's fascination with the stuff a little more understandable to me.

After that Duane asked me to play something of my own, and for the rest of the evening we all traded tunes back and forth there on

282

his porch. We sang, we told stories, we laughed and when we smoked the rest of that hand-rolled cigarette I played my fingers raw. When Duane heard me play Jobim he just sat there grinning his one-sided grin with tears at the corners of his eyes. Later he brought out a bowl of peaches and we ate our fill with juice running down our chins. The place, the love, the music, and even the terrible stress Val and I had endured the week before all combined to make that night the most carefree time I had experienced in years.

After Duane finally excused himself to bed Val and I sat on the porch steps for a long time gazing at the sky, entranced. The stars blazed with primal fire and beyond the moon's vicinity the Milky Way looked like a many-stranded river of light flowing down over the mountain. A symphony of cicadas rose up from the treetops and mingled with the music of the spheres, and when Valerie took me into her trailer we consummated the night with the sweetest, most unhurried lovemaking the two of us had ever known.

~

With great reluctance I left Val's side and slipped back into the house sometime before dawn. I climbed the steps to the loft barefooted, hoping there still would be bedding for me on the cot, and there was. I was asleep nearly before my head hit the pillow.

In my dream I stood in Mr. Plum's observatory looking down at the Coalbright pit and the mountains beyond. Streams of people issued from the mining tunnels while smoke poured out behind them. I felt the ground shaking, and watched in fascination as the whole scene began to rotate slowly. I was afraid for the house; the structure had not been designed to withstand an earthquake. But somehow the house remained stationary as the great bowl in the mountains increased its rotational speed. The people and structures became a blur as the bowl deepened further into a vortex. And then I felt the house slipping, crumbling as it began to be drawn into oblivion.

At first I was terrified, but instead of falling I felt myself floating up over the landscape, looking down. The structures and mountains disappeared and what first had been a vortex I saw now was a great wheel. As my perspective widened I could see other wheels around it, like gears in a vast machine, each one acting and reacting with its neighbors. One distant wheel seemed to be out of sync, spinning madly, slowing, and then engaging with a jolt that rippled outward like a wave through the system. I saw a battered wheel below me with its rusted cogs bent and broken, damaging the others around it, and yet its strong and steady turning contributed a vital force to the whole. I looked closer and saw that some true and unspoiled wheels actually helped mend their bent and damaged neighbors. None were unconnected; each had a specific influence upon some other.

I had a powerful sense of déjà vu and then the vision began to fade. Details were impossible to discern; I was looking down from too great a height. I felt an urgent need to keep the scene in view. I took a desperate plunge, and in the inexplicable way of dreams soared down until I saw another vortex forming below. I touched down on its outer rim where two people stood waiting for me. One was weeping, and I realized we had been in this place before. The three of us rotated slowly around an unfocused point on the ground. The weeping one cradled something to her chest, and this time I saw plainly what it was.

CHAPTER 21

A rooster crowed me awake, and it was already full daylight. I heard kitchen sounds and by the time I'd pulled my shoes on the aroma of coffee was tickling my nose. I made it downstairs just before Duane went out the door. He poured me a mug and asked if I'd like to walk with him up to the garden. I took my coffee and followed him out.

At first I thought we were going to the vegetable garden, but he walked through it into the woods. We ducked branches and twisted between trees, the dogs leading the way.

When we arrived in the clearing once again the fragrance of marijuana was overwhelming. All was quiet except for the singing of birds. Sunlight rifled through the trees and skimmed the flower tops. Duane walked among his plants, kneeling and probing the soil for moisture here and there. He gently touched plants as he walked by them, and took some of the flower clusters into his rough hands, buried his face in them and murmured sounds I couldn't understand.

"Looky over here," he said. I followed him back to the corner where Val and I had entered the clearing two days before, and he took a leafy branch in his hand. "Look close," he said.

I did, and saw the leaves were curled and slightly withered. It was something I would have missed unless he had shown me.

"Now looky here." He turned around and showed me another, and then another plant with the same feature.

"Will they be okay?" I asked.

"They'll be fine," he said. "They're almost back now. Come two more days you won't even see it."

"What causes it?"

"Strife." He looked at me with his face so earnest that at first I didn't get it. "There was something happened right here they didn't like. This here's the only place."

I looked more closely at the plants, and then noticed the pattern. It wasn't on all sides of any plant—it was only on the sides of the

285

plants facing where we stood, and it seemed to be contained in a circle no more than six or eight feet in diameter. It was as if a source of heat had radiated from the spot, scorching the plants. When the truth dawned on me I didn't want to believe it. This was exactly the place Val and I had our argument two mornings ago.

I knew Duane was far too canny for me to play dumb. "I'm sorry, Duane, I guess this was my fault," I said. "Val and I—"

"Don't worry, brother, it ain't going to hurt them," he interrupted, grinning with the good half of his face. "They'll be all right. I just wanted you to see how they talk to me sometimes."

There was no way to argue with that, and I was relieved he wasn't upset. He seemed happy that I'd seen what he wanted to show me. There was no doubt in my mind now that Duane had a conversational relationship with his plants. I couldn't help wondering what he might do with a vineyard if he lived in wine country. Walking back through the woods I had the sense of having seen wonderful things I would never be able to explain to anyone.

~

I had no idea of the complexity of the job Duane had taken on with my engine until I started helping him the day before. Now that the head was back on he went about reassembling the top end. Pushrods and valve rockers were installed in careful sequence, and then the valve cover. Finally we began putting parts back on the outside of the engine.

We had just replaced the air conditioning compressor and I was tightening the drive belt when the pulley caught my eye. Something about it triggered an image in my mind. For just one second it reminded me of wheels turning against each other. I had forgotten my dream altogether on waking but suddenly awareness of it began to churn inside me like a living thing struggling to be born. For the next hour I contemplated what I could of it, but it wasn't all there. All I could remember were smoke and people pouring out of the mines, and great wheels turning as far as my eyes could see.

286

We refilled the crankcase with oil, the radiator with water and finally turned the engine over. After a few seconds the truck coughed out a cloud of white smoke and then began to run cleanly. We let it idle for about ten minutes. Valerie came out to watch, and when Duane put the hood down I climbed into the driver's seat. I carefully backed Val's trailer into the flat grassy area in front of Duane's vegetable garden—a place that seemed made for it. When at last we unhitched the trailer I felt a tremendous sense of gratitude, rather than the greed and impatience to be gone that I had felt two days before.

As we leveled the trailer Val asked if we were hungry. "There's peach cobbler in the oven," she said.

We washed up at the barn spigot, and when we walked into the house the aroma of baking peaches overtook everything. "Lordy, if it don't smell like heaven in here," Duane said.

Val put sandwiches on the table and as we ate she took the cobbler from the oven. She carried it bubbling in a casserole dish to the counter and put it on a board to cool. She went to the cupboard for bowls and began scooping out servings for us. While she was working she touched the end of the casserole dish and yelped with pain.

I glanced up as she turned on the cold water and plunged her hand under the faucet. She looked over her shoulder with a doleful expression and then turned the water off, shook her hand and folded it to her chest. She put her face down and cradled her left hand in her right. I stared in amazement as the image I was seeing merged with another in my mind. Now I knew where my dream had ended this morning.

Val's fingers were only superficially burned, and the next minute she had our bowls on the table with a small pitcher of cream. I watched her curiously. I could hardly wait to ask the question that was banging to get out of my head. By the time my spoon hit the bottom of the bowl she had beaten me to it.

"So what's got you all eat up now?"

I wiped my mouth and leaned forward, looking her in the eye.

"What did you do with that bottle of cognac you and Tina found?"

Valerie looked like she had been slapped. "How did you know?" she whispered.

"I don't," I said. "That's why I'm asking."

"I put it back," she said in a tremulous voice. "Everything got worse after we found it and Rollie wasn't being careful, so I put it back." She touched her cheek nervously.

"Back where you found it?" I said.

She nodded, big tears welling. Duane stared at her and then at me, not understanding.

"Was that bad?" she said.

"No. It probably was the best thing you could have done."

She got a grip and leaned forward. "But how did you know?"

"I saw you in a dream last night like this." I folded my hands to my chest. "And I couldn't remember what you were holding until a few minutes ago, when I saw you standing like that by the sink."

She stared at me.

"You're the one who told me I should pay attention if I see something, remember?"

"Gold star for Bwana." This time her tone was respectful.

Duane had a puzzled look on his face, and then Valerie told him the story of finding the cognac at King's Tavern. She described everything—losing her earring in the wine cellar, how amazed she and Tina had been to find a secret compartment under the floor, and how excited they were when they saw the date on the bottle—1769. They were sure they had stumbled onto a treasure. But Rollin had been characteristically nonchalant, even reckless about their find. With Val's strong premonition about trouble ahead she felt compelled to put their discovery out of harm's way. "I wasn't an employee no more," she told Duane, "so I made myself invisible like you taught me." His interest grew as she told the story.

Right after she put the cognac back the two men calling themselves Smith and Jones walked in, so she stayed to see what would happen. She already had told Duane about the troubles at King's Tavern, but only in general terms. He hadn't heard about that

288

night and she didn't seem inclined to tell the details. "They were bad men," she concluded pensively, "and they were real ugly to Rollie."

I picked up the story and without being more graphic than necessary made sure Duane understood just whom the real player had been. "They made an example out of the bouncer," I said. "It took about five seconds. After that there wasn't a man in the place who would stand up to them." Val listened with her head bowed. "It took Valerie to put them in their place."

"They were homos," she spoke up again. "The big one tried to use Rollie like a woman in front of all his people. It was the worst thing I ever seen."

"Ahh," said Duane, shaking his head. "What did you do?"

"I don't remember all of it. I told him he was low and Rollie didn't deserve that. He slapped me and called me a bad name and I kicked him. And then mister philosopher here told them to leave me alone and they left."

"You did?" Duane asked me.

"It wasn't that simple, Duane. Believe me, Val took the fire out of them first. She was a hero—a giant."

"A giant," he mused. "Lordy, I wish I could of seen it. Good for you, girl."

"She was the only good thing that happened that night," I said. "Since then everything's gotten worse. Now they have a lien on the place for the old man's debt and they're turning it into a nightmare for Rollin."

"They beat up Tina real bad," Val said softly, her eyes brimming. "They were looking for me but they got her instead."

"Lordy." Duane sat stiffly. I tried to imagine what kind of hell he might unleash on men like those and then didn't want to think too far.

"What are you all a-goin to do?"

It hadn't occurred to me yet that there was anything more to do. Until this moment I had thought bringing Valerie's trailer back here was the end of my responsibilities. But no sooner had Duane asked than I knew the answer.

289

"I think we need to get that bottle out of there before Rollin loses the place. It's probably the last thing he has to work with now."

"A bottle of booze?" Duane said.

"I think it's more than that. A high-end bottle of cognac can sell for over a thousand bucks, but it's still something anyone can buy. This is something much older and rarer. Someone a long time ago went to the trouble of hiding it extremely well; there has to be a reason for that."

"You'd never find it," Val said.

"Sure I would, if you told me where to look."

"You might if you had all day, but you ain't going to get that."

"What are you saying?"

"I know right where it is."

"Val, you can't go back in there. I called Mike the night we got here and he said they've taken over the place. They even had drag queens dancing on the bar. For you to walk back in that place would be crazy."

"You don't think I can do it?" Her eyes flashed.

"They know who you are now, Valerie. You don't exactly blend into the woodwork when you're around."

"Oh no? Well then tell me who all knew I was there last time, mister know-it-all?"

"Nobody. But once you confronted them all that changed."

"Ray, not one soul knew I was there. You and Mike both looked right at me and never even seen me." Fire still flashed in her eyes and I felt my heart sinking. Duane said nothing, but he was listening.

"Besides, I'm gone now," she added. "They won't be looking for me no more. Since you're the one with all the importance I think the best way is for me and you to do it together."

I looked down at the table. I was embarrassed to argue further in front of Duane. The argument was premature, but somewhere in the back of my mind I thought Val just might be right. Maybe together we could do it, if the guys on my crew gave us some cover.

"You could give me credit once in a while," she said, leaning

290

forward and peering up into my face. "I may be a hick chick but I ain't stupid."

"I've never thought that, Val. I just don't want you in harm's way."

"Sometimes the truth hides other truths that ain't so noble."

"Girl, sometimes you got to take the good in a man for what it is." Duane's voice was patient but it had the rhetorical quality of repeating a thing that had been said before.

"We need to get you back to your car anyway," I said. "Mike said the guys are nearly done with it. We can figure out what to do on the way. No matter what we plan we'll probably have to improvise." I looked up.

Duane nodded once deeply. "Well said, brother. Don't take nothing for granted." We stood from the table.

~

Val started cleaning up and I went out to my truck to find the mobile adaptor for my cell phone. It was almost half past three when I punched in Mike's number, wondering if he would still be at work.

He sounded immensely relieved to hear my voice. "Man, I was beginning to think you'd gotten sick again," he said.

"Matter of fact, I nearly died," I said. "But I'm all better now."

"Yeah, right. You sound great. How's the truck?"

"We got it done this afternoon; I'll be headed out in the morning. If all goes well I should be back tomorrow night. How's everything up there?"

"Roof's done, windows are in. Everything's status quo on the job."

"How's Tina?"

"No change, Bwana. She's still in a coma but since I'm not family all I've been able to get from the hospital is a runaround. Everyone is unbelievably uptight right now. Even Rollie's hard to get anything out of. I've never seen him so down."

"Stick with him, Ace. He needs to hang in there. I have an idea;

291

it's a long shot, but if he gives up everything is lost."

"You have an idea?"

"Yeah. I can't talk about it now."

There was a long silence. "Well, that's more than anyone here has."

"Don't say anything—just keep everyone on task. Above all, keep Rollie's head above water. Tell him I'm on the way back if you want, but nothing more."

"Is Val coming?"

"Yeah. Better not tell anyone though."

"I think Spider and Mackey were expecting it. Her car should be ready by the weekend."

"Then have them keep quiet about it, if it's not too late. I sure wish there was a place to hide her for a few days."

"How about your place?"

"That's not safe enough. She needs deep cover."

"My sister lives in Pottstown. That's over an hour away."

"Megan? Isn't she sick?"

"Well, she's on chemo. But she still gets around."

"That doesn't sound too good to me."

Mike laughed. "Don't underestimate Meg —she's a tough cookie. And she'll do anything for me."

"I'll leave that up to you. But whatever happens has to be kept quiet."

"Don't worry. She works in security; she's very discreet."

"What's going on at King's?"

"Last night was just like old times, but over the weekend it was a freak show. We've been trying to have at least one or two guys in there every night just to keep an eye out and show Rollie some respect. They're toying with him now; I think they want him to sell out cheap and wash his hands of it."

"Don't let him even think that way, Mike."

"If I were in his shoes I might be thinking that way myself."

"It's too early for that. Remember what you told me—think positive."

"Yeah. We're trying."

"Look, I'll be back tomorrow night, okay? I'll call you when we get to Harrisburg and we can figure out where to meet."

"It sounds to me like you got your mojo back."

"What goes around comes around, bro. We're all just wheels turning against each other."

~

Valerie came out as I was finishing my call. She slumped onto the steps at the news of Tina. When I told her to have faith she looked up at me and said, "Faith in what?"

"In her inner strength."

"She don't seem to have much of that now."

"We have to believe, Val." I sat down beside her. "Nobody knows what's really happening inside her. All they can see is bone and tissue. Her spirit is something bigger than that."

"So you reckon your spirit is what saved you?"

"No."

"Well then maybe it was your inner strength."

"No. It wasn't that."

"You told me them little bacteria didn't believe in nothing but reproducing themselves."

"Yeah."

"Well, right now if Tina's brain don't stop swelling it won't matter much what her spirit thinks, will it?"

"I guess not."

"So explain what it is you want me to have faith in."

I was in a corner. "I don't know, Val. But we can't give up on Tina. What do you want me to say?"

"You don't need to say nothing. But maybe you ought not be so proud you can't even mention the name of the Lord without swearing. Unless you think what happened to you was some kind of everyday thing."

"I know better than that."

293

"Do you? Did you really stop to wonder why you ain't dead now? Or did you think all that just come to you because you're so special in the universe?" She was fighting back tears.

"I don't understand any of it, Valerie. No, I'm not special, any more than anyone else. And I'm very thankful, believe me."

"Well you had someone a-prayin up a storm for you, mister, and if you can't do the same thing for Tina then you ought to be ashamed."

"I don't know how to, Val. You learned those things as a child and I never did."

She laughed bitterly. "You act like it's so complicated to just say 'please' and 'thank you'. After what happened to you it seems like you'd be the first one to do it for Tina."

I was beaten. "You're right. I don't really know much about that kind of thing but it's the least I can do."

"You better hope you don't choke on your pride someday, mister importance."

"It won't kill me; it's not poison."

"Ain't that from a song?" She looked up skeptically.

"I thought it up just now."

"You're lying, that's Bob Dylan." She pushed my face away with the flat of her hand but she was coming out of her funk. "I want to see my mama; will you take me?"

"If you think she'll like me."

She gave another bitter laugh. "You ain't running for office—why does everyone have to like you?"

"I was just kidding. But if she does, maybe she won't worry about you coming back up to Pennsylvania with me."

"She already likes you more than you deserve," Val said, standing to her feet. "It's Daddy that thinks you're too worldly. He was afraid you might corrupt me with flattery and deception but I told him you don't flatter nobody but yourself."

"Well, that's great. I'm sure he'll be happy to see me now," I grumbled as I got up.

"I was just kidding, stupid," Val said, poking me in the ribs.

~

When we pulled up in front of the Tollivers' place the old Lincoln was nowhere to be seen. No children's faces peeped out the window. Val knocked at the door and called "Mama?" several times. The door finally opened a crack and Val said, "It's me and Ray. You remember Ray, don't you, Mama?"

The door opened wider and there stood Mrs. Tolliver with a hesitant half-smile on her face. Her sightless eyes swept between us as she reached up to smooth her hair.

"Don't worry, Mama, you look real pretty," Val said. "Don't she, Ray?"

"Yes, it's nice to meet you again, Mrs. Tolliver," I said, extending my hand. She seemed surprised when she took it in hers. She touched the depression in my palm and then moved her hands up my arm, feeling it carefully as a doctor might.

"I told her Ardie come to help you," Val said. "She knows all about it."

Mrs. Tolliver led us into the house, which was divided into four rooms. Later I found a tiny kitchen and bathroom at the rear, both added over a porch with a sloping floor. The front room was crammed with a ragged sofa, a rocker and an old recliner covered in vinyl. A battered coffee table crouched in front of the sofa with barely room to walk between them. Open on the table was a large Braille book with brown pages. I leaned over and lightly touched them.

"That's Mama's New Testament—she's learning how to read Braille," Val said.

"That must not be easy."

"She has real sensitive hands."

Mrs. Tolliver dropped her head with a bashful smile and took a seat on the sofa. Val sat next to her and I took the rocker.

"Duane finished fixing Ray's truck, Mama," Val said. "We're going back to get my car tomorrow."

I saw Mrs. Tolliver's mouth move several times but no sound came out. Her emotions were easier to read; anxiety lined her face and her eyes moved restlessly.

"It's okay, Mama," Val said. "I'm coming back. Duane's going to run water and electric to my trailer while I'm gone, so don't you worry."

Val talked about her new place in front of Duane's vegetable garden, and then told her mother about our evening before. She described the night sky, the crickets and cicadas in the meadow, and said we'd played the sweetest music she had heard since being away.

Mrs. Tolliver seemed enchanted by this and once again struggled to say something. Her mouth moved several times but every time I expected a word to come out she stopped. Her effort reminded me of a person who stutters, except she seemed unable to muster the courage to make a sound. Val took her hands and leaned in, and when their foreheads almost touched I heard her whisper, "What is it, Mama? You can tell me in my ear. Just whisper it." She put an arm around her mother's neck and pulled her close. "Just say it in my ear, okay?"

Mrs. Tolliver squeezed Val's hand anxiously, and I sensed her frustration. She drew closer and after what seemed like a terrible effort I saw her lips move. Val nodded with understanding once and then again, and then a big grin crossed her face. "That's wonderful, Mama," she said, and then hugged her. "I'm so proud of you!"

Mrs. Tolliver's face glowed briefly, and I saw that behind her shattered self-esteem there was a fragile loveliness. She must have been quite beautiful as a young woman.

Valerie whispered something back in her mother's ear, and I saw her mother blush with pleasure. Val turned to me and explained, "Mama started playing her autoharp again. She used to play with Daddy back when me and Vi was little, and we all sang together."

"That's great news. You had a family group?"

"Shoot, Daddy was the best guitar picker in Harlan County. Me and Vi learned to sing from Mama and we sang at church and revival meetings."

"Did Duane ever play with you?"

"He and Daddy used to play bluegrass when they was young 'uns, but after Daddy got saved he never would play worldly music no more. Or let us hear it." A shadow crossed her face but didn't linger. "Mama, would you play something? I haven't heard you in so long, and I know Ray would love it."

Mrs. Tolliver looked both pleased and distressed, and at first I thought she felt trapped. "I'd love to hear her," I said, "but I don't want to put her on the spot." I saw Val looking intently at me and then I spoke to her mother. "It's okay, Mrs. Tolliver. You do what makes you comfortable."

Mrs. Tolliver leaned in close to Valerie again, and Val put her arm around her and turned her ear close. Mrs. Tolliver was blushing like a schoolgirl, but managed to whisper enough that Val finally rolled her eyes and laughed.

"Sometimes. But don't let him fool you," she said, and they both giggled. "You don't have to worry about Ray. He already heard me a-playin Duane's mandolin so he's ready for anything."

I thought she would be too bashful but to my surprise Mrs. Tolliver left the room and returned clutching her autoharp in both arms. She sat and cradled it in her left arm like a baby and I felt her nervousness. She straightened, spread her left hand across a row of buttons and lightly brushed the strings with her right.

The sound was soft, almost ethereal. Her first few chords were tentative, but as the sound filled the room her nervousness disappeared and she began to play with confidence. I dimly recognized the tune from childhood and listening to it I understood Mrs. Tolliver was a real musician. The subtle harmonies in the chords she chose surprised me, and the way her hands moved revealed a long familiarity with her harp. She didn't just strum out chords; she swept her fingers individually across the strings finding arpeggios and counter-rhythms that I never would have imagined.

Valerie pressed a knuckle to her mouth and when the song was finished there were tears in her eyes. "Oh, Mama, that sounded like an angel," she exclaimed, and Mrs. Tolliver beamed. "When did you start playing again?"

Just then there was the sound of a car pulling up outside. Mrs. Tolliver stood abruptly with her harp in both arms. She walked into the back room with it more quickly than I thought possible while Val wiped her eyes, stood and looked out the door. She called out, "It's Daddy," and I heard a car door slam. Mrs. Tolliver reappeared without the harp and I stood just in time for Mr. Tolliver's entrance. He carried a bundle wrapped with butcher paper.

"Hi Daddy, you remember Ray," Val said as he walked in.

"I do," he said. He looked me over with his intense blue eyes as we gripped hands. "You look a right bit better today."

"I am," I said.

"We heard you took sick again."

"I think that's over. Thank you for your concern."

He nodded.

Valerie said, "Ray's taking me up north tomorrow to get my car."

"I see your truck is back a-runnin."

"Yes sir, thanks to Duane it's fine now."

He nodded again. "Would you all like to take supper with us? I got some pork chops. There's greens aplenty, and Vi left some potato salad."

"We had a late lunch, Daddy," Val said. "Duane and Ray was working on the truck past noon; we just wanted to see you again before we go."

Mr. Tolliver nodded again. "Have a seat," he said, and ducked through the door into the back room.

We sat again and Val whispered, "Does he know you're playing again?" Mrs. Tolliver shook her head slightly.

When Mr. Tolliver returned he sat stiffly on the edge of the recliner and said, "Valry says you build houses."

"Yes sir, I've worked construction ever since I was a teenager."

"Nothing like being a working man. I reckon you got a nice place of your own."

"Well, I have an old log farm house I've been working on for the last few years. It's not big but I like it."

298

"An old log farm house?" He seemed taken aback.

"It used to be a farm. I got five acres and the old house. It was in bad shape and I saved it. Built a new roof, put in new windows, plumbing and wiring. It's pretty decent now."

"That's good," he said gruffly. "Too many people tearing down the old things. They don't build worth spit anymore." He raised a hand to indicate the house around us.

"It all depends on who's doing the building, I guess."

"I reckon so. Your boss do good work?"

"Well, I hope so," I laughed. "It's my company and I think we do pretty good work."

"Your company?" He was surprised again.

"Tell him about your lawyer's house," Valerie piped up.

"You building a house for your lawyer?" Mr. Tolliver asked.

"He's not my lawyer, he's my client," I said. "But he has a law firm in Philadelphia."

"It's real big," Val said. "It's got an observatory for a telescope upstairs and a gym and a theater downstairs."

"A theater? In a house?"

"Yes sir," I said. "He's a pretty wealthy man, and I guess he's used to getting what he wants."

"Well, I'll declare." He shook his head like he'd learned something brand new. "Must have cost well over a hundred thousand."

"Yes sir. Quite a bit more." I didn't want to tell him the slate for the roof alone cost more than that. In fact I really didn't want to go any farther down that road, and changed the subject. "Valerie tells me you're the best guitar picker around."

"Well, now." He coughed and cleared his throat. "That might of been true long ago. Then again maybe not."

"Oh Daddy, you always were the best," Val said, and I saw the color rise in his face. Did he ever know she thought that about him?

"I heard you all had quite a fine family group," I said.

"Is that so? Well, ahhm—we did some singing and playing. But that's been many a year ago."

299

"I heard your brother last night, and if you played guitar as well as he plays the mandolin I'd sure love to have heard it," I said.

"He's still got his guitar, don't you, Daddy?" Val said.

"Well, ahmm, uh—" He fell into another spell of clearing his throat. "Can't say it would still hold a tune, really."

"Daddy, your guitar was the one everybody wanted when you quit a-playin. You ought to let Ray see it. He plays real nice, too."

He harrumphed and coughed a little more, and I just kept still. Valerie had him off his guard. He seemed pleased to hear her call him the best.

Val tilted her head and peered up into his face. "Please, Daddy? Can we just look at it? You really ought to make sure the mice haven't eaten it up." She was teasing him, but only a tiny bit, and the affectionate way she did it disarmed him. With his pride on one hand and his long-lost daughter's pleas on the other, he was between a rock and a hard place. By now I could tell that Valerie had been right. In spite of all he had done, Mr. Tolliver was not a wicked person. And he desperately wanted to put his best foot forward in front of the man his daughter had brought home. After a few seconds he looked up.

"Clara, do you know where that old thing is?" His voice was soft and humble, and when I looked at Mrs. Tolliver her face was a study in wonder. She rose to her feet and went into the back of the house and a moment later he followed. As he went out I glanced at Val and she looked even more stunned than her mother.

She grabbed my arm and said, "Ray, do you know how long it's been since he's touched that guitar? I was barely sixteen when he put it away!"

We heard his voice indistinctly from the back of the house, and a minute later he returned carrying an old hard-shell case. Mrs. Tolliver followed him and took her place again on the sofa. Mr. Tolliver sat on the recliner, laid the case on the floor and snapped the latches open. He lifted the lid and looked inside for a long time. I couldn't see beyond the raised lid but finally he murmured, "Well, she's still in there."

300

"Take it out, Daddy, let Ray see it." Val could barely contain herself.

He reached in and picked it up with his big hands, and I saw right away what it was. "That's a Martin, isn't it?"

"Yes, it is," Mr. Tolliver said. "D-28, made in nineteen and forty-one."

I whistled. He handed it to me and I took it in both hands. It was a thing of beauty. The rosewood sides were the color of wine and the spruce top had aged to a golden brown. There was considerable wear around the pick guard and sound hole but that's what you hoped to see on a guitar of this age. It had been played a lot, and the peculiar thing about a wood instrument is that the longer one is played the better it sounds. The finish everywhere else was still gorgeous and when I held the guitar up to sight down the neck it looked dead straight. I handed it back to him reverently. "That is one fine, fine instrument," I said.

"I been offered thousands of dollars for this guitar," he said quietly.

"I don't doubt it."

"To a poor man that's a lot of money."

"But you didn't sell it."

"No sir, I did not." He looked at me with fire in his eyes.

"Why?"

"Son, this guitar rings like Gabriel's trumpet and thunders like the day of judgment," he boomed, and he was just warming up. "It has a voice unlike any other creature, called forth to show the Lord's majesty and sing his praise. This guitar—" and then he choked. He sat there a long moment with his face frozen.

"It ain't nothing but pride and vanity," he finally muttered, looking down at the guitar still in his hands. "It ain't nothing but a piece of wood fashioned by the hand of man. Lord, forgive me. Hallelujah." His voice sank to a whisper. "Hallelujah."

Valerie's eyes and even Mrs. Tolliver's were wide and their faces looked stunned. I didn't know what to think except that I'd just heard a preacher start to unwind and it didn't sound much different

301

from what we'd heard on the radio coming down here. Val was the first one to recover.

"Daddy, it's a wonderful guitar." Her voice was low and intense. "Everything you said is true. If it makes you proud to play it then maybe you ought to thank the Lord every time you do. He'll turn it to a blessing. You didn't make it anyhow, some other man did. It don't make sense to turn aside a blessing because it's too good for you now, does it?"

Mr. Tolliver looked up, blinking. I think he was seeing his daughter in a new light and it was a shock to him, or maybe a revelation. But she wasn't done.

"You were a proud man back then," Val said softly. "You had a beautiful wife and two little girls and a little boy that loved you so much. But you had to learn more, and you took a hard way to learn. We all had to learn more." Her eyes were welling.

"Daddy, you ain't been proud in a long time. You've been living in a big old ball of hurt and shame. But you can't stay there if you want your light to shine, can you? You got to accept joy, even in a simple thing like music, and let it out if you want to bless others. Don't you, Daddy?"

His eyes were pained; he looked like all the wind had been sucked out of him. He turned to Valerie with a haunted expression. "I ain't got the right to that. You all better go along now."

"Daddy, you listen to me now." Val was insistent. "The Bible says the joy of the Lord is your strength, don't it?"

He looked back down at the guitar in his lap. His face was like a stone but I could sense a mighty struggle going on inside him.

"Don't it, Daddy?" She kept her eyes on him and I looked down, wanting to be a million miles away.

"I reckon so." His voice was barely audible.

"Don't that mean for every believer?"

"I reckon."

"Then you got as much right to it as anyone. Don't the Bible also say, vengeance is mine, saith the Lord?"

"What are you saying, girl?" He looked up at her again, his eyes

302

swimming.

"Daddy, you're trying to punish yourself when that ain't your job. Did you forget the Lord come to forgive sinners? He forgave Peter for denying him thrice, he even forgave the thief on the cross—don't you think he forgives you?"

His hands jerked on the guitar and a dissonant echo came from deep inside it. "My family—I want my family to—" Mr. Tolliver muttered hoarsely, nearly strangling on the words.

"I forgive you, Daddy." Val got up and took the guitar from his lap, laid it in its case and knelt and put her arms around him. "I thought I hated you for a long time but that's gone now. The Lord took it away; now you got to let him forgive you."

Valerie held him in her arms, and I couldn't see his face for all her hair. I stole a glance at Mrs. Tolliver and she was sitting there with an alert, almost electrified expression. Tears had gathered in her eyes but there was something else on her face too. It reminded me of streaks of light on the horizon long before the sun comes up. If I had to put a name to what I was seeing, it looked almost like hope.

I glanced around for the nearest exit. This was not a bad scene— it was infinitely better than the horror show I had watched three weeks before at King's Tavern. Nevertheless when Mr. Tolliver's big shoulders started shaking and he let go I felt profoundly embarrassed for him. Valerie just held him, and he sobbed like a child on her shoulder while Mrs. Tolliver made her way over to them, knelt beside Valerie and reached out her arms, weeping. Val pulled her into their circle while I ducked through the door.

~

I took my sweet time. I walked outside to have a look at the back yard and its tiny vegetable garden. An ancient freezer chest with a padlock was backed up against the house under a fiberglass awning. On the other side of the step a rusty propane tank stood outside the kitchen wall. Looking up and down the row of houses I saw clotheslines, several more gardens, a rickety swing set and a heap of old tires. Years of coal dust covered everything so completely that the very idea of color here seemed all but forgotten. The garden alone valiantly presented a few splashes of red and green.

Once again I wanted to be angry with Valerie for dragging me into the middle of other people's troubles, but couldn't. However painful the scene inside the house had been for me, somehow I realized my presence was the catalyst that had allowed it to happen. No matter that it was the last thing in the world I wanted to witness; no matter to what length I would have gone to avoid it. And no matter how I felt it was still a breakthrough, I realized. Maybe even a victory for the entire family.

I thought about my dream of the wheels, and how flippantly I had spoken to Mike a few hours ago. I didn't even understand it when I said it: We're all just wheels turning against each other. Some willingly and some not, but in the end no one could escape his own influence or the consequences of it. Valerie's words from weeks ago still echoed in my mind: Once you know something, you're responsible for it.

I had come down here so impatient and full of assumptions— only to confront my unraveling and have my pride poured out like water on the ground. All my notions of certainty in the universe and the rigid self-sufficiency I had lived by had been weighed in the balance and found wanting. For all the seeming naiveté of Valerie's arguments, in this place they had proven harder to refute than my own.

The mountain loomed beyond the rows of houses, and even the kudzu holding the embankment together looked gray. Vines had long since overtaken the woods above, covering everything with a shapeless mat of vegetation, and I guessed not many trees up there were still alive. Once upon a time people actually believed the stuff would save the world—now it was a bane that ate everything in its path. Assumptions often had tragic consequences. In the other direction the Coalbright pit yawned, its factory of bad dreams locked in rigor mortis. There was no sign of activity anywhere. I turned in the late afternoon heat and went back into the house.

Mrs. Tolliver sat beside her husband on the arm of the recliner, and I was pleased to see them holding hands. Valerie was sitting on the sofa. When I entered she turned to me and said, "We were just talking about Tina."

"Tina is a good girl," I said, grateful that the earlier situation seemed to be at a conclusion. "Nobody deserves what happened to her."

"Daddy's having prayer meeting tonight. He's going to ask everyone to pray for her."

"The doctor said it would be good to do that," I said, choosing my words carefully.

"Would you all like to come?" Mr. Tolliver asked.

There was an uncomfortable silence, and then Val said, "Thank you, Daddy, but I'm not ready for that yet. Maybe when I get back."

He nodded.

"Her family will be glad to know folks down here are thinking of her," she said.

"We'll make sure someone is a-prayin for her every hour of the day," he said gravely. "We'll be a-prayin for your trip, too."

"Thank you, Daddy. You look to Mama and Vi too now, you hear?"

"Girl, I would give my life for ever one of you," he said, his voice thick with emotion. "Your mama is more precious to me than silver or gold. I would never harm a hair on her head."

When we stood to go he shook my hand once more and said, "I want to thank you for bringing my little girl home."

"You're welcome, Mr. Tolliver," I said, and almost left it at that. "If you don't mind, I'd like to send you some new strings for that guitar with Valerie when she comes back. Just in case you decide to take it out again. It would be an honor to hear you play it someday."

He cleared his throat once more, but before he could respond Val said, "It would make me so happy to hear you and Mama making music again, Daddy—not me only, but lots of people. Will you just think about it?"

He sputtered a bit, and abruptly said "Alright." He opened his

305

arms to Val and they hugged for several seconds, and when they finished I saw his eyes were moist again. While Val hugged her mother I walked out the front door with Mr. Tolliver behind me.

"Looks like this place is nearing the end," I said.

"Yessir, it's plumb used up," he said. "Never was much to begin with."

"Where will you go if it closes?"

"We got us a half-acre of good bottom land over in Letcher County, but most here won't have a thing when this all shuts down." The front door opened and Val came down the steps.

"Well, good luck, sir," I said, and pumped his hand one more time.

"Luck's for them that don't know the Lord."

Val kissed his cheek and we climbed into my truck. Fortunately there was no time for more talk.

"Bye, Daddy—I love you," Val called out the window as we pulled away. I watched Mr. Tolliver in my rear view mirror, standing tall and alone in his little yard, until we turned the corner and the worn-out neighborhood disappeared behind us.

~

Thursday morning Duane and Val made a heroic breakfast of corn fritters, deer sausage, peaches and cream. Duane already had picked two bushels of fresh corn plus another basket of produce from his garden for us to take home. I asked if he ever gave any to his brother, and he laughed.

"I been trying for years to get him to take some for the folks around him down at the mine, but he won't. He says the Lord will provide."

"And does he?" I couldn't imagine not at least accepting help for his neighbors.

"He provided for you, didn't he?"

"I would have to say so."

"Duane takes a truckload down every week and leaves it at the

306

old commissary," Val said. "Daddy don't want no credit since he didn't grow it."

"Do people know where it comes from?"

"A few. Most think the welfare office pays Duane to haul it in, can you believe it?"

"Now, you don't know that," Duane said.

"Oh no? Did you forget I was there the time you told Mrs. Ludy off?

"She thought he was an angel of mercy and starts a-thankin him up one side and down the other, and he looks at her real cold and says, 'I'm just doing my job, ma'am,' and we drove off with her standing there like she been slapped. That was the meanest thing I ever seen you do, Duane."

"If everbody knew it wouldn't be no more help, now would it?" Duane said calmly.

"No, but you don't have to make ever last body so scared of you."

"People think what they want," he said. "I got no problem with that, except for your daddy. Maybe after what you done last night old Vance will come up and see me sometime."

"Maybe you should go see him."

He shook his head. "Not after last time."

"Duane, that was right after Mama got hurt. Things are different now. You even said him and Victor are talking again."

"I always thought that would take a miracle," Duane said.

"Maybe it's a time for miracles," I said.

"Well if it ain't mister skeptical, talking about miracles," Valerie said.

"I believe you're right, brother," Duane said. "Maybe it is." We finished eating and cleaned up the table without further talk.

Duane wouldn't accept a thing for all the work he'd done on my truck, not even for the parts. After lifting the produce into the back of my truck he asked, "Would you like some marijuana to take with you?"

Once again I was taken by surprise. I had no use for the stuff, but for just a moment thought about how happy it would make Mackey, Spider and a few other guys on my crew. "Thanks," I finally said, "but things are different back where I'm going. I'd better not."

Val heaved her backpack behind the seat and then hugged the dogs and finally Duane, for a long time. She got in the truck with tears at the corners of her eyes. Duane came around and shook my hand in both of his and I climbed in. He had jacked my door up to where it would latch, although now it dropped at a crazy angle every time it opened. He shut it firmly, gripped my arm and said, "Vaya con Dios, brother." I nodded and was surprised to feel my throat tighten.

We bounced wordlessly down the drive. After rounding the bend by the woods I slowed for the barricade and stared in disbelief. There by the lane stood Duane, holding the barricade open, still and erect as a statue. He snapped into a perfect military salute as we passed, and I couldn't help twisting around to look back at him. I didn't even trust my mirror. He held the salute for several seconds, dropped his arm and then began trudging the barricade back across the lane as deliberately as I had seen him do everything else. Only then did it occur to me that not once had I seen him in a hurry. He simply was where he needed to be, when he needed to be there.

"He's such a show-off," Valerie sighed, wiping her eyes.

CHAPTER 22

The drive home seemed effortless. The truck ran better than it had in years. Valerie was uncharacteristically quiet and serious; I felt jollier and even made her laugh once by singing "Thank God I'm a Country Boy" in a hillbilly accent along with John Denver on the radio. By then it was late in the day and Pennsylvania wasn't far ahead.

When I told Val about Mike's plan for her to stay in Pottstown with his sister she didn't seem too thrilled. She didn't know Megan and neither did I, although we'd met once or twice. I knew Val wanted to be with me but she couldn't argue with the need to keep out of sight.

"Am I going to be everybody's problem now?" she asked.

"No. You're not the problem, you're part of the solution. We just have to keep the problem away from you until the right time." She rolled her eyes.

As we crossed the Potomac River into Maryland Val stuck her head out the window and let her hair blow in the wind for several miles. When she pulled back inside it was a wild mess. "Feel better?" I said. She turned to peer at me through a jumble of hair. She didn't say a word but drew up her knees and continued to stare at me with long tendrils flying wildly out the window behind her. You're going to have fun getting those tangles out, I started to say, but something stopped me.

By the time we were approaching Harrisburg it was nearly eight and the sun was gone. I punched Mike's number into the phone and he picked up on the second ring. I asked how things were going.

"Umm, there's a slight complication," he said. "Meg is out of town; she won't be back until tomorrow. Can Val stay at your place just for tonight?"

"Have you talked to her about any of this?" I asked.

"Yeah, she's looking forward to it. But the chemo lowered her white blood count so they put her in the Reading hospital for IVs.

She'll be done tomorrow. She's been protesting the whole thing because she feels great."

"That doesn't sound too good. Maybe we should just find a motel."

"Trust me; she'll be fine. She wants to do this."

"Yeah, well, intentions are one thing, but—"

"Remember what I told you about Meg? She's tough, Bwana. She has her mind set on helping and if we back out now she'll never forgive us. And besides, she needs the company."

"How about the car?"

"It'll be ready tomorrow. Mack thought they'd have it ready today, but they weren't finished detailing it yet."

"Hmm." I chewed the inside of my cheek. "How's the Frye job?"

"All good. The police have been out there twice though. They've talked to all of us; they want to see you and Val too. They were asking how they could contact her."

"Did you say anything about her coming back?"

"Nope. I told them you're the only one who knows how to reach her."

"Any news about Tina?"

"That's the best news so far. The doctors said her cranial pressure started going down last night. She's still out of it but her reflexes are coming back."

"No kidding?"

"That's the word. At least things are going the right direction."

"Where are you?"

"I'm just leaving Reading. I was with Meg."

"Is she bringing herself home?"

"I'm picking her up in the morning. Spider and Mackey'll keep things rolling—I should be back by noon. How's your health?"

"Never been better."

"You sound great. I guess those meds are working."

"It's Megan we have to worry about now. I hope she's as well as you think she is."

After we signed off Valerie wanted to hear about Tina. When I

310

told her she seemed pleased but contemplative. "Have you been praying for her?" she asked.

I hadn't thought about it, and there was no hiding the fact. She looked reproachfully at me but changed the subject. "What's wrong with Megan?"

"She had breast cancer. She's on chemotherapy."

"So I won't be going to her place?"

"She's in Reading tonight; she'll be home tomorrow. Mike says she's doing fine."

Val seemed lost in thought. "You never prayed for her, either."

"You know me, Valerie, I never knew about that stuff before."

"Well if you can't say 'please' I sure hope you don't forget to say 'thank you.'"

"I won't. We need to get you a motel now, though."

"Get *me* a motel?" She was incredulous.

"Well, yeah."

"If I can't stay with you, mister big shot, then you can just let me out right now."

"I thought we went through this already," I said. "If anyone is snooping around my place I don't want you in harm's way."

"Fine. Then you can pull over right now, mister." Her voice was turning husky with rage. "And you tell Spider he can give my car to the cancer fund." She actually started opening her door.

"Whoa, wait a minute." I jammed my foot on the brake. "Where is all this coming from?"

"Just let me out. I ain't going to be nobody's extra baggage and you can't treat me like I am." Her door was part way open, and as I careened onto the shoulder several cars honked and sped by in the dusk.

"Val, you're not anybody's extra baggage." I slowed to a stop, pulling tight against the guardrail. "You are very precious and valuable, and I don't want anything in the world to harm you."

"And you want to dump me off in a strange place alone without even a way to go nowhere? That don't sound so precious to me, buster brown." Her eyes shot sparks from behind her wild hair.

"I'm sorry, Val, that was a terrible idea and it was very thoughtless of me." There was a lull in traffic and the sudden silence was unbearable. "Will you forgive me?"

She shook the hair out of her face and I could see the hurt look there. "I can't understand after everything that's happened why you would even think about doing that. How would that make you feel?"

"Sometimes I don't think enough about other peoples' feelings," I said, "but I'm learning. Can you be patient with me?"

There was another long silence. "So what do you want to do?" Her voice softened a little.

"We don't need to be anywhere tonight. Why don't we find a nice place together and worry about the rest tomorrow?"

"Okay," she said shyly. She closed her door and I pulled back onto the interstate looking for an exit into Harrisburg.

~

I was able to get us a suite at the Hilton Towers downtown. The desk clerk was polite in spite of our scruffy appearance, but the valet didn't seem too enthusiastic about parking my truck until I palmed him a twenty and told him not to worry about scratching it.

The hotel had been renovated recently, and at first the ambience seemed terribly synthetic after the natural harmony of Duane's place. But when Val looked out the big windows and saw the fading sky reflected from the broad Susquehanna River below and lights coming on all over the horizon she seemed enchanted. She was wide-eyed at nearly everything in the place. "There's even a refrigerator and ironing board," she exclaimed. "And a hair dryer!"

"And room service," I said.

We looked over the menu together and she picked a summer fruit platter and a baguette with brie. I studied the wine list and selected a highly regarded Cabernet which would add almost a hundred dollars to our bill, but considering what nearly had been lost it felt like a bargain. I called room service and added some Lebanon bologna, smoked salmon and a second baguette to Val's choices

312

while she made a face at me.

Val dug in her pack and took a few things to the bathroom where there were more squeals of delight at the wonderful amenities that probably couldn't be found in most of the bathrooms around Hurt, Kentucky. She came back out with a hairbrush and pulled a chair around to face the windows that looked over the panorama below us. "Can you make the light lower so we can see outside?" she asked.

I found the lamp switch and turned it off. The city lights outside came alive with the change.

"Will you brush my hair?" She stretched her legs out, lifted her heavy hair and let it fall down over the chair back. Then she leaned way back, peering upside-down at me standing behind her in the semi-dark.

"Okay." Nobody had asked me to do that before. She handed me her brush and I sat behind her and clumsily began brushing from the top down.

"Ow! Not that way," she yelped. "You start with the ends, silly."

So I started with the ends, and soon got the hang of it. I took a section at a time, working my way up through her thick mane, and in the dark found it was a sensual task. "You're going to have fun getting all the tangles out," she murmured. My mind reeled and I could tell it took all her will power to keep from giggling.

It took many minutes but I kept working until there wasn't a tangle anywhere. Finally I began running my fingers up into her hair and down through the length of it, and Val was practically purring. It felt like heavy silk falling over my forearms. I leaned forward and buried my face in her hair, thoroughly aroused now and stunned by its fragrance. I didn't understand why it always smelled so exotic until she said, "Didn't nobody ever tell you about pheromones?"

And then she got up from her chair, bent over me and kissed me deeply, her hair falling like a curtain around our faces. She went to her knees and whispered, "Didn't I tell you you'd have fun getting the tangles out?" She had unbuttoned my shirt and was gently addressing my nipples when there was a loud knock at the door.

Never in my life have I been so reluctant to greet the arrival of a great wine. I groaned and stood unsteadily. "Don't you think you ought to pull that shirttail out?" Val said. And then she did it for me, playfully smoothing it over the front of my jeans. She kissed me hard once more and giggled as I groped for the light switch and made my way, aching with desire, to the door.

Room service was efficient and polite, and the young bellhop who delivered our meal seemed anxious for me to approve the wine before he left. After he set the tray down I let him uncork the bottle and pour a splash into a wine glass, which I swirled for a few seconds and sniffed deeply before tasting. I closed my eyes as a million nerve endings twinkled on behind my face. The wine was stellar. I fumbled in my pocket and handed him a bill without even checking the denomination, and he smiled broadly. "Thank you, sir, and congratulations," he beamed, and then he was gone.

Valerie howled with laughter after the door closed. I wanted to say "where were we?" but the mood was broken; the fruit platter beat me by a mile. It was an elegant presentation and the bread was still warm from the oven. I poured two wine glasses about a third full, set them aside to breathe and found some classical music on the radio.

Valerie turned her nose up at the bologna and salmon but she attacked the rest with enthusiasm. When she watched me pick up one of the glasses, swirl and sniff it she tried the same thing. "Mmmm," she said, closing her eyes and sipping.

We ate our fill with gratitude. It was a simple meal but all of it was the best quality, and it was clear Val appreciated that too. She was responsive and funny and the air between us was charged. Her hair tumbled over her shoulders with a life of its own and her eyes sparkled with interest as we ate, laughed and teased each other.

After the last drop of wine was gone I took both her hands in mine and got serious. "I'm really glad we're together, Val. I can't believe I was going to leave you here alone. You're the best company I've had in a very long time."

She searched my face and murmured, "I know. Me too."

We kissed and before I knew it we both were undressed and

314

burning with desire. I switched the lamp off and Valerie whispered, "Let's do it here, watching the lights." She leaned at the railing and I held her from behind, and we had sex high above Harrisburg while the Susquehanna River flowed dark and wide below. Again we climaxed at the same moment and she cried out as the lights on the horizon rushed together and exploded in our vision. We collapsed into the chair with Val curled against me, our hearts pounding in perfect rhythm.

Later she tied up her hair and we bathed each other in the fanciest tub she had ever bathed in. We went to bed and made love again and for the first time since I had known Valerie we fell asleep together, and I do not remember dreaming anything at all.

We woke Friday morning and from our king-sized bed watched cars crawling over the bridges, while a small airplane pulled a banner advertising health insurance high over the morning traffic. This was a big city compared to Gladburg, and I knew Val was marveling at how different it all was from the life she had known in the mountains back home in Kentucky. And I wondered without trying to veil my thoughts if she ever could ever find happiness in such a place.

~

After breakfast we threaded our way out of downtown Harrisburg, and a few minutes later were back on the interstate.

"Thank you for the hotel." Val looked over at me. "That was the nicest thing anyone ever done with me."

"You're welcome," I said. "Now comes the hard part."

"What do you mean?"

"I'm not sure. I guess if I knew it might not be so hard."

She pondered that and neither of us talked much the rest of the way to Gladburg. As we approached our exit Val turned around, hung over the seat and began digging in her pack. When she sat again she gathered her hair up and twisted it into a knot on top of her head. She put on a baseball cap and a pair of bulky reading

315

glasses and buried her face in an old woodworking magazine from under the seat. I tried to keep from grinning. She turned her head sideways to look at me. "Is something wrong?" she asked.

"No, I was just waiting for the mustache," I laughed and she rolled up the magazine and whacked me on the head with it, blushing.

I took the long route around town. We stopped at two lights on Reservoir Boulevard and at both of them Val hunched over the magazine, not looking up until we were back to speed. We turned onto Link Road and crossed the old iron bridge over Falling Creek before she finally put it down.

For some reason my stomach was churning, and then I realized where it was coming from. "Relax," I said.

"Just pay attention to driving, mister cucumber."

"Cucumber?" I guffawed.

"You know what I mean." She blushed again. I was mister cool.

By then we were on Old Mercer Road, and when I made the turn into my lane I could practically feel Val's antenna quivering. She had been here only once, back in the glory days. She hadn't seen my place since, and my mind began making an inventory of the mess inside even before we came to a stop. My grass hadn't been cut in weeks and the place looked shabby.

I got out, took my duffel from behind the seat and was ready to unlock the door when Val said, "You're not going to check it out first?"

"Check out what?" I said. I turned the key and walked into the kitchen. Nothing but a stale smell greeted me. I dropped my duffel on the floor as Val walked in behind me. There were still dishes in the sink and a general look of disarray about the place.

My dining room was my office, with a desk facing the big window that was long enough to hold a computer monitor and printer, plus spread blueprints on. A big drafting table dominated the living room. All of it was in sight of my kitchen, where I usually ate at the counter.

I picked up the desk phone to call my voice mail while Valerie went to the sink and began cleaning up. "You don't have to do that," I said, but she paid no mind. There were nine messages; two of them were from the Gladburg police department. A detective named Dennis Delcorlia was inquiring about Valerie and both times left his number asking me to call as soon as possible. The last message was from Rollin. It was from this morning and against all my expectations he sounded upbeat—even exuberant.

"Ray, I wanted you to be the first to know. Tina regained consciousness this morning—not for long, but the doctors think she's through the worst of it. She took a drink of water and recognized her parents, and she even asked about Valerie. She's still critical but it looks like she's going to make it.

"Give me a call when you get back to town. I heard you had some truck problems—man, I was sorry to hear that. But I sure am glad you got that girl home safe. Hope to talk with you before the weekend. Ciao."

I sat the phone in its cradle and turned to Val. "Tina woke up. The doctors think she's through the worst of it."

She sighed with relief and turned her face upward with her eyes closed. I saw her lips move.

"The police want to talk with you, Val. Mike said they've been out to the job twice looking for us."

I carried my bag to the bedroom and was pulling out dirty clothes when I noticed the window over my bed. It was smashed and there were big depressions on the bed that looked like footprints. My heart sank. I looked around the room and saw nothing else out of place. My dresser was littered with the usual mess. I yanked the closet door open and nothing was missing. I looked in the bathroom, then ran upstairs and looked in both rooms and nothing was amiss. I came back down and grabbed the flashlight from its charger over the kitchen counter. Valerie turned to look as I headed down to the basement. I shone the light behind the furnace, the water heater. Nothing. I went back up the stairs and Val was staring at me.

"What's wrong?" she demanded.

I led her to the bedroom where she immediately saw the window.

317

Broken glass was strewn over my pillows.

"Have you got a gun?" she said.

"Why would I have a gun?"

"Why would you have a gun?" She looked away like there was a bad taste in her mouth.

"One gun between the two of us is enough, don't you think?"

"We ain't got that now, have we?"

"There's nobody here, Val. This happened days ago."

"How do you know there's nobody watching?"

"The son of a bitch is a coward. For all we know this might be unrelated."

I looked at Val's defiant face and aggressive stance and realized she was scared. I opened my arms and she let me hold her but she wasn't comforted. She stayed rigid and kept her arms between us; there was no getting through her guard.

CHAPTER 23

When I got Delcorlia on the phone he sounded glad to hear from me. He had a straightforward manner that I liked but I was cautious.

"Mr. Anderson told me you took Miss Tolliver to Kentucky."

"I just got back. Mike said you've been out at the job."

"Is there any way we can contact her?"

"That might be hard. Her community is pretty poor and as far as I know none of her relatives has a phone. I thought the idea was for her to disappear for a while."

He chewed on that. "Can you come down and talk? We've got some evidence from the scene where we found Miss Utterbach, and we were hoping someone might be able to make sense of it."

I considered telling him about the break-in but decided to wait. I didn't want cops swarming over my house yet. "I can be there in about thirty minutes," I said.

"You know where the station is?"

"Downtown. I used to drive by it every day."

"Great." He sounded happy. "You park anywhere you want, Mr. Brauner. Ask for me at the desk. You get a ticket and I'll personally void it out for you."

"Hopefully that won't be necessary. I'll see you." I hung up the phone.

"That was pretty good," Val said.

"Well, there's no point in spreading the news around. He says they found some evidence they want us to see."

"Can I finish this first? Your floor is gross. You really ought to take better care of this place, you know."

"It's been kind of hectic."

I let her wash dishes while I finished unpacking. I took inventory of my bedroom and everything was intact. I gingerly pulled my dresser drawers open with a handkerchief and found nothing missing. My own guitar still rested in its case so I knew this hadn't been a burglary.

319

Ten minutes later my dishes were done, the kitchen sink and counter were sparkling, the floor had been swept and we were on our way downtown. Again Valerie kept a low profile and I could feel her humiliation at having to hide like this. I hated it too. When we arrived at the station I parked near the front entrance in a police space and we slipped inside.

While Val hung back I asked the desk officer for detective Delcorlia and handed him my card. He disappeared and about thirty seconds later a man my age wearing civilian clothes and a shoulder holster came around the corner.

"Mr. Brauner? Dennis Delcorlia. Thanks for coming," he said. We shook hands and I noticed he was already graying, but he looked fit and sharp. "Come on back." He seemed not to notice Valerie, who stood quietly by the wall.

We had walked a few steps down the hall when he wheeled sharply around. "May I help you?" he said.

Val was following a few steps behind me and I said quietly, "I believe she is someone you wanted to see."

A look of astonishment spread over his face but he recovered quickly. Once we got into an office down the hall and the door was closed he smiled broadly. "Miss Tolliver, I presume?"

"Well it ain't Mister Livingston," Val said, taking off her cap. She pulled the knot from her hair and shook it out around her shoulders.

"Well, I'll be damned." Delcorlia stood staring at her, and then remembered his manners. "Thank you for coming. Please have a seat, both of you. I guess I have some catching up to do. I thought you were in Kentucky." He sat down after us.

"We were," I said. "We took her things down with my truck because her car was broken. A couple of my employees have been fixing it while we were gone. They're the only ones who know she was coming back and we'd really like to keep it that way."

He sat stroking his chin and nodding, but I could tell he was delighted. "Very well. We'll keep it that way. You were renting a trailer out at the Streidl farm, Miss Tolliver, is that correct?"

"It was my trailer," Val said. "Ray here was good enough to pull it back home with his truck."

"And where is home, Miss Tolliver?"

"Hurt, Kentucky. It's in Harlan County."

"Harlan County? That's a pretty hard place from what I hear."

"You'll never know unless you lived there."

"I heard about the night in King's Tavern when you stood up to those two thugs. I must say that took a lot of courage."

"There wasn't nobody else doing nothing. Sometimes you got to speak up."

"From what I hear you were quite a hero."

"I heard you wanted to talk about Tina."

"Yes," Delcorlia said, getting down to business. He hunched over a clipboard. "Do you know of anyone who might have wanted to hurt her?"

"No. She was good to everybody, all the time."

"Did you know her boyfriend?"

"Curtis? Not too good, but he wouldn't hurt her like that. He's a drunk and he has a mouth on him but he ain't that bad."

"Are you aware that he struck her at least once, and was seen shoving her in front of witnesses last month?" He looked up.

"I know he hit her before, and I think she was crazy to stay with him. But he ain't that strong for one thing, and he don't care about her enough to hurt her like that."

"How do you know this?"

"The doctor said Tina had skin under her nails. Can't you tell whether it was him from that?"

Delcorlia's eyes fell to his clipboard. "How about anyone else? Have there been any customers who might have had some fixation on her?"

"Everybody liked her, mister. There's been a new bunch a-comin in lately with the old man's trouble, and I don't know nothing about them. But folks around town love her. How about some of them ugly people that's been pushing Rollie around? It seems to me you ought to be checking them out."

"That's the problem. We've checked them out, and every one of them was somewhere else that night. There are reliable witnesses for all of them, placing them far from Miss Utterbach's apartment at the time of her attack."

"Well, they got people behind them, you know."

"We know. And believe me, we're working on that. Miss Tolliver, do you know anyone else who might hold some personal grudge against you?"

She snorted. "Lots of people. I ain't never been that popular."

"Have you ever had a quarrel with a customer at King's Tavern?"

"One time I knocked down a man who grabbed my butt, but that was nearly two years ago."

"Can you tell me what happened?"

"I just did."

"Did you know him? Was he a regular?"

"He was a steelworker from out of town. I believe there was a crew of them a-workin on the water tower."

Delcorlia made a note on his clipboard. "Can you describe him?"

"He was about six foot, kind of heavy with reddish hair. It wasn't him neither, I can tell you. He was just a rowdy and all his buddies bought him a beer down the street and laughed about it afterward. Some of the regulars from King's seen them there."

Delcorlia continued scribbling. "I understand you were quite a ping-pong champion," he said before looking up again.

Val took a deep breath and blew it out slowly. "Well, I hated it. It was like being in a freak show. That was just the old man's way of getting people in."

"Did you have any regular opponents? People who might have been obsessed with beating you?"

"It was ping-pong, mister. Nobody took it that serious."

After nearly an hour of this Delcorlia apologized for taking so much of our time. "I realize some of these questions seem trivial, but there's no way of knowing what may help us later. Would you like a sandwich? I'm going to have someone run out to Campelli's."

~

322

After phoning in our order he turned to me. "I understand you two were together the night Miss Utterbach was attacked."

"That's right," I said. "We had dinner at a brew pub over near Stroudsburg."

"And you came back to King's Tavern after leaving Miss Tolliver at her trailer?"

"Yes. But we sat and talked in her trailer for over an hour first. During that time I went out to my truck and surprised someone outside. When I came out he ran up the drive toward the road, and I heard a car drive off."

"Really?" Delcorlia seemed startled.

"Yes. It was a little before midnight."

I was surprised at first that nobody had told him. Then I realized not a man on my crew would give up a thing to the police unless it was their own business. Now I was pretty sure Delcorlia had no inkling of the episode with Tony in the men's room at King's Tavern.

"And you didn't call the police, or stay around?"

"It's not like I didn't try. But no, I didn't."

"I wouldn't let him," Valerie interjected. "He wanted to stay but I sent him home. I had a shotgun with me and I ain't scared to use it."

"You had a shotgun with you?" Delcorlia's eyebrows lifted.

"Mister, I wasn't raised around here. My uncle was a sniper in Vietnam and he taught me to take care of myself."

"I see." He digested that for a few seconds, and then turned back to me.

"So this person you surprised—it was a man, is that right?"

"Yes. I saw him in the shadows when he started running, and then got a better look by the security light up at the farmhouse. He tried to stay out of it but he couldn't entirely."

"Any description?"

"Not much. He had dark clothes on, dark hair I think. That's about it."

"Hmmm." Delcorlia tapped his fingers on the clipboard.

323

"I think he must have figured I was there for the night and he didn't want any complications. So he went for Plan B. The funny thing is, he could have had the drop on me but he didn't take it; he ran."

"That's because you're mister untouchable to those guys," Val interjected again.

"What do you mean?" Delcorlia asked.

"That night in the tavern they all showed respect for mister importance here, but he was the only one."

"Val, that was just those two clowns. The other guy certainly had no respect for me or anyone else. It was a quirk." I felt a flash of irritation that she was still harping on that.

Delcorlia made more notes on his clipboard, and soon the sandwiches arrived. While we were eating Val asked if there was any more news about Tina.

"Well, right now it looks like the perpetrator avoided a murder rap. This morning she was coming out of her coma; we're hoping she may be through the worst of it."

"Can we visit her?"

"I doubt it. Her doctors don't want us talking to her yet. That young lady is going to be in critical condition for a while."

"Is she under any kind of guard?" I asked.

"Twenty-four seven. Nobody gets through her door except doctors, nurses and family."

We ate in silence for a few minutes, and when I was nearly done decided to get the inevitable out of the way. "I found a window broken at my house this morning," I said. "Someone came in through my bedroom."

Delcorlia looked up. "Why didn't you say so?"

"I don't have time to deal with that now. Besides, I'm pretty sure it happened days ago. Nothing is missing as far as I can tell."

"Did you touch anything?"

"No. My father was a cop, too. I do understand some things."

"No kidding? Where was that?"

"Montgomery County, Maryland."

324

"Huh. You better let me send some fellows out to dust your place and check it out. Can we do that when you get home?"

"It won't be until late. I've got to get out to my job and then get Valerie squared away. In the meantime I'd really rather things be left alone."

"How long are you going to be here, Miss Tolliver?"

She looked at me and shrugged so I answered. "A couple days. She has a few things to wrap up. But she won't be staying in Gladburg."

"I see. Is there a number where I can reach her?"

"We don't have that yet. But you'll be able to find her through me."

He sat behind his desk frowning slightly until Valerie spoke up.

"I heard you found something."

"Yes. We did." He opened his desk drawer and pulled out a clear, flat plastic bag that had been heat-sealed at the top and slid it across to Val. "We found this underneath Miss Utterbach when the paramedics put her on the gurney. Nobody recognizes it; I wondered if you might have seen anybody wearing something like it."

She picked it up, fingering it absently through the plastic, and I saw that it was a gold crucifix on a chain. The chain was broken. Suddenly an electric shock shot up my spine and I felt every hair on my body stand on end. Valerie dropped the bag like a red-hot thing and recoiled violently from it with a guttural sound.

"Oh lordy," she said in a husky voice, turning to me. Her eyes were wide. "It's him. It's him, Ray. Oh lordy, I think I'm going to be sick."

She put her hand over her mouth and rose from her chair, and Delcorlia rushed around to escort her out of the room. I followed them into the hall in time to see her plunge through a door. Seconds later a uniformed officer flew out the same door zipping his fly and the three of us stood there listening to the sound of Valerie being sick, and it was not pretty. I was shaking violently all over, freezing cold even though I'd been warm only seconds before.

"Are you okay?" Delcorlia asked, staring at me.

325

"Not yet. I will be." I stuck my hands into my pockets to try and stop them from shaking but my whole body was out of control. I felt an abstract sort of relief that at least I wasn't sick.

After a minute we heard the sound of water running and Valerie coughing and clearing her throat. I was still fluttery and turning limp from the adrenalin surge when she came out. Her face was ghastly white but she was composed. The other officer had disappeared.

"Are you okay?" Delcorlia asked her.

"Yeah." She looked at me. "Are you okay?"

"Yeah, fine." I felt like I'd been wrung out.

"You want to talk about it?" Delcorlia said. "Either one of you?"

"Can you get me some water?" Val said.

~

Sunlight came through narrow blinds and fell across one side of Delcorlia's desk in blinding strips. He shuffled papers for a few seconds while an intermittent hum droned from the fluorescent lamp overhead. He picked up a paper clip, scratched the side of his neck with it and threw it down. He finally leaned back in his chair, looking back and forth between us. "Would somebody like to tell me what just happened?"

And then Valerie began speaking in a voice so soft Delcorlia had to lean forward again to hear her.

"When I was a little girl I started feeling things that others was feeling. Sometimes I could tell just what they was thinking too, without even wanting it. It's been that way ever since, off and on. Back home the old folks call it a gift. Most times I try to ignore it because it kind of gets in the way of things, if you know what I mean."

Delcorlia's face was expressionless.

"When Ray and me got to be close the same thing started with him. He don't really understand it, cause mostly it just happens with me. But it happens real strong between me and him sometimes. I don't even understand it myself, but I'm used to it and he ain't." She

326

turned to me. "I'm sorry, Ray, I didn't mean to scare you like that."

"It wasn't your fault."

It took Delcorlia a while to digest this. "How about the gold cross?" he asked, massaging his neck. It still lay on his desk.

"I know who it's from," Val said, her voice turning cold. "It was a man I met two years ago when I first come up here. But it wasn't here, it was in Scranton."

"How sure are you?"

"Mister, I guarantee you."

"Do you mind if I tape record the rest of what you say here?"

"You go right ahead," she said.

And then Valerie related the story of how she had left Kentucky because of problems at home, and traveled up the Appalachian Mountains to the one other coal mining region of the east, hoping to make a new start. But quickly her money ran out. Her car was barely running, she hadn't eaten in two days and she was desperate to find work. It was at a little restaurant in a run-down section of Scranton, near a railroad bridge crossing a river, where a man had taken pity on her. Or so it seemed at the time.

"None of the nice places would hire me because I didn't have any address," she said. "I was sleeping in my car; I didn't even have a place to wash except for gas stations. That's why I had to look in the lowest kind of places for a job—anything to get myself turned around.

"When I went in this one place the woman said she couldn't hire me, but she felt sorry for me. She asked if I was hungry and gave me a plate of food and a big glass of milk. I was sitting in the corner eating when this man come over and sat himself down.

"At first I thought he was a kind man. He looked like a businessman and he talked real nice. He said he was from New York but he had some property nearby he was checking up on. He said I looked like I needed a break, and he wondered if I ever made commercials. I told him I hardly ever watched a TV and he seemed surprised. I guess I told him more than I ought to, but he was real

327

polite and listened to me.

"When I was done eating he said he had to go take care of some business, but he'd like to see me that night if I was free. Like I had some kind of a busy schedule." She laughed bitterly. Delcorlia sat quietly with his hands folded.

"He said he made instruction videos and commercials and he thought I was pretty. He told me if I got cleaned up he would make a sample video to take back to New York, and maybe he could get me a job where I could earn lots of money. He gave me a twenty-dollar bill for gas and wrote an address on a piece of paper and told me to come that night and hope for the best." Val squeezed her eyes shut at the memory.

"I went to the address. There was this strip of old metal buildings; I think there was a radiator shop or garage or something like that next door, and some other dirty places that was all closed up. And I seen his car, it was a gold Mercedes, by a door and I knocked on it.

"When he come to the door he looked different. He had on a shirt that was unbuttoned partway down, and that's when I seen that cross. He even reached up and touched it once. He said to come in, and when I walked inside there was some lights and a stand with a camera on it but it wasn't nothing like I expected. There was a real bad feeling to the place." She shuddered and I felt it all the way up my spine.

"I knew I shouldn't stay there, but he kept talking to me real easy. He told me he was sorry the place was so dirty and he said it wouldn't show in the pictures. When he started talking about the pictures again is when I seen it."

She stopped. Voices could be heard in other parts of the building, snatches of static and radio conversation. Traffic noise drifted through the window, while overhead the soft buzzing of the fluorescent lamp came and went.

Valerie was sitting erect with her eyes squeezed shut, and tears were beginning to come. Delcorlia fumbled in a drawer and produced several tissues, which I took and pressed into her hand.

She wiped her eyes and then blew her nose. "Thank you," she murmured wetly, gathering her composure.

"Seen what, Miss Tolliver?" Delcorlia asked.

"Death." Val sat erect, and coldness came back into her voice. "I looked at him and I seen death. I could hear the sound of women crying, women begging. It was like a nightmare, and then I knew what he wanted me for."

"Where were these women? Did you see anyone else there?" Delcorlia seemed puzzled.

"It was a-comin from inside him. They was women he had hurt, and he killed them. He liked it. I could see it in his eyes, plain as looking in a window."

Delcorlia sat there with his hands folded and kept very quiet.

"I knew if I didn't get out of there I'd be another one just like them. I said I didn't feel good, I'd have to come back later, and he saw I knew. He got between me and the door and said it was too late for that. He grabbed me and tried to put a cloth over my face and then—" She stopped and her eyes fell to her lap, where her fingers were twisting the tissue into shreds.

"And then what?" Delcorlia asked quietly.

"I guess I went sort of crazy on him." She took a deep breath and pulled in her lips and I could feel her struggling. The room was dead still.

"Went sort of crazy?" Delcorlia's voice sounded strained.

"I told you my uncle was in Vietnam. He taught me how to take care of myself when I was going through a rough time." Val spoke softly but her composure was back. "When that man grabbed me it was like everything Duane taught me come to a point, and there wasn't no holding back. I think he didn't hardly know what hit him, and neither did I until it was over. It happened real fast."

"What happened?"

"When I got loose I knocked the wind out of him. Then I busted his face and his arm and took him down. He might have got a couple busted ribs too, plus I kicked him in the scrotum real hard. When I left him he wasn't in no shape to hurt nobody for a while."

329

"Good Lord."

"Do you think I done wrong?"

Delcorlia cleared his throat. "Miss Tolliver, I wasn't there and I can't pass any judgments. But if everything you've told me is true, and I have no reason to think it's not, it sounds like a simple case of self-defense." He picked up a pencil and fiddled with it. "How can you be sure this is the same cross you saw that man wearing?"

"Ask him." Val tilted her head at me.

"Mr. Brauner?" Delcorlia looked at me.

"Look, I don't know how anyone can explain these things," I said. "But a few weeks ago out on one of my jobs I got hit by two hundred forty volts of alternating current and it was the worst shock I had in my life. That is, until the second Valerie recognized that thing. You saw with your own eyes what it did to me. It's not something I want to feel again. Frankly I'd be more comfortable if you put that back in your evidence locker."

He reached across the desk, took the bag back and slid it into his drawer. "Is that better?"

"Yeah. Thanks."

"Miss Tolliver, did this man have a name?"

"He wrote 'Tommy' on the paper with his address. I don't believe that was his real name though."

"Can you describe him for us?"

A slight whirring sound and then a click came from the tape recorder. The cassette had run out. Delcorlia reached over and took it out. He began rummaging in his drawer for another, and then Valerie spoke up.

"You don't need that. I can draw you a picture."

"You can draw me a picture?"

"If you loan me your pencil and some paper."

"You really are full of surprises, aren't you?"

"Mister, I ain't here to entertain nobody. I'm here to tell you what happened, and what you want to do about it is up to you."

"I apologize, Miss Tolliver. I didn't mean anything negative by that. It's just that you get to a point in life when you think nothing

330

can surprise you any more, and boom." He threw his hands wide, and shrugged. "Let's just say you've taught me a few things I never expected to learn."

He shuffled through the credenza behind his desk and found a pad of unlined paper, which he slid across to Valerie with his pencil. She moved closer, picked them up and began sketching. Her eyebrows furrowed in concentration. Delcorlia leaned back in his chair with his fingertips together watching her. I had a better view of the pad. She started with an oval for the head, placed a line for the eyebrows and then roughed in the neck and shoulders. I felt the heat of her concentration as she went back to the face and drew a nose and mouth. The more details she filled in the more I felt a strange anger boiling up inside, but it was focused and purposeful. I watched as the face began to take on a specific personality, and realized with a start that Valerie was an excellent artist. Full of surprises indeed, I thought.

"Keep your thoughts to yourself," Val muttered as she penciled in an open shirt and then the cross hanging at the man's neck. By now his face was complete right down to the wrinkles and shading around his eyes, and a tiny droop at the corners of his mouth. Using her fingertips she even smudged in the shadow of a beard, although he was clean-shaven. He looked to be in his mid-forties, dark hair, not quite handsome but trustworthy, almost melancholy. After a few more minutes she leaned back, picked the pad up and held it at arm's length and seemed satisfied. "That's him," she said, and slid the pad over to Delcorlia. "About five eleven, two hundred pounds. Nearly tall as Mister Brauner here, only heavier."

"Good Lord." Delcorlia stared at the drawing. "Where did you learn to do this?"

"My mama always was artistic. She taught me lots of things. My daddy just thought it was pride and vanity."

"Well, Miss Tolliver, I believe your pride and vanity are going to help us find the man who attacked your friend. And if everything you told me is true we might also put a serial killer out of business. Your daddy may be proud to know that someday."

~

There wasn't much after that. Delcorlia thanked us in a heartfelt manner for our cooperation. He promised to keep Valerie's identity confidential but said her picture would be faxed to every police department between Allentown and New York City. Once more she put her hair up inside her cap and we left the station exhausted.

I felt quietly thankful that something unknown at last had been dragged from the shadows into the light of day. Now the problems at King's Tavern began to assume more manageable proportions. Dangerous as they were, no longer did I regard the bumbling bruisers there as killers. As for "Tommy", his days of anonymity were nearly over. I was thinking I surely would hate to be him once that picture hit the wires, but then realized Valerie was struggling with darker thoughts. Having to relive the events of that night had brought a nearly unspeakable horror back to life, but it took me a while to understand there was something more on her mind.

"That detective don't know I stole from that man," she finally said.

"Delcorlia doesn't need to know that, Val. That man has blood on his hands. You said it yourself—it was your life he was aiming to take and he didn't deserve to walk away clean. Let it go."

"What if they catch him and he tells?"

"If they catch him there is nothing he can do or say to hurt you any more. Anyone could have rolled him after you left him there, and if his DNA was under Tina's nails he's done. Hell, his DNA is probably on that necklace. One single hair is all they need."

"What if they ask me to testify?" She didn't seem persuaded.

"You already did. I think you need to eat something now. Breakfast was a long time ago and you might not get another chance until pretty late."

"I'm not hungry."

"Trust me, you will be. Look, we can't go out to the job for another hour—let's go back to my place and make you a nice fat sandwich and boil up some of that corn. Look at all that stuff back there." I jerked a thumb at the bushels of Duane's produce and veered into the lot of the IGA.

While Val slouched down in the truck I ran in and picked up a gallon of milk, two loaves of bread, some butter, Provolone cheese and mayonnaise. On the way back to the house I plugged my cell phone into the speaker and punched in Mike's number.

"You're a hard man to reach," Mike said when he heard my voice.

"We've been at the police station," I said. "We're headed back to my place to grab some grub and then we'll be out there. There's news, some major developments."

"Oh, no." Mike sounded chagrined. "None of this would have anything to do with a broken window at your place, would it?"

"How did you know about that?"

"I broke it," Mike's voice crackled over the speaker. "I forgot to tell you yesterday because I was so involved with Megan."

"You broke it?"

"One of the blueprints got ruined in a rainstorm and I had to get into your computer to find the clearances for the ductwork."

"You bastard!"

"I thought I'd have it fixed before you got back but it was insulated glass so I had to order it. I've got it with me now. Next time you leave town you ought to burn me a CD with all your mojo for the job on it."

A sweet feeling of relief flooded over me, and I couldn't keep from laughing out loud. Then Val started, and pretty soon Mike joined us over the phone, and by then the three of us were laughing so hard I nearly missed the turn off Link Road onto Old Mercer.

CHAPTER 24

After replacing Val's lost lunch with a much better one and cleaning the broken glass off my bed we headed out to the Fryes. I called Mike again on the way and he said the last guys were leaving. When we arrived he was coming down a ladder with a tube of caulk under his arm. I stared in admiration at the addition. The siding was done; the exterior was nearly complete.

When Mike got down the ladder he greeted Val first. She responded shyly; then he stared in amazement at me. "Whoa! What happened to you?"

"I'm back, Ace." I stuck out my hand and Mike gripped it and pulled me close.

"Something has changed. Val, tell me I'm not seeing things here. What did you do to this guy?"

"It wasn't me," she said. "I think he better tell you."

"I'm back," I said. "Is that so hard to understand?"

Mike looked me up and down. "Where's your pump, Bwana? Let me see that hand."

I held my hand out and he looked closely at it. He squeezed my forearm all the way up to the elbow and shook his head. "Someone put the mojo on you, my man."

I felt Valerie staring at me, and finally I said, "Yeah. It was a miracle, so to speak. In fact—well, that's just about what it was. It's kind of an unusual story."

"I'd really like to hear that story."

"I'm not sure there's time for it right now."

"You seen your doctor yet?"

"No."

"That's going to be interesting," Mike said.

"Yeah. I think it may be."

"You know, it really wouldn't hurt you to give God the glory once in a while," Val said.

"Speaking of which," Mike said, "do you know that two nights ago after work Mackey got the guys together to say a prayer for Tina?"

"You're kidding."

"I'm not. I think he's been feeling pretty guilty about what we did to old Tony in the men's room, and you can't imagine how down he's been about Tina. Hell, everyone has been. After work he told the guys he was going to pray for her and asked if anyone wanted to join him."

"Really?" I could just barely picture it.

"Yup. I thought they were going to laugh at him, but Spider was the first one to come over, and then I did, and after that the other guys hung around to listen. Old Mack did himself proud. He prayed a real nice prayer for Tina and everyone kept real quiet and said 'amen' at the end. And damned if she didn't start getting better the next day."

"I guess there's no end of surprises," I said.

"Now why would you be surprised?" Val retorted. "You really ought not be so ashamed to say 'please' and 'thank you', Bwana. With you being so smart and all." Her eyes were drilling a hole into me.

Gratefully at that moment I spotted Mr. Frye walking up from his barn. His face opened into a smile when he saw me.

"Well, hello there, young man," he said, sticking out his weathered hand.

I pumped it and said, "Are my guys taking good care of you?"

"We are so pleased," he said. "Lucy can hardly wait to get back from vacation, and we haven't even left yet." He shook his head and laughed his pure rich laugh. "Say, you're looking a lot better," he remarked, looking closely at me. "I guess the time away did you some good."

"Yes, it did," I said. "I should be back here Monday—there'll be more time to catch up then."

"Well, it's good to have you back. These boys have been doing a fine job—you ought to be proud of them."

I thanked him and he continued into the house, and about that time we heard the sound of a car. Valerie's Jetta was coming up the drive, followed by Mackey's old red Dodge. Before it got close enough for a good look it disappeared around the drive circling the house. Val stood there looking mildly interested that her car actually was running, but when it reappeared around the back of the house her expression changed to one of puzzlement.

"Where's my car?" she asked, sounding disappointed. This car looked and sounded like a brand new 1987 Jetta, right down to the tires.

"I believe that would be it," Mike said.

She had a look of disbelief on her face as Spider stopped in front of us. He got out while Val stood there uncomprehending. "That's my car?"

"Yes ma'am, it is," Spider said. "'Sup, boss," he said, sticking out his hand, and then he did a double take. "Holy moly, what happened to you?"

By that time Mackey had pulled his truck up behind the Jetta and emerged with a grin. Valerie had her hand over her mouth and was at a loss for words.

"We fixed it up a little for you," Mackey said, his big face beaming.

"You fixed it up?" Val said tremulously. "Is that really my car?"

"It's really your car," he said.

"Oh, lordy," Val said. She walked over, stuck her head inside and wailed, "What have you done?"

I looked over her shoulder and saw that even the inside looked new. The seats were immaculate, there were new floor mats and a stereo sat snugly in the console where only a big hole had been before.

"Don't you like it?" Mackey asked, sounding a little worried.

"Like it? Nobody ever done anything so nice for me," she said, laughing through her tears.

"We, uh, appreciate what you did for Rollie." Mackey cleared his throat and looked down.

"Thank you so much," she said and hugged him tight. He

blushed, and then Val turned to Spider.

"I never did give you enough credit, Spider," she said. "I hope you forgive me. Thank you," and she hugged him too. He hugged her back, and I could tell he was moved.

"How did you get all that done so fast?" I was impressed.

"It was Mack's idea," Spider said.

"My buddy Jimmy teaches at a vo-tech outfit," Mackey said. "They teach high school kids body work and sometimes they need cars to work on. I helped him build his deck, so after we fixed the motor we took her over there. When we told Jimmy who it was for he said they'd do the full treatment on it. You got a lot of respect by standing up for Rollie, ma'am," he said to Val.

She dropped her eyes and ran her fingers over the shiny new paint.

"What all did you do to it?" I asked.

"Spider tuned her up and I helped—new plugs, wires, belts, hoses, flushed the radiator, everything. Jimmy and his kids did the body, plus they put in a radio and new exhaust and brakes and did a front-end alignment. I took up a collection for the tires. They're Michelins." He looked pleased as could be.

"Took up a collection?"

"At King's and from the guys here."

"Did you tell anyone she was coming back?" I asked.

"No, I just said it was for Val's car and it was a surprise."

I shot Mike a glance and he shrugged. It was already done and there was no helping it.

"What's your secret, boss?" Spider said. "You look like you've been eating some red meat."

"Well, I did have a little bit of good deer meat at Val's uncle's place," I said. "We brought you back some of his produce too."

I walked over to my truck and took one of the baskets from the bed. Mackey and Spider came over and I lifted the other two out to them. We carried them into the addition and I invited the guys to take what they wanted. They helped themselves and we left the rest to divide with the crew on Monday.

337

"What happened to your door?" Mackey asked.

"We had a mishap," I said. "Rolled backward and it caught on a tree."

"I believe you had a real adventure," Spider said, looking strangely at me.

"The Lord healed you, didn't he?" Mackey said.

"Yes." That was the simplest answer possible, and I took refuge in it.

"I knew it the minute I saw you," he said.

"I got sick again," I said. "My IV pump broke and I thought I was going to die down there, but instead I got healed by a little girl. She said the Lord brought me there. I really don't understand more than that."

"Hell, you look better than I ever saw you before," Spider said.

There was the distant sound of a phone ringing somewhere in the Fryes' house. Mike said, "How did it go with the police?"

"We know who hurt Tina," I said.

"No shit?" said Spider. All three of them stared at me.

I looked around for Val but she was outside sitting in her car, playing with her radio.

"It was none of those clowns from King's. It was someone Val ran into up in Scranton before she ever came to Gladburg. We think he may be from New York. It took him two years, but he finally tracked her here."

"You're sure about that?" Spider said.

"Dead sure. That's another long story I can't tell right now. They've got physical evidence and a picture of him. We don't know his name but he's a real sicko, probably a serial killer. That's why it's imperative that nobody knows where she is now. Nobody." I stared at Mackey. His face was white.

"I appreciate what you did for Val, Mackey, but if anyone knows she's around here, even for one day, it's more dangerous for her. Anybody asks you how she liked her tires, you just say she loved them all the way back to Kentucky. Not a word more."

"Yes sir," Mackey said in a small voice.

338

"I'll keep you filled in as much as I can. It's going to be at least a week before I get caught up on everything. I haven't talked to the Plums yet and I need to see my doctor again. But you guys should know I'm proud of every one of you. You've done a great job here, and what you did for Valerie is beyond words."

I slapped Mackey on the back. "Tell your friend Jimmy I owe him one. After we get through this mess we'll have a big old party, all on me."

~

After Spider and Mackey left I asked Mike if anyone else knew Val was staying with Megan.

"Not a soul," he said. "As far as Spider and Mack know, she's with you."

Valerie walked through the door with a happy look on her face.

"You said something about a plan to help Rollie?" Mike said.

"Well, it's better than nothing," I said. "Val, tell Mike about that bottle you and Tina found."

She recounted the story to him, just as she had to Duane. Mike listened intently as she described the compartment under the floor in the wine cellar, and how excited she and Tina had been to find the old bottle of cognac. She ended with it sitting on Rollin's office fireplace mantel. Then I picked up the story, describing the bottle in more detail and how I had advised Rollin to put it away. I recalled Rollin's visit in the hospital when he told me it was gone, and how hopeless I had felt.

"We really didn't know a thing about it, but to me it seemed like a metaphor for everything that was happening. I thought Rollin was letting everything slip through his fingers. The night we heard the old man's tape seemed to put everything into a death spiral.

"And then three nights ago I had a dream. I saw Valerie holding that bottle like she was taking it somewhere. The next day I asked her about it."

Mike was following with a bewildered expression, not

339

understanding how any of it connected, and then Val picked up the thread.

"The night those two bad men come into Kings I took that bottle out of Rollie's office and hid it back where Tina and me found it. It just didn't feel right leaving it up there where he had it.

"I made myself invisible like Duane taught me, and just finished when them two come in. So I sat back in the corner to see what would happen. I seen you both when you come in."

"Who's Duane?"

"That's her uncle," I said. "We stayed with him in Kentucky; he fixed my truck. He's a Vietnam vet."

"He was a war hero," Val said. "He's a mountain man now. He taught me how to take care of myself when I was going through a bad time."

"And he can make himself invisible?" Mike said.

"You and Ray didn't see me until I stood up, did you?"

"I guess not," Mike said, scratching his head. "But what does this have to do with helping Rollie?"

"I think we need to get that bottle out of there before he loses the place," I said. "I don't know why, but someone went to a lot of trouble to hide that thing. It's got more than sentimental value. My guess is that compartment was made for it when they built the hotel, and to me that says something."

"Hmm." Mike contemplated that.

"If Rollin sells out he'll never be the same again, Mike. I don't know where the old man is, but he's a proud man. I think he's laying low somewhere, just praying that Rollin comes up with whatever he needs. If Rollin loses that place I don't think he'll ever see his dad again. He'd probably die on the boardwalk somewhere in Atlantic City before coming home to that kind of disgrace. We can't let that happen."

"And you think that cognac is the ticket?"

"I don't know. But I think it's worth finding out."

"So what's your plan?"

"I wanted Val to tell me where the compartment is and try to get

340

it during a service call. But the way things are now I probably wouldn't be left alone long enough to find it. She knows right where it is, so going in there together might be the only way to do it."

"You want to go back to King's?" Mike said to Val.

"Nobody saw her the last time," I said. "Maybe she could be one of my helpers, carrying tools or something."

"I don't know about that, Bwana. These guys are walking a fine line and they know it, but that means they're paying attention to everything. They've even got a night watchman now."

"Then maybe we should do it when everyone's partying."

"That's probably more feasible. But damn, it's crazy." He stood there scratching his head.

"We should have some of the guys there for cover," I said. "Create a diversion, if necessary. How long will it take, Val?"

"Maybe five or six minutes."

"How hard is that?" I said.

Mike shook his head. "Not hard at all, if everything goes right. But what it doesn't?"

"We'll have to improvise. But we need to decide now what the best night is. When is the biggest crowd in there?"

"Tonight and tomorrow. No way," Mike said. "The place will be loaded with their own people. Rollie is having a band both nights but I dread the thought of it. I told you about last weekend, didn't I?"

"You both worry too much," Val said. "You got to have faith and then make your action pure. Everything else hangs on that."

Mike stared at her.

"Duane taught me that. It's how I saved my life one time. Except my action wasn't all pure and that's why Tina got hurt."

"Give it a rest, Val," I said. "Your action is the only reason the cops are going to catch this guy, so let it go."

She looked down. "We can do it," she said. "It should be Sunday night. That's when it's mostly locals and everyone's laid back."

"Sunday night it is," Mike said.

"Sunday night, by God," I said.

"You better mean it when you say that," Val said.

341

I walked Val to her car and slipped her two hundred dollars while Mike carried the glass for my window to my truck. He already had given her his cell phone. As she followed his van down the drive and away toward Megan's place she was singing to the radio and her Pirates cap was bopping.

~

I slept soundly in the fresh air coming through my broken window. In the morning I called Dr. Panos and got his answering service. I left my name and it wasn't ten minutes before he called me back from the golf course.

"This is the first chance I've had to do nine holes in six months," he said. "You'd better not have any bad news."

"No, things are going very well."

"You keeping up your meds?"

"Well, the pump broke. But I don't think we need it any more."

"Young man, that is not something to joke about. Are you keeping up the meds?"

"Doctor," I said, "the pump really did break but I'm fully recovered now; I think you'll agree when you see me."

"Please don't do this to me. Mr. Brauner, do you understand anything about antibiotics, and the super-resistant bacteria that can develop when you don't finish a full course of medication?"

"Yes, I do. But what happened to me is outside of science. I was stranded on a mountain in Kentucky when the pump broke, and I got really sick again. It wasn't funny at all. I was healed by a young girl, doctor. I can't explain it but I'm perfectly well. My burn is like an old scar now. You can run every kind of test you want; in fact I'll feel better about it if you do. But you won't find a thing wrong with me."

There was a long silence, and then he blew up. "You really know how to wreck a man's day."

"I wasn't trying to do that. I apologize; I should have waited to call you. Please don't worry; play your best game and I'll see you

342

later."

"No, that doesn't cut it. I will see you at the emergency room in one hour. Of all people I expected to have more sense than this, it was you." He was too angry to speak further, and I kicked myself for telling him anything. I should have lied and just made an appointment, but it was already done.

I arrived at the hospital a few minutes early. When Dr. Panos walked in wearing full golf attire I wanted to smile. He went to the desk and made an inquiry, and when I spoke from behind him he turned and gave me a look as if he'd just swallowed a bad oyster. I watched his eyes open wide as his irritation turned to surprise. He quickly hustled me into an examining room.

"Let me see your hand."

I showed it to him and he rubbed the depression in my palm like he expected to uncover the real wound beneath. He felt my arm up to the elbow, then compared my two arms and looked astonished.

"Tell me what happened," he said.

I told him I'd missed more than a full day of medication before realizing the pump was broken. Moreover I had been under enormous stress in the days prior to leaving, and hadn't been eating or sleeping well either.

"When I got sick I desperately wanted to get to a hospital, but the man whose house I was in told me later things were too far gone for that. He said he'd seen sepsis in Vietnam. He brought the girl to me."

And then I related my encounter with Ardie—her foul-tasting tea, the retching, and how her hands had simply stopped it. I described how her eyes seemed to change hue as she looked at me. I told him she thought my injured hand looked "just like Jesus' hand," and Dr. Panos was mute. When I told him how she clamped my hand over her breast he looked aghast. I described the sensation of heat leaving my body, how hot her breast and then her whole body became. I even told him about sensing some kind of light or energy traveling up my arm and into my body. His eyes never left mine the whole time. I told him I finally fell asleep.

343

His face wore an expression I've never seen on anyone before. When I described waking the next morning and urinating a powerful, dark brown stream he was visibly shaken, then he muttered "Yes, of course."

When I described my amnesia, how Valerie responded when she saw me, and how she had to help me remember the events I had just been through, he started to get animated. He asked to see my hand again. Now he understood why the depression in the middle of my palm was so perfectly shaped. He had me clench my fist and squeezed my arm up to the elbow once more and then he said, "We'll have to do blood tests, you know. That and a urinalysis would be more conclusive. Will you wait just a minute?"

He left the room and returned a few minutes later with a tech who drew two vials of blood from me. She gave me a specimen cup and asked me to fill it in the bathroom just outside the examining room. When I brought it back Dr. Panos told her to guard the samples with her life until she got further instructions from him, and sent her out.

"Mr. Brauner," he said, "I've been a practicing Christian all my life. Greek Orthodox. Everybody has heard stories from the literature of miracles but I never thought I would live to see such a thing. Do you know who that girl was?"

"Only her name. She's from a poor Appalachian family. I was told not to try and contact them."

"Why?"

"They're simple people and now they have to nurse her back to health. Apparently every time she does this she takes the sickness into herself, but somehow she always recovers. I was told she once healed a woman's rabies and nearly didn't make it afterwards."

"Rabies!"

"I only know what I was told. But I tend to believe it. Doctor, I was pretty bad off when that girl got there. I don't think I'd have made it without her."

"Do you realize you have been visited with divine grace?"

"I don't know anything about that. The girl said the Lord brought

344

me there. That's how folks down there think, and now I'm starting to believe they're on to something. I guess it was a miracle."

"You guess?" he almost sputtered.

"Yeah. I guess it was."

"You're a stubborn man," he said, shaking his head.

"Maybe so. But I'd still like to know what you find out from those samples you just took."

"Don't worry about that—you haven't seen the last of me. I strongly feel we should start over with the clindamycin though. You could be the picture of health but if there are still only a few viable bacteria left inside you they could be back with a vengeance."

"Ain't going to do it, doctor. Not unless you find something real. I hated that thing."

"We're going to follow this very closely, and be testing you a few more times." He was looking at me hard. "You're quite a contrary fellow, aren't you?"

"I don't try to be. I just like to keep things simple."

~

Before leaving I asked Dr. Panos if there was anyone I could talk with about Tina. He steered me to admissions and told a woman there that I was a close friend of a critical patient, and asked her to do what she could for me. She took Tina's name and spent a minute with her computer. Then she took my name and asked me to have a seat while she made a call.

A few minutes later to my surprise she told me I had been cleared to visit Tina's room for five minutes. She gave me directions through a labyrinth of hallways and up two floors on an elevator, and said someone at the nurses' station would direct me from there.

When I arrived at the nurses' station a uniformed police officer was waiting for me. He studied my driver's license and patted me down, and took me down a hall to a room where another cop stood at the door. I was glad to see they were taking security seriously. He checked my identification again and I was allowed to enter.

345

Mr. and Mrs. Utterbach barely greeted me. "Tina wanted to see you," was all her mother said.

I was hardly prepared for the sight of Tina. Her head and face were heavily bandaged with only one eye uncovered. Her left arm was in a sling and the exposed part of her face was still discolored from bruising. There were monitors and machines all around the bed. I saw the spark of recognition in her eye but wouldn't have known her until I saw the half-smile.

"Hey, handsome." She tried to put some perk into it but sounded heavily sedated.

"How are you feeling, Tina?" I said through an unexpected thickness of emotion.

"Oh, you know." She lifted her right hand and then it fell. "You're no stranger here. Wait till I tell those nurses who came to see me."

Her words sounded like they were being pushed up from a great depth and had barely enough amplitude to cross the distance between us.

"Valerie's been really worried about you."

"Is she okay?"

"She's safe and sound. I pulled her trailer down to Kentucky and met her family."

"Kentucky?"

"She went home, Tina. Her father said their whole church is praying for you."

"Tell Val—tell Val—"

"Tell her what, Tina?"

"Tell her be careful. Tell her I miss her, okay?" She was fading.

"I'll do that. You get well, Tina. You've got a lot of good friends who can't wait to see you again."

"Okay. Thanks." And her eye closed, and she lay so still and fragile on her pillow that my heart clutched.

Her father followed me out of the room. He looked like a pretty tough guy but in the hallway he struggled to hold back tears. "That's the most she's talked since she woke up," he said.

346

"What do the doctors say?"

"We thought she was a goner," he said. "The doctors didn't give us much hope either, except for Hallock. He told us to keep our faith up. When she started coming back two nights ago it was like a miracle."

"Maybe it was."

"Did you see the paper this morning?"

"No. Why?"

"They think they know who did this." His eyes burned into mine. "They even printed a picture of the guy."

"They'll get him," I said.

"I sure hope so."

"Mr. Utterbach, you count on it. His days are numbered."

There wasn't much else. He thanked me for coming and said I would be welcome any time, we shook hands and I left. On the way back to Gladburg I called Valerie and told her what had just happened.

~

I called Mr. Plum when I got home, and found he already had moved his telescope into the observatory. He said he planned to be out at the house most of Sunday. We needed to talk about landscaping and a few other things so I told him to expect me in the early afternoon.

After lunch I went out to my shed and started my old garden tractor and spent the next two hours mowing. I repaired my broken window and then weeded the flowerbed in front of the house. By evening my yard looked neat again, and the exercise lifted my spirits. I had a good dinner and stayed up playing my guitar until after ten o'clock.

I went to bed expecting to fall asleep easily but images of Tina lying in her hospital bed kept intruding. And her voice, so tiny and attenuated, rising from her bandaged face. I kept hearing Mr. Utterbach saying, "We thought she was a goner," and "when she started coming back it was like a miracle."

Until a few days ago I hadn't believed in miracles. As I told Dr. Panos, I liked to keep things simple. Now I had not only Valerie, but also Mackey, two doctors and Tina's father on my periphery reminding me of my deficiencies.

I knew why religion repelled me. I associated all of it with hysterical preachers barking their phobias to superstitious, acquiescent congregations. I had no doubt that many of the same preachers went home and abused their families as Val's father had, or consorted with prostitutes and built empires on the penury of their pious parishioners. Some even went into politics and attempted to transmute their claptrap into the law of the land.

But that was a prejudicial view, a defensive outer bulwark erected to protect a more vulnerable spot in my belief system. Miracles scared me because of an idea I had believed long before Valerie came along: There is no such thing as a free lunch.

I never had believed in Santa Claus or the tooth fairy, and when I became a young man learned quite early there was no such thing as free sex, either. You paid and paid for whatever you got; sometimes with things money could buy like dinners, gifts or trips, but more often in much harder currency. Even with most marriages I'd seen people continued to pay in emotional distress long after the thrill was gone. And who alive hadn't seen "The Godfather"? What reasonable person wouldn't expect prayer to work the same way? You take favors from someone higher up and eventually the bill comes due. Not being in a position to negotiate the terms it seemed wiser to me to just go it alone.

Now for better or worse I had been the recipient of—what was it Dr. Panos called it? Divine grace, if there was such a thing. It had fallen into my lap like a golden apple and the trick of it was, I hadn't been in a position to say no. Now there wasn't a thing I could do about it. I held my arms over my chest and felt my right bicep. I was stronger than I'd been in months—maybe ever. I continued down my arm to my hand, and explored the cavity in my palm with my fingertips. The skin was thick and supple, an old wound now by the feel of it. Had this been some cosmic bribe, or an out-and-out gift?

And how about Tina's unexpected turnaround? I couldn't see that as a quid pro quo; she had done nothing wrong but likely would be hurting for a long time even with the best prognosis. After visiting her I almost would have changed places with her, if only she could have been situated under the golden apple tree. But there were no if onlys allowed; the apple had fallen on me.

In that hollow place deep inside my soul I could tell myself I owed nobody anything because I hadn't asked for what happened. But somehow Val, Dr. Panos and a growing number of others had gathered into a Greek chorus in the back of my mind. Their persistent refrain was starting to get to me: Why do you have such a hard time saying "please" and "thank you"?

I knew that sometimes I feigned superiority over others for no greater reason than to hide my own insecurities. More than once Val had nailed me for my pride. Did she realize the truth? The world has no sympathy for weaklings, I thought, and I refused to walk through life radiating fear like Clarence did. Better to rub a few people the wrong way than to have the world run you over. It was a grand rationalization—my offense became my defense, hence it mattered not what anyone thought, not even Valerie.

But what Valerie thought did matter and I knew it. She made me see myself in a new light, no matter how unflattering it might be. At times she was like my cold shower in the morning—grabbing me by the neck and shocking me awake because that was the only thing that worked. Some days I hated those showers, dreaded them like the plague, but they were my portal to the waking world and I had to get through the door to find what was beyond. Sometimes Val made me afraid; not of her but of the things she showed me about myself. Things I often did not like.

Why was it so hard to say "please" and "thank you"?

I shut my eyes against the glow from the digital clock and pressed my eyelids with my fingertips until fireworks pinwheeled out from some dark place beyond my understanding. I watched the show for a few seconds and then lay still. "Thank you," I finally said out loud.

349

"Thank you for my life back again."

~

Coming up the drive to the Plum property felt like old times. Sunlight dappled the woods and when the house appeared I felt the same timeless sense of harmony flowing through the scene I had felt at Duane's place. I noticed the observatory port was open southward. Mr. Plum's blue Porsche sat by the garage and I pulled up next to it.

The house smelled pristine, of wood, paint, drywall compound— aromas I had grown to love over the years. Walking from the living room into the atrium I felt a marked difference of atmosphere. The air was purer here and the water's music lifted something inside me. I knelt by the stream, cupped my hand and drank, and its cold, pure sweetness invigorated me.

I recalled the day we hit this spring, and how fast the hole had filled with water. How Digger's curses had filled the air, and the sinking feeling that after months of dreaming, planning and meticulous work everything was going to collapse like the dirt walls nearly did around Digger's backhoe. I still had to smile at the memory of his face as he realized he couldn't just put the scoop of dirt back and plug what he had uncovered. He'd raced up to me babbling something about hydraulic cement while the water rose around the tires of his tractor. When I pointed to it he just stared unbelieving with his mouth open. Finally when he splashed down to get it out, the whole scene had been so comical I'd laughed in spite of the gravity of the situation.

I ended up renting a big pump and calling my old engineering professor from grad school, Colonel Strickland, who flew up in his turbocharged Mooney and showed us how to deal with our little problem. It had been a mess for many days. Two new guys quit, saying they had hired on as carpenters and not to drown themselves. Mike had been instrumental in persuading the rest to stay. Without him and the Colonel I might have lost much more, but their faith

350

never wavered. Things were chaotic for a while but we not only got the situation under control, we turned it to our advantage.

Barely a year later the old Colonel was half paralyzed by a stroke; he ended up having to be spoon-fed by a niece in Arizona and saddest of all, he could no longer fly. He loved flying his plane like nothing else, and it was only while we were working down in that muddy hole together that I came to understand the man had the soul of a poet.

Now all of that was history; the house stood solid over the spring and once again I felt compelled to acknowledge whatever powers had allowed us to prevail with it. I dipped my hand into the water and drank once more. "Thank you," I said out loud. "But isn't it Tina's turn now?"

~

"Am I interrupting something?"

My reverie was broken. I turned to see Mr. Plum by the door and quickly stood. He met me halfway and gripped my still-wet hand.

"Raymond, it looks like you've made a deal with the devil," he said, looking closely at me.

"What do you mean?"

"Just a figure of speech," he laughed. "I've never seen anyone as sick as you were looking so well so soon."

"The time away did me good," I said. "There were no deals involved."

"Forget it, I was kidding. Would you like to see the observatory?"

"Sure," I said, shaking off my irritation. What the hell went on inside his mind?

I followed him to the back of the house and up the winding stairs in the tower. He had moved some equipment into the computer room, and when we got to the top I saw his telescope had been moved in as well.

I was impressed by it. The primary mirror, he told me, was twenty inches in diameter. The back end of the scope was a fat

351

cylinder with carbon fiber trusses extending forward that held a smaller mirror, which gazed back into the belly of the thing. It had cost over forty thousand dollars. Mr. Plum said the focus could be adjusted in increments of one ten-thousandth of an inch. The scope was bolted to a massive mount, counterweighted and driven with servo motors that could keep it aimed at the same spot in the heavens while the earth rotated on its axis. I had seen a few of Mr. Plum's photos of galaxies on the walls at his law firm and knew that others had been published in astronomy journals.

He sat in a folding nylon camp chair by the telescope and put on a pair of reading glasses. A small tool kit was open beside him, and at his feet sat an electronic device that was wired to the telescope. A laptop computer lay open beside it. Why he would juggle such a demanding technical pursuit with his lawyering mystified me. Something inside him seemed too cold to be moved by the beauty of the heavenly bodies and too proud to be humbled by the infinity of space.

"Have you always been interested in science?" I asked.

"Science?" He peered at me over his glasses.

"Yeah. I mean, this is all pretty difficult stuff, isn't it?"

He chuckled. "Not so difficult. You learn how to use it and it's just operating a piece of equipment. No, science never was that interesting to me." He picked up an Allen wrench from the floor and carefully put it back into his kit. "Necessary, maybe, but so are cars, and I'm no mechanic."

"Then why astronomy? Why not gardening, or golfing?"

"Gloria likes gardening," he said. "One of us is enough for that, I think. I never really liked putting my hands into dirt, although I understand the appeal of it in an abstract way. It gives her that kind of pleasure.

"As for golf, I'll never be more than an average player, and there are physically gifted people who dominate that field. But out there," he gestured at the open sky, "That's where immortality is. That's where anything is possible."

"Like what?" I didn't get it.

352

"If you knew how the search for new planets is heating up," he mused. "There are so many things to be discovered out there. A few years ago I missed naming an undiscovered comet by three days. Three days! Instead it went to a Japanese gentleman with a very large pair of binoculars."

"But why is naming it so important?"

"Don't you realize comets keep coming back? How long do you think it will be before the name 'Halley' is forgotten? Every civilized person who lives a normal lifespan knows it. My only consolation with the Japanese comet is that it won't be back for forty thousand years, and by that time even Halley might be forgotten."

"Is it so much better to name something than to just enjoy it?" I asked.

"Raymond, you are a builder of things. You've left a piece of yourself behind on the earth that will probably outlast you. All I know how to make is money. Money is like a river—it's always out there flowing, anybody can get wet in it; hell, you can even drown in it, but nobody can change its essential character." He took off his glasses and looked at me.

"Making money means nothing to me. What has meaning is to own a piece of history, to define or possess something unique and irreplaceable. There aren't many things left on the earth like that. So I look up there for things more ancient than anything down here. For me, that's the place to find immortality."

"Have you had any success?"

"Only clues." He patted the barrel of his telescope. "But it's very big up there, and with this new instrument I can look deeper into space than I've ever been able to before. My last one had only a twelve-inch mirror."

"What does Mrs. Plum think of all this?"

"She loves the pretty things. There are so many of those up there—maybe too many, because they just distract from the search. You know how women are." He looked up and shrugged.

I started to suggest maybe those were the very things that held the answers, but then realized he would never understand that. Or if

353

he did, it would have to come from some epiphany I could never provide.

We talked about the house, about final details. Mr. Plum preferred to hold off discussing landscaping until his wife could be present. I was starting to feel my time today had been wasted, but before leaving I asked Mr. Plum if he had heard anything about the events at King's Tavern.

"As a matter of fact, the place has been the subject of some talk," he said. "A shame, really. Mr. King had quite a nice project for such a modest investment, and to lose it in that fashion reveals a terribly primitive character, don't you think?"

"I'm not aware that it's been lost," I said.

"Maybe not, but the boy? I don't hear that his talents exceed his father's."

"I think they probably lie in different areas."

"That may be more accurate," he agreed. "They certainly don't seem to lie in business."

"I'd like to help him save it."

"Raymond, Raymond." He laid a hand on my shoulder. "Your future is ahead of you, not behind. The entity you helped create now exists apart from you; whoever happens to own it shouldn't matter to you."

"But it does," I said. "Mr. King put his heart into that place, and if it weren't for his confidence in me we'd never have accomplished what we did there."

Mr. Plum smiled. "His confidence was much like the confidence you've enjoyed from me, wasn't it?"

"Very much."

"But suppose I find myself too deeply in debt to handle my mortgage—would you then recommend that I be allowed to keep the house anyway?"

I spun my wheels in that for a few seconds while he watched me. Finally I said, "I'd do anything within reason to help you."

Again he smiled. "It's charming to be an idealist when one is young. But when a man grows up, he had better be a realist. You are

354

not responsible for my success or failure. If I lose what you made for me, someone else will get it; there's nothing you can do to stop it. You could buy the place if you could afford to, of course, but I would still lose it. It's the nature of reality. If Mr. King loses his hotel you are in exactly the same position."

I sighed. "Well, I guess that depends on Rollin now."

"Cheer up, Raymond. Your future is assured whatever happens to that place. You have great things ahead—don't spend your life looking over your shoulder."

"Nobody's future is assured, Mr. Plum. We only live like it is because we have faith."

"Faith in what?"

"I'm still trying to figure that out. I think it may be something different for each of us."

He laughed heartily at that and gripped my hand again. He told me to call later in the week to make an appointment with him and Mrs. Plum together. I took my leave, glad to be nearly finished dealing with a lawyer who searched the heavens for his own immortality.

CHAPTER 25

There was a message from Valerie waiting for me when I got home. She was giggling and said she and Megan had been having a grand time together. She wanted me to call.

The thought of what we were intending to do tonight began to make a knot in my stomach. I had no qualms about walking into King's alone, but showing up with Valerie was another matter. Neither of us could expect anonymity there, but at least I had a reputation for keeping to myself so people usually left me alone.

We should arrive separately, I decided. She could slip inside invisibly as she had before; then the two of us could sneak downstairs. She'd pulled it off once and I had faith she could do it again. I didn't understand the psychology behind it, but my time at Duane's made me believe such things were possible. As long as Val didn't screw up all I had to do was be mister cool. But what if she were seen?

I called Val, and heard laughter in the background as she answered. She sounded as carefree as I felt apprehensive.

"Sounds like you've been having quite a time," I said.

"Oh, quite a time. And you?"

"It's been a strange weekend, but not bad. I saw Mr. Plum this morning."

"Your hotshot lawyer?"

"The very one."

"Did you ask him about King's?"

"Actually, I did. He's so full of himself I don't think he's capable of feeling a thing about it. He's working on his telescope, all fired up about finding immortality somewhere out in space."

"Then forget about him. We think you should take us out to dinner."

"You and Megan?"

"Well, I don't see nobody else here. Have you eaten yet?"

"No, it's barely five. You want me to come down there?"

"Don't you remember we have a job to do? We'll come up there."

"What's Megan going to do when we finish dinner, Val? We still haven't figured out how to get you into King's. Don't you think it might be better to wait until another night for this?"

"You worry too much. We're coming to take you out then. We'll pick you up at seven."

I started to protest but before I knew it Val had clicked off. I considered calling her back but decided that would probably backfire. I looked at the mess around me and knew what had to be done.

Being busy helped stave off my anxiety. After vacuuming and straightening the house there was enough time to shave and take a long shower. I had dressed in sage chinos, a ribbed charcoal tee and my black linen jacket when I heard a car coming up the drive. I looked out and saw a silver Mustang pulling up behind my truck.

I paced nervously around my kitchen waiting for the knock. When it came I waited a few seconds and nonchalantly pulled the door open. There to my surprise stood two very attractive women who were strangers to me. My first thought was that they were lost and had come up my drive by mistake. One was dressed in black pants, an elegant black and white striped top with a silk scarf around her head; the other was a tall blond wearing a lightweight burgundy sweater with a short black skirt. I must have looked confused because the woman with the scarf smiled, stuck out her hand and said, "Ray? Remember me? I'm Mike's sister, Megan Anderson."

"I'm sorry," I laughed, and took her hand. "Please come in. It's been a while, hasn't it?" Now the face was familiar—I remembered her with long blond hair, but of course she had just come through chemotherapy.

They stepped inside and the other woman watched with an amused expression while Megan introduced us. "Ray, this is my friend Elaine Carlton; Elaine, this is Valerie's friend, Ray Brauner. He's my brother's boss."

I took Elaine's hand and we shook politely. Seeing her up close I

357

realized she was more than attractive—she was a knockout. And the way she looked at me made me drop my eyes; the last thing I needed tonight was another distraction but it seemed events already were spinning out of my control.

"Was Valerie following you here?" I asked, hoping not to sound anxious.

"She should be here any minute," Megan said, turning around to look out my front door. "Wasn't she right behind us?"

"Well, I believe she was," said Elaine.

I recognized the voice immediately, and then Megan and Valerie both lost it. They high-fived and danced around whooping with laughter while I stood gaping. The illusion had been complete.

"You ought to see your face, Bwana," Val said. "I never seen anyone look so funny since the time I found you up the tree." And then they both fell out laughing again, and I joined them, not knowing whether to feel more foolish or relieved.

When we were finished laughing I looked Valerie up and down. "Good grief, Val," I said. "How in the world did you do it? You look absolutely like another person." And she did—even her eyebrows were lighter below her blond bangs, they were thinner and perfectly arched over her blue eyes, which looked bigger than I'd ever seen them. Her lips were a new color; her nails were elegant and manicured to glossy perfection. She looked polished as a cover model.

"It's all her fault," Val giggled, pointing to Megan.

"We girls need to pamper ourselves now and then, you know," said Megan airily. "Sometimes you just have to take yourself to the salon."

"Meg thought I should wear her wig," Val said. "It's real hair. How do I look?" She pirouetted once, looking at me over her shoulder.

I studied the hair. It looked completely natural, shiny and straight to where it curved in just above her shoulders. "Very convincing," I said. "But I think it was the eyebrows that fooled me. How did you do that?"

358

"Bleach. Look, they even did my arms." And she pulled up the sleeves of her sweater and I saw the hair on her arms was blond enough to make her look Scandinavian.

"You could pass for Kim Basinger's younger sister," I laughed. "That's truly amazing."

"Wooo! You go, girl," said Megan.

"Who's Kim Basinger?" said Val suspiciously.

"Don't worry; she's hot," Megan laughed.

I watched Megan and Valerie interact. I guessed Megan was about ten years older than Val. I didn't know much about her except that she was a serious and accomplished person. I'd heard that she had come to Mike's rescue when he was in trouble once or twice in earlier times. She had been in the military but took an early out due to physical problems. She looked more fragile than I remembered but didn't seem to lack spunk. I was glad to see how well they had hit it off.

"So where do you ladies propose we dine?" I asked.

"Now where would you think?" Val retorted.

"You want to have dinner at King's?" I was horrified.

"I told you he'd be like this," Val said to Megan. "Of course we're going to have dinner at King's. If you don't want to come with us that's up to you."

"But Val, everybody knows your voice! Does Megan know—" and then I turned to appeal to her. "Has Val told you what we're up against tonight?"

"Actually, Mike told me all about it," Megan said. "And Valerie told me what you have to do tonight. It seems to me the best way to disappear is to spend some time becoming part of the environment. After a while people will turn back to whatever they normally do. Or would you rather try sneaking off together right after Elaine walks in, when every eye is on her?"

They both looked at me while I spun my wheels in that. It took about two seconds to realize I was defeated.

"Elaine is a friend of mine," Megan said. "You're just the lucky guy I introduced her to—all you have to do tonight is be a gentleman. Do you think you can manage that much?"

"Well—sure," I said. "I can do that."

"You know, we just might make something of him yet," Megan said to Val with a nudge.

Megan drove us to King's with me folded into the cramped back seat of her Mustang like a grumpy afterthought. The car had a big V8, and she liked to drive fast. All I could think was that once again things had spun completely out of my control, while the two of them chattered away in the front like schoolgirls.

When we arrived at King's my relief at climbing out of the back was neutralized by mild terror at what lay ahead. I was getting ready to walk into a role for which I felt completely unprepared. When I stood out of the car Val said, "You look real nice, Ray. Don't he look handsome, Meg?"

"Just like a big hunk of eye candy. After everything you and Mike told me I feel like I'm in the presence of a legend. You do look adorable, Ray," she said, patting me on the lapel.

My mind already was sputtering at Megan and Val's audacity; I was beginning to feel like nothing so much as an accessory to their evening. My feet no longer had any traction in my own world—and yet here we were, preparing to walk into the very place where I had carved out my identity in this town. And the train was already rolling; there was nothing left to do but hang on.

"Shall we, ladies?" I said, extending an arm to each of them.

~

We walked through the marble-floored vestibule of King's Tavern and I held the big glass door open for Valerie and Megan. A black mesh bag hung from Val's shoulder. We stood inside the entrance for a few seconds before the hostess approached and asked if we were there for dinner.

"Yes, for three," I said.

"Did you have a reservation?"

"Ah, no," I said, hope springing. "Will that be a problem?"

"Not at all. If you'll wait just a sec I'll see about a table for you."

The bar was busy but not yet full. Rollin stood halfway down to the waiters' station polishing a wine glass. Looking past him I felt a little surge of adrenalin—there sat Jones, the dark-haired bruiser. He seemed preoccupied with the bar and paid no attention to us. Before long the hostess returned and asked us to follow her. I kept my eyes away from the bar as we walked closer, turned right past the booths and descended two steps into the elegant dining room.

I heard Megan draw in her breath and then she murmured, "Wow, I forgot how nice it is in here."

And it was nice. The modern chandeliers were from Italy and the carpet had been woven from the finest wool, in a three-dimensional pattern that only one mill had been willing to make for us because it had required retooling their loom. The wainscoting was made from the same rare chestnut as the bar top, and the invisibly lit, circular recess above the ring of chandeliers was painted with a faux sky so subtle and realistic it seemed like a big round portal opening into a perfect evening above.

The old man wanted Old World luxury in here—but with flair, with a streak of New World flamboyance that represented his own optimism and Rollin's sunny idealism. I thought we'd done pretty well balancing the two. Looking around the room was like tracing a chapter in my own history; there were stories behind nearly every detail.

The hostess seated us, and Megan seemed quietly dazzled. Even Valerie looked around like she was seeing everything with new eyes. "Have you had dinner in here before?" I asked.

"No," said Megan. "I've just sat at the bar and had lunch in a booth once or twice."

"Me neither," said Val. "I never expected to."

I'd dined here several times with the Plums and once with my mother but it had been nearly a year ago, and now I was almost as smitten as Megan and Val were. A friend of Rollin's wearing a tuxedo jacket with jeans was playing jazz on the Steinway baby grand piano. Islands of greenery surrounded tall ficus trees, exuding vitality

361

and a welcoming atmosphere. They made the sky blue overhead seem even more real, while the chandeliers subtly directed warm light down to the tabletops and flattered the face of every diner.

"I do believe you hit a home run in here, Mr. Brauner," said Megan.

"Now don't get his head all swole up or it might float through that hole up yonder," admonished Val, and we all laughed.

I was thankful the room wasn't crowded. Nobody was close enough to hear our conversation and I didn't see anyone I recognized. A pretty brown-haired waitress named Allison introduced herself and described the dinner specials, and Megan asked me to select a wine. I waited until our orders had been placed and chose a young Oregon Pinot Noir. I thought it would have enough body to stand up to Megan's lamb chops and should be perfect for Val's stuffed peppers and my tuna fillet.

Valerie didn't bat an eye at our meat orders, and I was beginning to think we were going to get off easy until the waitress left. Then she turned to Megan and said, "Do you know mad cow disease comes from sheep too, and it can't be killed by cooking?"

"I've heard that," Megan said. "Did you know that mad Megan disease comes from messing with me and my food?"

Val seemed to weigh that, and didn't say another vegetarian word the rest of the evening. I figured strength of character must run in Mike's family.

"So what kind of work are you involved in?" I asked Megan. "Mike said something about security."

"Yep. I'm a vice-president of a security company."

"That could cover any amount of territory to me. What kind of security?"

She laughed. "It does cover a lot of territory. We do everything from protecting corporate secrets to crowd control at rock concerts. When I was in the Army I worked in security, so this was kind of a natural extension of that."

"Rock concerts? What groups?"

"We've worked with shows as different as Neil Diamond and

362

Alanis Morissette. Lots of country artists. Ninety percent of it happens either through their agencies or their venues. Most of the artists aren't even aware of us—our job is just to make sure everyone has a safe time."

"Ah—so you have experience with what we're doing tonight," I said.

"Heavens, no," she laughed again. "Most of my work happens on the computer these days. But what I'm doing tonight is having fun— let's please not drag work into it."

Allison returned with a basket of bread and our wine. She uncorked it and poured me a sample. I held the glass up and studied its color, then swirled it and took a deep sniff as Valerie watched. I tasted and declared it superb, and it wasn't long before Val and Megan were swirling, sniffing and babbling happily about the nuances of the wine.

Suddenly their conversation dwindled and I saw their eyes cutting across the room. I turned and to my dismay saw Jones' hulk mincing like a linebacker in heels toward our table. His face wore a beatific smile.

"Mister Brauner, what a wonderful surprise to see you," he gushed, clapping his hands together. "I do hope your evening with us will be a pleasure." He looked around the table. "Oh my, what elegant friends you have! I just love that scarf, dear—is it a Hermès?"

"Thank you—actually, it's Versace," said Megan mildly.

"Oh, my God." He rolled his eyes. "How could I miss that? He was such a huge talent, such a darling man, what a horrible tragedy! He will be so missed." He wrung his hands and I was hoping that would be all, but he didn't want to leave anyone out.

"Honey, your hair is to die for," he said to Elaine. "I have not seen such a gorgeous, perfect head of hair in this place before. But your eyes are just so striking—if you trimmed those bangs up just a teensy bit you would be absolute cover material. I mean, Vogue, Cosmo, Elle, you could take your pick."

She didn't say a word, but fixed him with an icy smile and turned those eyes onto him like steel. He recoiled and cringed.

363

"Oh dear—a Republican. I am so sorry." He backed away from our table biting his knuckle and disappeared from the room on tiptoes.

I glanced around to see several other diners looking discreetly in our direction. Val's face was a study in consternation. Megan had one hand over her face and her shoulders were shaking. Finally she gave it up just as Allison arrived with our salads.

"Was that man bothering you?" she asked.

"Not at all," Megan laughed. "I just could hardly believe my ears. Oh, God, what a riot!" And then she fell out again. "If I tried to tell anybody what just happened nobody would ever believe me." She sighed and wiped her eyes on her napkin.

"Well, I apologize," Allison said unhappily. "My boss didn't want him to come out here, but unfortunately nobody can tell him what to do. He's kind of nutty sometimes. He and that other man act sort of like they own the place but I don't think they do. We all just wish they would go away." She looked around as if she were afraid someone else was listening.

"Honey, don't you worry about them," Megan said, patting her arm. "You're doing fine, and that's what counts. You tell your boss we appreciate being here."

"Thank you," Allison said with relief in her voice. "Is everything else okay? Can I bring some fresh pepper for your salad? Your entrees should be ready soon."

~

By the time our dinners arrived Megan had us laughing with stories from her younger years. I knew she and Mike had lost their father in Vietnam when Mike was just a toddler; even Megan was barely old enough to remember him. The two had grown up close in Harrisburg. She had been Mike's defender in childhood and although their roles had changed, their loyalty was fierce. She told a funny story about a date she had been on years ago, how Mike had disapproved of her suitor and put ball bearings behind his front

364

hubcaps while he was inside the house trying to extend his good night. The poor guy drove all the way home to Altoona thinking his wheels were about to fall off.

Rollin got a minute to come back and say hello. He hadn't met Megan before, but when he learned she was Mike's sister he welcomed her like family. He seemed especially charmed by Elaine, who hardly spoke at all. She demurely kept her eyes down for most of his visit to our table. He apologized for Jones' intrusion but Megan waved it off and said she'd found him entertaining.

"He and his colleagues are not very entertaining for us right now, unfortunately," Rollin said.

"I know that. But we weren't going to let him ruin our evening, so we just let him act out," she said. "Give them enough rope, people like that usually hang themselves."

"I sure hope you're right," he said, and excused himself back to the bar.

We were nearly through our meal when Mike stuck his head around the corner. Megan saw him first and waved him over. By that time the dining room was practically empty; even the pianist had left and the speakers were pumping out quiet rock. Mike strolled over, kissed Megan's cheek, slapped me on the shoulder and took a seat directly across from Valerie.

"Mike, have you met my friend Elaine?" Megan asked.

"I don't believe so." Mike sat there staring at Valerie for several seconds. He rubbed his face and looked again. "I do not believe this," he said. He burst out laughing, and then he just buried his head in his arms on the table, laughing. He finally looked up again. "I still don't believe it. Pleased to meet you, Elaine," he laughed, sticking out his hand. Valerie took it and they shook while she blushed.

Mike leaned forward. "You look fantastic! How did you do it?"

"Don't you know your own sister's wig?" Val said dryly. "Some men are such suckers for a blonde."

"It's girl magic," I said. "We're not meant to understand; we're only meant to follow."

"I was afraid of that. You'd better be careful, Bwana," Mike

365

laughed. "You could follow that right into some trouble."

"Not tonight. This is strictly business. We're just waiting for the right time to zip in and out."

"We were thinking about getting a little ping-pong going," Mike said, leaning forward confidentially. "Make some noise, get Rollie to play some good music, you know, give you two a chance to do your thing."

"Do the guys know anything?"

"Only that there's something important you need to do downstairs."

Just about that time there was a quiet whistle from the doorway. I looked around to see Spider sticking his head into the dining room. Mike motioned him over, and Mackey followed.

"You guys remember Megan," Mike said when they arrived at our table. "She brought her friend Elaine along to see our famous handiwork. Megan, you remember Spider and Mack."

Spider took Megan's hand first and said, "How are you feeling, young lady?"

"Great," she said. "Elaine heard all about this place, and she wanted to meet the legendary architect behind the sensation. You'll have to pardon her for not speaking much—she's had a bad case of laryngitis."

"Hello there, Elaine," Spider said, looking closely at her.

"Hi," she said in a breathy voice, offering her hand.

When it was his turn, Mackey seemed completely smitten. "Hello, ma'am," he said shyly, and took her hand in his big paw.

"So are you guys going to stick around a while?" I asked, trying to take attention off Elaine.

"Long as it takes," said Spider. "You're looking pretty slicked up there, boss."

"Well, we decided to do the dinner thing, and I didn't want to embarrass the ladies by coming as my normal self," I said.

"I think everyone reverts to their real selves by the end of the day," Megan said.

"Now that's a wise woman," Spider declared, while Mackey just gawked at Elaine.

"Hey, we'll let you finish your meal in peace. See you later on," Mike said.

"Nice to meet you, ma'am," Spider said to Elaine.

Allison returned with a selection of desserts. I was so nervous I couldn't eat another thing, but the ladies were still hungry. Megan settled on a raspberry crème brulée and Val chose chocolate truffle cake, while I downed the last bit of wine to calm my nerves.

~

By the time we sauntered out of the dining room it was after nine. A ball game on TV dominated the bar, which was beginning to stack up with the local crowd. Rollin was busy and Jones was reading a magazine. Where was Smith tonight? I could hear music coming from the ping-pong parlor so we wandered back to have a look.

There were games going at both tables with about a dozen people watching. Once more Rollin had classic blues on the sound system. At the moment Clarence Gatemouth Brown was singing and it sounded great. Mike was playing one of the locals at the table closest to the door, and we stood watching. A waitress I didn't know asked if we wanted a drink. I declined but Megan and Val each ordered a Rolling Rock. Spider lifted his bottle from across the room and we acknowledged him.

I was in favor of accomplishing our errand sooner rather than later, but we had agreed that once it was done we would leave quickly. I hadn't spoken to Rollin except for his brief visit during dinner and didn't want to seem rude by leaving too soon. Megan and Val's Rolling Rocks arrived, and I considered having a beer. I'd had two small glasses of wine with dinner and didn't feel them at all, but didn't want to take any chances. I was arguing it out in my mind when Val took my arm and pulled me close.

"Relax," she said into my ear. "You're worrying too much."

"Okay," I said. I signaled the waitress for a beer, and she nodded. I looked over and saw Spider watching us. What was he thinking? A

367

part of me wanted to chuckle at that but I couldn't; my stomach was knotting up.

Spider was going to the far table for a game when the waitress came in with my Rolling Rock. I pulled a twenty from my pocket to pay for the three beers and was waiting for her to make change when my blood ran cold. I knew without looking who had come into the room. I took my change and peeled off a couple ones for her tip. I felt tension coming from her hand, and saw it in her eyes when she said "Thanks."

Smith was standing by the doorway not more than six feet away from us coldly surveying the room. "Ping-pong," I heard him sneer. "Fucking ping-pong." He shook his head in disgust, and then looked around. When he saw me he seemed surprised, and then his lips peeled back. I didn't much like the smile; in fact everything about him seemed wrong.

He walked over and looked me up and down. "Well, Mr. Brauner," he said. "I see you've been on vacation. You look, how can I say it? Rowrrr." He made a growling sound deep in his throat and laughed at his own joke. "You have much better taste tonight. She is more your speed." He tilted his head at Elaine. "Her, not the bald one."

I stared at him, anger rising.

He put back his head and laughed his quiet, hissing laugh. "So what do you think of ping-pong?" he asked. "Don't you think this place would be much better with billiards?"

"It seems to be working." I did not want the conversation to continue.

"Ah, a diplomat," he said.

I could feel Valerie's hackles over his remark about Megan. I turned back to the game, trying to dismiss him, and sipped my Rolling Rock.

"Would you think more of me if I could play ping pong?"

"I would think more of you if you left us alone."

"Oh, but you're breaking my heart, Mr. Brauner."

I kept my eyes on the game. Mike looked quizzically at me for a

368

split second and when he missed the next return I realized he was struggling to keep his concentration. Across the room Spider was playing and seemed to be unaware of what was going on here, but Mackey was looking in our direction.

"I will play the winner, then," Smith said. "Next game," he announced to the room at large. "I will be playing for Mister Brauner's favor."

The situation was deteriorating fast. We had to get our business done quickly but there seemed to be no way of slipping out unnoticed. If Smith played a game, that might be our only window of opportunity.

"She is a debutante. I can please you in ways she would never imagine," Smith said into my ear. A dry, hissing laugh followed. He stood so close I could feel his breath on my neck.

I considered taking Val and Megan and just leaving. Why not come back another night? But there was no assurance any other night would be easier. It took all my will power to focus on the game.

Valerie put her arm through mine. I pulled her close and whispered in her ear, "When he plays." She kissed me, and when I looked across the room I saw Mackey staring in amazement. To my left, Smith's presence felt like a festering mass of danger; remaining outwardly calm required all my effort. Valerie kept her arm in mine. I was aware of a primal stoicism emanating from her and it calmed me somewhat. I had no idea what Megan was thinking until I heard her clapping and cheering, and then realized Mike had just won.

Smith strode to the other end of the table and picked up the paddle just as Spider's biker friend Gus approached. Mike said, "I believe someone else was before you, sir."

"I am playing ping-pong for Mr. Brauner's favor," Smith said.

"That's fine with me, but you have to wait your turn," Mike said.

Gus held his hand out for the paddle. He didn't look quite so big facing Smith. "You get the next one, boss," he said. "House rules— you can't butt in line." I admired his audacity.

I saw Smith's nostrils flare. He took the biker's hand, put the paddle in it and closed his huge fist around it. I cringed, thinking surely he would crush it. I think Gus may have had his own misgivings for a second or two but then Smith backed off.

"Play your little game," he sneered. "It doesn't matter. I will play the winner for Mr. Brauner's arrogant ass." He folded his arms and stood to the side, anger radiating from him. I realized most of the room had begun watching, and felt Valerie's grip tighten around my arm. It crossed my mind that to some it might look like I was passively waiting for Smith to claim his prize, but I couldn't afford to worry about what anyone else thought now.

Mike and Gus began their game. Before they were far into it, the game at the other table had changed. I saw Spider and Mackey standing together, looking in our direction. They worked their way around the perimeter of the room, and when they got closer turned their attention to Mike and Gus. The knot in my stomach was too tight for me to pay more than superficial attention to their game, but they were playing well. Smith stood about eight feet to my left, close to Gus's end of the table. I took tiny sips of beer and it tasted rank to me.

After what seemed an eternity Mike had fallen behind by six points and the game was approaching its conclusion. I was relieved; we needed him for a lookout while we were downstairs. In a few more minutes the score was 20-17, game point, and when Gus slammed and Mike's return went wild, it was over. The two of them laughed and shook hands, and Mike came around and handed his paddle to Smith.

The big man took it, bowing sarcastically. As he walked to the end of the table he turned and gave me an air kiss. "This is for you, love," he said in a silky voice. "Isn't it exciting?" The whole room watched as he and Gus volleyed for serve. I was dismayed to see that he was a very good player. He projected a sneering attitude of condescension as he won the volley, and the game began.

Mike stood to my left. I noticed Spider and Mackey had worked their way around the corner of the room and now stood on the other side of Megan. I looked over at Spider and beckoned with a tilt of my head. He casually slouched over, and when he got on the left side of me I asked if he and Mackey would take our seats for a few minutes.

"Sure thing, boss. Is she going with you?" He looked quizzically at Elaine, who was still clinging to my arm.

"Yeah. We shouldn't be long. Whatever happens, try to keep everyone in here."

I watched for a minute. Smith was a power player, slamming the ball with ferocious speed, and his arms were so long it didn't take much movement for him to cover the whole end of the table with ease. He was getting into it. Elaine and I stood and without looking back I slipped out the door pulling her behind me. Nobody was in the hall except Allison, who smiled and started to say something. I put my finger to my lips and we scooted past her. Rollin's office was closed on the left; the door to the stairs was just past it on the right. I looked over my shoulder and saw nobody. I pulled the door open and we were through.

~

We flew down the stairs, left around the corner at the landing and right through the old brick archway that led into the wine cellar. I flipped on the light while Val kicked off her shoes, shrugged the bag from her shoulder and dropped to her knees. She was examining the floor somewhere around the end of the third row of shelves when suddenly she stopped. "Shit!" she moaned, clapping her hand to her forehead. "Shit, shit, shit!"

"What?" My heart jumped into my throat.

"A knife! I forgot to bring a knife," she said. "We can't get it open without one."

"Keep looking," I said. "I'll find something."

She went back to searching the floor. I had nothing metal in my pocket except for keys and a few coins, and started looking randomly around for anything else we might use. Unfortunately one of the old man's final accomplishments had been to reorganize the wine cellar.

It was spare and clean down here now—no clutter of any kind. I pulled open the door into the mechanical room that housed the refrigeration unit. I found the light switch and flipped it on, and looked the tiny space over. Nothing except for a small circuit breaker panel that fed electricity to the refrigeration unit and the dumbwaiter.

I looked closer at the panel cover and saw it was fastened to the box with four big pan-head screws. I fumbled in my pocket for change and found a penny. It just fit the slot in the screw heads, but the screws were tight. I turned with all my might and broke the first screw loose, then tackled the second. I was starting on the third when I heard Val say, "I found it!"

"Come help me," I said. She squeezed into the space beside me and I indicated the loosened screws. "Twist those out while I get these started."

They were long screws that went over an inch into the body of the box. By the time I had broken the last one loose she had only removed the first one, and I started madly unscrewing two at a time. It seemed to take forever, but then the cover swung loose and hung by the remaining corner.

"Here, let me," I said, and frantically twisted the screw the rest of the way out. The sheet metal cover dropped into Val's hands and we ran with it back to the spot where she had left her shoe as a marker.

She tried to work the corner of the cover into the tiny crevice between the flagstones but the metal seemed too thick. I watched her hands shaking and found myself praying that it would work. No sooner had I thought, "Please, please let it work," than it dropped in. She wiggled it back and forth carefully, and to my amazement the entire flagstone in front of her began to move. Not just back, but upward as well.

When it had moved far enough to get my fingertips into the gap I began pulling and just like Val had said, it came out. I slid the stone to the side and there about two inches below floor level was a rectangular panel that looked like asbestos, about ten inches wide and over a foot long. An iron handle was riveted to it. Val lifted it and I saw the top of the bottle deep in the compartment. I reached in and picked it up with both hands, and was surprised by its weight. I slipped it into Val's bag as she held it open. I looked down into the hole as she started to replace the lid. "Wait," I said. "There's something else down there."

She peered in as I reached deep inside and felt around the bottom of the compartment. There was a sizable lump along one side, and when I tested it with my fingers it seemed to yield. I kept pressing it away from the wall until I could work my fingers down the length of it, and finally pried it from the floor. It was a soft, waxy cigar-shaped object nearly a foot long. "Eww, gross," Val said, but I tossed it into her bag as well.

She was cinching the bag closed when we heard voices from the hallway overhead. I clapped the lid back down and we were frantically sliding the flagstone back into place when the door opened at the top of the stairs. Val slung her bag over her shoulder, kicked her shoes into the arch and then to my surprise grabbed me by the shoulders and drove me back into the brick column so hard it nearly knocked the wind out of me. The breaker panel cover still lay on the floor.

"What—" I started to say but suddenly her face was locked onto mine. She kissed me hungrily and massaged my groin with her left hand as heavy steps descended the stairs. A wisp of blond hair was stuck between our mouths and as I reached up to pull it away she hooked her leg around me. I found myself madly aroused, and by the time the steps reached the bottom we were churning against each other like two horny high schoolers. Somewhere in the back of my brain I understood exactly what she was doing, and would have laughed if I hadn't been so turned on.

I heard a sharp intake of breath as the intruder rounded the corner. Elaine didn't let up; she just pressed into me harder. I thought I heard a squeaking vocal sound, and then came an awkward throat clearing. At length Elaine let out a frustrated moan and reluctantly pulled away from me. She stuck out her lip in a beautiful pout and turned slowly to face Jones, who stood wringing his hands together with a matchless expression on his face.

"Oh my. Oh dear. Ahhmm, Mr. Brauner, this is so—so—" and again he squeaked and cleared his throat, completely at a loss for words.

I sighed. "Is there a problem?" I said.

"Oh no—well, yes—but it's not you, Mr. Brauner."

Once again Elaine circled my neck, kissed me deeply and then put her mouth up to my ear and sucked at my earlobe.

"Oooooh. Oh, dear," Jones said over and over, until Elaine turned around again with that glorious pout and finally untwined herself from me. She shook the blond hair from her face and looked petulantly at Jones while she pulled her shoes back on.

He was biting his knuckle, and again I sighed. "Forgive us for finding a quiet place," I said dryly. "I guess we'll be leaving now."

"Mr. Brauner," he said again, his voice cracking. "My, ah, colleague is a little, ahhm, hyper right now. If he found you here this would not be good, oh no. You really must go. I think maybe out the back door. I'm sorry, miss—you really are gorgeous, just simply gorgeous. Oh my. Oh dear." He wrung his hands again, rolling his eyes upward, and seemed agitated beyond reason. All I could hope now was that my guys would give us enough cover to get out.

We started up the stairs, Jones in the lead. Val's bag hung heavily from her shoulder, and as I ascended behind her I noticed the blond wig was a bit tousled. I had no idea what her makeup looked like.

~

As we entered the hall upstairs Smith was just coming in through the back door after looking for me in the parking lot. Our escape that way was blocked, and in any case we had to find Megan. Mike and Gus were standing between the exit and the door to the wine cellar, and they slowed Smith's progress after he saw us in the hall. But they couldn't stop him.

"Mr. Brauner!" he yelled. I pretended to not hear, and tried to present a relaxed demeanor as Elaine and I sauntered into the ping-pong parlor. My heart was pounding like a jackhammer and when I

374

saw Megan and Spider talking together I felt giddy with relief. They saw us, and Megan rose expectantly to her feet. Spider took one look at Elaine, then me behind her, and disbelief spread over his face. I might as well have been bringing a date home with her skirt turned inside out. Spider was nobody's fool, and at that moment I knew he felt completely betrayed.

I didn't see Mackey at first, but he saw us and by the time he made it to where we stood, he too was gawking at Elaine's disarray. Megan knew it was time to go but before anyone could say a word Smith came around the corner pushing Mike and Gus aside like bowling pins.

"Mr. Brauner," he said over my shoulder. His voice softened in a way that made my skin crawl. "What made you leave the room while I was playing for your favor? Do you know what an insult that was to me?"

Spider, Megan and Mackey were all looking up at him behind me. I slowly turned while something strange and strong gathered itself inside me. "Sir, I'm not your friend or anything else of yours. My favor is not up for sale. I'm sorry if you misunderstood that."

"I misunderstood? No, my little flower, you misunderstood." His big sausage finger punched the air in front of my face.

"I played ping-pong with that biker prick over there for your arrogant little ass and I believe everyone present heard me say that. I beat the cocksucker in a fair game and now you are mine." He was breathing hard, his nostrils flaring. He stared at me from scarcely two feet away and spoke softly again. "I don't care if you built this entire town, lover boy, you are going to dance with me right here or else everyone in this room is about to have a very educational experience."

He turned to the room. "Where's Mr. King? Have him play something nice and slow."

His face was flushed and his eyes were hazing, the lids drooping while the veins in his neck stood out like knotted ropes. Looking up at him I realized no man in this place except maybe Jones could offer him more than token resistance. Trying to walk away wouldn't get

375

me far. There was nothing I could do that wouldn't make things worse. Would Rollin call the cops, please? I thought that might be a prayer. I was ready to try it now, but somehow that didn't seem like the right formulation. Just how were you supposed to say it? Please was all I could remember. Please.

And then from beside me Elaine spoke. And remarkable as this may sound, it was Elaine's own unique voice. It was the only time any of us ever heard it—a soft but unmistakable southern accent with perfect diction, crystal clarity and irrefutable logic. "No, mister. That other man doesn't have any claim on Mr. Brauner. For him, you have to play me."

There was something so matter-of-fact about the statement it seemed beyond argument. Everyone stared at Elaine. Her porcelain beauty and perfect calm neutralized the messy makeup and disheveled hair. "Here," she said, picking up a paddle from the table and putting it in Smith's big hand. She walked to the far end of the table. She slid the bag off her shoulder and handed it to Megan, then picked up the other paddle and innocently stood there as if she had all the time in the world.

Smith looked mesmerized. He stared at the paddle in his hand, at Elaine calmly waiting, and then began to laugh. Not the hissing, reptilian laugh but an adolescent giggle, involuntary and nervous. With effort he pulled himself together. "Okay," he said. "I will play the debutante for Mr. Brauner." He tried to laugh again but it came out like a spastic snicker. He rolled his big shoulders and then his neck, and walked to the end of the table.

Rollin had turned the music down. He always did when things got too rowdy. Quiet rock now played, but it was only background to the conversation that had just happened. Everyone heard it and suddenly the room was filling up; the walls were lining with quiet spectators. Megan stood behind Elaine holding her bag; I stood on the side of the table closest the door. Mike and Gus stood to my left while Spider and Mackey flanked my right. I looked over my shoulder in time to see Jones appear at the door. He was twisting his big hands together nervously, and after looking into the room his

376

eyes rolled upward and he crossed himself before disappearing again.

Elaine began the volley for serve with a high, timid backhand. She kept it going for several returns and then Smith slammed the ball by her so hard I thought it would be smashed. Elaine stood with a startled look on her face.

"I think you should leave, Bwana," muttered Spider from the corner of his mouth. "She's giving you the time; you better take it."

I didn't reply. Smith served, mimicking Elaine with an exaggerated, girlish backhand. Again there was a brief volley and again he slammed the ball past Elaine while she stood there holding her paddle in wide-eyed wonderment. A second, third and fourth serve produced the same result, and the tension in the room was growing palpable. Spider nudged me and tilted his head toward the door but I shook my head. Consternation gathered on his face. Elaine kept her patrician composure, but after the fifth serve whizzed by low and fast she indulged in a little pout as she picked up the ball and threw it across the net to Smith.

"No, it's your turn," he grinned, tossing the ball back to her. He was full of piss and vinegar again. The score was five to nothing; all he needed was two more points to finish the game. I felt a trickle of perspiration running down my back.

Elaine made her first serve high again, like someone just learning the game, and Smith slammed it viciously past her, a huge grin breaking out on his face. I glanced over at Spider. His head was bowed, shaking slowly back and forth. Beyond him Mackey stood looking straight ahead, motionless and pale as a sheet.

"Oh-six, game point," Smith said, barely able to contain himself.

A low murmur began running around the room. I stole a peek at Mike and his face was pale and full of concentration. When I looked back at Elaine she had put her paddle down and was taking off her stylish shoes. She looked more comfortable without them. She picked up the paddle and ball again but her stance was different somehow. She was looking Smith in the eye and suddenly she fired a serve so low and fast he didn't even react until it had already passed him. He snarled and threw his hands up. It was one-six; now he would have to play the game out. He didn't realize he had scored his final point already.

Elaine kept her eyes fixed on Smith's. He didn't like that very much, and after she served three more straight past him he began fraying. When his serve came he was still ahead, but only by two points. He served with a vengeance. Elaine fell back and returned beautifully, catching him off guard again. He barely returned her ball and then she moved into it with a wicked forehand that finished the play. He began scrambling to adjust, but didn't understand quite yet that it was hopeless.

Elaine won the next two volleys, then feigned a broken nail and switched to her left hand. Smith lunged at the advantage, but it was a mirage. Nothing else changed. She hardly looked at the ball, she just kept her eyes on his face while her paddle arced, sliced, parried and lunged. All the while she wore an expression of total innocence and acted surprised at each new point. By the time the serve went back to Smith at six-fourteen he was looking desperate and the room was buzzing with excitement. Nobody had seen anything like this since the glory days, and something about the way Elaine moved was stirring memories. As for me, I was seeing Duane's shadow.

Spider and Mackey were beside themselves. They still only thought Megan had discovered a new ping-pong sensation in Elaine, and that we had brought her here to buoy up business for Rollin, but their cheer was back. The crowd was ecstatic, and to my left Mike stood quietly grinning. He knew we were seeing something we'd probably never see again.

When the score got to six-eighteen and Elaine began switching hands, tossing her paddle back and forth in the middle of the volley, a roar went up from the crowd. Nobody had seen such a thing before. Valerie always had shunned theatrics, sticking to the job and grimly seeing it through night after night. But never had she played anyone repugnant as Smith, and never in any game at King's Tavern had the stakes been so high. I turned around to see Rollin by the door, and then Jones, wringing his balled-up hands like an excited child. Smith lost the volley and pounded the table in rage. He was beginning to understand it was hopeless.

At nineteen-six it was Elaine's serve and now she had Smith where she wanted him. Once more she toyed with him, serving as she had in the beginning a high, backhanded ball that begged to be slammed. But he was cautious and focused mainly on returning it. During the volley one of his returns barely made it over, and as she dove to the net for a brief instant her body formed the familiar, striking-snake signature we had seen so many times during the glory days.

"You know..."

I turned to see Spider stroking his chin. "I'd swear if it wasn't for the hair..." he said, and then shaking his head let it go. He turned to me with a shrug. I grinned, and he gave me a quizzical look. And then it was twenty to six, game point. We turned to watch the finish.

Again Elaine gave Smith an easy, high serve and this time he had nothing left to lose. He furiously slammed it but somehow she already knew and her paddle was already there. The volley went on for several exchanges before the curtain fell over Elaine's face. Suddenly there was that old look—a flat, almost pained expression that said, "I'm not interested." With a quick overhand flick she put an end to it. It was coldly efficient as an execution, and the fact wasn't lost on Smith.

The room went wild. Nothing so exciting had ever happened in King's Tavern. No Super Bowl game could have matched it. When the cheering died down everyone was laughing and talking at once. They pressed around Elaine to congratulate her, but after slipping her shoes back on she was intent only on leaving. She took her bag from Megan and smiled briefly at the well-wishers around her, and forged her way toward the door while Smith stood at the other end of the table breaking his paddle into splinters.

Suddenly he lunged around the far side of the table, knocking people aside as he pushed his way through the swarm. Neither Elaine nor Megan saw him coming. "Who are you?" he demanded from behind Elaine.

The crowd melted away like wax. The two women looked around

379

and saw Smith. They turned their backs on him and continued pressing toward us, and the exit. The hubbub in the room quieted noticeably.

"Who are you?" Smith snarled again. This time he grabbed Elaine's shoulder. She whirled around with fire in her eyes and he backed off, but only for a second. I noticed to my alarm that her wig looked dangerously askew. No sooner had the thought crossed my mind than Smith reached out and yanked it right off her head. A collective gasp went up from the room, and for the next few seconds the only thing that could be heard was the guitar finale from "Hotel California" softly wailing over the sound system like a tragic coda to everything we had just witnessed.

Smith stared at the wig in horror, and then dropped it, revulsion twisting his features. Valerie's mass of black hair was pinned up all over her head. One lock had come loose and curled down past her shoulder. Her face was red with fury.

"YOU!" Smith roared, and then pandemonium broke loose. Valerie raised her right knee and drove her heel down hard into the top of Smith's foot. The big man doubled over. I heard him grunting in pain as he wobbled on one leg, trying to cradle his damaged foot in his hands.

And then before I knew it Val was holding her bag high in the air. My heart jumped into my throat. "NO!" I yelled.

But it was too late. She brought it down and a loud thwock told me the bottle inside had met its target. Smith toppled sideways. She bent down, snatched up the wig and clutched it with the bag to her chest. Her face was still fiery red. She stuck out her chin defiantly and the crowd parted as she and Megan marched around the table. Mike and Gus formed a vanguard as I fell in with Valerie, while Megan, Spider and Mackey brought up the rear. Rollin and Jones stood by the door gaping, and the room erupted into wild cheering as we exited. We hurried by the vacant bar and plunged through the big glass doors, out of King's Tavern into the night.

CHAPTER 26

We didn't stop until we got to Megan's car. By that time Val was cooling off just a little. Megan and Mike were laughing so hard they could barely stand, and all Mackey could say was "Great googly moogly." Spider and Gus were looking blankly at me for an explanation but all I could think about was the bottle in Valerie's bag.

She leaned back trembling against the car and took several deep breaths. "Whoo-whee!" she finally said, and then she started laughing quietly to herself.

"Val," I said, "can I see the bag?"

"Oh, lordy," she said, and Mike groaned.

Spider, Mackey and Gus had no idea what any of it was about. Valerie still had the bag and wig clutched in front of her. She handed the wig to Megan and murmured, "Sorry for that." She opened the top of her bag and gingerly felt around inside.

"There ain't nothing wet," she said.

"Can I?" I asked.

She held the bag open and I put my hand inside, feeling all the way around the bottle. I put my other hand in and carefully lifted it out with both hands. Four of us breathed a sigh of relief.

"The glass is so thick on the bottom it saved us," I said, squinting at it in the security light. I cradled it in both hands so the others could have a look. "This, gentlemen, was the object of our quest tonight. I don't even want to think about what might have happened. We got it out safe, thanks to you."

"What is it?" Spider said.

"I'm not even sure. But it's a long story and this is no place for it."

A small group of people came around the corner from the tavern entrance laughing and talking, and I slipped the bottle back into Val's bag. "Can you guys see that Rollin gets out of here in one piece and bring him over to my place?" I said to Spider. "I'll explain then. I don't care how late it is—just don't say a word about this. I want him to see it with his own eyes."

"Sure thing, boss," Spider said. "Valerie, you ought to get some kind of medal after tonight. I would feel truly honored to shake your hand." He stuck his hand out, but instead of taking it Val reached around his neck and gave him a hug.

"That's awful kind of you," she said. "But the wig and everything was Meg's idea, and the whole thing was Ray's idea, so I guess it took all of us. I think we better go now." More people were drifting out of the tavern, and although it wasn't close to closing time this was anything but a normal night.

"Not a word to anybody about the bottle," I said, looking at Mackey.

"Yes sir," he said.

We slipped into Megan's car while Mike sprinted to his van. This time Valerie took the back seat, and as we turned onto Market Street and away from King's Tavern, the deep note from the Mustang's pipes was like music to my ears.

~

Nobody talked on the way home. In the back Val unpinned her hair and combed it out with her fingertips while Megan softly hummed along with the local oldies station. At one point she stomped on it to pass a dairy truck poking along in front of us. The acceleration pulled my head back and pressed me into the seat. We were riding in the getaway car with the booty intact. I felt a righteous sense of relief settling over me.

We made it home in a blur, pulled up behind my truck and hurried into the kitchen. Mike arrived a few minutes behind us. After he came in I locked the door, took the prize from Valerie's bag and set it on the counter. The four of us stood staring at it.

The bottle had sloping shoulders typical of a French burgundy, except it was broader and much heavier at the bottom. In bright light the glass appeared greenish in color and hand-blown, with tiny

382

bubbles and imperfections. The contents looked deep red. The condition of the seal was excellent. Remarkably, the bottle seemed to have lost nothing to evaporation.

"What does 'Pour Louis' mean?" Valerie asked.

"I think it means 'for Louis'," I said.

"In 1769 that would be Louis the fifteenth, I believe," said Megan. "The next-to-last last king before the Revolution."

"You mean this was made for a king?" Val said, wonder in her voice.

"Not necessarily," I said. "The king authorized all kinds of commerce. The label might just mean it was licensed by the court."

"How can we find out?"

"We need to get it appraised. There are experts who know about these things."

"I'll bet that bottle could tell some stories," Mike mused. "Too bad there wasn't any documentation with it."

"Didn't you tell me you and Tina found some old papers along with this?" I asked Val.

"We gave them to Rollie," she said. "He never paid much mind to them; I don't know if he even saved them."

"Hmm." A glum silence fell over us.

"You all want something to drink?" I asked. "I've got a few bottles of decent wine, there's whiskey in the cupboard and I think there may even be a couple beers hiding somewhere in the fridge."

"One more glass of wine would be lovely," Megan said.

I went downstairs and returned with a good Italian Barolo and a fancy California wine the Plums had given me for Christmas. I wanted something special to open for Rollin when he arrived. Mike poked around in the refrigerator and found four beers, but left them for Mackey and Spider. Valerie excused herself to the bathroom while I uncorked the Barolo and took glasses from the cupboard.

Val came back to the kitchen scrubbed of makeup except for a bit of pencil that brought her eyebrows back close to their normal color. She looked more herself now. "What is this thing in my bag?" she asked, distastefully holding out the cigar-shaped object I had

383

pried from the floor of the compartment in the wine cellar. I had forgotten all about it.

I took it from her. It was dirty brown and a bit sticky. The softness of it reminded me of cloth, and as I turned it in my hands thought I saw a seam. I picked it with my thumbnail until an edge came up, and then started peeling it back. Then I realized it was a rolled-up piece of muslin that had been sealed with beeswax. I laid it on the counter and continued gently pulling the edge back until the length of it was free.

"Hold that," I said to Val, and when she had the edge firmly gripped I began rolling the rest of it back. After the first couple of layers it became easier. Pieces of wax crumbled away from the ends the farther we went. Mike and Megan stared. After about twenty inches the cloth ended and there inside was a rolled up paper—two papers, as it turned out.

I carefully unrolled the largest, ivory-colored with age and smooth as vellum, on the counter. It was slightly taller than a standard notebook page and filled with handwriting, entirely in French. The penmanship was fine and looked feminine, with swooping descenders. The date at the top was 9 July 1785. I peered more closely at the heading and started with shock at the name there.

"Oh my God," said Megan in an awed voice as she bent in beside me. "Somebody please tell me I am not dreaming."

"What is it?" Valerie demanded.

"Do you see that?" Megan said, pointing to the name I'd already seen. "It's a letter to Ben Franklin! Look, it's signed by the Countess du Barry." She pointed to the end, and there at the bottom I read the signature: La Comtesse du Barry.

"Who's that?" Val said.

"She was the mistress of King Louis the fifteenth."

"What does it say?" I was stunned.

"I don't know; my French isn't good enough to read this." Megan was poring over it, shaking her head.

"Lordy, can't someone read it?" Val was nearly bursting.

"Rollin!" I said. "He speaks French—he'll be able to read it."

Mike was excited now. "What's that other one there?"

I unrolled the second paper and noticed my hands were shaking. It was smaller and looked more fragile than the letter, and bore signs of having been folded several times. The handwriting was bold and masculine, this time in English. I gently held it flat while Mike read aloud:

"Bill of Lading—Rec'd from M. Le Veillard at Havre, One crate of Remy Martin brandy for delivery to Mr. Ben Franklin at Philadelphia. I have received all due fees & considerations and pledge to keep these goods in my quarters, guarded insofar as possible from the vicissitudes of sea and weather, if God be pleased to grant us safe passage. Signed 20 July, 1785 R. Jennings, Capt."

I felt the hair prickle on the back of my neck.

"Lordy," Val said. "It's old Ben Franklin's brandy."

"Let's get these things away from the sink." I swept up the papers and carried them to my desk, away from the kitchen and the open bottle of wine. I laid a stainless steel ruler across the top edge of both papers and carefully uncurled them one at a time. I laid a small weight at the bottom of each one, and switched the lamp on.

Valerie carried the bottle of cognac over and set it gently between the papers and my laser printer. I walked back into the kitchen feeling giddy, picked up the wine and began pouring glasses. "I propose a toast," I said. "To Valerie and Tina, for the discovery of a lifetime."

"To Val and Tina," said Megan and Mike.

"To old Ben Franklin," said Valerie, and we touched glasses and drank.

~

It was just past midnight when we heard the sound of two Harleys coming up the drive. I peered out the window and watched as they pulled into my yard. Rollin's Subaru was behind them and Mackey's truck brought up the rear. We walked outside to greet them.

"You closed early," I said as Rollin got out of his car.

"My God, it was nearly a disaster," he said. "When that guy got up I thought he was going to tear the room apart. What in the world possessed you all to do such a thing?" He was pretty distraught.

"I'm sorry, Rollin. It wasn't intended to happen that way, believe me."

"What were you trying to do, Ray? The ping-pong was great, but don't you think leaving would have been better than making him so mad?" He was nearly in tears, and I realized what an unnerving night it had been for him.

"I have something to show you," I said, putting an arm over his shoulder. "Come on in, guys." I led Rollin into my dining-room office and stopped in front of my desk. "See anything familiar here?"

Rollin's jaw dropped. He pointed at the bottle and then looked back at me, unbelieving. "Is that—is that the same one?"

"The one and only. That's what we came for tonight, Rollin. Everything else that happened was just the obstacle course we had to run to get it out of there."

"Where was it?" He stared back and forth between the bottle and me, uncomprehending.

"You'll hear the whole story in just a minute. We also found something else with it." I pointed at the two letters.

Rollin bent close to look, and seconds later he gasped. "But—this is impossible! These were with that bottle?"

"They were. We didn't know what we had until we got back here. In fact none of us can read the letter. We were hoping you might be able to help us out."

Spider, Gus and Mackey crowded in to have a look. "Holy shit, boss, that's Ben Franklin's brandy," Spider said.

"No shit?" said Mackey.

"Hey, back up, guys," Mike laughed. "You'll all get to see everything, but right now I think you should let Rollin read us the letter."

"Woo-hoo!" exclaimed Val and Megan. "Read the letter!"

"Wait." Rollin was still having a hard time comprehending any of it. "Where were these things? How did they come to be here?" He seemed altogether overwhelmed.

"I'm sorry, Rollin. I'm being a bad host here. Look, let's sit down and we'll start at the beginning." I indicated the kitchen counter, and Rollin took a stool. "You guys want a drink? There's beer in the fridge, whiskey in the cabinet and glasses up there."

While Mike helped Spider and Mackey to the beer, Gus poured whiskey over ice and I began opening the other bottle of wine. "I've been saving this for you, Rollin," I said.

"You got a Screaming Eagle?" he said, dumfounded again. "Where did that come from?"

"A gift from a rich client. You met the Plums."

"Ray, that's a collector's item. Please don't—it's far too valuable."

"Payback time, Rollin. It's only a bottle of wine; I'm sure it's worthy of your friendship and the occasion." I grinned and pulled the cork and thought his eyes would leave his head. "That, over there," I tilted my head toward the cognac sitting on the desk, "That's the collector's item." I poured Rollin a glass and set it before him.

"Valerie," I said, "would you mind telling Rollin about the day you and Tina found that cognac?"

And so she did, starting once more with the lost earring, and ending with her slipping the bottle back to its hiding place the terrible night Smith and Jones had made their first appearance. Spider and Mackey could hardly believe we had missed finding a secret compartment in the wine cellar but I assured them it was real. When Valerie came to the point of hiding the bottle again Rollin hung his head.

"I wasn't very careful, was I?" he said quietly.

"None of us knew what it was, Rollin," I said. "The important thing is that Valerie put it out of danger. I had no idea what happened to it until we were down in Kentucky. I saw Val holding that bottle in a dream one night, and the next day when I asked her about it she told me what she'd done. That's when I decided we had to get it out of there."

387

"So this whole night was your idea?"

"Not exactly. I wanted to get it during a service call, but I didn't know where the compartment was. Val thought we should do it together. She and Megan came up with the disguise. I really balked at coming in there like that, but now I can't see how it would have worked any other way. I apologize for things almost getting out of hand, but—" I shrugged. "Life happens in odd ways sometimes."

Rollin nodded slightly. He was calming down now.

"What took you so long downstairs?" Mike asked.

"I forgot to bring a knife," Val said, "so Ray had to unscrew the cover off the electric panel with a penny. We used a corner of that to move the stone back. After we got the bottle he seen that roll down there and had to dig it out. And then that big man was a-comin down the stairs, so I pushed him into the wall and started kissing on him like crazy. Of course mister cool here just thought it was cause he was so sexy and all."

Everyone hooted with laughter. "It was a close call," I said. "But the look on Jones's face when he found us like that was priceless. For that matter, so was Spider's when we walked back in upstairs. He thought for sure I'd beaten him out for a shot at Elaine." Everyone cracked up again, and even Rollin was laughing. It was the only time I ever saw Spider blush.

"I swear, Valerie, you looked like an angel tonight," Mackey said wistfully.

"You mean I don't look so hot now?" she demanded.

"Oh, no ma'am," he blushed. "I didn't mean it like that—" and then Val fell out laughing and punched his shoulder.

"I was just kidding," she said, and hugged his neck, and the moment was magic.

"Are you going to taste that wine, Rollin, or will we have to drink it for you?" I said.

"Ray, do you realize that bottle cost hundreds of dollars? People wait on a list for years to buy this stuff."

"It didn't cost me a penny, so tear it up. If you enjoy it we might even help you."

Rollin sipped, closed his eyes and seemed to meditate. We watched his face. After a long time he swallowed and quietly said, "This is magnificent."

I poured a bit for each of us, and after sampling it we all agreed it was indeed wonderful. "How's your French, Rollin?" I asked after he'd relaxed a little. "You think you might read us that letter? Megan says it was written by a countess."

"I'll give it a try," Rollin said, "but my translation might be a little rough."

"We don't care about that; just give us the gist of it."

We followed him to the desk and all leaned in behind him as he bent over the letter.

~

"My dear Monsieur Franklin." Rollin began haltingly. "A report has come to me that your work in Paris has ended. My heart is heavy to learn of your departure. We hoped to enjoy many more conversations with you.

"I am honored by your visits to Louveciennes. The Duke of Brissac speaks often of the wisdom of the American philosopher Ben Franklin. The gratitude of the duke is only a small portion of mine. You have given respect to every person, with no difference for blood or royalty.

"When my sun was extinguished at Versailles I felt my world had ended. Yet always fate has given me more joy than sorrow. How can I complain, who have known the best and worst of men, and after all these things have a friend such as you?

"Perhaps I will visit America someday and see the Republic you hold so dear. Now please accept for your memory of our beloved France, a gift of the brandy from Cognac.

"My lord Louis often said this brandy holds all the beauty of France. Share it with friends who cherish your gifts. Please reserve one bouteille for someone born after you. In this way we both leave comfort to those who follow, in times we cannot know.

"Adieu my friend. Never forget your time in Paris, for Paris will not forget you. Your faithful friend, La Comtesse du Barry."

By the time he reached the end Rollin was having trouble with his voice. He wiped his cheek and stayed bent over the letter for a long time.

~

Megan was the first one to break the silence. "Do you realize what this means?"

I glanced around. Everyone in the room looked stunned.

"Nobody even knew Ben Franklin and the Countess were acquainted," she said almost reverently.

"Who was the Countess?" Mackey asked.

"Madame du Barry was the mistress of King Louis the fifteenth."

"Then who was Marie Antoinette?" Mike asked.

"Marie Antoinette was the wife of Louis the sixteenth, the last king of France."

"Did they know each other?" I asked.

"Oh, yes. Antoinette despised du Barry for being a commoner and a lady of questionable repute. But if you ask me, she was jealous of the Countess's greater beauty and wit.

"After Louis the fifteenth died of smallpox, the Countess was banished to a convent. But two years later Louis the sixteenth released her. In the end he let her keep Lucienne—the estate she had been given by his grandfather. I think he knew they really had been in love. She was a patron of the arts, and in her later years she entertained musicians and philosophers at Lucienne."

"How does my sister know all this stuff?" Mike asked.

"Back in grade school I used to pretend I was the queen of France. I romanticized the royal court without knowing much about it."

"I remember you parading around with all your veils and costumes with your nose in the air."

Megan laughed. "Embarrassing, but true. Later I studied

European history more seriously. When I was stationed in Europe in the Army I finally got to visit Versailles and Lucienne on leave. The more I learned what it was really like the more I appreciated living in the present."

"Pretty messy, was it?" Spider said.

"They all ended losing their heads. The Countess actually survived longer than Marie Antoinette, but in the end it didn't matter. The Revolution swept them away like a flood."

"But look what she left behind," Gus mused. "It looks like the Countess has the last word after all."

"That letter alone could be worth a fortune," Megan said. "Together with the cognac and bill of lading..." She shook her head in awe.

"To the Countess," Mike said, lifting his glass.

"To the Countess," everyone echoed.

"To the Countess, and old Ben Franklin's diplomacy," I said, and we all touched glasses and drank. The wine's complicated aromas echoed beautifully and long, and each of us fell pensive.

"I think the Lord put all this together long ago cause he seen how you'd be needing it, Rollie," said Valerie at last. "I've been a-prayin for something good to happen for you."

"Aye," said Mackey, his voice thick with emotion. "The Lord did it."

"We still don't know if this is real," I cautioned.

"Oh, ye of little faith," said Spider. "Of all the people in this room."

"If only Dad were here to see this," said Rollin.

"Maybe he'll see it yet, Rollie," Megan said, slipping her arm around him. "You can't unravel the whole ball at once. Just take one little knot at a time, you know?"

"Thanks." He hugged her back.

"Do you know what you're going to do next?" Mike asked.

"I've got to talk with Buddy first thing in the morning," Rollin said. "This puts a different cast on things. I guess we'll have to play it by ear."

"Do you remember Val and Tina giving you some papers with that bottle when they found it?" I asked.

"They're in my file cabinet."

"It might be good for you and Buddy to have a look at them."

"It will be done. Can I leave these things with you for the night, Ray? We can get a safe deposit box for them tomorrow."

"No problem," I said. "Are we all sworn to secrecy here, folks?"

"Aye," said Mackey.

"Not even your wife, Mackey, until this business is settled."

"Yes, sir."

"Everyone?" I looked around the circle. Everyone nodded.

"Work tomorrow starts whenever we get there. Just try to not be too late."

After Spider, Mackey, Gus and Rollin took their leave I asked Mike if he would keep the cognac until morning. I didn't want all Rollin's eggs in one basket here at my place, even for a single night.

"I don't think so, Bwana," he said. "It wouldn't feel right. I think you know who ought to take it."

I turned to Val. "Will you, please?"

She nodded and slipped the bottle into her bag.

"Will you keep this lady safe?" I asked Megan.

"I don't need nobody babysitting me," retorted Val. "But at least she ain't too prissy to keep a gun on her, like some people I know."

"Now don't you go giving away my secrets," said Megan.

We walked Val and Megan out to the Mustang and hugged them; then Mike climbed in his van and followed them away down the drive.

CHAPTER 27

Rollin was good as his word. The next morning he found the papers Valerie and Tina had first discovered with the bottle, and met Buddy Sykes with them at the Aero Diner out by the township airport. I would give a pretty penny to have heard that conversation. If Rollin had given those papers even a glance in the beginning he might have taken things more seriously and saved us all a good bit of trouble. As it turned out they legally entitled the owner of the property to "all items on the premises of the Grand Hotel", going so far as to specify "one bottle of Remy Martin brandy, date 1769" and "certain documents pertaining to the estate of Benjamin Franklin."

The prior owner of the items, whose signature appeared on the papers in several places, had been one Archibald Forrest Franklin, who died in the fire that consumed the lakeside lodge outside Gladburg the night of January 15, 1927. According to records on file at the courthouse Mr. Franklin had owned a quarter interest in both the lodge and the Grand Hotel. He had neither wife nor children and died intestate. Combing through newspaper accounts of the fire later at the library Rollin could find nothing further about Mr. Franklin except that he had been born in Albany, New York in 1885. Buddy advised him to let that investigation wait for a more convenient time. Right now the cognac and all the documents with it were incontestably Rollin's, to dispose of as he wished.

With this assurance Rollin wasted no time getting the additional loan to put the old man's trouble behind him. None of us had a clue what the cognac was worth, but a bigger note with the Gladburg Mercantile and Trust was no longer something Rollin couldn't see beyond.

Val brought him the cognac and I gave him the documents, which promptly were secreted in Buddy's office safe. On Tuesday afternoon Rollin and Buddy brought a cashier's check for two hundred thousand dollars to Angelo in exchange for a quitclaim deed for the lien on King's Tavern. It still wasn't clear who had suckered the old man into their web except for "Xybacz Properties", the name that appeared on their papers, but that mattered little to Rollin. As suddenly as they had come, his tormentors were gone.

On Wednesday Delcorlia called to tell me that police in the Bronx, New York had arrested a suspect who had been identified from Valerie's drawing. The man, whose name was Reinhold Massey, already had a long rap sheet for mail fraud and trafficking in pornography. The search of a storage locker registered to him yielded a collection of snuff videos so vile that the police who viewed them were shaken. One of them showed the face of a woman in close-up being forced to kiss a gold crucifix on a chain held by her killer before he pushed a knife into her head from under her chin. My blood curdled listening to Delcorlia's calm voice describe this through the telephone.

"They emailed us a couple screen shots of the woman kissing the cross. Real nice camera work. The thing caught the light and it looks just like the one we've got here. The one Miss Tolliver, uh, recognized."

"No kidding?" I felt numb.

"They swabbed him for DNA; with the skin we found under Miss Utterbach's fingernails I think we're going to have a conviction."

"Are they going to nail him for the videos?"

"Oh yeah. His work has been known for a while, but nobody knew where it was coming from. This thing just blew it wide open. That creep is never going to see the light of day again."

"Who gets him first?"

"We do. After that he goes back to New York for everything they can put together on him. He's done, Mr. Brauner. He's out of circulation. You can thank Miss Tolliver for that."

"I'm sure she'll be relieved. Have you talked to the Utterbachs yet?"

"Yes."

There was a long silence, and Delcorlia spoke again.

"If you don't mind me asking, are you and Miss Tolliver, uh—is

394

she your girlfriend?"

"I don't know."

There was another long silence.

"We appreciate your help, Mr. Brauner." His voice sounded strained. "You can tell Miss Tolliver thank you for a lot of people."

"Yes. I'll do that."

By the time I talked with Valerie she already had heard about Massey's arrest. She had gone to see Tina early in the afternoon and said Mr. and Mrs. Utterbach welcomed her like family. She said Tina laughed when she told her about our wild night at King's Tavern. Of course the story had been abbreviated. Tina was still badly hurt and by no means ready for regular visitors, but I was sure Val's visit, along with news of her attacker's arrest, cheered her considerably.

I asked Val if she would like to stay with me for a few days and she said she'd think about it. I expected her to be eager and was a little disappointed by her reluctance. But she agreed to have dinner with me the next evening, so I put my feelings aside to deal with essentials.

~

Being on the job gave me back a lightness I hadn't felt in weeks. The Fryes were vacationing now but work on their addition was proceeding well. The honest pleasure of carpentry and the sight and smell of new construction around me gladdened my spirit. The arithmetical precision of it all anchored me in a comforting way to the certainties I had taken for granted before the events of the past few weeks had shattered everything.

The keening of saws, the drone of the compressor and the reliable thwack of nail guns all helped mute the questions that had been swirling in my head ever since I'd waken up to find myself the recipient of divine grace—a thing I still struggled to get my mind around. Even with the intervening distraction of King's Tavern that gift was complicating my inner life greatly. And it was hard to forget the moment I had said "please" my first primitive prayer had been

395

answered in a manner most unexpected. As for the hidden treasure of King's Tavern being coughed into Rollin's hands at the moment of his greatest need, all I could feel was wonderment, along with no small relief for him.

I wanted to push all those things aside and lose myself in the simple, therapeutic motions of building. But even my physical movements seemed filled with grace as I realized how impossible they would have been just two weeks ago. I'd been walking around hooked up to a medical device, watching my crew watch me skeptically as I waned on the cusp of collapsing. And now here I was, working alongside the strongest of them.

I was sure this remarkable transformation indebted me somehow. Not just to Valerie, although she had been a huge part of it. But I really didn't want to think about that—all I wanted was to savor the little time we had left. And to clarify, preferably without words, whether there was a chance we might preserve the closeness that had grown between us.

After the chaos of the preceding weeks I found myself looking forward to coming home in the evening, and decided to invite Valerie to my place for dinner instead of taking her out. It had been a long time since I'd cooked for anyone else, and I had little idea how to plan a vegetarian meal. I stopped by the organic food store after work and picked up a variety of ingredients, flying pretty much by the seat of my pants. Once I got home I had things figured out.

I put a Maurice Ravel CD on my stereo at high volume and set a pot of rice on the back of the stove to cook while I cut up a ripe mango for salsa. I diced half a red onion and lots of cilantro into it, along with a bit of habanero pepper chopped very fine. After squeezing a fresh lime into the mix it was perfect.

I mixed up a green salad, slicing in Duane's radishes, paper-thin onion rings and throwing in a handful of his cherry tomatoes. I blanched carrots and fresh broccoli, also from Duane's garden, and set them aside. Then I found my old wok that hadn't been used since Jillian walked out and heated peanut oil while I cubed a block of tofu. I tossed in the tofu, shitake mushrooms, pine nuts, cloves of garlic and fresh ginger, and was stirring in the baby carrots and pieces of broccoli just as Valerie arrived.

"Mmm, that smells scrumptious," she yelled over the music, kissing me on the cheek. "Can I help?"

"You can go downstairs and find a bottle of wine," I yelled back. "The rack's under the stairs."

Valerie brought up a bottle of Sauvignon Blanc while I turned the stereo down, and began opening it as I set out the salsa with chips for an appetizer. "Whoo-whee," she said after tasting the salsa. "Hot hot hot."

"Not half so hot as you."

"Well, ain't you the ladies man."

"You should have let me chill that bottle first," I said. "Do you have a pitcher?"

"Of what? I've got lots of pictures."

"I said a pitcher, stupid. Like for water."

I smacked myself on the forehead. "Sorry. I think there should be one somewhere in that cupboard." I pointed to a lower cupboard while I put the salad out.

Val found a big plastic pitcher and put the wine bottle into it. She scooped handfuls of ice from my freezer and dropped them around the bottle until it was covered to the shoulder. "There you go, mister particular. Your champagne bucket."

"Lovely. This stuff should be ready in a second."

I took down wine glasses and laid out the dinnerware, then I heaped the rice into a serving bowl, sprinkled threads of saffron over it and set it on the counter.

We sat down and she dropped her eyes and said a silent grace.

"Do you always do that?" I asked when she was finished.

"Inside my head I always do. Don't you?"

"The first time I ever did was at Duane's. I guess I never thought of it before then." We began eating. "Tell me about your visit with Tina."

"She was real happy to see me. When she found out they caught that man she cried. She said God saved her life by telling her to fight

397

back."

"Do you believe that? That God told her?"

"Why wouldn't I?"

"I thought Christians were supposed to be pacifists. You know, turn the other cheek and all."

"That don't mean to let someone take your life, Ray. Only God has the right to do that."

"Did anyone say how long she's going to be in there?"

"Nobody said. But she's real hurt. They have to do more surgery on her face, plus her mama told me she'll probably need physical therapy. I don't think she's going to be back for a while."

We dug into the main course, and only after Valerie declared my stir-fry wonderful did I say my own little grace. She told me more about Megan and her ordeal with cancer, of which Mike had spoken only little. I knew Val and Megan had become quite close in the few days they spent together. When the subject of Rollin and the tavern came up, I suggested the door might be open for her to come back and work there if she wanted to.

"I don't think so, Ray. I learnt a few things while I was there. One was I'm not much of a waitress."

"What would you really like to do most of all?"

"You know I've got to go see my family now. I didn't get much time with Vi except for that day you took sick, and I was kind of upset then. I haven't seen my brother for over two years."

"How do you think that's going to go?"

"It might be a little rough at first, but not bad as it was. Back before I left nobody was talking to each other, and now—well, you seen what it is."

She was pensive. "I think I got my work cut out for a little while. If they shut that whole place down there's going to be some people that need help. I'm not sure what I can do, but it feels like I ought to be there now."

"What would you like to do beyond all that?"

She thought for a minute. "Maybe go to college. You know I had nearly a four point in high school."

398

"Wow, Val. You never told me that."

"I could even begin speaking properly, if I really had to."

I laughed. "I knew you had it in you. What would you like to study?"

"Social work. Or maybe even law—something to help the people that always get stepped on. I liked what Johnny Cottrell done after he become a lawyer, taking on the coal companies for tearing up the mountains." She shook her head and gave a rueful laugh. "I don't know how I ever could, unless Duane helped me. I don't want to take nothing from him though. I think it's enough with me living there."

We finished eating and sipped wine slowly, caught up in our own thoughts.

"I'm going to miss you very much," I said.

"Me too." Her voice was soft. "But don't you think it's best this way?"

"Why would I want you to go away, Val?"

There was a long silence. "I thought you didn't want to talk about it."

"I've changed my mind."

She sighed, looking down at her empty plate. "I've been thinking a lot about it the past few days. I know you hate me saying things from the Bible, Ray. But I can't get out of my mind how it says for believers to not be unequally yoked with unbelievers."

She looked up. "Even if we love each other but we can't agree about something real basic like that, how much chance do you reckon we'd have? Not to mention you being so smart and all, and me being the hick chick."

"Val, I've never, ever called you that. I've never even thought that way about you."

"But are you a believer?"

I struggled with the question. "I'm not an unbeliever, Val. That's impossible after what happened to me. But I don't have the context to understand it like you do. I can't lie to you; I have no idea what this requires from me and it scares me if I think about it."

"Why does it have to be so hard? The Lord does good things for us because he loves us. Maybe you could start by just being thankful."

"Don't you think I am?"

"I think you are inside, but you're scared to show it. It's not my place to tell you how to be, Ray. But if Mackey ain't ashamed to speak up and pray for Tina, how come you won't give God the glory after he saved your life?"

Now I looked down. "I don't know, Val. I guess it's because there are so many—so many fanatics out there, pumping religion, using that language, and I don't find anything in their values or culture that speaks to me. It's not God that bothers me; it's all the unpleasant people who claim to represent him."

"Then maybe someone like you could set a better example."

"Like me?"

"Why not, Ray? You're smart and kind, and people respect you. Maybe you could show the Lord done you a great good, without being like them other people. Did you ever think maybe that's why he give you all your importance?"

"I'm not a preacher, Val."

"I never said nothing about preaching. Everybody has their own calling. You glorify God by doing good work, by being honest and kind. But you ought to tell the truth without fear when he done something so marvelous for you. If you wasn't so worried about what other people think, it would be natural as a bird singing his own song."

I could still hear that mockingbird singing outside Mr. Plum's observatory, and the thrush we heard pouring its heart out in the meadow below Duane's place a few evenings before. I remembered the simple grace Duane said over our meal the night we arrived, and the unaffected way Mackey asked if the Lord had healed me. There was no pretense in any of it—they all were just being in the moment. Honest as a plumb wall, pure as a clean chord ringing from a guitar. Nothing like that radio preacher we'd heard in the truck on the way down to Kentucky.

"You can't let people hollering on radio and TV, dragging the Lord's name in politics, tell you what it is," Val said. "Some of them are as bad wrong as everybody they're against. When that governor down in Texas killed that Christian lady who murdered someone when she was young—that just showed he don't even know the Lord. Nobody with the love of God in their heart could do a thing like that."

I remembered the incident and how much it had upset Val at the time, but I hadn't thought about it since. Now little more than a year later that same governor was running for president. I never had agreed with the death penalty, but to me a convicted murderer didn't seem like much of a loss to the world.

"That's what I was tempted to do before I left home, Ray. I wanted so bad to punish my daddy when he hurt mama. But that's the way of the world. The Lord's way is forgiveness and reconciliation. If my daddy can forgive his own self he can still be a blessing to so many around him, like that lady in Texas was before they killed her. People can grow in grace. There ain't a one of us that wants to be judged on the worst thing we ever done."

"I can't argue with any of that," I said quietly.

"That's why I think so much of Rollie now," Val said. "His own daddy done him a terrible wrong, but he still loves him so much. And you know Rollie ain't even religious—he's just got love in his heart, even for someone who hurt him." She looked up at me. "He taught me something when I saw that, Ray. That's what I mean when I say you can be an example. It don't take being a preacher."

"That's a lot to think about."

"Well, don't you go thinking yourself into a hole now, mister serious." She got up from the counter, came and put her arms around me from behind, and kissed my neck. "I can help with the dishes if you want to put some more nice music on."

~

Valerie spent the night with me. It was tender and agonizing in a

401

way I never expected to feel again. I knew she would be leaving tomorrow after visiting Tina in the hospital. We made love and then talked deep into the night. Before falling asleep she told me she loved me, and I told her the same. It felt like the first time I'd said the words; it was the first time ever I had felt them so deeply.

I woke with a start in the morning to find Valerie gone. At first I was frantic with grief, and then I found her note on the kitchen counter:

Dear Ray, I hope you will forgive me for leaving like this, but the last thing you said was so sweet I want to remember that instead of goodbye. I wouldn't hurt you for anything. You know where I'm going and what I have to do. I will get some good strings for Daddy's guitar on the way home.

You can write me in care of Duane at P.O. Box 117 in Hurt. Please don't leave me hanging. I know we will see each other again. Remember there is no fear in love, for perfect love casts out all fear.

I love you Mister Brauner.

Valerie Tolliver

Below her name was a tiny, funny caricature of herself blowing me a kiss that was mostly hair, eyes and lips, with her hand represented by two gracefully curved lines. It was so perfectly drawn that anyone would recognize her. I laughed through my tears and folded the note carefully into my wallet.

I worked hard all day but wouldn't be drawn into a conversation with anyone. There just weren't any words to express the things I was feeling.

~

To my surprise Sotheby's of New York dismissed Rollin's treasures. They wouldn't handle the auction of distilled spirits due to state liquor laws, and never returned his calls regarding the Franklin documents until he already had found a buyer. I can't help but think when all was said and done that someone up there must have been sorry.

Thanks to one of Buddy Sykes' old law school friends an appraisal was arranged. The friend, Milo Witkowski, had been a lawyer until he quit the legal profession to spend more time with his family. He started an import business that eventually made him wealthier than he ever dreamed of being as a lawyer. And he was a collector of rare wines and spirits.

Milo later told Rollin of his initial skepticism when Buddy first called him about the find. For decades, it seems, an old tale had circulated among collectors that there existed a bottle of King Louis's brandy, brought over by Ben Franklin from Paris, and that its authenticity was supported by some sort of document. Nobody could say exactly what that document was; the brandy itself once was regarded as the holy grail of the wine collecting world.

From time to time over the years one enterprising huckster after another had tried to counterfeit that bottle of brandy and pass it off as the find of the century. It had happened just often enough that the story was mostly regarded as a hoax now by serious collectors. That may have explained the initial reluctance of Sotheby's to become involved.

When Buddy called him, Milo was certain that old hoax had surfaced again until Buddy told him where the things were found. Milo had researched that story for years as well. The most credible account he ever came across seemed to be tied to a hotel somewhere in Pennsylvania. Almost nobody knew that little detail—it had ceased being part of the tale long before.

Buddy had great respect for Milo, and we soon discovered why. If his personal credentials were impressive, his connections were stellar. Milo lived outside of Princeton, New Jersey. Using his contacts he assembled a team of appraisers, consisting of a retired cellar master with a career spanning nearly three decades at Rémy Martin, a French historian from the Sorbonne currently visiting at Princeton University, and a document specialist from the British Museum who had spent years working for the National Security

Agency.

After comparisons with documents from the period, including known samples of the handwriting of Countess du Barry, and laboratory testing, it was determined that both the documents and cognac were authentic beyond doubt. The gentleman from the British Museum further allowed that Rollin had something of a national treasure on his hands, and his colleagues agreed.

With Rollin's permission Milo leaked the information to a select group of collectors, along with executives at Rémy Martin. Not surprisingly, Rémy Martin contacted Rollin first and made him an offer in the high six figures for everything. Although the offer turned his head for a few days Rollin felt the documents were more part of American history than French, and he couldn't accept it.

For several weeks lesser offers trickled in from here and there, and then one day his patience was rewarded. A lawyer for the world's richest man called Rollin, and told him that a certain Mr. Gates would be very interested in ownership of the documents and artifact. Rollin was ecstatic.

"I'm not supposed to tell anyone," he confided nervously to me that evening over the phone. "Ray, he wants to give me over a million dollars for them. In fact, the offer is closer to two. What do you think?"

"What does Buddy think?" I said.

"He thinks I should hold out. We'll owe Milo a little percentage for helping us, but Ray, this is more than I ever dreamed of."

"I think you should listen to Buddy," I said. "Two million bucks is like bath water to Bill Gates, and what you have is unique and irreplaceable in the universe. Let him upgrade and reboot, and see what happens."

"I'm not much of a gambler, Ray."

"Then trust your gut. Is the man helping you or himself?"

"Well, maybe I'll just sit for a few days and think about it."

That was on a Tuesday. Thursday of the same week a fit looking, middle-aged guy named Larry showed up at King's Tavern. He was outgoing and friendly, and it wasn't long before Rollin found he was

404

a pilot. They hit it off instantly and for the rest of the evening they traded stories—mostly Rollin's, at first. When Rollin found that Larry had just flown into Allentown from San Jose in his own jet he was slack-jawed with admiration.

But Larry wanted to know more about Rollin's mountain climbing, and inevitably they ended up together in Rollin's office, looking at his wall of photos. After hearing most of the stories behind them Larry finally laid a hand on Rollin's shoulder and asked if he'd ever sailed on a racing yacht.

"We're kind of landlocked around here," Rollin laughed.

"Would you like to?" Larry asked.

"Well, sure—who wouldn't?"

"I think that could be arranged," Larry confided. "But you've got something that interests me, and I'd like to talk about that a little bit first."

And then Larry pulled out a business card and handed it to Rollin—when Rollin tells the story I find it amusing that guys like Larry even have business cards—and Rollin nearly shat himself. For he had been spending his evening prattling to one of the world's richest billionaires, the CEO of a software empire, a man whose secondary mission in life was to make Bill Gates look like a piker.

"You're Larry Ellison?" Rollin gaped, and Larry put back his head and laughed.

"The one and only. I'm interested in a history lesson, and I understand you have some visual aids."

And so it was that Rollin met the buyer of the Franklin artifacts, as they came to be known in the news. It was a no-brainer, really. Larry was a hands-on, fully engaged guy who didn't delegate things he was passionate about to subordinates. No lawyers called—the man himself came, and to Rollin that meant everything. Not to mention the fact that Larry's offer indeed made Bill Gates look like a piker.

Larry arranged to meet Rollin and Buddy at Lehigh Valley Airport in Allentown the next day, took them onboard his Gulfstream jet, and they did a quick flight up around Martha's

405

Vineyard and back with Rollin in the co-pilot's seat. When Larry's Gulfstream took off that night for the West coast it was carrying a bottle of cognac from 1769 and the Franklin documents, and Rollin King was a multimillionaire.

~

With Buddy's help, the first thing Rollin did was to set up trust funds for Tina and Valerie, generous enough to provide for them both well into the future. They'll be able to attend school anywhere they choose now with no financial worries. In addition Rollin is giving Tina's family a little extra help until she's fully recovered. Construction just started again on the Grand Hotel, which has been in limbo ever since the old man's disappearance.

The discovery of the Franklin artifacts is suddenly a national gossip item—a welcome diversion from the presidential campaign now underway. Rollin was interviewed last week by the Today Show and NPR, and in both venues he was reserved and modest, giving all the credit to the "fantastic employees" who found the items. He won't name them out of respect for their privacy, and has said nothing about his own generosity on their behalf. Neither has he mentioned any of the circumstances surrounding his father's disappearance. What I found most poignant in both interviews was how frankly Rollin yearned to be back climbing a mountain somewhere, as soon as his personal affairs allow it. I knew that was a veiled plea for his father to come home.

Tina laughed and cried when she heard the news. She's recovering quite well; I've visited her several times and gotten to know her folks a little better. She says she can hardly wait to come back to work in the newly designated historic district in downtown Gladburg.

Megan opines that maybe now the extraordinary Countess du Barry will receive her rightful share of attention, after having been overshadowed for so long by the much thinner character, Marie Antoinette. I laughed and told her it would take a movie to do that,

406

and she bet me a bottle of good wine that someone does it within two years.

My crew, of course, takes great pleasure in Rollin's deliverance and in seeing King's Tavern have a second helping of fame. None of them could get over the hiding place we all had missed in the wine cellar. As soon as Rollin's tormenters vanished several of us traipsed downstairs for a good look at that compartment. On close inspection it became clear that whoever designed it accomplished an engineering feat worthy of old Ben himself. Under the flagstone there is a carved stone channel that runs around the inner lid, with drainage holes into a mysterious void. My guess is that a good-sized reservoir was built under the compartment to handle any flooding that might happen. The asbestos inner lid is grooved to fit tightly over the raised lip of the compartment, and the groove is lined with a gasket of silk cording saturated with beeswax. I've always been a sucker for craftsmanship, and whoever went to all that effort—I can only assume it was Archibald Forrest Franklin—deserves no small credit for preserving a valuable piece of American history.

After three sets of tests Dr. Panos told me my blood chemistry shows no indication that I was ever ill. And what's more, a minor heart murmur I've had since childhood has disappeared. In short, I've never been healthier.

I'm also learning how to say thank you—I try to do it every day now. If not to someone unseen, I try to find somebody that I can sincerely thank for something, no matter how small. My crew even seems to think I'm a nicer guy these days, but I think they've become more thoughtful too.

I've written Val twice; things have been busy and there are some new things she doesn't know. One is that my relationship with the Plums has changed a lot in recent weeks. That's natural once a job is finished, but this feels stranger than usual. It isn't Gloria, but Mr. Plum seems distant, preoccupied and melancholy. After moving in they invited me to their housewarming party. I felt awkward and completely out of place. Not a single conversation went anywhere; I felt more like a novelty object—an accessory to Mr. Plum's large

407

new appliance, his cyber-controlled mansion with its eye to the sky.

A couple days later going through some old documents from early in the job I found one of the plats of their land. It had been notarized at Mr. Plum's law firm, and when I saw the notary's signature I felt a subtle click in the back of my mind: Albert Travino. For just an instant I saw red hair, beautifully highlighted in the glow of the wall sconce at King's Tavern—Liz Travino's hair, and then a ribbon of blood arcing in the same light as that young bouncer's face assumed terrible new proportions in full view of all.

A coincidence? I don't know. The old man is still out there somewhere, and with Tina's attacker in custody nobody is pressing any new charges. Rollin's position has solidified greatly in recent days, and my relationship with the Plums is at an end anyway.

I remember Valerie telling me the Lord's way is forgiveness and reconciliation. I don't think whoever went after the old man has the slightest interest in forgiveness or reconciliation, but it isn't my place to stir around in the affairs of others. And now I believe maybe forgiveness and reconciliation do even more for those who forgive, than for the forgiven. Need I say how grateful I am that Valerie left home to burn out her anger up north instead of turning it against her father, as she first was tempted to? Like a ripple in an infinite pond, like wheels turning as far as the eye can see, it was a decision fraught with consequences that will never end.

For now I'm letting the Travino matter rest. Yesterday Rollin asked me to contact Val and tell her about the trust he's set up for her. I could do that in a letter, but it feels like a thing that should be done in person. Of course I'll let her know I'm coming. There are some papers to give her, and living where she is I'll bet she doesn't even know yet what's happened with old Ben Franklin's brandy. There will be some things to talk about.

READING GROUP DISCUSSION QUESTIONS

1. After finishing this novel can you find more than one possible meaning in its title, *The Redemption of Valerie Tolliver*? How many characters in the story experienced some kind of redemption?

2. At the beginning of the story did you feel Valerie's reputation was deserved? How did your opinion of her change as the story progressed? Did your opinion of Ray change as well?

3. Does this story strike you as having mythological aspects? If so, which story threads or characters most give you that impression?

4. Did you feel limited by a first-person point of view? Imagine how this story might have been told if Valerie were the narrator, instead of Ray.

5. What events or objects were most pivotal to the story? Don't forget events that happened before the story opens. Talk about how things might have unfolded if characters had made different choices, and how that could have affected the outcome.

6. Which of the characters do you feel most strongly about, either positively or negatively, and why? Which one would you most want to know, if they were real people? Which of the secondary characters would you like to have seen developed more fully?

7. Two married couples were depicted: Mr. and Mrs. Plum, and Val's parents. Talk about their relationships and how they coped with their difficulties. Does one couple seem more likely to grow or change than the other, and if so, why? Realizing the differences between Ray and Valerie, do you feel they could ever build a successful long-term relationship?

8. How did the three central buildings in the story anchor the plot (the Plum house, King's Tavern and Duane's house)? What part did their owners play in Ray's journey and evolution? Do you feel the Plum house crumbling into the Coalbright mining complex in Ray's dream in Kentucky held significance? If so, why?

9. Discuss Ray's dreams and how they affected his awareness. Did Ray's dream about the wheels turning make you think about your role in the lives of other people, or their place in your life?

10. Did Ray's miraculous experience in Kentucky challenge your suspension of disbelief? Do you feel there is such a thing as divine grace? If so, has it ever happened to you, and how?

11. Talk about your impression of Ardelene Younger. Was she a heroine, or was she only doing what she had to?

12. Who do you feel was the greater scoundrel—Old man King or Mr. Plum, and why? Do you believe Mr. Plum was behind the old man's troubles? If so, what makes you think that?

13. Was the ending satisfying to you? Of the various plot threads, do you feel any were not resolved satisfactorily? Does real life always tie up every loose end? Were there aspects you would have preferred to end differently?

14. Did your opinion of this book change significantly over the course of reading it?

15. Would you recommend reading *The Redemption of Valerie Tolliver* to others?

Connect with the author:

www.facebook.com/valnovel

www.smashwords.com/profile/view/dcrews

www.dcrewsphoto.com